KU-653-557

Gary Gibson

STEALING
LIGHT

First Book of the
Shoal Trilogy

TOR

First published 2007 by Tor

This edition published 2013 by Tor
an imprint of Pan Macmillan
20 New Wharf Road, London N1 9RR
Associated companies throughout the world
www.panmacmillan.com

ISBN 978-1-4472-2409-9

Copyright © Gary Gibson 2007

The right of Gary Gibson to be identified as the
author of this work has been asserted by him in accordance
with the Copyright, Designs and Patents Act 1988.

All rights reserved. No part of this publication may be
reproduced, stored in or introduced into a retrieval system, or
transmitted, in any form, or by any means (electronic, mechanical,
photocopying, recording or otherwise) without the prior written
permission of the publisher. Any person who does any unauthorized
act in relation to this publication may be liable to criminal
prosecution and civil claims for damages.

5 7 9 8 6

A CIP catalogue record for this book is available from
the British Library.

Phototypeset by Intype Libra Ltd, London SW19 4HE
Printed and bound by CPI Group (UK) Ltd, Croydon CR0 4YY

This book is sold subject to the condition that it shall not,
by way of trade or otherwise, be lent, re-sold, hired out,
or otherwise circulated without the publisher's prior consent
in any form of binding or cover other than that in which
it is published and without a similar condition including this
condition being imposed on the subsequent purchaser.

Visit www.panmacmillan.com to read more about all our books
and to buy them. You will also find features, author interviews and
news of any author events, and you can sign up for e-newsletters
so that you're always first to hear about our new releases.

PART ONE

PART ONE

ONE

Standard Consortium Date: 03.06.2538
25 kilometres south of Port Gabriel, Redstone
  Colony
Port Gabriel Incident +45 minutes

It was like waking up and finding you'd just sleepwalked through the gates of hell.

Dakota drew in a sharp breath, feeling like she'd first awakened into existence only a moment before. She stood stock still for several seconds, the touch of freezing rain clear and sharp on her skin.

Trying to take it all in.

Bodies were scattered all around her, under a slate-grey sky from which snow fell in sporadic squalls. Most had been cut down as they ran for safety. It was a scene of appalling carnage.

She remembered with dazzling clarity what it had felt like to kill them.

Her hands hung limply by her sides, Consortium-issue assault pistol still held in one fist. Fat-bellied Consortium transports rumbled far overhead, dropping

3

down from orbit, looking to salvage something – anything – from the disaster of the assault.

The worst thing was that she remembered so much. Every moment, every scream, every death: it was something she was going to have to live with for the rest of her life.

That made the decision to kill herself a lot easier.

Dakota wandered away from the transport and the bodies of the Freeholder refugees it had been carrying, walking along the side of the highway and seeing where bodies had slumped into the snow-filled ditch running parallel to it.

A woman had died tangled up in the thick, hardy roots and foliage of a jugleaf bush. Dakota pulled her free, ignoring the plant's sharp barbs that tore at her skin and survival suit. She laid the woman down on the side of the road, peering into her face. Middle-aged, motherly looking, a few strands of grey among the black roots on her scalp.

Dakota closed the dead eyes and remained kneeling by the corpse for a minute or so.

Finally she stood and looked around, listening to the rasp of freezing air coursing through the filtration systems in her breather mask, and felt her lungs heave into a scream that felt like it would never end.

Eventually her chest began to hurt from the exertion of screaming, and she stopped.

She started walking again, stripping off her survival suit bit by bit as she went. She dumped the suit in the roadside ditch, then pulled off her insulated under-garments, until she stood naked under the Redstone morning sky.

The subzero temperature was instantly numbing. She kept her breather mask on, however, because a quick death by asphyxiation in this alien atmosphere somehow felt too easy an end. Flecks of snow danced over the soft pale flesh of her bare shoulders, and against the close-cropped stubble of her scalp.

Dakota managed to stumble a few more steps, her vision blurring as she stared over towards the trucks and buses and long-distance haulers that had been carrying the refugees to safety. Some of them were burning, staining the Redstone sky with oily smoke.

She collapsed beside the statue of Belle Trevois, the Uchidan child-martyr, that stood in eternal vigil by the roadside. Its arms reached up into the air in a gesture that seemed all the more forlorn in such a lonely and desolate spot. The plinth was stained with ugly Freeholder graffiti.

Dakota realized death was very close, and curled up in a ball beneath the statue's feet. From there she gazed up at its blank features.

Inside her head she could still hear the sound of running feet, the sound of the refugees' screams as they burned.

Then she heard other voices – soldiers shouting to each other, coming closer.

Coming to rescue her.

TWO

City of Erkinning, Bellhaven Colony
Consortium Standard Date: 03.02.2536
Two years prior to Port Gabriel Incident

Dakota stared out over the distant rooftops of the shanties clustering beyond the city's grim stone walls. The seven stars of evening shone down on her like an Elder's blessing.

The instant she glanced up at the night sky, her new Ghost circuitry – freshly installed within her skull – unloaded a deluge of mostly useless information into her thoughts: without any effort she knew instantly how far away each star was, its declination in respect to the galactic equator, and how many planets and dark companions orbited each of them. A rich cornucopia of similar detail in relation to thousands of other stars, all scattered within a sphere hundreds of light years across and centred on Bellhaven, waited on the fringe of her mind. She imagined she was a spider at the centre of some vast cybernetic web, her implants like thousands of dainty multiple limbs that could reach out and tug suns and moons out of the sky for her to play with.

She pulled her gaze back down, her breath frosting in the cold night air after escaping from under the scarf wrapped tight up around her mouth and throat. A chill winter wind whipped across her freshly shaven skull where it emerged, exposed, from beneath the protection of the thick leather cap she had pulled over her head and ears. She glanced behind her to see Tutor Langley standing only a short distance away.

Langley wore a small goatee beard against his dark skin, and his long black coat resembled that of a preacher from some past century, its high stiff short collar pressing tight around his neck, while its skirt fluttered around his boots. It was a uniform intended to remind citizens of the authority of the City Elder's controlling religious oligarchy.

Dakota noticed the expression on his face and flashed him a grin. She didn't mind that her shaven scalp still looked bruised and battered from the surgeon's intrusions.

In the streets far below the Garrison, on whose roof she stood, she could see people clustering at food stalls lining a busy crossroads she had wandered past a thousand times. She could just make out their faces gathered in a few small patches of light. Snatches of their conversation drifted up to her, along with the smell of cooking, making her hungry.

Dakota was suddenly aware how easily these odours

could be broken down into specific categories. Words like *hydrolysates*, *esters* and *caramelized sugars* popped into her head, broken down into percentages that changed with each sudden gust of wind. Far below, people hid from the winter cold and rain under sheet-metal awnings, or warmed themselves around communal fusion heaters set up at each corner of the crossroads.

Jesus, Uchida, Buddha; these and a dozen more effigies glowed in incandescent hallucinatory colours from dozens of niches as they did in so many other parts of the city. They bestowed their luminous blessings on the fossilized layers of posters and public notices pasted over and over again on every available flat surface.

Just then she realized Marlie had joined her by the railing, her mouth wide in a grin under dark eyes.

'Did you hear the latest about Banville? Now they're saying he's defected, gone over to the Uchidans, and abandoned his family in the process.'

'Are you sure?' Dakota replied. 'Last I heard, they were claiming he was kidnapped.'

This was significant news. Banville was the scientist personally responsible for much of the cutting-edge Ghost tech on which the world of Bellhaven had long built its scientific reputation. Both Marlie and Dakota, and everyone else with Ghost implants, carried a piece of Banville's work inside them.

Marlie shrugged happily. She had a way of smiling completely regardless of what she was actually saying, which indicated a lifelong – and to Dakota deeply irritating – dedication to perkiness beyond reason. 'I picked up a *City Bulletin* just before I got here. Looks like he left voluntarily, after all, and the Elders are going crazy because of it.'

Dakota nodded. The news of Banville's disappearance had already inspired riots in the Grover Communities, as the Elders preferred to call them. *Shanties* would have been a better word – they'd been growing out beyond the city walls for three years now, packed as they were with refugees flooding in from the failed Grover colony a thousand miles further north.

Dakota quickly performed the visualization routines that opened her subconscious to a flood of data and news from the local tach-net. Her eyes widened in shock as a torrent of new information was dumped into her skull: Banville had disappeared less than a day before, but within the past few minutes a recorded message had surfaced in which he claimed to have joined the Oratory of Uchida willingly, and had left Bellhaven for ever.

She looked over at Marlie, knowing instantly that she was getting the exact same information.

'This is bad,' Dakota said unnecessarily.

Marlie nodded. 'Yes, Dakota, it's very bad.'

There were reports of a dozen more riots erupting across the globe as the shock revelation of Banville's defection spread. Dakota watched a pall of smoke rising from two different sectors of the Grover camps as she stood on the flat roof of the Garrison's East Quadrant Tower, the perimeter of which was ringed with ancient battlements. Steel and ceramic mountings for pulse weapons, which had defended Erkinning during the First Civil War, lay pitted and rusted from a century and a half of neglect.

Given the current circumstances, the celebrations surrounding Dakota's graduation were a touch muted. Still, as the night wore on, Langley had set up his telescope as he'd promised, upon this selfsame rooftop, so they could all take a look at the new supernova sliding towards the horizon as dawn approached.

The telescope looked positively medieval to Dakota, a fat tube of gleaming copper and brass mounted on a rotating equatorial base, as if some machine-arachnid invader from beyond the known worlds were stalking the city rooftops.

'Did you say something, Dakota?' Langley peered over towards her.

She gestured upwards with her chin, indicating the supernova. 'I said, I'd like to go someplace like that some day, and see what a dying star looks like up close.'

Her gaze met Aiden's and she faltered, her pale skin flushing red as she recalled their fumbled intimacies in the dormitories.

'You're kidding, right?' said Aiden, a touch the worse for wear from drinking. 'Go visit the *supernova*?' he laughed, eliciting nervous chuckles from any remaining students who were still awake and hadn't already passed out. Marlie sat cross-legged, ignoring the damp tiles under her as she fixed her attention on Langley, who in turn was fully aware of her unrequited longing. Martens' owlish features were distracted by some personal reverie, lost to the world around him. Otterich and Spezo looked bored and tired, while the rest had since made their apologies and retired for the night. Exploding stars didn't hold much interest for some students.

Langley himself flashed Aiden a warning look. Then he glanced at Dakota, apparently satisfied at last with the minute adjustments he had been making to the telescope. 'I share the sentiment, but the Large Magellanic Cloud is a little further away than the Shoal are prepared to transport either you or anyone else.'

'Yeah, what is it again?' sneered Aiden. 'Hundred and sixty thousand light years, right?' He flashed Dakota a grin, and she shot him back a look of pure hatred. 'So we're seeing an event from about the time the Shoal first developed faster-than-light technology. Loooong way away, right?'

The first supernova had appeared six years before, early in the autumn, and just a couple of days after Dakota's sixteenth birthday. It had blossomed like cold fire, briefly one of the brightest elements in the night sky, before gradually fading out over the following weeks. Then, over the next several years, dozens more had appeared at irregular intervals, shining brightly for a few brief weeks before again fading back into stellar anonymity. And all this had occurred within a relatively tiny sector of a neighbouring galaxy.

'What you're all forgetting,' Langley told them in his soft-spoken way, 'is that these novae still represent a mystery. And there's nothing people like more than a mystery. It's in our nature.'

He stepped back from the telescope and rested one hand gently on its glinting carapace. 'Martens, since you've been studying the novae, why don't you remind us of some of the background detail? What is it that's so remarkable and unusual about them?'

Martens wasn't entirely sober himself, and he blinked and stuttered, caught unawares by the Tutor's potentially dangerous line of enquiry. 'Uh, Sir, up until now our understanding was that most stars that go nova are part of a double-star system.' His foot kicked over an unfinished bottle of beer that sat forgotten by his foot. He reached for it, but changed his mind halfway. Dakota caught the look on Aiden's face, and even he suddenly looked a lot more sober. 'One of these stars sucks up material from its companion, and as a result you get a stellar detonation. But, as far as anyone can tell, none of these new novae was either massive enough to go nova, or even part of a double-star system.'

'And there's also the double neutrino bursts,' Dakota added impulsively, whereupon Martens looked grateful not to have to say any more. Langley turned to her with a look of appreciation, even admiration, which made her blush.

'Deep space scanners have always recorded a neutrino surge occurring a few minutes before any visual observation is made,' she continued. 'But every one of the recent Magellan novae has been preceded by a neutrino echo: not one but two neutrino bursts, separated by a few seconds, followed by the normal visual confirmation. Yet that should be impossible. Maybe a couple of novae appear every century in our own galaxy, but now there's a couple of dozen occurring in a neighbouring galaxy made up of only a tenth as many stars as our own Milky Way. That's in the space of a few years, and almost literally next door to each other. It just doesn't make sense.'

Langley smiled. 'See, that's a girl with genuine curiosity, Aiden. She likes to ask questions, while you just sit around and complain.'

There was nervous laughter from Martens, which Otterich joined in with after a moment. Aiden forced a smile as if to say *You win*, and Dakota suddenly found it hard to remember what it was she'd liked about him enough to let him climb on top of her not so long ago. She put it down to a combination of alcohol and the undeniable fact that he was far from unattractive.

She sighed and pulled her thoughts away from the memory of their bodies tangled together between warm sheets. It was one thing for them to climb up here on a frozen rooftop because yet another new star had appeared in the sky, but even coming close to asking the reason why could, in some quarters, lead to problems.

When those first novae had appeared, the City Elders, who ruled Erkinning and all the other cities of the Free States, had been quick to label such stellar manifestations as part of God's Ineffable Purpose, and, therefore, not open to scientific or indeed any other kind of speculation.

The Consortium – the name by which the administrative and military body that controlled human-occupied space was known – had little interest in local politics, yet the fact remained that of Bellhaven's several different nations, the Free States had been heavily invested in by the Consortium itself due to the remarkable advances that technicians in Erkinning and certain other Free State cities had achieved in developing Ghost technology. Under the circumstances, this clampdown on public speculation over the novae was little more than sabre-rattling: an attempt by the Elders to show they remained the real authority in Erkinning, when everyone knew otherwise.

Aiden looked grim. He had an uncle sitting on the Council of Elders, and getting involved in this kind of speculation wasn't going to help advance his career. Dakota's next words came out in a rush, lest Aiden accuse Langley of deliberately courting heresy.

'The supernovae have thrown everything we thought we knew about stellar mechanics out the window, but the Shoal won't even discuss them, which makes everyone think they're hiding something.'

For a moment, there was only silence, and the sound of the night wind blowing across the parapets.

'All right, then,' said Langley, unable to suppress a grin. 'I brought this telescope out here for a reason. The Consortium expects a good return on its investment, so you have to understand just how much you'll still need to learn after all your studies here are just distant memories – and by then, you won't have to worry about the Elders telling you what you can or can't think.'

He tapped the side of his head with one finger. 'Nothing ever happens without a reason, and that includes a neighbouring galaxy lighting up like an explosion in a fireworks factory. So here's a question to consider. Assuming some as yet unknown force has caused a considerable number of very distant stars to detonate, despite apparently lacking sufficient mass, does that suggest the same thing could eventually happen here?'

'But that's an unanswerable question,' Aiden protested, a touch of defensiveness now apparent in his voice. 'Even the Shoal's ships would take centuries to get there and investigate, and whatever happened there, it happened when we were still swinging around in the trees back on Earth. There's no point in speculating if we'll never be in a position to find out the answer.'

Langley closed his eyes for a moment, and Dakota thought she heard him swear quietly under his breath. When he opened his eyes again he looked over at Dakota and motioned to her.

'Dakota, would you like to be first to take a look?'

She stepped forward, bending over to peer through the telescope's viewfinder. Clearly, Langley hadn't responded to Aiden's statement because what he had said was true. The only reason humans had ever reached the stars had been down to the help of the Shoal. Twenty-second century experiments in long-distance quantum entanglement had resulted in tach-transmission, a form of instantaneous communication already long put in use by the Shoal's vast interstellar fleets of coreships. Among all those millions of inhabited star systems, they claimed to be the only race who had developed a faster-than-light drive, and in return for a promise that humanity would never attempt to replicate this technology, mankind would be allowed to colonize other planets within a specified bubble of space approximately three hundred light years in diameter.

It was an offer that couldn't be refused, but there had been stories and rumours of subsequent human attempts to replicate the transluminal drive, regardless of the Shoal's original threats. But all those attempts had apparently ended in abject failure. Similarly, there was never any public admission that human governments used covert satellites and remote observation technologies to constantly observe Shoal coreships in those vital moments before they translated into transluminal space, yet it was widely believed to be the case.

Without the Shoal, therefore, there would now be no colonies, no interstellar trade, no carefully licensed alien technologies provided by the Shoal's other client races, and certainly no original colonists to build Erkinning, the Free States, and all the other human cultures here on Bellhaven.

Without the magnanimity of the Shoal, none of this would ever have happened.

Dakota pressed closer against the telescope's viewfinder, feeling the cool circle of plastic against her eyebrow and cheek. Points of light then jumped into sharp contrast. Once again she was made very aware of details concerning the stars she now viewed that she couldn't possibly have registered without the aid of her implants. But her Ghost was already learning to anticipate her desires, so the information evaporated as quickly as it had appeared.

It was true that orbital telescopes and distributed radio scanning networks were far more accurate for the business of stargazing, but there was still a visceral rush in the physical act of peering through a simple lens. It made her feel like Galileo looking at the moons of Jupiter for the first time.

'Maybe somebody blew them up,' Dakota muttered. 'The Magellanic stars, I mean.'

Aiden laughed uproariously, and Dakota's face grew hot with embarrassment.

'If you've got any better ideas, feel free to share,' she snapped. At that point, Marlie, clearly embarrassed by the sniping, stepped forward to take her turn in peering through the telescope.

Langley's features had reverted to their usual granite-like impassivity, but he was doubtless taking in every word they said.

'You know, Aiden,' he said at last, 'it's entirely true that the Shoal have us over a barrel. There's thousands of other species out there, we're told, but we've so far only ever encountered the Bandati and one or two others. But you never know. Maybe it won't always be that way.'

Aiden smirked, but Dakota could see he wasn't so sure of himself anymore. 'Tutor, those are dangerous words in some places,' he said quietly.

Langley's stony features didn't even flicker. 'Then let's just say that once you, too, realize just how many restrictions the human race labours under, then you'll know how it feels to dream of changing the status quo. Then you'll know how frustrating it is to get only so far, and be told you can go no further.'

'Well, it's still far enough, isn't it?' Aiden replied, looking slightly bewildered. 'I mean,' he continued, a cocky grin now tugging up one corner of his mouth, 'it's still better than sticking around here for the rest of our lives.'

Dakota caught the look on Langley's face, even if Aiden was oblivious to it.

'You have,' Langley muttered, each word rasping as it emerged from his throat, 'a worrying lack of adventure.'

THREE

Shoal Homeworld, Perseus Arm
Consortium Standard Date: 01.02.2542

The creature's name was Trader-In-Faecal-Matter-Of-Animals, and he fell from orbit, contained within a field-protected bubble of brackish fluid, towards an unending expanse of blue.

Far above him, only a very few stars shone down. During its long and lonely flight, the Shoal homeworld had been lost in a dense cloud of interstellar dust for almost ten millennia, and was not expected to emerge from the other side for another millennium at least.

The part of the homeworld towards which Trader descended was currently in day, the requisite heat and light providing life given not by the long-departed star under which Trader's kind had first evolved, but instead by a myriad of field-suspended fusion globes arranged in a tight grid hanging a few thousand kilometres above the planet surface.

The homeworld moved alone through the vast expanse of the Milky Way, heading for the relatively empty spaces between its great spiral arms. There, at least, might be found safety from the war that would surely come one day.

Oh woe, thought Trader, as the watery surface of the homeworld approached at an alarming speed, *that we should ever reach our fabled destination!* His manipulator tentacles writhed under his body in an approximation of grim humour, snatching wriggling live-foods from his briny encasement and slipping them into his quivering jaws. Ten thousand years travelling and, with any luck, ten thousand years more, and another ten thousand years after that, and after that, and after . . .

The world of Trader's birth was an ocean world. A long time ago there had been continents, too, but careful management of the natural tectonic system had lowered these continental surfaces until they could be safely drowned beneath the life-giving waters. Now all was ocean, for ever and ever, except where carefully shaped energy fields cut great holes down through the surface of the waters: gaping abyssal spaces into which the vast pressures of the ocean yearned to plunge. These fields sliced high up into the atmosphere, generating vast areas of vacuum that led all the way down to the seabed, and even further.

It was to one of these tunnels running through the world that Trader dropped, his enormous blank eyes staring out from the skull of his piscine form, but safe within his protective bubble.

The ocean rushed towards Trader and then past,

as the creature dropped down one of the vacuum shafts, the blue surrounding waters rapidly turning black as he descended, leaving just a bright circle of light far above to mark his point of entry.

In the fraction of a moment it took Trader to twitch one of his palpebra, he was plunged into darkness except where the occasional fusion globe hovered in defiance of the laws of nature. These lit the way into sub-aquatic portals where a Shoal-member might pass at last from deadly vacuum and into the slippery embrace of Mother Ocean.

Down, down, down. Trader fell yet further, then twisted to one side with impossible speed in his inertia-free bubble, a fusion marker reduced to a fleeting point of incandescence as he sped by it in a flash. Then he was deep within the healing waters of Mother Ocean.

This was the place where the Deep Dreamers dwelt, in unending blackness at the very bottom of the world.

The decision to remove the Shoal homeworld from its orbit around the star that had birthed it had been made long before Trader had come into existence. But Trader himself was very, very old. He had employed a thousand names but, when he came to dealing with the humans who were his current area of interest and employment, the sobriquet Trader-In-Faecal-Matter-Of-Animals had seemed apposite.

It was a joke between Trader and the humans, some of whom found the honorific deeply offensive while knowing there was literally nothing they could do about it.

And neither they nor any other client race had the faintest notion of the deep rifts that ran through Shoal society. Nor would they, ever, if Trader and those of similar employ had anything to do with it.

Trader drifted further across the sandy ocean floor, where the vast watery spaces were broken into distinct regions by field projections. Massive buildings and administrative blocks grown out of ancient coral rose above the seabed like living colossi, though this was a region to which few were allowed access. Other Shoal-members darted about, following their own paths, busy in the gigantic task of administering to the Dreamers' needs – feeding and caring for them, aeon after aeon, on and on into a future which the Dreamers had been specifically engineered to detect and analyse.

The landscape was marked by yet more fusion globes that cast a luminescence over the chillingly vast shapes scattered across the face of the abyss. The Deep Dreamers would be aware of Trader's approach, as they were aware of so much else in their godlike capacity to see where the roots of coming events lay within the present. Trader drifted on over the edge of a precipice, and then spotted the Dreamers directly ahead, great bulbous shapes with sightless eyes, their gargantuan tentacles draped across and dwarfing the smooth hummocks of what had once been an undersea mountain range.

The land for hundreds of kilometres around the Deep Dreamers was devoted to sea farms that generated the thousands of tonnes of food necessary to feed them. Hundreds of tenders constantly roamed around the Dreamers, like acolytes waiting to be consumed by vast and terrible black gods.

'If you go among the Deep Dreamers,' Trader's superior had warned several days before, 'it's very likely an agent of the Mother Star Faction will seek to destroy you.'

They had met at an arranged rendezvous in an orbital park, a water-filled environment constructed partly from physical materials and partly from shaped energy fields. The homeworld had been visible far below, its waters wreathed in summer storms, lightning flickering across the southern hemisphere where a hurricane raged, whipping the surface waters into foam-capped waves beneath a tight curl of coriolis.

Above the atmosphere, and beyond the warming light of the fusion globes that surrounded it, the planet was ringed from longitude to latitude by glittering silver bands like a jeweller's cage. These were manifestations of certain fundamental energies that allowed the Shoal homeworld to be guided through the depths of interstellar space, keeping as far as possible from any neighbouring star systems.

Trader and his superior – an ancient, leather-skinned

individual known to him only as Desire-For-Violent-Rendering, a title reflecting his past involvement in the messier and bloodier affairs of government – had swum in parallel course through the public space, appearing to any casual observer as merely two ancient fish lost in their reminiscences of times long past.

'It wouldn't be the first time they've tried, I assure you,' Trader had replied. His answer had been enunciated as a cascade of watery clicks generated by its secondary mouth. 'I know how to handle myself.'

Desire-For-Violent-Rendering had clicked assent, but Trader could discern the other's nervousness manifest from the way he twisted his manipulator tentacles.

'Attention has been drawn to your working methods within higher levels of government,' Desire continued. 'Officially of course you are a free agent, long retired from active service. Nevertheless . . .'

Nevertheless. Trader had felt a certain wry humour listening to Desire's carefully phrased statement. Even an old murderer like Desire got the shits in Trader's presence. But as far as Trader was concerned, given that their ultimate purpose was to guarantee the continued survival of their species against so many enemies, real and potential, any successful approach was the right approach.

'You think me amoral and careless?' Trader had replied casually. 'Yet if I had not acted in the past according to my own judgement, the outcome might well have been far more terrible than some of our cadre frankly are capable of comprehending. This agent of the pro-solar faction, would its name be Squat-Devourer-Of-Enemy-Corpses, by any chance?'

Desire-For-Violent-Rendering fell silent, and Trader enjoyed a small flush of triumph at this response.

General Squat was a Shoal-member with a reputation even more terrifying than that of Desire, who had been taking charge of many a military campaign since long before many of the Shoal's client species had been huddling around their first self-made fires. Yet Squat seemed to have grown weaker with old age, more . . . liberal.

At that point, Trader had shot out a tentacle and snatched up a mollusc swimming by, ripping its shell open and stuffing the contents into his primary mouth with particular force. Even thinking about Squat provoked strong feelings of anger.

'Squat is close to the truth,' Desire-For-Violent-Rendering then warned Trader. 'We know the General was approached by Mother Star representatives, after making some enquiries of his own, and has since been recruited to their cause. Do not underestimate either the power or the influence that—'

'With respect, I am hardly to be underestimated myself.'

'But you are becoming careless, I think,' had been Desire's instant reply. 'You wouldn't be the first agent to get swallowed up by his own hubris. This name you have chosen for yourself . . .'

'Trader-In-Faecal-Matter-Of-Animals?'

'Yes.' Desire-For-Violent-Rendering's distaste had become clear in the writhing of his manipulator tentacles. 'A joke for a name, a very human joke at that. You have, I think, spent too long around those wretched creatures. Not only that, your methodology has become eccentric, for want of a better word. As if you're testing fate by giving those you seek to manipulate the opportunity to uncover your very manipulation. One might believe you to be suffering a certain, well, existential despair, as is not unprecedented amongst agents of the Dreamers.'

Desire had halted close to the border of a vacuum shaft, clearly waiting for a reply.

Trader's own manipulators had writhed in amusement. 'Are you suggesting I *retire*?'

'Perhaps not immediately,' Desire had conceded, 'since the Deep Dreamers appear to confirm the central nature of your role in coming events. Do you intend to visit them soon?'

'Yes, very soon. I will . . . have to deal with the General, it appears.'

'If word got out of the Great Secret, of the true reason for abandoning our home star and carrying our homeworld so far from any other solar body . . .'

'I understand.'

Desire appeared satisfied with this reply. 'It seems more than likely the General will approach you during your visit to the Dreamers, since you're otherwise unlikely to return to the homeworld again for some time. A meeting there would be . . . efficacious.'

Trader had flicked his massive eyes to either side of them out of habit. A multitude of peripheral devices scattered throughout the length and breadth of the park made it clear, however, that no one was in a position to overhear anything they said to each other.

The Deep Dreamers were the result of tens of millennia of selective breeding and genetic manipulation that had resulted in creatures as near to immortal as could be imagined, even by the standards of the exceedingly long-lived Shoal. The Dreamers' biological neural networks constituted a massive engine of quantum parallel-processing designed to navigate the chaotic foaming surf of the very near future, and thereby discern the rough shape of coming events. They could sift through near-infinite numbers of conflicting and competing quantum uncertainties, and predict where certain trends might bear fruit, or where certain historical processes might either grow in impetus or grind to a halt. They were also one of the Shoal's best kept secrets.

Generally, the Dreamers' predictions produced relatively few real surprises. Trader had long known that the war they all feared was an historical inevitability, something to be postponed as long as possible rather than entirely avoided. Nevertheless, the Dreamers could often produce remarkable – if occasionally unreliable – results on a far more basic and personal level.

It was for this reason Trader-In-Faecal-Matter-Of-Animals had chosen to make this personal trip to visit the Deep Dreamers for the first time in centuries. Extremely secret communiqués had predicted his prominent role in certain worryingly apocalyptic visions recently generated by the Deep Dreamers.

Never one happy to accept information at second hand, Trader had naturally requested a direct audition with the Dreamers, in order more accurately to decipher his role in coming events.

This close to them, it would have been easy to mistake the vast undulating shapes of the Deep Dreamers for a particularly sinuous and disturbingly organic-appearing range of hills and valleys. Hills that, from time to time, moved.

Occasional tiny sparks of bright energy fizzed around the surface of Trader's protective field bubble, as it adjusted to a soul-crushing pressure far higher than that in which Trader's species had first evolved. Other bubbles of bright energy, each containing a Shoal-member, rose up towards Trader from the direction of the Dreamers. These were the priest-geneticists that spent their lives tending and guarding their mountainous oracles here in endless, solemn darkness.

Trader soon became aware of the presence of another, approaching him rapidly from another direction. Trader slowed, allowing General Squat-Devourer-

Of-Enemy-Corpses to come parallel with him. They swam on together, progressing in the direction of the Dreamers.

'There you are!' cried the General with forced joviality. 'Trader-In-Faecal-Matter-Of-Animals, eh?' His manipulators rattled together with a series of clicking sounds, the Shoal equivalent of raucous laughter.

Trader suffered a momentary frisson of panic. Could the approaching priest-geneticists be fully trusted in their imminent dealings with the General? They were all, supposedly, insiders, loyal to Desire-For-Violent-Rendering's decision to suppress the unpalatable truth from the likes of General Squat.

But what if Desire had in fact already betrayed Trader? What if Desire's warning about Trader's working methods had really been a kind of ultimatum?

What if? What if?

Trader scolded himself even for such a momentary lapse of faith. If death came this day, he would die with the knowledge he had served the Shoal Hegemony far longer than most. There was grace and nobility in that thought for, after all, the notion of dying a natural death seemed preposterous.

And if not this day, then he would die on another. So be it.

Trader ceased his worrying. He cast a sideways glance at Squat, noting what an ugly brute the General was, his scaly hide scarred and weather-beaten. One eye – albeit easily repairable – was milky-white and blind, with a visible rent in its surface. A formidable opponent indeed, but Trader had faced worse.

General Squat rammed his field bubble into Trader's, and the water around them boiled as their energies clashed. Trader rapidly skipped his protective field away from the General, taking a moment to realize Squat was not in fact attempting to kill him.

'General—'

'Caught you there, eh?' The General came rushing back up, ancillary mouth snapping and tentacles writhing. 'Need to stay sharp! Never know when you might get a knife between the fins.'

'And you, General' – Trader was regaining some of his composure – 'what brings you to the Deep Dreamers?'

'Well, you see, the future's been rather on my mind of late too,' Squat replied.

At this comment, Trader kept his tentacles noncommittally bundled.

Something very like a human shrug rippled across the General's scarred exterior. 'There are rumours . . . very dark rumours, my friend.'

'I had no idea,' Trader replied.

'I hate to listen to unfounded gossip, but you'd be amazed the things that are presently being muttered in some very high-ranking circles.'

'Such as?'

Trader looked askance at his companion. They were close enough now to the Dreamers to see the sheer scale of the beasts; each tentacle-sucker could easily consume a hundred Shoal-members all at once. They were deep within the Dreamer's influence now, caught in the eddying tide of the very near future, even as it prepared to crash into the present.

'Well, I wouldn't care to elaborate,' Squat replied in a conspiratorial tone. 'And if I did, I might subsequently be forced to kill you.' The General's tentacles swirled around with humourless mirth.

'I have heard rumours myself,' Trader replied, 'that the Dreamers all predict a war is coming.'

'Yes!' The General seized upon this. 'Now don't get me wrong, war is a wonderful thing – in the right context, with the right enemy, and as long as you win. But these rumours, they concern an *unwinnable* war, as preposterous as that notion seems. Unwinnable?'

'Perhaps some of our associates have been talking too freely, General. It really wouldn't do to frighten the ordinary population.'

'Indeed,' the General replied.

Trader glanced ahead and noticed the priest-geneticists were almost upon them.

'Have you heard about old Rigor-Mortis?' asked Squat. 'Dead, I'm afraid.'

'Is that so?'

Trader failed to conceal his surprise. Rigor-Mortis had long been a prime mover among those who, like Trader, were privy to the Great Secret.

'Yes. Rigor gave himself to the Dreamers not so long

ago, apparently unable to bear the burden of some preposterous secret he had carried all his life. Or so the old fool told me, before he became voluntary squid food.'

'I see. And what might this secret be?'

'Preposterous nonsense, obviously. But I wanted to ask you about it, considering you were close pals with old Rigor for, oh, so many centuries. He claimed he knew the real reason we've been fleeing our own sun for so long. What he said was . . . remarkable. Of course, if you were to lend credence to such stories, it would raise rather a whole slew of other questions, wouldn't it?'

Trader steeled himself. 'I wouldn't know, General. What secret? Which questions?'

'Officially, the decision to remove our world from the original home system was due to inherent instabilities within our own star, which were likely to result in particularly destructive solar flares. Correct?'

'This is old news, General.'

'For this reason,' Squat blithely continued, 'we have since been travelling through the eternal darkness of space at a sublight crawl for millennia. Yet there are plenty of viable and stable star systems we could have guided our world toward before now. But we haven't done so. Why?'

'General—'

The General ignored Trader and continued. 'Yet we continue eternally on this quixotic quest, believing misguidedly that it wouldn't possibly occur to any of the tens of billions of Shoal-members living today that this story doesn't hold up nearly as well as a bucket of fish guts on the sunniest day of the year. Otherwise, why would the Mother Star Faction have gathered so much support for the idea of simply finding a viable star and going there! And then, of course, there remains the question of why we don't simply construct the biggest transluminal drive in the galaxy, and just fly this bloody great mudball to some other perfectly compatible star in an instant. Oh, so many questions, my dear Trader. And yet old Rigor seemed remarkably certain he had all the real answers.'

'General, Rigor believed in a lot of things, but his mind became increasingly addled since he was forced to retire. You'll recall he was captured in some middle-of-nowhere conflict and came very close to being made into a stew.'

'Be that as it may, everything the General told me made perfect sense. And don't keep trying to play the innocent, Trader. Your own name turned up often enough during his confessions.'

Trader sighed inwardly, and mentally prepared himself to murder General Squat at the nearest convenient moment. Now, however, he would have to listen to his idiotic heresies for a few minutes more, until the priest-geneticists were close enough for Trader to flash them the prearranged signal.

Squat continued in his blustering way. 'Remarkable, Rigor's revelations, particularly his suggestion that our faster-than-light technology was in fact *stolen* from another species.'

'General, would you really see the Shoal Hegemony collapse after a hundred and fifty thousand years? Is that what you're seeking? Would you still be proud of giving away the secrets of some dried-out old idiot too tired of life to stick around to see what damage he could do before he died?'

'Of course not. The days of our earliest interstellar travels are now long ago and half-forgotten. And, as we know, the few records that still exist are sketchy at best. Yet he didn't stop there. According to Rigor, the trans-luminal technology has other uses so remarkable that merely possessing the knowledge of it would entirely explain our long flight from the home star . . .'

The dozen priest-geneticists, in their bright, colour-coded pressurized bubbles, were almost upon them, feigning as if to pass on by in the opposite direction. Trader watched the General glance towards them, and struggled not to do the same.

'All right, General, tell me what your price is. Please don't tell me it's anything as banal as power and influence. I'd be disappointed.'

'Half a million years of unbroken rule would hardly become unbalanced by a more candid attitude towards our fellow citizens,' came Squat's immediate reply. 'If the Mother Star Faction's demands can't be met, then at least give them a reasonable explanation of *why* they can't.'

'That won't happen, General. Those to whom I answer will have none of it.'

'Then you're facing the risk of revolution, Trader-In-Faecal-Matter-Of-Animals,' came General Squat's immediate reply. 'Now that I think of it, perhaps your chosen ambassadorial name sounds more appropriate than I realized. Most Shoal-members live far from the homeworld, but they would all rather see it orbiting securely around a stable star than lost for ever in a frozen dust cloud. Otherwise . . .'

Otherwise, what? was Trader's unvoiced reply. It was clear the General was not going to listen to reason.

'Otherwise,' General Squat concluded after a pause, 'others like me will be sure to disseminate the truth – particularly if anything drastic were to happen to me.'

Trader gave the signal. Suddenly the dozen priest-geneticists came rushing forward. Their energy bubbles flashed as they collided with the General's, while Trader himself retreated to a safe distance.

Thirteen balls of coloured light suddenly merged into one, with General Squat caught in the middle. The priest-geneticists now fell on the old warrior-fish, their tentacles ready-tipped with diamond-edged blades. The General fought valiantly, but he was old, and had been taken by surprise.

Your agents, dear General, are compromised, Trader thought to himself. Squat's plans stank of rank amateurism.

It was over so quickly. After a few moments the

priest-geneticists fell away from the General's ripped-up corpse, which began spiralling down towards the seabed, preceded by a field disruptor weapon the old fool had kept concealed about his person.

'Feed the General's remains to the Dreamers,' Trader instructed one of the priests, a near-albino known as Keeper-Of-Intimate-Secrets-Of-The-Unwittingly-Compromised. 'They can enjoy his memories.'

Keeper blinked his massive eyes at this request. 'If we submit the General's remains to the Deep Dreamers, his once-conscious matrix will merge with and further inform the Dreamers. The memory of what has happened here would survive and, so long as it remains within the matrix of the Dreamers, what he knew at the time of his death might be rediscovered by others.'

Trader sighed, emitting a long stream of bubbles. 'And it is your duty to sift through, interpret and censor such information as it comes to light, is it not? Rigor-Mortis gave himself to the Deep Dreamers precisely because he believed the truth would emerge just as you describe, and it's your duty to ensure this *never* happens. Is that understood?'

'Understood, yes,' the priest-geneticist replied, with a rapid string of clicks.

'Very good. Now take me to the Deep Dreamers.'

*

For some reason, some of the priests – including Keeper-Of-Secrets – appeared to regard Trader as almost as much of an oracle as the Deep Dreamers themselves.

'And you truly believe the war to end all wars is upon us?' Keeper-Of-Secrets asked yet again, as General Squat's body was delivered to the vast spirochetes of the nearest of the Dreamers.

Trader's reply was dismissive. 'What the Dreamers tell us is . . . well, it's rarely conclusive, is it? Sometimes, sad to say, it's even useless.'

Keeper was clearly scandalized by this suggestion, but Trader blithely continued: 'Instead the Dreamers give us clues vague enough to appear to mean one thing, then turn out to have a wildly different interpretation once it's too late to influence the course of events. Keeper, I think we rely on them too much. They're just a convenience the Hegemony can point to so they can abdicate all responsibility for their own actions. Look, they just say the Deep Dreamers predicted this, and the outcome was inevitable, whatever they might have done.'

Trader flicked his tentacles in a shrug. 'So ultimately that means an unfortunate few like myself are forced to take on responsibility for what must be done, and divert the flow of history.'

'Perhaps, but it must be . . .' Keeper hesitated.

'Continue.'

'I'm afraid of speaking out of turn.'

'You have my permission.'

'It strikes me as a lonely and thankless occupation,' Keeper-Of-Secrets continued. 'So few are permitted to know that such as yourself must manipulate events throughout the galaxy for the general benefit of our species. Yet, since such manipulations are based on the Dreamer's own predictions, and you appear not to think highly of the Dreamers . . .'

'I couldn't live with myself, if I thought any inaction on my part led to our destruction,' Trader replied. 'So, you see, to act is morally unavoidable, whatever the source of the intelligence.'

They had by now almost reached the first of the Dreaming Temples – a hovering robot submarine that granted the privileged few the means to interface directly with the Dreamers.

Trader made his farewells to his new partners in murder before finally slipping into the wet embrace of the Temple. The machine's innards opened up automatically at his approach, mechanical mandibles reaching out and securing his field bubble, which merged on contact with the Temple's own energy fields.

Trader found himself in absolute darkness, greater even than that prevailing beyond the Temple's hull. This hiatus lasted only seconds, however, before the Temple made contact with the Dreamer's collective consciousness.

Trader felt as if his mind had expanded to encompass the entire galaxy within a matter of seconds. Powerful images and sensations assailed his mind, far stronger than those faint intimations he had sensed on his journey here. He witnessed a hundred stars blossoming in deadly fire across the greater night of the Milky Way, a wave of bright destruction unparalleled in all of Shoal history, outside of the Great Expulsion.

Trader felt sickening despair. This was the worst possible outcome: a seething wave of carnage sweeping the Shoal Hegemony into dusty history. To become a had-been and never-would-be-again civilization, forgotten in the annals of the greater history of the cosmos.

Yet hope could still be detected even in the face of apparently unavoidable doom. Over the next few hours, working within the Temple, Trader was able to identify potential key factors: individuals, places and dates that might well influence the initiation of the conflict.

And even if war could not be prevented, it might still be reduced in the scale of its destructive impact. With gentle manipulation, it might even be contained, rendered harmless: turned into a historical footnote rather than a final chapter.

Sometimes, Trader had found, fate really did lie in the hands of a few sentients such as himself.

He began to make plans to ensure he would always be present in the right places to witness – and influence – these pivotal events. And perhaps even divert them away from an astonishingly destructive war that otherwise threatened to erase life from the galaxy.

FOUR

Trans-Jovian Space, Sol System
The Present

Warm, naked, her muscles tense with anticipation, Dakota floated in the cocoon warmth of the *Piri Reis* and waited for the inevitable.

Ever since she'd departed Sant'Arcangelo, the ship had gone crazy at precise thirteen-hour intervals: lights dimmed, communications systems scrambled and rebooted, and even her Ghost circuits suffered a brief dose of amnesia, while heavy, bulkhead-rattling vibrations rolled through the hull.

Every incidence was worse than the last. And every time it happened, Dakota thought of jettisoning the unknown contents of her cargo hold, only to end up reminding herself just why that was a really bad idea.

Twenty seconds to go. She put down her rehydrated black bean soup and flicked a glance in the direction of the main console. Streams of numbers and graphs appeared in the air, along with the image of a clock counting down the last few seconds. She stared at the numbers, feeling the same flood of despair she'd felt every other time this disruption had happened.

Deliver the cargo. Ignore any alerts. Don't interfere with either the cargo bay or its contents. That's what Dakota had been instructed, and that was exactly what she intended to do.

Absolutely.

'*Piri,*' she said aloud, 'tell me what's causing this.'

<I'm afraid I can't>, the ship replied in tireless response to a question she'd already asked a dozen times, <without violating the terms of your current contract. Would you like me to analyse the contents of the cargo bay anyway?>

Yes. 'No.' This wasn't the way her life was meant to work out. 'Just leave it.'

The clock hit zero, and a sonorous, grating vibration rolled through the cabin. Floating 'alert' messages stained the air red. Meanwhile her Ghost implants made it eminently clear the source of the vibrations was the cargo bay. 'Alerts *off,*' she snapped.

Everything went dark.

Piri?

No answer.

Oh crap. Dakota waited several more seconds, feeling a rush of cold up her spine. She tried calling out to the ship again, but it didn't respond.

She felt her way across the command module in absolute darkness, guided by the technological intuition her Ghost implants granted her, pulling herself along solely by her hands, while her feet floated out behind her. The bulkheads and surfaces were all covered with smooth velvet and fur that was easy to grip. Cushions, meal containers and pieces of discarded clothing whirled in eddies created by her passage, colliding with her suddenly and unavoidably in the darkness.

The only sound Dakota could hear was her own panicked breathing, matched by the adrenaline thud of her heart. Convinced the life support was about to collapse, she activated her filmsuit. It spilled out of her skin from dozens of artificial pores, a flood of black ink that cocooned and protected her inside her own liquid spacesuit, growing transparent over her eyes so as to display the darkened space around her in infrared.

Instrument panels glowed eerily with residual heat, and she saw hotspots where her naked flesh had touched heat-retaining surfaces, making it easier for her mind to wander into fantasies of being trapped on a deserted, haunted ship.

She found herself at the rear of the command module. Three metres behind her lay its cramped sleeping quarters, two metres to the right, the head. Nine metres in any direction, the infinity of space beyond the hull. She ducked aft, into the narrow access tube leading to the overrides.

Piri?

She tried switching to a different comms channel but still couldn't get an answer.

'Fucking asshole Quill!' she shouted into the darkness, her fear rapidly transmuting into anger. At least her Ghost circuits were still functioning: she let them flood her brain with empathogens and phenylethylamine, brightening her mood and keeping outright terror at bay.

Dakota started to breathe more easily. It was only a minor emergency, an easily fixable systems fault. She soon found the first of several manual override switches and punched it a lot harder than necessary. Emergency lights flickered on, and a single klaxon alert began to sound from the direction of the command module. The life support, however, remained resolutely inactive.

One thing she was certain of. Whatever the source of her present troubles, it was surely within the cargo bay.

'I can't take that kind of chance,' Dakota had warned Quill several days earlier.

The asteroid Sant'Arcangelo's central commercial complex was visible through the panoramic window filling one wall of the shipping agent's office. Vehicles slid constantly along cables slung across between the two sides of a mountainous crack cutting deep into the crust of the Shoal-boosted asteroid. Birds flew in dizzy flocks through air so thick and honeyed you could almost drink it, while trees sprouted from slopes as broken and jagged as they'd been on the day of creation. On either side, both slopes were festooned with buildings and shopping complexes that literally hung suspended from tens of thousands of unbreakable cables criss-crossing the enormous void.

Just a few hundred metres above this city of Roke's Folly, the narrow wrapping of atmosphere ceased abruptly at the perimeter of the containment field wrapped around Sant'Arcangelo. Beyond that lay the cold wastes of the asteroid belt.

'Dakota.' When he spoke, Quill combined all the verbal qualities of a stern teacher and a favourite uncle. 'There is no risk involved. What could be simpler? My client loads an unspecified cargo into your ship. You fly your ship to Bourdain's Rock, where you then allow my client to retrieve his cargo and go on his way. Where's the risk in that?'

Quill shook his head, apparently incredulous. 'Look. If it weren't for the fact I'm not a pilot with a reputation as good as yours *used* to be, I'd do the job myself.' He moved over from where he'd been standing next to the window, and sat down opposite Dakota. 'So tell me how it's taking a chance.'

She stared at Quill and laughed. 'For a start, you can stop pretending I don't know that we're talking about Alexander Bourdain himself. I know things about Bourdain that would make the hair stand up and creep off your head. I've dealt with him a couple of times before, and I'd rather take my chances stark naked in a cage full of hungry wolves. And, on top of that, I won't even know what it is I'll be delivering to him?' Dakota shook her head. 'Gangsters like Bourdain—'

'Wrong,' Quill interrupted. 'He's not a gangster.' He glanced back towards the window, momentarily hiding his face from her. 'All those charges were dropped, remember?'

She wanted to take Quill by the throat and ram his head against the window behind him. It took an extreme effort of will not to start shouting at him. 'Well, I heard how one witness died mysteriously in an accident, and by remarkable coincidence all the others changed their testimony within a couple of days of that. Excuse me if I don't feel totally convinced.'

Quill returned his gaze to her briefly. Then he walked over to the door of his office and opened it. 'You, I think, need to get some trust into your life.' He gestured her out of the door with his head. 'Or are you telling me you don't need this job so badly anymore?'

'Shut the door. I haven't changed my mind.'

Quill closed the door and went to stand over her, arms folded. Just then Dakota felt like she'd never hated anyone more in her whole life. 'But it's . . . it's too much of a risk shipping something when I don't even know what it is I'm delivering. That's just asking for trouble!'

Quill pursed his lips. 'You've still got some time to think about it: another eight hours before they need a definite answer. Though I should add, he's . . . *my client* is in a hurry to finalize arrangements. Maybe I'd be better off getting someone else to—'

Dakota shook her head, suddenly weary. She was just making a fool of herself pretending to Quill she might have any choice. If she didn't do this job for Quill, she'd forfeit her ship the *Piri Reis* to him. He'd been responsible for acquiring much of the highly illegal counter-surveillance and black ops devices now installed on the vessel, and Dakota still owed him for that equipment.

'No. I'll do it.'

'Maybe I'll—'

'No.'

'All right, then.' Quill nodded and sat down again behind the low marble desk where he did much of his business. 'We won't need to worry too much about official channels, since I'll be providing a manifest detailing something entirely innocuous—'

'Don't,' she said sharply, cutting Quill off. 'Just leave it. Load the cargo, tell the Consortium whatever you like, and just let me do the job. I don't want to know anything more than I absolutely have to. I don't even want to be having this conversation.'

Quill gazed at her blankly for a moment, then a small smile twitched at one corner of his mouth.

'You know, you wouldn't be stuck like this if you hadn't messed up that job out at Corkscrew. Way I heard it, you were lucky the Bandati didn't dump you in a hive and feed you to their grubs. They like doing that kind of thing, I hear.'

'I delivered – but the people I was delivering to tried to kill me rather than pay me.' Dakota's voice rose in pitch. 'I'm a machine-head, yes, but I'm not a fucking psychic. I didn't know what they were going to try.'

'Shame Bourdain's now got you running jobs like this as penance, I guess.' Quill smiled, watching Dakota rage in impotent silence, then gave her the details.

'Okay, you're going to have to rendezvous with another ship at these coordinates . . .'

A few minutes after the *Piri Reis*'s systems had ceased functioning, Dakota stepped into space and secured herself using intelligent lanyards. These snaked out of a belt she wore around her waist, and embedded themselves in the hull, constantly retracting and shooting out again to attach to a new point as she pushed herself on around the hull in the direction of the cargo bay.

She was still getting used to the filmsuit she'd stolen from the Bandati during her visit to Corkscrew. It coated her naked flesh just like a thick layer of dark chocolate, protecting her from the vacuum and radiation just millimetres from her skin. It smoothed out her features, making her appear, to any potential observer, like an animated doll. Her lungs were stilled, their function temporarily taken over by microscopic battery units she'd had implanted in her spinal column. She was, in effect, a one-woman spaceship, though there was a clear limit to just how long the suit would keep functioning before the batteries needed recharging.

But if by some miracle this trip to the Rock worked out, it would have been worth the deception – and worth her botching the Corkscrew delivery.

The vibrations had faded by the time Dakota exited the ship. But when her Ghost suddenly fired a pulse of nervous attentiveness into the middle of her thoughts, she braced automatically, and a moment later the ship had jerked hard enough to propel her away from the hull. She drifted a couple of metres away before the lanyards roughly yanked her back.

That's it, she thought. *Screw Quill, and screw Bourdain. I'm going in to look.*

She found her way to the cargo bay's external airlock. The crew of the ship she'd rendezvoused with for the pickup had spent a busy hour installing security devices inside the cargo bay, while she herself waited inside the command module.

Dakota reached up and pulled the manual override key, which she wasn't supposed to possess, off the narrow wire she'd loosely strung around her neck. Bourdain's installed security was good – the best money could buy – but it was off-the-shelf, and could be circumvented.

She adjusted her position, tightening the lanyard until her feet were firmly planted on the hull, and with one hand took hold of one of the hand-grips extending from the airlock door, still clutching the key in her other hand. She held this position for a minute, recalling her conversation with Quill, thinking about the risk she was about to put herself at.

If I do this and Bourdain finds out, losing the money

and the Piri'll be the least of my problems. Maybe it's not worth it.

She reached out with the override key, and paused again.

But then again, I have no idea what it is I'm transporting. What if those vibrations get worse? What if it's something that could destroy the Piri itself?

She tried to imagine a new life without the *Piri Reis*, her only home for several years now, and found she couldn't.

Once more she reached out with the key. Once more she paused.

On the other hand, with the life-support apparently irretrievably down, she couldn't even hide in the *Piri*'s medbox until she made it to the Rock, nor would her filmsuit last long enough to keep her alive in the meantime. Her only other option was the tiny one-man lifeboat she always kept on board, but it also had limited air and battery power.

Fuck that, she thought, and started to insert the key, just as she felt a familiar tingling at the top of her spine.

<Dakota?>

Piri?!

She froze, the key still poised in one hand. For a moment she thought she'd only imagined the ship's voice inside her mind. A wave of exhausted relief flooded through her.

Piri, what happened to you? You were out of contact for, for—

<Approximately twenty minutes, Dakota. Life-support systems have been reactivated. I have no records relating to the downtime.>

Dakota let go of the key. Then her eyes closed for several moments behind their slippery film, and she sent out a fervent prayer to no one in particular. It was over.

Aboard the *Piri*, she lowered the lights and crawled exhausted into her sleeping space. She'd have to clean up before disembarking on the Rock. That meant good-bye to now familiar body odour: regular hygiene was easy to forget in the long, lonely weeks between departure and arrival. She barely noticed the random detritus of her hermetical existence that now floated in freefall throughout the living space, even drawing a kind of comfort from it.

As so often these days, loneliness and depression swept over Dakota, lying alone in the dark. The ship's soft fur felt warm under her skin, yet something was missing.

It didn't take long for the *Piri* to respond to her unspoken need.

She was facing the wrong way to see a familiar shape detach itself from one wall, but she could imagine it easily. A tall, warm-bodied effigy of a man, its face as smooth and bland as its artificial flesh, its machine eyes imbued with fake emotion.

In the dim red light seeping through from the command module, she saw the silhouette of its smooth curved buttocks as it kneeled over her, soft moist lips kissing her gently on her naked belly.

'Dakota?'

Her ship spoke to her through the lips of the effigy. It had soft brown hair, almost indistinguishable from the real thing. Cables like umbilicals ran from its spine and into the wall-slot where it spent most of its existence – her ship made flesh.

She was so used to it now, it was beginning to feel natural.

'Dakota, your nervous system is again flooded with high-grade Samadhi neural boosters. Perhaps you are over-indulging—'

'Don't lecture me, *Piri*.' Dakota smiled, both her thoughts and body warm and fuzzy.

'Yes, Dakota. However, it does concern me that—'

That I'm not dealing properly with my past. Dakota felt a surge of anger, but it was soon gone under a flood of neurochem that washed the bad feelings away. *If you were really intelligent and not just doing a remarkable imitation of sentience, I'd—*

Dakota wasn't sure what she would do, but it would be mean. Mean and nasty. She smiled as she felt the effigy press down on her, smooth and soft and almost indistinguishable from the real thing in the warm dark.

*

Bourdain's Rock measured fifteen kilometres along its widest axis, eight along its narrowest. Before Concorrant Industries had drilled out the asteroid's core and plugged a planet engine into its empty centre, it had drifted for the better part of a billion years on a looping elliptical orbit, taking it close to the edge of the heliosphere before circling back in past Jupiter and Saturn. Several years before, Concorrant-built fusion jets had manoeuvred the asteroid into a permanent, stable orbit out beyond the most remote of Jupiter's native moons.

Dakota had seen pictures of the asteroid before Alexander Bourdain had paid the Shoal to work their magic on it. The images had then reminded her of a fossilized turd she had once seen on display in a museum. To some extent it still looked like a fossilized turd, but one that had been sculpted with explosive nuclear chisels until its shape approximated that of a rough-edged flattened sphere. Its surface was still cratered with deep cracks running along one side, but had now been transformed into a chiaroscuro of blues and greens, like a child's drawing of a tiny world with exaggerated people and buildings towering over its minuscule surface area.

The planet engine created a field of gravity by some arcane trick of physics that still baffled those human scientists who took it upon themselves to try and figure out the Shoal super-science behind it. The engine also generated a series of shaped fields that surrounded the asteroid, containing a pressurized atmosphere that extended no more than a few hundred metres beyond the asteroid's surface while also filtering out radiation and retaining heat. It was a grand, baroque gesture on the part of a man who had inherited a fortune reaped from the helium-three mining operations at the heart of Jovian industry. More, it was a demonstration of the power the outer-system civilizations now wielded.

Once the gravity field and atmosphere were in place – the latter drawn from the substance of the asteroid itself – Bourdain had clearly spared little expense furnishing his new world with a complete flora and fauna, all prevented by Shoal magic from spontaneously floating away into interplanetary space.

Like Sant'Arcangelo, Bourdain's Rock looked like a god's discarded toy. Some of the buildings on the asteroid were tall enough to push through the atmosphere-containment fields like fingers poked through a soap bubble.

The *Piri Reis* had been decelerating for half an hour now, its engines pointing towards the asteroid in a braking manoeuvre. Strapped into an acceleration couch, Dakota looked up at a viewscreen showing densely wooded forests that fell away into deep crevasses. A herd of deer moved past grey cliffs, while the distant face of Jupiter was reflected in the crystal waters of a lake.

Light came from incandescent fusion units mounted on poles that also extended out above the thin cladding of air. She watched the Rock turn before the ever-watching eye of Jupiter, banks of lights strung along the asteroid's longitude winked out to create a simulated night across one misshapen hemisphere.

It was utterly beautiful.

It took Dakota a while to find her way from the docking bays, across the asteroid surface and into the Great Hall. Enormous deerhounds ran past as she entered its vast space, their claws skittering and slipping on the polished mirror-like sheen of the marble flooring. The Rock's gravity had been set to about two-thirds Earth-normal. Beyond, in the distance, the sound of revelry echoed from the curved stone buttresses of a cathedral-like ceiling that looked at least a thousand years old, but had actually been in place less than five.

In the distance she saw two Shoal-members, each floating in their separate water-filled containment fields, each bubble supported by tiny anti-grav units. A retinue of Consortium bodyguards accompanied each of the creatures at a distance. Long tables held food and drink, all served by human waiting staff.

Dakota had dressed quickly, in loose light multi-pocketed trousers, and the one clean t-shirt she'd been able to find in a frenzied search through the zero-gravity maelstrom of her ship in the moments prior to docking.

She'd waited for several minutes in the antechamber that led into the main hall itself, composing herself and trying to quell the hammering in her chest. She had nothing to worry about, not really. Bourdain would be busy throwing endless parties in order to attract new investors, but she hadn't expected to find herself attending any of these lavish dos.

All she wanted to do was sort out her payment, then leave immediately, and start a new life somewhere very far away.

Nothing could be simpler.

'*Piri*, can you hear me?' Dakota asked the air, unnecessarily.

<Loud and clear,> the *Piri Reis* responded. <System response at maximum. Further directions?>

The computer's voice was sharp and masculine, and Dakota had a mental flash of *Piri*'s effigy. *Piri* wasn't really intelligent, of course, any more than her Ghost implants: that latter technology had been created in response to humanity's failure to yet develop anything close to true artificial intelligence. But, even so, there were times when it felt close enough.

None, Dakota sub-vocalized, stepping forward into the noise and light of the party. *Just keep an eye on things.*

Sheets of transparent crystal allowed her to look up between the vast stone buttresses of the hall towards the black sky above. For the next few hours, it would be night on Bourdain's Rock. Beyond the windows she could see where a sheet of rock rose sharply to a knife-edge peak, its vertiginous incline dripping with mosses and blue flowers. Everything she saw had been designed for maximum impact.

There must have been several hundred people at this particular gathering, but even they managed to look a little lost in such a vast interior space. She was very conscious of the clack of her boot heels as she crossed the marble floor.

The noise of the party grew louder, with a full-blown live orchestra, positioned on a raised dais, playing light classical music. Parakeets and finches flew overhead, darting towards nests built in carefully sculpted twists of ivy that grew up the walls. Unlike the Sant'Arcangelo asteroid, which had been designed as a financial centre for the outer-systems mining industry, Bourdain's Rock was developed solely as a theme park for the obscenely rich.

Apart from the two Shoal-members, almost all the guests present were human. A couple of dark-furred Bandati had settled down on various perches just above the milling heads of the guests below, their vast roseate wings twitching above their tiny bodies while they conversed, via translator devices, with a group of men and women who had the hard-faced look of deep-space miners.

Dakota felt a small thrill of nerves when she saw the Bandati, but the chances they might have any idea who she was, or that she had stolen something from them, were vanishingly tiny . . .

'Miss Merrick?'

She turned to see a gaunt-faced man in a formal suit, his hands clasped in front of him. She'd met Hugh Moss before on previous trips to the Rock, yet every time she managed to forget how badly he creeped her out. He had, as ever, the demeanour of a bloodless corpse that had been resurrected on a mortuary slab less than five minutes before and already regarded the experience with a warm nostalgic glow.

'Miss Merrick,' he repeated, in a voice drier than a desert grave. 'If you'd care to follow me, Mr Bourdain is waiting for you.' He gestured towards a door set into one wall, and began to turn away.

'Wait a minute.' She put up both hands as if physically trying to stop him. He halted and regarded her with a baleful eye. 'I don't have any intention of going anywhere unless it's absolutely necessary. I've done my job. Just pay me now so I can get out of here.'

Moss smiled, revealing a row of yellowing tombstone teeth. 'It seems Mr Bourdain wants to talk with you first.'

Dakota chuckled nervously. 'C'mon, what for? He must have a hundred cargo shipments coming in here every day. What's to discuss?'

'That's a matter for yourself and Mr Bourdain.'

Dakota studied him for a moment. 'Is there some problem?'

Moss shook his head. 'No problem.'

'But there's no point in my meeting him now I've done my job, right? I could just get paid and go. How does that sound?'

Moss regarded her silently for several moments, then

shook his head slowly. 'Speaking to Mr Bourdain is now a condition of payment' – that tombstone smile again – 'and then you can be on your way.'

Dakota thought for several seconds, the sudden pounding of her heart merging with the sounds of the party around them. 'I'm going to tell you right now, I don't like this.'

One corner of Moss's mouth curled upwards. 'Nonetheless.'

Dakota made an exasperated noise, shook her head and waved a hand at Moss. *Go on, then*. He started moving towards the door again, and she followed him.

They passed a whole circus of people in their progress. There were at least a dozen Catholic priests standing together in a loose knot, a few of them engrossed in conversation with an entirely human Imam wearing the gold earring of the Ministry of Islam. She caught a glimpse of a woman in a long dark gown, her hair pulled back in a tight bun – one of the many avatars of Pope Eliza, who stood in the centre of this gaggle of metal-skinned priests. Perhaps they were explaining to the Imam how they were free of sin because they were free of corruptible flesh.

Gas paintings partitioned the hall into sections, forming curtains of dry ice that trailed down from the ceiling, with images of mythical beasts projected on them, creating the illusion of ghostly monsters rampaging high overhead or wheeling through arched spaces on vast ribbed wings. In the centre of the hall a small artificial lake lapped at shores of finely crumbled marble, again creating the impression that the walls around it had stood here for millennia.

Mosses and vines wreathed the statues scattered here and there around the perimeter of the miniature lake, while clearly non-Terran shapes moved through its waters, sending up spumes of water from their blow-holes as they surged from one side to the other. Hidden holo-projectors painted the air with abstract patterns of light through which guests passed as they walked from one fresh attraction to the next. Significantly, each constantly evolving pattern was based around the logo for Concorrant Industries.

Despite her qualms, Dakota felt a tug of excitement at the sight, mingled with deep unease. There was no doubt that Sant'Arcangelo was impressive, being one of the first asteroids to be equipped with a planet engine, but this one had it solidly beat.

But a darker side to Bourdain's Rock quickly became evident. She followed Moss through the door, and then along a corridor opening into an enfilade of cavernous spaces that managed to make her feel claustrophobic after the sheer epic scale of the Great Hall behind them.

There were even more guests gathered here, but their activities were rather less salubrious. In a pit a pair of mogs – half-human, half-dog hybrids – fought with steel-tipped claws, while a crowd cheered and jeered encouragement from above. The beasts were vicious, lupine things, their human element barely recognizable in the dull vacancy of their eyes.

Even by the relatively lawless standards of the outer solar system, for all its lawlessness, breeding mogs was stunningly illegal. By such a display, Bourdain was openly flaunting his power and influence in the face of the Consortium.

Moss led her along past the edge of the pit and she glanced down on hearing an agonized howl. Just then one of the mogs collapsed, bright red blood gushing from its eviscerated torso.

The next cavern they entered was given over to the darkest sexual desires. There were mogs here too, hairless muzzled bitches with perfumed bodies, caged and set on plinths and awaiting the attentions of those whose tastes were so inclined.

Moss led her blithely through this cavern and on into the next, where human whores cavorted or copulated or danced with their clients, many glassy-eyed from the skin euphorics Bourdain's employees had painted on their flesh. None of this would have bothered Dakota, except that some of these whores, male and female alike, were bead-zombies.

Moss escorted her through a final door, and into a large office space so relatively mundane that it took Dakota a moment to adjust. Subdued lighting cast gloomy shadows across expensively upholstered couches and chairs arranged casually around coffee tables.

Bourdain had clearly been waiting for her. He stood up from behind a vast desk made of dark wood and stepped forward to greet her, instantly recognizable from a thousand newscasts and any number of scandals reported in the media.

'Dakota, I'm delighted you made it to my little party.' He smiled, revealing a row of expensive teeth. 'Go on, admit you're impressed,' he continued, his smile broadening as if he meant to take a bite out of her.

She glanced around and noticed that Moss had taken up a position by the door, as if to block her exit, his hands folded casually in front of him.

'If I have to be honest, I'm a little surprised you wanted to see me in person,' Dakota replied, not able to keep a quaver out of her voice. 'If there's anything wrong with the consignment, it's nothing to do with me, I assure you.'

Bourdain perched on the edge of his desk, with his arms folded in front of him, and gestured with a nod towards one of the visitor's chairs near by.

'Sit down, Dakota. I promise this won't take long. I just want to clear up one or two small things, and then you can be on your way.'

Dakota stared at him, not moving. She heard Moss step up behind her.

Piri? Are you there?

Only silence. She felt the first swellings of real panic.

'I can't contact my ship.'

Bourdain shrugged. 'Sorry about that, but I'd like

anything we say here to remain private. Now, the sooner this is over the better, so please do sit down.'

Dakota obeyed with a show of reluctance. 'All right, tell me what's wrong, Mr Bourdain.'

'Nothing,' interrupted Moss from behind her. Dakota twisted her head to study him, and then realized Moss had been addressing Bourdain. 'No scanning devices, recorders, weapons, nothing inside or outside of her body apart from her black-market machine-head implants. And we're blocking them, of course.'

'Nothing's necessarily *wrong*,' Bourdain finally said in reply to her question. He hadn't even glanced at his subordinate when he spoke. 'But I'd like to know for sure if, at any point, you carried out a remote scan of the contents of your ship's cargo hold.'

'Never.' Dakota shook her head. 'I've got no idea what you've got in there.'

'You were involved in the Port Gabriel massacre, am I correct?' A fresh grin spread across Bourdain's face. 'Don't look so startled, your secret's safe with me, Dakota. You see, I don't like too many surprises.'

She stared at him, for a moment more surprised than afraid. 'That's none of your business,' she snapped. 'I . . .'

Bourdain laughed as Dakota faltered, then he flashed a look at Moss. Dakota glanced to the side and saw the corner of Moss's mouth twitch upward again in an attempt at a smile. Watching it made her think of a corpse exhibiting the first symptoms of rigor mortis.

'You were subsequently tried for war crimes,' Bourdain added. 'That's one hell of a thing to have in your résumé.'

'Wait a minute.' Surprise gave way to renewed anger. 'What does any of this have to do with me being here?'

Bourdain leaned forward. 'I want you to realize there's nothing you can tell me that I don't already know. All I'm asking now is that you tell the truth. Did you ever try to find out what was in the cargo hold of your ship?'

'No, of course I didn't. I—'

Moss grabbed her head in two vice-like hands. She struggled desperately, but he was deceptively strong.

Then her sense of survival kicked in, and she let herself suddenly relax. As she felt Moss's hold on her ease marginally, she thrust herself away from him and towards Bourdain.

Two strong arms yanked her back down into her seat, and held her there. Moss's fingers dug hard into her flesh, Dakota screaming as overwhelming pain ran through her entire body.

She glanced down at Moss's hands where they held her, and she saw he was now wearing insulated gloves coated in fine metal mesh.

Lightning gloves.

Dakota tasted blood and realized she'd bitten her tongue. Bourdain continued looking at her as if nothing had happened. Somewhere behind him a concealed door slid quietly open and two ambulatory nightmares stepped into the room: bead-zombies.

The door closed silently behind them, and they stood behind Bourdain, awaiting orders.

Bourdain was speaking again. 'Port Gabriel was, what, almost a decade ago? Now look at you. Scraping a living in a stripped-down cargo ship that can barely haul itself from one lump of space-borne slag to another. And then this unfortunate business with the Bandati on Corkscrew?' Bourdain shook his head, and looked almost sympathetic. 'I heard a little rumour you took something from them, and didn't tell me. Now, what kind of way to do business is that?'

Quill.

How else could Bourdain have found out so much about her?

The first thing she was going to do, if she ever got out of this, was find Quill – and kill him.

'Fuck you,' she swore weakly. 'I don't respond too well to torture, so fuck you. Just tell me what you want and let me go.'

'Not the answer I was looking for.' Bourdain turned to the two bead-zombies, each of which came around opposite ends of the desk to stand on either side of Dakota. One male, one female, both tawny-skinned. Dakota wondered who they'd been when they were still alive, and why Bourdain had them killed.

Their heads had been surgically removed, and then cloned skin grown over the neck wound. Tiny low-level control beads implanted into the top of each of their truncated spinal cords allowed the bodies to respond to external orders, as well as controlling the basic functioning of the body and acting as a guidance system hooked into the local computer networks. Their bodies had been steroid-pumped, the skin shining and glossy. Each was dressed in a complex arrangement of fetishistic leather straps wrapped over their shoulders and under and around their groins, barely concealing the naked flesh underneath.

Bourdain nodded to Moss. Dakota gritted her teeth and heard herself scream when a high voltage current ripped through her once more.

Once it passed – surely the jolt had lasted only a second or two, but it was starting to feel like she'd been in Bourdain's office for a couple of hours – the power of speech took a moment to return to her.

'I don't *know* what's in the cargo hold,' Dakota croaked, with such an overwhelming sincerity in her voice it surprised even her.

Bourdain stood up and went to kneel next to Dakota's chair, laying one hand on her thigh in an almost paternal gesture.

'Let's get it straight exactly how much shit you're in right now, Dakota.' His hand slid up closer to her crotch and she tried to jerk away, but it was impossible with Moss holding her so tightly. 'If you're legitimate, you walk away. That's the truth. If I'm anything, I'm fair. But if you're lying' – he looked up, nodding at each of the headless monstrosities on either side of them – 'this is what Hugh's going to do to you, too. That right, Hugh?'

A breathy sound from behind her, like air escaping from a flatulent corpse. It was too easy to picture those greasy yellow teeth bared expectantly.

'So I think you'll agree, Dakota, that doing what I want you to is really going to be in your best interests.' He stood and looked down at her with what appeared to be real sorrow. 'I hate this kind of situation because it's so distasteful, you know? But that's business.'

'I haven't done anything!' she screamed. 'And, besides, the cargo is still in my ship, Bourdain. You can't get hold of it without my say-so, you understand me? If you go near it—'

Bourdain shook his head sadly, cutting her off. 'I own you, Miss Merrick, same as I own Quill. We know that someone or something probed your ship, and also probed the control systems for the cargo. Maybe you knew about it, maybe you didn't. If you didn't, I'm sorry, but I just can't afford to take any chances. Hugh, let her speak to her ship for a second, then . . .' He waved a hand towards her. 'Then find out what you can. Just make sure you clean the place up before I get back.'

Moss nodded as Bourdain walked out of the room, before leaning down to whisper in her ear.

'My dear Dakota, it's so good to be alone together at last. I can't tell you how much I'm going to enjoy you, after I remove your head.'

<Dakota?>

Piri!

Panic-stricken relief swept through her. She probably only had a few moments before Moss managed to close the connection again.

I need you to get me out of here.

<I am afraid to inform you that as you are no longer the registered owner of the *Piri Reis*, I am obliged to refuse you command as of seventy-five seconds ago.>

What? Override that, Piri.

<Only the appropriate personnel can permit over-rides.>

Dakota twisted around to face Moss, seeing the look of triumph on his face. It was the same look she'd seen on Quill's face once she'd agreed to take this job. Who else would have been able to supply Bourdain with the necessary overrides?

What 'appropriate personnel'?

<Mr Alexander Bourdain is the registered majority shareholder in Quill Shipping.>

Dakota closed her eyes, opened them again. Moss chuckled quietly.

'You and I are now going to have a long talk, Miss Merrick.' He deliberately drawled the word *long*.

Emergency systems override, Piri.

<Emergency systems overrides can only be facilitated by the appropriate registered senior personnel. Please note that—>

Parsley, Sage, Rosemary and Thyme, she subvocalized, rattling the words together in her panic.

<I am registering a stage-one intrusion alert.>

Remember me to one who lives there, she continued.

Somewhere inside the *Piri*, carefully hidden higher-level systems were coming alive as Dakota spoke her own secret code phrases.

<Second-stage intrusion alert: I am alerting the appropriate registered senior personnel. Further intrusions on higher-level autonomous functions will be severely—>

She once was a true love of mine, Dakota finished in a blur as Moss leaned in towards her ear.

'Your connection's cut,' he said. 'Now it's just you and me.'

<Hello, Dakota.>

Dakota's heart skipped a beat.

Create a distraction, Piri. Anything.

One of Moss's fingers stroked her ear, and she winced at the stench of his breath. Then he suddenly stood bolt upright, but kept one hand resting on her shoulder.

'Sir?'

Dakota twisted around further and saw Moss seemed to be talking to the air, one finger to an earlobe. She guessed he was speaking to Bourdain.

'I just received an automatic alert, sir. Comms report receiving warning of a terrorist threat through a secure police channel.'

Moss nodded to the empty air. Dakota could almost hear the sound of her heart trying to bludgeon its way through her ribcage, her hands gripping the chair.

'It's a secure channel routed through the Consortium Outer System Patrol offices,' Moss continued, for the benefit of his invisible employer. 'They're claiming an unmanned helium dredge has been programmed to alter course and hit the Rock within the hour. No details beyond that, at the moment. And given the number of guests we now have in the Great Hall . . .'

<Dakota, I have generated a false police warning and routed it through the Rock's alert systems.>

Piri, I love you.

<You're welcome. Does that mean you would like me to fuck you on your return?>

Please.

Bourdain reappeared a moment later, so clearly he hadn't gone far.

'It's still only an automated alert,' Bourdain snapped. 'I need someone human to tell me what's going on.' He reached up and tapped his earlobe, looking over Dakota's shoulder. His eyes gradually unfocused, and she guessed he was seeing and hearing someone on his technical staff as if they were standing next to him.

'Tell me what's happening,' he suddenly demanded of the empty air. His expression got grimmer. After a moment, Bourdain shook his head, clearly unhappy.

He appeared to suddenly notice her, as if he'd forgotten what had only just taken place in his office. 'This isn't over,' he told her, venom in his voice. 'Hugh, come with me.'

She heard Moss shift away from behind her. 'Stay here,' he warned her. 'Don't make it any worse for yourself than it already is.'

They left, closing the door as they exited.

She was on her own.

Almost.

The bead-zombies remained standing on either side of her, like frighteningly detailed statues. Dakota realized, with a start, that neither Moss nor Bourdain had yet given them any orders, and without directions they were about as dangerous as a pair of well-muscled vegetables. She sat there frozen for a couple of seconds more, filled with sick fascination at the steady rise and fall of the zombies' chests as they hovered beside her. As they would wait, for ever, or until instructed to go elsewhere.

Dakota stood up carefully, ready to bolt if either of them so much as twitched a non-sentient muscle in her direction. A wave of nausea swept over her and she leaned against the back of her chair just in time to stop herself from collapsing.

<Systems indicate,> the *Piri Reis* informed her, <that you might require medical attention.>

The bead-zombies remained as impassive as ever.

Thank you, Piri. Thank you from the bottom of my heart. You saved my life.

<Comment noted.>

Can you please, please get me out of here?

<It may take several seconds. The local security systems have a high level of encryption.>

Somewhere inside Bourdain's Rock, the *Piri*'s offensive routines were subordinating the systems that ran the asteroid's primary computer networks, forcing them to channel erroneous information to Bourdain's technical staff.

Even so, it wouldn't take Bourdain long to realize that Dakota was the cause of it all.

She went to the door and tugged at it experimentally, unsurprised to find it locked. *Come on, Piri.*

<Please wait. Please wait. Please—>

She rattled the handle for the tenth time in as many seconds, and suddenly the door swung open. She peered out into the corridor beyond, knowing her problems were far from over. All she'd done was find her way out of his office. Now she had to get past Bourdain's security set-up, and safely off the asteroid itself, and that was going to be an entirely different challenge.

She touched her lips and her hand came away sticky with blood. Dakota closed her eyes and thought hard. If she tried to find her way back to *Piri* in her present battered state, she'd just be making herself easier for Bourdain's security to spot.

A frantic search located a bathroom some way along the corridor outside Bourdain's office, but fresh despair filled her when she saw herself in one of the mirrors.

Blood smeared her mouth and chin from having bitten her tongue.

She grabbed a wad of toilet paper and soaked it under a tap, then began cleaning the gore off her face, her hands shaking so badly she kept dropping the tissue, cursing as she bent down to retrieve it. And all the while, she pictured Bourdain or Moss coming back to look for her, while she stood here defenceless.

A few moments of effort and she still looked deathly pale. Not the best image to present, but it would have to do. Fortunately her dark t-shirt made the bloodstains less noticeable.

She edged through the door at the far end of the corridor and found the party was still in full swing. She waited a moment, composing herself, then stepped forward, fresh neurochem flooding into her blood-stream. By a miracle there was no obvious sign of either Bourdain or Moss.

She cut a straight line through the first of the sequence of caverns, heading for the Great Hall and the antechamber beyond, and after that the docking bays.

Can you locate Bourdain?

<Yes.> There was a pause as *Piri* negotiated the Rock's databases. <He is at the very far end of the Great Hall from your current location.>

What's he doing right now?

<He is speaking with the man named Hugh Moss.

Wait. Wait. They are now returning. They will reach your current location in approximately two minutes.>

Dakota found her way past a group of whores cavorting lasciviously in a cushioned depression in the floor, busily servicing a dozen male guests. Meanwhile, harsh and brutal music pounded from hidden speakers. She picked up traces of euphorics from the sweat of the onlookers around her each time one of them brushed against her bare arms. This contact generated tiny, unwanted bursts of pleasure in her body as she passed by.

Two inebriated men lurched eagerly towards her. One of them she decked without warning, pausing just long enough to grab the other on either side of his head, before lowering him to the ground and kneeing him hard in the stomach. He curled into a foetal ball and twisted away from her, gasping in agony.

She was only distantly aware of drunken cheering in her wake; the euphorics were starting to affect her senses. *Got to get out of here.*

She hurried on into the next chamber, where the female mogs were located. Out of the corner of her eye, she caught sight of a male whore copulating with one of the caged creatures on its plinth, for the benefit of a roaring crowd. The sight goaded her on with renewed and grim determination.

Dakota emerged at last into the Great Hall, but didn't pause for a second. She brusquely pushed her way into the deepest, densest part of the crowd in search of cover, ignoring the startled stares her passage provoked and a few knowing looks cast toward the door she'd just come through.

'Welcoming hello, meeting you please?'

Dakota stumbled to a halt, as one of the Shoal-members drifted up close to her. None of its human, Consortium bodyguards were anywhere in sight.

She blinked in surprise, studying the creature more closely. The bubble of water in which it floated extended perhaps two metres in width, and the anti-grav units holding it above the marble floor took the form of tiny metal discs placed at equidistant points around the containment field.

The Shoal-member itself possessed about half the body mass of a human, but its shape was that of a large chondrichthian fish. Rainbow-hued fins and tail wafted within the surrounding waters, and the several tentacles it used for manipulation extended downwards from its belly region, while the gills appeared as long dark slashes halfway along its torso.

Other, much tinier, non-sentient fish darted around it and, as Dakota watched, a few of the creature's tentacles lashed out to ensnare a clutch of them, stuffing them greedily into its ancillary mouth. The alien's translation and communications systems failed to disguise the cracking and chewing sounds as the fish were messily ingested.

'Pleased to meet you too,' Dakota said insincerely.

She glanced around to see if she could catch sight of either Moss or Bourdain. 'Now if you'll excuse me—'

'Miss Dakota Merrick?'

The Shoal-member had her full attention now. It wasn't conceivable the thing was working for Bourdain rather than the other way around – or was it?

No, of course not. Concorrant Industries couldn't survive a day without the beneficence of the Shoal's technology and expertise.

'Hungry fish swimming for minnows,' the Shoal-member's translation software informed her, more than a little obscurely. 'A shallow pond. Mr Bourdain seems unhappy. Safety in numbers. Co-operation is key.'

She didn't have the time for alien riddles.

'I'm sorry, I really am in a hurry.' She began to move away.

'Small and alone in deep water, more likely to be consumed by predators,' continued the alien, rather less obscurely, floating along beside her as she strode rapidly through the hall. 'A free lunch. Some feed from skin of larger fish, live. Safety in numbers, in survival strategies. Two is better company than one.'

'You . . .?' She had the uncanny sense the creature was offering to help her. 'How did you know my name?'

'Shoal know all,' the alien replied mysteriously. 'What is dark to you is light to us. Clarity itself. Shoal hold open book of dreams, waiting to be read. All locks are broken with Shoal science, all secrets laid bare. You dart through deep waters with Mr Bourdain, yes? He attempts to force words from your head. Where Mr Bourdain is concerned, many smaller fish get eaten, and much blood is spilt.'

Dakota finally caught sight of Bourdain and his side-kick out of the corner of her eye, and she quickly ducked around the other side of the alien's floating bubble. She was pretty sure they hadn't seen her yet. The creature inside it swivelled to face her once more, while the bubble itself floated along by her side, matching her steady progress towards the main exit.

She knew it was impossible to read human emotion into the alien's face, but she couldn't help but believe that it looked amused, somehow.

'You know what happened to me in Bourdain's office?' she enquired, then started to move faster, almost breaking into a jog. People around them stared as they passed. 'Is that what you're telling me? How do you know?'

'Affirmation most appropriate answer. Shoal know all.'

'Look, Bourdain is out to kill me, and I don't know why.'

'Shoal is thinking affirmation. Much tail-thrashing, much gnawing at deep waters. Query, Miss Merrick . . .'

It took her a moment to realize it wanted to ask her a question. She kept darting glances from side to side, feeling deeply vulnerable from the lack of anything even resembling a weapon with which she could defend her-self. It took a great effort of will not to make a dash for the antechamber; with the alien floating along beside her, she was drawing too much attention to herself.

'What?' she snapped, wondering if she should simply make a break for it. But Bourdain would surely have placed security teams at every access point to the docking bays. Yet she saw nothing menacing as the tall archway leading out of the Great Hall drew closer.

But of course, she thought furiously: mounting an impromptu security operation to catch her right in the middle of a public extravaganza like this would draw far too much attention for Bourdain's comfort, especially after all his recent legal troubles. And with so many witnesses . . .

She had to remain calm. She kept moving forward, briskly. Her arms and neck were already damp with sweat.

<Dakota, I am being scanned by the primary local defence systems.>

Can you deal with it?

<For the moment.>

Keep me updated and prep for launch. I'm on my way.

She quickened her pace again, willing herself not to start running. In the meantime, the alien kept pace with her, which had her cursing under her breath. It was as good as having a giant flashing arrow pointing straight towards her, for the benefit of the dozens of people already watching their progress with bewilderment or amusement.

'Late to explain sorry sincerely. Embarrassment, as of

revelling in self-fouled waters. Query: your craft is filled to capsizing with darkly operating systems, all unheard and invisible to dry-floating-island's listening machines. If discovered by your Consortium, these non-legal modifications would consign you to ocean-bottom darkness for eternity, far from the common shoal, and with the loss of your craft. Follow?'

Darkly operating systems? And then it hit her what the Shoal-member was telling her. It knew the *Piri* was rigged with illegal black-ops modifications.

<I am registering massive systems intrusions. Initiating defensive measures.>

'What are they doing to my ship?' she demanded of the alien.

'Please to be curious,' the creature replied. 'This Shoal-member's scent glands recognize the presence of much else that is questionable recently residing within the belly of your craft. For instance, to be enquiring as to means whereby Miss Merrick came into possession of GiantKiller?'

'I don't . . .' Dakota's mouth worked uselessly for a moment and she almost stumbled. 'Did you say GiantKiller?'

'Pleased to be affirming this.'

For the briefest moment she forgot about Moss and Bourdain. 'You're telling me I had a fucking GiantKiller on my ship?'

'Shoal is pleased to note contrition arising from this unfortunate issue. Much unpleasantness. Human phrase "children playing with matches", curiously apposite, with apologies and humour. Dealing in such non-leased, highly restricted goods is most non-Consortium behaviour, resulting in banishment for all concerned far from surface waters, chained upside-down in deepwater cell for eternity. A sorry end.'

Shit. 'I didn't know,' she stammered. Somehow she found the strength of will to keep moving, despite a sudden weakness in her legs. 'I swear, I didn't know.'

But then, she reminded herself, she hadn't *wanted* to know. She'd deliberately and carefully avoided so much as speculating what might be contained within the *Piri's* cargo hold. Which was exactly why she'd spent the long days and nights of transit between Sant'Arcangelo and Bourdain's Rock in a state of sustained borderline panic.

Dakota enjoyed a moment of personal re-evaluation, as if she could step outside herself and witness the events of the past several months for the very first time. And in that instant, she knew she was back where she'd started, that all her efforts had come to nothing, and she would never receive the rest of her much-needed money, ever, from Bourdain.

She balled her hands into fists, forcing the nails hard into the flesh of her palms, finding some kind of solace in the sudden flash of pain it brought to her.

Piri? What's happening?

<I have initiated further emergency defensive software protocols. I am awaiting further instructions.>

'Shoal-member has suggestion.'

Dakota stared at the huge, fish-like creature floating in its ball of brine and wondered again if she could read amusement in its bulging black eyes.

'Suggest away.'

'Safety in numbers.'

'You said that already,' she snapped.

'We will move as a shoal, towards the shelter of caves. In meantime, would like to suggest acceptance of gift.'

'Gift?'

'Precisely.'

Dakota glanced around the side of the Shoal's bubble and saw, with a start, that Moss and Bourdain were staring straight towards her from nearby, but were still keeping their distance. After all, the alien was one of Bourdain's clients, one of his primary sources of income.

The alien floated closer to the archway, and Dakota hurried to keep up with it. She understood that the longer she stayed beside it, the longer she was likely to stay alive. She noticed it now held something in its tentacles. A box.

The tentacles holding the box flicked outwards to the rim of its encompassing briny bubble. Dakota watched as the water first swirled around its restraining fields, then began to pitter-patter down onto the marble tiles as a small puncture appeared in one side of the bubble, just wide enough for the alien to push the box through. As it clattered to the ground, the restraining field healed itself immediately.

Dakota stared at the box stupidly for a moment

before realizing she was meant to pick it up. She snatched it up and turned back towards the exit.

Bourdain stared towards her balefully and she turned away from him, feeling more naked and alone and frightened than she had since the ordeal in Port Gabriel. She clutched the alien's gift in one hand as, breathing hard, they arrived at the archway.

'OK, what is this thing?' she asked the alien.

'A gift. Accepting this, yes?'

'I'm not sure. Why should I?' she replied, with a stab of alarm. 'What's inside?'

'If Miss Merrick accepts gift, Shoal-member will endeavour to restrain Mr Bourdain from eating Miss Merrick. Shoal-member will also instigate legal reparations against Mr Bourdain for suspected illegal acquisition of non-leased technology, most specifically aforementioned GiantKiller. This in turn will allow Miss Merrick opportunity to sail for safer shores, facilitating hopefully rapid escape.'

Dakota opened her mouth, closed it again, opened it again. 'Why?'

'Beneficence of Shoal-member,' the creature replied. 'Much of existence is mysterious. Accept fate as fickle – or determined by whim. To gift Miss Merrick is pleasing.'

Dakota felt the cool texture of the gift wrapping against her hand, slick and waterproof. 'And in return – you're going to help me to escape?'

'Affirmation with pleasure.'

As soon as she passed through the archway the alien halted, placing itself between Dakota and her pursuers.

'I don't understand any of this,' she said. 'What's in this box?'

'A gift,' the alien replied obtusely.

She heard shouts from somewhere beyond the antechamber, echoing in the complex of tunnels and caverns that threaded their way through the immensity of Bourdain's Rock. The alien was clearly going no further.

Run. Run now. She stuffed the box in a convenient pocket and fled, soon leaving the Shoal-member in its containment field far behind her.

A minute or two later Dakota found herself in a crystal-roofed forest, under a starry night. Winding paths cut lazily through dense green foliage and between vast tree trunks with a too-regular mottled bark that indicated high-speed vat growth. Her Ghost circuits guided her back along the exact route she'd followed on her way to meet Bourdain, and she jogged down a lane that snaked between tall trunks looming on either side.

It didn't take long for her to sense that someone was coming after her. She could hear the twigs snapping underfoot as an unseen pursuer moved towards her at an angle through swaying grasses, but avoiding the path itself and staying out of sight.

Birds suddenly scattered in an explosion of wings,

vanishing far above Dakota's head as they sought new perches higher up. She pushed between a couple of benches and darted aside, behind the cover of some high bushes, crouching there in the grass and peering through dense foliage back the way she had come.

Moss emerged a moment later from the depths of a copse, and began looking around wildly. Blue flashes flickered around his lightning gloves, starkly visible in the artificial night of the surrounding forest. It lent him the appearance of some primeval nightmare god of electricity.

By the faint glow of his eyes, Dakota could tell his sight had been artificially enhanced. She watched as he scanned the trail just a few metres away from her, and when his eyes locked on the bushes that concealed her, it was as if nothing stood between them.

'Come out, Miss Merrick,' he ordered calmly.

She was so distracted she almost didn't hear someone else sneaking up on her from behind.

She stood, turned and kicked hard, catching the side of a helmet as one of Bourdain's security men moved towards her in a crouch. Burning pain flashed up her leg and she yelled out loud. The guard leapt forward and made a grab for Dakota. Ghost-boosted instinct caused her to let herself fall backwards as he slammed into her, his own forward momentum sending the guard sailing over her head.

She rolled back on to her feet by the edge of the path, almost colliding with one of the benches. She watched the guard as he crashed into his superior. Moss clutched at the tumbling man in surprise, and lightning snapped from his steel-meshed fingers. The guard screamed hideously, and Dakota caught the unmistakable stench of burning flesh.

She turned and dived along a different path, running blind now. As more shouting erupted nearby, she could hear Moss scream and curse somewhere behind her.

A moment later she realized that the local net was denying her Ghost access. And she was lost.

Piri, I need you to get me out of here.

<I have you on the live security feed. Proceed directly ahead and enter the third access tunnel on your right. This will return you to the docking bays via the shortest possible route.>

The forest gave way to an arcade of empty shop fronts strung along a wide walkway that eventually disappeared out of sight as it followed the natural curve of the asteroid's circumference. It was like a street constructed up and over the summit of a rounded hill.

Shots whined from somewhere behind her, sending more birds flying upwards in panic from their nesting places in numerous sculpted nooks. She heard the sound of running feet, coming from the far end of the arcade that was still hidden from her by the curve of the asteroid.

She slid into deep shadow between two shop fronts, then noticed that it was the mouth of a narrow alleyway. She ran further into it, and paused.

'Get the lights up!' somebody yelled. 'Get them up now!'

Panting hard, Dakota crouched with hands on knees. She guessed they were trying to get the main lights of the arcade switched on: the only illumination at present came from faintly glowing globes placed at discreet intervals, and which were clearly intended to be decorative rather than practical.

With one hand, she touched the alien's gift in her pocket.

Piri, why can't they turn the main lights on? Are you the reason?

<Yes.>

Then she noticed Moss's eyes flickering, luminous and satanic, in the dim light of the arcade beyond. They turned in her direction and he started straight towards her.

Dakota hauled herself back upright, wondering how much longer she could keep going like this, and why she was even bothered to try. They'd never allow her to get near the docks. Never.

At its far end the alleyway opened on to a covered plaza. This wide open space was filled with yet more trees whose dense foliage reached up towards narrow walkways that ringed the lofty surrounding walls. Drunk on adrenalin, she scrambled up a tree trunk, and then dropped off a branch and on to one of these walkways, water dripping on her from the wet leaves surrounding her. She hurriedly looked around, her head spinning from so much physical effort.

Muffled shouts as figures began to emerge at the far end of the plaza below. A sudden shot whined off the stonework of the wall, just inches from her head.

There's something I want you to do, so listen carefully, Piri. Apparently we were carrying a GiantKiller in the hold.

<Understood. Initial scans indicate there are restricted classified files in regards to their operation currently stored within local databases. Do you wish me to attempt to access them in full?>

Yes! I need to know if there's a way we can trigger it. Can you trace the GiantKiller itself, since it was unloaded?

<Affirmative. I have its location.>

She continued at a crouch towards the far end of the walkway, then saw to her horror that Moss was already waiting for her there. Torchlight flickered below, its narrow beam shining in her eyes for a moment. She ducked away from it, desperate to find some kind of cover.

Ahead of her, Moss held his hands out and blue sparks flickered through the gloom, crossing and spitting between the lightning gloves. His enhanced eyes glowed as dim ovals in the dark silhouette of his face.

He started towards Dakota, moving fast. She scrambled back the way she had come, then pulled herself up a stairway towards the roof. It brought her to the entrance of a wide gazebo set astride the wall at one corner of the plaza. Below its roof stood an intricate water sculpture.

Water gushed from the mouth of a marble dolphin set high on a plinth of finely sculpted rock, tinkling as it descended and splashed into a wide but shallow pool through which myriad finned shapes darted incessantly. Grassy ferns and occasional palm trees surrounded the fountain, dripping water like rain on to the sculpture so that it constantly glistened.

There were no other exits from the gazebo. Dakota turned to see Moss appear at the entrance, his unnaturally illuminated eyes finding her instantly in the dim half-light. She felt a sudden, terrible despair flood through her. She was trapped.

<I have located the protocols required to activate the GiantKiller, but it will take considerable time to fully decrypt and implement them.>

How long exactly?

<I estimate between twenty hours and fifteen days, Dakota.>

Dakota felt all hope evaporate. She'd been planning on a complex bluff, in case Bourdain might back down if she threatened to set off the device.

Someone else, she didn't doubt, had scanned the contents of the *Piri*'s cargo hold on its voyage to Bourdain's Rock. The critical question now was, *who?*

It had to be the same Shoal-member that had spoken

to her in the Great Hall. How else could it have known what was inside her ship?

GiantKillers were a near-mythical technology, supposedly originating from a Shoal client race somewhere else in the galaxy, which humanity hadn't yet been allowed to come into contact with. It was a tool of reportedly enormous destructive power, supposedly designed to reduce large bodies – such as asteroids, heavy with valuable mineral resources – to dust within mere minutes. Her Ghost's knowledge stacks were filled with a century of wild speculation concerning how such a technology might work.

As Moss moved slowly toward her, she decided to take a chance.

'Back off!' she yelled. 'Let me through to the dock or, I swear on the Pope's tits, I'll activate the GiantKiller from here!'

Moss paused. 'Nice bluff, but it really won't work.'

'I mean it!' she yelled in terrible despair. 'I've got the activation protocols uploaded to my Ghost circuits,' she lied. 'I can read every last fucking one of them back to you right now, or I can blow the shit out of this asteroid. Got a preference?'

'Lying slut, I'll open you from neck to navel and devour your innards while you watch.' Deadly blue sparks leapt lazily from one hand to the other as he again moved cautiously forward.

'Do you really want to try me, Moss?' she screamed,

backing around the fountain, away from him. 'Seriously?'

Then something remarkable happened.

The GiantKiller had already been moved to its new home in a secure storage facility deep inside the body of the asteroid, several kilometres below its outer surface. The *Piri Reis* had meanwhile been monitoring the Rock's communication channels, disguising its presence from moment to moment by simulating any one of thousands of maintenance programs, with a degree of sophistication equal to the covert systems used on board many of the Consortium's finest military vessels.

Suddenly, the *Piri* was no longer alone in its explorations. Something vast came crashing through the Rock's data stacks, devouring information like a lumbering virtual behemoth. For a few moments the *Piri* became deaf, dumb and blind as this new presence swept through the Rock's computer systems with all the subtlety of a sledgehammer being used to smash a doll's house.

By the time Dakota's ship recovered, the Giant-Killer's protocols had been wiped clean from the records. Alarm circuits blazed throughout the asteroid.

In appearance, the GiantKiller itself was little more than a mottled silver ball several centimetres in diameter, still held in the same field containment chamber it had been placed in prior to its trip aboard the *Piri Reis*. A casual observer might notice that this silver ball appeared to be flickering in and out of existence from moment to moment. But, rather than flickering, this was in reality a series of rapid expansions and contractions occurring almost too fast to register with the human eye. The GiantKiller was in fact testing its prison walls, lashing out in its pre-programmed desire to consume.

A microscopic analysis of the GiantKiller's surface would reveal something very like capillaries inside an organic body, channelling resources and information through a highly complex bundle of exotic matter held in check only by the shaped fields that contained it.

Without warning, the shaped fields that surrounded the GiantKiller vanished, and the silver ball now dropped to the floor of its containment chamber deep within the heart of Bourdain's Rock.

That same microscopic analysis would have then revealed those containment fields dissipating without warning, allowing a torrent of programmed matter to crack through the dense walls of the chamber, in just a few millionths of a second.

It was exactly as if a bomb had gone off.

The alien device underwent explosive decompression, extending microscopic feelers deep into the ancient flesh of the asteroid, spreading and dissolving the molecular bonds of almost everything it touched, reducing the solid matter of Bourdain's vast, pressurized folly to dust and gravel in an instant.

The irony was that the GiantKiller had been

intended as a practical resource for mining rather than as a weapon. And now it was transforming the asteroid into essential components that could, under more typical circumstances, be more easily collected by mining ships.

Dakota kept edging backwards, keeping the fountain between her and Moss. She was pretty sure he'd be careful about getting too close to running water while he was wearing . . .

And then it came to her. Everything here, the trees above, the ground under her feet, was wet, so there must be some kind of sprinkler system, some method of generating artificial rain . . .

Piri! If there's any way to turn the water on in here, do it now!

In response, *Piri* fired fresh instructions into the local network, again feeding false information to the asteroid's computer systems.

Dakota hauled herself up over the lip of the fountain and dropped into the pool, standing up again next to the splashing foam emerging from the dolphin's mouth. Moss stood scowling at her, but kept his distance.

Something rattled and spat in the dimness overhead.

They both glanced up.

All at once, throughout the entire Rock, it began to rain from ten thousand steel nozzles.

A torrent descended from the dome above, soaking them both immediately. Dakota propelled herself instantly away from the fountain and hit the ground rolling. Moss began screaming as the artificial rain shorted his lightning gloves, and she almost gagged from the awful stink as he jerked and writhed in an expanding cloud of steam. Fresh torrents continued to drench him from above.

The stricken man staggered blindly towards her, and then he fell face-forward right into the pool.

Just then a sonorous boom sounded from somewhere deep within the asteroid, so faint at first that Dakota wondered if she'd imagined it.

But more, heavier vibrations followed, rippling underfoot in regular pulses, each growing slightly stronger than the last. She heard yelling, and voices calling to each other, back in the general direction of the plaza. But then the voices faded, as if moving further away.

Then there was a sound like the sudden onrush of an ocean tide. It lasted several seconds, before silence fell again.

Dakota remained rooted to the spot for another few moments, desperately wondering what the hell was going on.

She then crept back along the walkway leading to the plaza, noticing how the lush, damp grass below her now shone with thousands of fragments of shattered crystal from the gazebo roof. Without warning, the entire plaza shook so hard she was almost sent tumbling over the railing to the ground some metres below.

No wonder Bourdain's soldiers had fled. Whatever was going on here, Dakota wasn't their priority any more.

The rumbling faded as quickly as it had started, whereupon Dakota made her way down to the ground level as fast as she could. She was conscious of glass crunching noisily underfoot, but that hardly mattered now there was no one around to hear.

Or so she at first thought. Two security personnel, their weapons already raised, emerged from where they'd taken cover under the dense foliage. Dakota gave a shriek and dived out of the way just as bullets whined off the tree trunks right next to her.

The ground rolled and rumbled beneath her with considerably more violence. Then it tipped sideways, suddenly transforming into a vertical plane.

Dakota went tumbling into some bushes, her senses spinning with the sudden shift in gravity. Her stomach twisted with a surge of nausea, and she desperately grabbed some branches, her legs dangling in empty air. The sidewall of the plaza was now several metres beneath her swinging feet.

Something was very, very wrong with the planet engine.

One of the two security men had grabbed hold of a tree trunk somewhere above her, then lost his grip and plummeted past her with a yell. He crashed into a concrete pillar supporting one of the walkways, his neck twisting at a sickening angle. His companion already lay dead nearby.

A steady shower of broken glass fell past her and on to the two corpses, but fortunately the dense foliage of the bushes sheltered her from most of the tumbling shards.

Then gravity began to right itself, just as she could feel her grip starting to weaken. A few seconds later the world had returned to normal, and Dakota found herself kneeling on the soft, wet grass again.

It took her a while to find the courage to stand upright.

Someone had clearly activated the GiantKiller.

Someone who wasn't her.

There came another series of dull booms from far beneath Dakota's feet, each one sounding closer than the last. Cracks began to appear in the nearby walls and in the grass. The plaza suddenly split into two halves, drawing away from each other. Dakota threw herself over the yawning chasm, landing safely on the other side, and ran for her life back the way she had come.

The constant tug of the Rock's artificial gravity began to fade. Suddenly Dakota was swimming through the air, carried forward by her own momentum. A howling maelstrom of escaping atmosphere roared up from the lower levels of the Rock, spilling out through the yawning crack in the plaza's floor and rushing upwards through the shattered roof.

Dakota activated her filmsuit and, under her clothes, it coated her bare flesh within moments. Her lungs shut down automatically and, as always, it took her a moment to get over the sensation that she was suffocating.

She then hurriedly discarded everything she was wearing, wanting to move as freely as possible. But first she removed the Shoal's gift from the pocket it nestled in, and clutched it firmly in one night-black hand.

Unfortunately for them, nobody else on the Rock enjoyed the benefit of stolen Bandati technology such as her filmsuit. Most of those guests she'd seen in the Great Hall earlier were either already dead or very soon would be. The only others likely to survive were the Shoal-members and the occasional Bandati she'd seen there. The priests she'd spied with their Pope-avatar were vacuum-proofed and radiation shielded, of course, as all their kind were. But whether they were alive or not in the first place was a matter of conjecture and religious inclination.

Now the only thought in Dakota's mind was how to escape.

'What did you say to her?' Bourdain demanded from inside his own protective bubble of shaped fields. In a corridor filled with people desperate to find a way out, he'd caught up with the Shoal-member that had spoken with Dakota earlier. 'How could you let her go?' he screamed. 'For God's sake, look at what she's done!'

There was no sign of Moss, but Bourdain had

received a verbal report from one of the squad he'd sent after her of how she'd threatened to activate the GiantKiller. Bourdain raged at the thought of her actually following through, and right behind that thought came the appalling awareness that he had so badly underestimated her.

As soon as he had things under control, he was going to hunt that murderous little bitch down remorselessly. And when he had her – well, he was going to take his time over what happened then. It would require time and imagination.

'Simple enquiry made concerning Dakota's cargo, nature of,' the Shoal-member that called himself Trader-In-Faecal-Matter-Of-Animals replied. 'Perhaps to peruse Mr Bourdain's thoughts concerning afore-mentioned matter?'

Anarchy now reigned throughout the ruins of the Great Hall. One of the ceiling buttresses had given way during the initial panic, sending a mighty spray of water across the cavernous space as the structure began to tumble into the artificial lake. Small decorative fish twisted frenetically in air that was misty with water now free of gravity's grip.

Like Bourdain, a very few humans were wealthy enough to afford personal shaped field technology. Those had long fled, along with anyone else who had been able to reach the docks before the atmosphere gave out. But most of the rest hadn't got that far, and their corpses littered the air all around.

Trader recognized that Bourdain was angry. It was very amusing to observe.

'Your planet engines are guaranteed *never* to fail,' Bourdain bellowed, his eyes showing white around the rims.

A strong gust of wind whipped constantly past them, rapidly increasing in intensity.

'I'll rip your fucking fish guts out in court. I'll see you in hell. I'll—'

'Terrifying power of the most illegal variety has been unleashed, a much prized and non-leased technology, most dangerous in hands of irresponsible species. A GiantKiller, I believe you would phrase it.'

Bourdain sucked in a deep breath, and his eyes narrowed. 'Prove it.'

'With ease. But also note that planet engine fully operational under normal optimal circumstances, such circumstances invalidated by presence of activated GiantKiller. Therefore the Shoal can accept no blame.'

'I should never have done business with your fucking kind,' Bourdain snarled. 'Really, outside of your box of magic tricks, all you lot are fucking tubeworms with attitude.'

'Correct surmise,' the Shoal replied. 'But very powerful, very wealthy tubeworms. Note also that safety lies within personal protective bubble, as world dissolves like salt. Mr Bourdain advised to make use of such tubeworm technology by way of escape. Should reparations be sought, if still unhappy after conclusion of this sad woeful day, honourable tubeworm suggests further thoughts concerning embarrassment of criminal charges for procuring GiantKiller. Non-loss of species access to leased technologies in the face of such criminal acts might be considered extremely lenient.'

Bourdain was starting to say something else, but Trader failed to catch it as a vast crack rent the Great Hall totally asunder, rapidly opening out into a chasm below them.

Trader propelled himself upwards as the roof collapsed, revealing the stars beyond. He left Bourdain to find his own exit, ignoring his continuing protests over their shared comms band.

Trader's human bodyguards were long gone in search of safety, and, truth be told, they were only there for show. If Trader had one real skill – beyond subterfuge and deceit – it would be a knack for survival.

He nimbly skirted a great section of the roof as it tumbled towards him, then navigated past several other sizeable chunks of falling debris as he made his way to safety far from the disintegrating asteroid.

Light sparkled from far above as the atmosphere's retaining field vainly attempted to repair itself before finally giving out completely. Now he was well out of danger, Trader glanced down for the rare privilege of watching an entire world – however tiny – disintegrate before its eyes.

The ambassadorial cruiser had departed the Rock the instant the first signs of catastrophic engine failure had manifested. Any sooner and Trader would have run the risk of arousing suspicion during any subsequent investigation.

'Please to be estimating surviving population of Bourdain's Rock,' Trader messaged his human staff aboard the cruiser.

'Of two thousand, two hundred and thirteen individuals, of which two hundred and thirty-five were registered staff, there's an early estimate of just seventy-five survivors, Ambassador.'

What would happen next depended on how much Trader chose to trust the information provided by the Deep Dreamers. Prior experience had taught the alien that the chances of someone successfully following a predicted course of action could be improved by narrowing down the alternative options.

So far, the Dreamers had been entirely accurate in their predictions of key events. In some way as yet unfathomable to Trader, the woman Dakota Merrick now stood at the beginning of a path that, without judicious interference, would lead to the most terrible war the galaxy had ever witnessed.

Now Trader's priority task was to make sure of staying with her every step of the way, until the root cause of that impending conflict could be discerned – and then carefully eradicated.

*

Before blacking out, the last thing Dakota remembered was a wall of rock rushing straight towards her. As she awoke, she was therefore considerably surprised to find she was still alive.

She remembered the plaza ripping apart down the middle, with a sound like an army of gods grinding their teeth in unison. She recalled seeing rivers of silver work their way through the ancient exposed rock, as she'd been carried upwards in a rushing tornado of air. Then a chunk of mountain had come flying towards her, lines of silver spreading through that too, before it visibly dissolved into gravel before her eyes.

The filmsuit, she knew, had kept her alive. She'd been aware that it could absorb kinetic energy to some fantastic degree, but ensuring her survival after colliding with a mountain was on a whole new level of scary.

A section of slowly tumbling debris about the size of a stadium came rushing up towards her. There was no way she could avoid it, but she braced herself nevertheless, hoping against hope.

She came into contact with the hurtling debris at bowel-emptying speed, yet she felt nothing. For a few moments, her filmsuit glowed a dull red while the rock underfoot began steaming and cracking. It seemed the filmsuit could somehow reflect the enormous kinetic energy of the impact back into itself.

Dumbfounded at this knowledge, Dakota bent her knees and kicked, pushing herself away from the shattered asteroid fragment. Her filmsuit slowly faded to its usual black, any remaining energy radiating back into space. It was hard to believe the Bandati liquid shield could be capable of so much.

Gradually she built up a momentum taking her away from Bourdain's Rock by pushing herself off other chunks of passing debris. Once she was far enough away, she finally took the opportunity to look back. Patches of dying forest were still visible, clinging to shattered asteroid-fragments that spun slowly away from each other or else collided and continued to disintegrate.

Dakota didn't even want to think about what had happened to the people left behind.

As she watched, a huge chunk of the Rock's shattered horizon split apart in a shower of grey and black dust. Trees and lichens still clung to one segment and, against all the odds, some localized emergency power circuits were still functioning, illuminating the interiors of ripped-open corridors, equipment bays and living quarters. Combined with the glow of sporadic electrical fires here and there, these lights gave the impression of a hellish grotto. She caught glimpses of the flash-frozen corpses of deer and horses floating near by, then they were gone, caught in a disintegrating maelstrom of dust and rock that was likely to grind them down to nothing.

Piri was feeding her news reports of the disaster, as local ships escaping from the Rock continued firing live feeds into the local tach-nets. Her Ghost subsequently picked out a description of a woman urgently being sought for questioning. A woman carrying illegal machine-head implants.

But I didn't do anything, she protested within the safety of her own thoughts. Maybe they were talking about some *other* machine-head.

They were going to kill me. I had no choice . . .

But no choice as to what? She hadn't followed through on her threat. She'd tried to bluff Moss, and failed pathetically.

But *someone* had followed through. She had absolutely no doubt the Rock had been destroyed by the same GiantKiller she'd transported here earlier.

The appalling notion that she had been set up oozed into Dakota's thoughts like a pool of coagulating blood. People were looking for her, people who thought she was responsible for this outrage.

But who could be easier to blame than a machine-head, an illegal?

Old anger and frustration flared deep inside her thoughts. She remembered all too clearly the day they'd forcibly removed her original Ghost implants, after the fatal flaw in the technology had become clear. Just as vivid was the memory of her subsequent near-suicidal depression, a bleak period that had lasted several months. Then came her decision to acquire some crude black-market clones, furtively installed in a backstreet surgery, before slowly starting to piece her life back together.

Without doubt she was the perfect scapegoat, for no one really trusted machine-heads. Not after . . .

For a long moment, Dakota imagined her broken and beaten body being tossed aloft by a jeering mob.

Come and get me, Piri.

<I am already on the way, Dakota. It may take me some time to reach you, however, due to the risk of compromising hull integrity through further impacts. It is therefore advisable for you to maximize distance between yourself and any debris.>

That's fine, Piri. Just make sure you get here before my filmsuit runs out of juice.

She was drifting towards a boulder measuring about a hundred metres across. As she got closer, she recognized the tiles adorning part of its surface: it was a fragment of the Great Hall. Both she and it were moving in the same direction at roughly similar velocities, so she managed to land on it gently. She was about to push away again when she caught sight of a human body floating nearby – a partly naked woman, with the few remaining scraps of an evening dress still straggling from her torso.

The corpse's eyes were glassy and frozen, the mouth open in a soundless scream. Dakota recognized her as the avatar of Pope Eliza.

As Dakota finally pushed off into the darkness her Ghost circuits tugged her gaze in a particular direction, where she saw light glinting from the rapidly approaching shape of the *Piri Reis.*

It would take days for her to shake the hideous memory of the avatar's corpse from her restless dreams.

The *Piri* hove closer, changing from a dull silhouette barely visible against the stars to a grey hull comprised of three joined-up sections. From a distance it resembled a fat metallic insect. From the ship's underbelly, a forest of grapples extended, seeking her out.

Dakota fell into her ship's machine embrace, like a swaddled child falling into the arms of its mother. At that moment she became aware of the Shoal's gift still clutched, by some miracle, in one black-slicked hand.

FIVE

Freehold Democratic State
Redstone Colony, 82 Eridani

Lucas Corso blinked, trying to stay alert, and focused again on the bleak landscape beyond the windscreen. He was getting tired after the long drive, the snowy vastness merging into an unending pale void as he aimed the tractor transport at a point midway between two distant volcanic peaks from which thin trails of smoke dribbled.

Fire Lake was visible to the east, spreading beyond the horizon, its icy foam-topped water crashing against a desolate shore. Canopy trees towered in the near distance, like black umbrellas sprouting from the corpses of buried giants. The largest and oldest of them easily reached fifty or sixty metres into the air. One-wings circled around the high, veined shrouds of the trees, their organic photovoltaic upper-wing surfaces sparkling as they circled in the fading light.

Corso checked the co-ordinates they'd been given: almost there now.

Sal was asleep beside him in the passenger seat, arms

folded over his chest, head back, occasionally blinking awake and peering around for a few moments as they trundled across the frozen landscape. He'd long since given up arguing with Corso, of trying to prevent him – as Sal put it – from committing suicide.

'Nothing you do will bring Cara back or get your father out of jail,' Sal had repeated for the hundredth time. 'Not even murdering Bull Northcutt. God knows I'd like to see the psychotic son of a bitch dead and skewered, but the fact is, if either one of you is going to wind up in a coffin, it's probably not going to be him.'

Corso had slammed the wheel with the heel of his hand, angry at Sal, but also with himself for letting Bull manipulate him so transparently. Bull had murdered his fiancée, knowing Lucas would inevitably call him out on a challenge. Lucas Corso, the son of a liberal Senator who'd renounced the whole system of challenges, before expediency and war had forced the Senate to outlaw them anyway.

Cara had disappeared on her way back from the medical facility in a small mining community south of Fontaine, where she'd been working on loan. A few weeks later, her remains had been found in the burned-out wreck of a short-haul landhopper on the road to Carndyne Valley. Her teeth had been pulled out and her fingers cut off – the trademark of Senator Gregor Arbenz's death squads. Her face had been so badly mutilated they'd had to identify her from DNA records.

It was all Corso had been able to think of for a

month now, that same floating image imposed between his eyes and the rest of the world: his Cara, not smiling but mutilated, torn, destroyed.

He couldn't prove that Bull Northcutt had done it, but Bull liked to boast. And Senator Northcutt's son was widely known to be in charge of one of the death squads.

Then one day a few weeks before, Corso had been on his way back from the research library in Carndyne Valley's East Tent and come across Bull Northcutt lounging outside the hydro farm with several other off-duty police, standing around a couple of tractor vans, getting drunk.

Corso kept walking, and tried to ignore the leering, grinning faces that turned to follow his progress. There was no one else around. They were here solely because they knew he came this way, every day. They fell silent, while watching him pass.

'By the time it was my turn to stick my dick in her,' Corso heard Bull say loud and clear, 'she was pretty good and loose. I don't think she'd ever been fucked properly in her life. What do you think, Corso?'

Corso had stopped, fists clenching at his sides, any last remaining scrap of doubt concerning the identity of Cara's murderer suddenly vanished. That was when he had challenged Bull. They could have easily arrested him there and then: since the Freehold had found a real enemy to fight in the Uchidans, the challenges had been outlawed. Too many soldiers were dying in duels when they were needed on the front.

But Bull had just kept grinning, and accepted.

Sal snapped awake as the tractor rolled down and then back up the banks of a stream, before Corso finally hit the brakes.

'Oh shit, I'm still here,' Sal yawned, blinking sleepily and staring around. 'Guess that means you're still going to get yourself killed, huh?'

Corso shot him a sharp glance, and Sal shrugged, turning to look out at the lakeshore, falling silent again.

Senator Northcutt, Bull's father, was in charge of the Senate investigation against Lucas's father, Senator Corso. Murdering Cara was Senator Northcutt's way of sending a violent message, not just to Lucas but also to his old man. Witnesses had already been bribed or coerced into claiming Senator Corso had organized secret meetings with the Uchidans; that he'd supplied them with vital military information and worked against the Freehold in order to destroy it; that he'd kidnapped Freehold children, handing them over to the Uchidans for mind-control experiments.

Men and women, friends and confidants, all frightened, all bruised and bloodied from long, violent hours in Kieran Mansell's police cells. All had testified against Senator Corso and his supporters, before the assembled Senate.

Lies, all lies.

A brief squall of icy rain spattered across the windscreen. Corso peered into the distance, and saw a couple of black dots standing around another tractor, a couple of flares driven into the hard icy soil, marking the site of the challenge by the shores of the lake.

'We're here,' Corso muttered, surprised at how calm he sounded.

Corso pulled on his winter gear before following Sal from the cabin, dropping several metres down the ladder to snow churned up by the tractor's tracks. He checked the seal around his breather mask one last time, then looked around. They stood on loose shale and rock dotted with tiny green and blue growths that pushed through the permafrost. The cold burned his skin wherever it was exposed, 82 Eridani's orange-red orb dropping towards the horizon as evening descended on Redstone.

Corso rubbed at the red fuzz of his beard where it was uncovered by his breather mask. Its protection was essential because the partial pressure of the nitrogen in the air was enough to cause a potentially fatal case of the bends after just a few moments of unaided respiration. It was possible to talk through the mask, which had built-in electronics that processed the voice, but what emerged sounded flat and metallic, like a robot speaking.

Harsh laughter, faint and distant, carried towards them from the other tractor. Corso clenched his fists tightly, anger reasserting itself under a black tide of adrenalin.

'Lucas. Listen to me. Remember what I suggested? Just walk in there, accept the challenge, and surrender without fighting. Then you can walk away with honour – and with your life. According to the code of conduct he has to accept that or he loses his honour, right?'

'No, Sal, I need to kill him. If I don't, they don't get the message. They'll go on thinking we'll never fight back.'

Sal then lost his temper. 'For God's sake, even if you won, that doesn't make you a Citizen! Challenges are *illegal*.'

'I'll present it to the Senate as a fait accompli. They'll arrest me, sure, but I'll go on fighting from inside prison until they take notice. Things have got to change here. Arbenz himself wants to re-legalize challenges. If I win and he still refuses to recognize me as a Citizen, he'd be committing political suicide.'

Sal snorted. 'Yeah, and either way, you're committing *real* suicide.'

The Freehold was based on ancient ideals. To become a Citizen – to enjoy certain privileges, to be able to vote – you had to be prepared to fight on its behalf. This inherently warlike philosophy had seen the Freehold forced out of colony after colony until the Consortium had relented and granted them a development contract for Redstone. With no actual enemies to fight, at least until the arrival of the Uchidans, and comfortably far from Sol and the bulk of the Consortium, the system of challenges had developed there.

But times were changing and, increasingly, only extremists like Arbenz and his gang of followers held up the old principles. The fact they were losing the war with the Uchidans, a constant tit-for-tat exchange of guerrilla fighting along a constantly fluctuating border, made the ground on which the old guard stood even less sure.

Six bright flares shone around a circle demarcated by stones carefully selected from the nearby shore. In the flickering light, Corso noted the same faces he'd seen that day outside the hydro tents when he had issued his challenge. Drunken cheers went up as he and Sal approached the base of the two-storey transport Northcutt and his cronies had arrived in earlier.

'All right,' Sal said, exhaling long and slow, as if he'd just come to a momentous decision. 'So you're really doing this.'

Corso nodded, without even glancing at his friend. 'I'm doing this.'

Eduardo Jones was Bull's right-hand man, and the last of Northcutt's crew to swing himself down from the lofty transport's cabin, agilely stepping down the ladder with practised ease. From the lake, a warm breeze blew over them, tinged with sulphur from the hot springs a couple of kilometres further along the shore.

'Hey!' he shouted as Corso and Sal drew closer. Jones began playing the hard man, pushing his breather mask up on top of his head and briefly sucking in the raw, nitrogen-heavy air like there was no tomorrow. 'What's this shit about you challenging a real man, Corso?' he yelled, after dropping his mask back down, so his voice emerged as a metallic rattle. 'Don't you know the rules – don't pee in your own bed, don't screw your sister, and don't get into a fight you know you can't win?'

One or two others chuckled. Bull Northcutt laughed the loudest. His face was twisted in an arrogant sneer above his powerful shoulders, eyes bright from heavy military-grade neurochem abuse.

'This is bullshit,' Sal yelled back to Corso's amazement. 'This isn't a fair challenge. There's not one of you,' he shouted, anger emerging from him in waves as his voice rose, 'that doesn't know it.'

Northcutt burst out laughing. 'You've got to be kidding me,' he spat, in a voice filled with ugly derision. 'Corso, right after you're dead, I've got a date with that sister of yours. Figure she could entertain me, and all my friends here, yeah? How'd you like that, you fucking piece of shit!'

A few of Northcutt's crew cheered, passing a bottle around and yanking their masks down to take quick pulls like they were celebrating a winning bet. Corso had no doubt every one of them had participated in Cara's murder. And, before Cara, others too.

And now they were gathered to watch him die.

Sal, as Corso had realized some time earlier, was deep in denial. He believed he could appeal to Northcutt's basic humanity, but Corso had seen Cara's body lying in the morgue and wasn't under any illusion he was dealing with normal human beings here.

If he was going to die, he'd rather go out fighting and do his damnedest to take Northcutt with him. Northcutt, who stood waiting, his eyes bright with enhancement drugs that ate away at his brain and nervous system, year after year after year.

Corso noticed the way Bull Northcutt's hands trembled uncontrollably, the fingers jerking slightly, the slight tremble in the muscles under his chin. Fighting Bull would be dangerous, very dangerous, but Corso's opponent wasn't as young as he had been.

Men like Bull rarely survived to grow old, because they got called out again and again, till they made mistakes, got slow.

Feeling momentarily light-headed, Corso closed his eyes. When he opened them again, he stared out over the shores of the lake, thinking, *If this is the day I die, then fine.*

*

113

Two long, double-edged knives with carbon steel blades already lay crossed in the centre of the circle where the challenge would take place. Corso watched as Senator Northcutt's son began to strip off his outer layers of protective gear, revealing a physique that was tall, lean and muscled. He stared slack-jawed as Northcutt continued to strip right down until he was bare-chested, though his skin was slathered in some kind of insulating grease. One of his crew threw a heated blanket around his shoulders, holding it in place.

'He's trying to psych you out,' Sal whispered, one arm resting on Corso's shoulder. 'It's his way of saying the fight's going to be over long before he'll freeze to death.'

Which would usually take no more than a minute or two, so if Corso could draw things out, Bull would get dramatically weaker. But clearly Bull was assuming his opponent would be an easy kill.

Corso had kept his inner insulating layers on, suddenly aware how much they restricted his mobility compared to that of his opponent. He kept himself in shape, but Northcutt resembled some kind of barely human predator, sleek, wiry and feral.

Jones stood in the centre of the combat circle and gestured for them to take their positions. 'Time's here,' he announced, and Northcutt's crew cheered, while Bull himself paused on the edge of the circle of stones, staring, unblinking, at Corso.

'Last chance to back out,' Jones taunted Lucas, with a grin.

'Fuck you,' Corso shouted back at him.

Jones turned in a slow circle. *How long are they going to delay this?* Corso wondered. With Northcutt half-naked, if they waited much longer, there wouldn't be any challenge to fight.

'Whoever wins will either attain or retain their citizenship, and as such he can then in turn be challenged by any non-Citizen who chooses. This is ordained under the eyes of the Most Holy, our Lord and Saviour, current fucking legalities regardless. Amen.' Jones then trotted out of the circle.

Corso had only half-listened, surprised and shocked by the sense of keen excitement welling in him, a surge of fire that spread through his chest, making every breath deeper and harder. Blood pounded in his skull like the roar of an ocean.

They stepped into the circle from opposite sides. Northcutt made the first move, darting like lightning towards the crossed knives.

Corso was big enough and strong enough to take Northcutt on, but Northcutt moved with an unnerving, fluid grace. Corso got to the knives a fraction of a moment after the other man, in his haste slamming into Northcutt's shoulder as they each grabbed a weapon. He felt something hot flash against his upper arm, followed by the splash of his own blood on the frosty ground.

Corso scrambled out of reach, quickly pulling himself upright just inside the circle, but now feeling the reassuring weight of the steel knife with its rubber grip in his right hand. They prowled around opposite extremes of the challenge perimeter, waiting to see who moved first.

'Fucker,' Corso swore under his breath, and kept swapping his knife from hand to hand, in an attempt to confuse his opponent.

With a shriek, Northcutt came running straight at him, his blade weaving patterns in front of his naked chest. He kept shifting from side to side so Corso couldn't be sure which way to head in order to evade him.

They slammed into each other, Corso grabbing the wrist of Northcutt's knife arm, feeling taut muscles tremble under the frozen skin. He twisted aside, attempting to slash up at his enemy's jugular, but Northcutt floored him with a single kick.

Northcutt moved in fast, intent on making his killing blow while Corso lay prone. Without any protective gear, he could move far faster than Corso could respond.

But Northcutt had clearly expected to make a faster job of it: Corso wasn't a trained killer like his opponent, but that didn't mean he was unable to defend himself. If the contest didn't end within the next few seconds, Northcutt was going to be in serious trouble from hypothermia. Corso could see how the other man was getting slower, even as he towered over him.

Without thinking, Corso brought his knee up, slamming it hard into Northcutt's testicles. Northcutt lost his balance, sliding to one side . . .

. . . red flared across Corso's vision and he felt the hot flow of fresh blood across his cheek. He blinked, suddenly light-headed, then tried to lift himself up, but slipped on the ice.

There was a lot of blood on the ground nearby. His blood.

Northcutt straddled him, his blade held vertically over Corso's chest, while his free hand pressed down on Corso's ribcage.

'Time to—' Northcutt started to say, before bright lights suddenly flared across them, accompanied by the deafening *whup-whup* of 'copter blades.

Two helicopters dropped down next to the combat circle, while Northcutt's crew looked around, stunned. Forgetting about Corso for the moment, Northcutt yanked himself upright and moved rapidly over to the perimeter.

Corso meanwhile rolled over and on to his knees. Panting wildly, he glanced over towards Sal, standing just beyond the circle with a hopeless expression on his face. Northcutt's crew began running around, shouting; rifles had magically appeared in the hands of most of them. Jones was already conversing with someone who had just stepped down from the nearest helicopter.

Corso looked over and recognized him as Kieran Mansell, Senator Arbenz's right-hand man.

'Hey!' Sal began shouting at Northcutt, who seemed just about to step out of the ring of stones. 'You can't leave the circle, Northcutt!' he yelled. 'That's quitting!'

Shit. Sal was right, Corso realized. Whatever the circumstances, leaving the circle amounted to surrender. Because challenges were illegal, Northcutt wouldn't actually forfeit his place in the lower Senate, but word of his shame would get around. Meanwhile his crew couldn't even toss him a blanket to keep warm, because outside help was strictly forbidden under the traditions of challenge.

Corso pulled himself upright and gasped as he felt the deep wound. It made him feel sick and weak to touch it, but he was pretty sure it wouldn't be enough to kill him.

Another couple of minutes spent out here in the freezing cold would do that just fine.

Mansell was escorted by heavily armed military clad in white and grey camouflage gear. Northcutt's crew began to raise angry voices. Mansell strode on straight past Bull Northcutt and into the centre of the combat circle, sparing Corso himself only the most cursory of glances.

Corso hauled himself into a sitting position, still clutching his chest. He noticed that Mansell was wearing body armour under his long overcoat, his hair like a stiff blond brush above the square-jawed face. There was something pitiless and inhuman about the man's eyes. Meanwhile the soldiers who had accompanied him began fanning out across the icy beach, their weapons lowered but at the ready.

'You all know who I am' – Mansell's voice was rough-edged and coarse – 'and I'm here on Senate authority. This challenge is illegal, and is over as of now. You' – he lifted one gloved hand to point at Northcutt – 'need to get inside. Now.'

'I'll kill you,' snarled Northcutt, simply but clearly. 'You're inside the circle, and that means you're taking up the challenge yourself. First I'll kill you – and then I'll kill him,' he added, with a brief nod towards Corso.

Mansell glanced back at him with a derisive expression, while Northcutt's crew remained silent. Corso saw that Bull was now becoming irrational from whatever warrior drugs he'd been taking. For a moment he thought Mansell's security team might intervene, then he saw the man make a hand gesture, and the soldiers remained where they were.

'I'll forget you said that, son,' Mansell replied finally. 'Go join your crew. Normally I wouldn't want to interfere, but I'm here on government business, and that makes all the difference. Got that?'

As he said these words, he turned and fixed Corso with a steady gaze.

He's here because of me, thought Corso with a start. He could see Sal still hovering on the edge of the circle, wanting to run over and help his wounded friend, but unable or unwilling to risk taking on Bull.

'No.' Northcutt was shivering violently now, his neck muscles outlined like steel cables under his skin. He moved towards Mansell. 'I don't give a fuck who you are. This is a challenge. You wouldn't be where you are now if you hadn't killed the right people. That's how we do things, right? There's precedent. You enter somebody else's challenge, that makes you fair game.'

'Go home, Northcutt.' Mansell sounded bored. 'You're not fit to talk.'

Corso felt a wash of dizziness pass through him. Northcutt was holding his blade out threateningly towards Mansell.

'I've never lost a challenge yet,' Bull snarled, moving closer to Mansell, who remained stock-still. 'And I won't start now.'

What happened next, happened fast.

Bull pushed himself forward in a series of motions that appeared almost ballet-like to Corso. Then it was over so quickly it took him long seconds to understand what had in fact happened.

Mansell turned a little to the side so that, as Northcutt moved in fast for a stabbing blow, the other man appeared to embrace Northcutt around the shoulders, as easily as if Northcutt were a life-size rag doll being tossed towards him.

Corso heard a pitiless crack and it was over. Mansell

lowered Northcutt's suddenly lifeless body to the ice, the latter's head lolling at a sickening angle.

Corso glanced over at Northcutt's crew, still scattered around the perimeter of the combat circle. Some of them looked like they were thinking of using their weapons in retaliation. Mansell's men dropped their own guns off their shoulders, and for a moment Corso thought things might end in a bloodbath.

'Stop right there,' said Mansell, addressing Northcutt's followers. 'The challenge is now over. He took me on and I won fair and square. Any of you care to disagree with that?'

A pair of hands began to pull Corso upright. He turned and realized it was Sal. Corso draped one arm over his friend's neck and together they staggered out of the circle.

It's really over, Corso realized, *and I'm still alive.*

Sal, with the help of one of Mansell's soldiers, carried him over and heaved him up into the back of one of the 'copters. Corso stared up at the rotating blades above his head, feeling curiously calm as other faces moved above him, their silhouettes blocking out the stars.

Another soldier bent over Corso and touched the side of his bare neck with something icy. A few moments later the ice spread through his thoughts, numbing him. Corso grinned, and started to laugh. Mansell meanwhile pulled himself inside the same 'copter just as it began to lift from the ground, leaving Sal behind them.

Corso looked down and saw the same hopeless look

still on his friend's face, as the shoreline dwindled with distance.

The next thing he knew, he was strapped into a webbed seat in the rear cabin of the 'copter, staring up at the aircraft's ribbed steel interior. Some internal clock told him hours had passed meanwhile.

'Feeling better?' Mansell was eyeing him intently.

'I don't know. Maybe.' Corso's clothing had been cut away around his heavily bandaged wounds. 'I need to get back,' he muttered weakly. 'My family . . .'

'Your family are fine, for now,' Mansell reassured him. 'But that's one of the things we need to talk about.'

'I really didn't think . . .' Corso trailed off, staring at Mansell.

'Really didn't think you'd still be alive?' he finished for him, a sour grin flickering across his curiously square features. 'If I hadn't turned up, you wouldn't be. Bull Northcutt was one of the best fighters in the Freehold before he turned into a liability.'

Corso shook his head. 'I don't understand any of this. Where are we going?'

'Tell me,' Mansell asked as if by way of reply, 'what do you think our chances are of winning this war with the Uchidans?'

Corso felt his stomach tighten. 'Why do you care what I think?'

'Speak freely. I'm being serious,' Mansell reassured him, noting his disbelieving expression. 'It's one of the reasons you're still alive.'

'In that case, perhaps you ought to speak to my father, Senator Corso. Assuming your boss drops those false charges against him.'

'Unfortunately, your father doesn't share your particular area of expertise.'

Corso opened and closed his mouth. 'Excuse me?'

'You're a scholar, not a fighter,' Mansell continued. 'Not hard to tell from that shambles of a fight back there. You're a specialist in alien programming languages.'

Corso squinted at the man, now completely confused.

'Shoal communications protocols,' Mansell prompted. 'Correct?'

Corso nodded dumbly. His area of expertise was ancient alien languages, going back possibly hundreds of thousands of years: part of the constant human effort to pick apart the available knowledge base of the Shoal Hegemony, trying to find the magic key that might open a world of infinite knowledge and power.

No one had ever come close to succeeding, however. Corso had merely expected a quiet life working away at the University with the help of a Consortium grant.

'Senator Arbenz is going to ask you to do something that will very likely affect the entire future of the Freehold, and you're going to say yes to him, because "no" isn't an option. Do this for us, and all the current charges against your father will be dropped, nor will the rest of your family be forced into indentured labour. You have my word on this, and the Senator's word, too.'

'And if I say no?'

Mansell's smile showed all his teeth. Corso looked away from him, feeling a deep chill settle around his heart that had nothing to do with the frozen air surrounding the helicopter.

'You're going to help secure an absolute victory for the Freehold over the Uchidans and rid them from Redstone for ever,' Mansell continued. 'But we don't have much time. You're being taken off-world, first to the Sol System, then to another location. We have been given command of a frigate called the *Hyperion*, for this express purpose, and we'll be rendezvousing with it in less than twenty-four hours.'

Corso struggled to take all this in, and his fit of shivers was not entirely due to the lack of heat in the tiny cabin. 'You're serious, aren't you? And this has something to do with my research? We're talking some pretty obscure academic material there, you know.'

'I need your answer, Mr Corso.'

Corso reviewed his options and realized there weren't any. He had no doubt that his refusal would result in a bullet through the head and his body being tossed down on to the icy wastes below. 'All right. Whatever it is, yes. But I need to—'

'No buts. Consider your position, Mr Corso – and

remember my reputation. I don't enjoy wasting time on arguments. You'll do as your world requires.'

'But what exactly am I meant to do?'

'The trip on the *Hyperion* shouldn't last more than a few weeks, and then we'll rendezvous with the nearest coreship heading to our final destination,' Mansell continued, ignoring his question. 'Don't even think about asking where it is we're going. We'll be joined by Senator Arbenz along the way. I believe you've already met him?'

Corso blinked several times. For the first time since he had been a very young child, he longed for the power to make his troubles go away simply by closing his eyes very tightly. 'You could say that. So Arbenz is responsible for . . . this?'

Mansell smiled again, and Corso really wished he hadn't.

'He needs your help, Mr Corso.'

'And in return?'

'Do this for us and you could wind up a hero – a war hero. That's better than getting a knife in the back for betraying your own people, wouldn't you say?'

SIX

Redstone Colony
Consortium Standard Date: 28.05.2538
5 Days to Port Gabriel Incident

Dakota's shuttle fell out of the infinite night, dropping
from orbit in a graceful arc towards a white and blue
streaked pearl set against starry velvet.

Until that moment lost in the complex approach
vectors her Ghost was channelling through her forebrain, she glanced back at her sole passenger. 'Sorry, did
you say something?'

Severn had a look on his face like he was waiting
for an answer. He popped into his mouth a narrow-
bladed green leaf that had the unmistakable patterning
of Redstone flora and began to chew on it. The
Freeholders had given this mildly narcotic plant the
remarkably original name 'chewleaf'. It seemed to be
available everywhere on board the orbital Consortium
ships, even though they'd only been in-system for a
matter of days. Too little time for anyone with enough
authority to get round to banning it.

'I was *saying* it feels good, yeah?' Severn repeated. His face betrayed a Mediterranean ancestry by its pale-olive skin.

Beyond the necessary details of their rapid descent to the planet surface below and the constant dialogue of traffic control, Dakota's thoughts had been focused on the ice-locked continents below, increasingly visible through the craft's windscreen. But she didn't complain about Severn's interruption. Every now and then, the way she saw it, there were moments when you realized something that was happening was really happening: like a kind of epiphany. This felt like one of those moments.

Shit, I'm really here – and it isn't all just in my head. That was what she had been thinking: how Bellhaven was a long way away and, even though unfathomable reaches of interstellar space had been crossed, somehow it seemed as if she was only now really coming to terms with the decisions, the life choices that had led to her being here in this place, and at this time.

Dakota shook her head. 'Sorry?'

Severn sighed dramatically. The craft shuddered around them and Dakota tensed automatically: they were skimming the atmosphere now, surfing the upper levels of the stratosphere at several thousand kilometres per hour, like a skipping stone skimmed expertly across the surface of a lake.

'I *said*, it's good when you finally get to go down below, get walking around on solid ground and, OK, maybe not breathing fresh air, but it's a lot better than being stuck on a fucking rock for years on end, y'know?'

Severn grinned and reached out with a fist to wallop the bulkhead next to his acceleration couch, presumably in order to emphasize this slice of homespun philosophy. Most of the way down, he'd been talking about the interior of Dakota's shuttle.

She had decorated the cabin of the little craft with small items originating from the Grover shanties back home. Fetish dolls hung from different points around the cabin. Dakota was hardly the religious type, yet the Revised Catholic icons epoxied on to a shelf above the entrance to the aft bay reminded her strongly of her own formative years in Erkinning – effigies of Peter, Anthony, Theresa, Presley and Autonomous Ethical Device Model 209, all rendered in gaudy clashing colours, their features beatific and childlike.

'You should know I'm not a Rocker, I'm from Bellhaven,' Dakota told him. 'Life on the boosted asteroids isn't so bad. Is it?'

'Yeah? Well, the kinds of places I grew up, they don't have the time or resources for fancy shit like field-retention atmospheres or artificial gravity.'

Dakota shrugged in response, twitching the control stick as the craft juddered. She could have guided the ship down using only her Ghost implants, but the general practice was to keep things reasonably physical. Even with implants, the mind could wander.

She'd left Bellhaven for the very first time three

months before, and she was still learning just how adaptive the technology inside her skull could be. Already her ship was starting to feel like an extension of her body.

When it became clear, by the end of the twenty-first century, that anything resembling true artificial intelligence was still a long way off, scientific research had shifted instead to a far greater emphasis on mind-machine interfaces. Dakota's implants were learning how her mind worked equally as she was learning just how they worked. It was like possessing a backup subconscious – something that could almost anticipate what you were thinking, thus allowing a degree of control and flexibility verging on the superhuman. An extra ghost in the machine.

They had a name for people like her: machine-heads.

'You're new to all this, aren't you?' Severn asked.

'Thought we were *all* new here.' The shuttle bumped and rattled as it came into closer contact with the atmosphere, the view beyond the windscreen fading as the optical filters reacted to the blazing heat of re-entry. A break in the cloud cover far below revealed the ruins of the town that surrounded the Redstone skyhook: this had spent half a year under bombardment by Uchidan forces, using conventional explosives before they'd scraped together enough resources for a couple of nukes.

The nukes had been high in radiation yield, but low in destructive capacity, insufficient to seriously damage the skyhook's structural integrity. Nevertheless, only the arrival of the Consortium had prevented the Uchidans making one last push and taking away the Freehold's only remaining link to the rest of the universe.

Dakota flashed a smile over her shoulder. 'You're a machine-head too, right?'

'Wow, how could you tell?' he replied in mock amazement. 'Worse. I'm a pilot as well, though this is gonna be the first time I do my job inside an atmosphere. Maybe you should hold my hand 'case it gets rough on the way down?' he leered, brushing a hand across the rough stubble of his scalp.

Dakota grinned and shook her head. Severn laughed at his own wit, and she noted they'd be landing in just under thirteen minutes, give or take the vagaries of ground control, and whether they'd managed to find enough secure landing spots for all the hardware currently on its way down from orbit. It would have been easier to ride down on the skyhook, but there was no telling whether the Uchidans might strike again with more nuclear mortar fire. Apparently there were still one or two pockets of resistance holed up down below.

'I'm Dakota.' She shoved one hand behind her seat for him to shake, and felt Severn grasp it after a moment's hesitation. 'Dakota Merrick.'

'Chris Severn.'

'Yeah, you see I knew that.'

'Mind reader.'

'Manifest reader.' She tapped the readout screen

printed on the thigh of her trousers. 'Same thing, just more boring.'

'Lean forward again so I can see more of your butt, and then I'll stay interested.'

'I could tell from how much your hands are sweating. Hang on.'

During the final descent, tortured air ripped around the tiny craft as she manoeuvred them into a tight spiral that factored in Ghost-fed random shifts designed to make it harder for any enemy forces to target them on their approach. She'd heard rumours that the Consortium were bargaining with the Shoal to acquire the same kind of inertialess technology they used on the coreships that had brought her and the rest of the fleet to Redstone, and fervently wished they'd get the hell on with the deal as her insides rattled in their bony cage.

'Listen, I got a confession to make. This is my first time on the surface,' Severn murmured.

Dakota took a moment to process this information before it made sense to her.

'On a planet, you mean?'

Severn nodded.

'Ever?'

'Ever,' he repeated excitedly, a grin spreading across his face. 'Seventh-generation Rocker. My daddy never set foot on nothing more Earthlike than Mesa Verde. Said he didn't like the smell of the place. Figured anything green that grew outside of a hydroponics tank wasn't natural.'

Dakota merely nodded, and sank once more into the multiple Ghost-mediated conversations flowing between herself and traffic control, and included several other pilots at once. Sometimes a dozen separate strands of conversation would merge for a few moments into one babbling cacophony, at other times unravelling and becoming more distinct, the words flowing like some arcane magical tongue.

<Sittin' steady guys, can you give me an update on local conditions?>

<Roger that, your delta vee is good by the way. Patching in weather feed – uh oh . . .>

<¿Cuál es él?>

This last from Severn who, Dakota had not noticed until that moment, was hooked into her comms feed. She could hear the tension in his voice, and she realized his Ghost must have picked up on the weather feed reference, subsequently pulling fresh data from a string of appropriated local weather sats.

<Got converging thermals off the coast,> came the report from Kirov, one of the traffic control staff. <Projections show a storm is likely by 1400 hours local time. You'll be here way before, but we might suggest some course corrections just to stay on the safe side.>

<Roger that, thanks for the info.>

<Hey Dakota, last time I saw you you looked like you stuck your head up a bear's butt and fell asleep—>

<Fuck you too, you lousy shit,> this followed by a

braying laugh from Kirov that made her smile. <That was your mother's butt.>

<Yeah, you need to stop drinking so much, we're taking bets down here how many bits we find by the time you hit the ground.>

The ride got yet bumpier, the craft tilting nose-up as her Ghost (or was it her? It was almost impossible now to tell the difference) implemented the re-entry procedures. The glow beyond the windscreen brightened, then darkened again as the filters compensated once more: the ship was slicing through the atmosphere at an increasingly sharp angle. Dakota pictured themselves as they might appear from the surface, burning their way across the sky in a fiery hypersonic parabola.

A few moments later heat shields slid down over the windscreen, cutting off any view of the landscape or sky beyond.

Smoke trails bled across the sky around the base of the skyhook, which rose into the blue exactly like a never-ending tower. Dakota had been warned that following it with your eyes up and up to its visible vanishing point could make you dizzy. She brought her gaze back down: the advice had been sound. Instead, she kept her eyes fixed more or less on the horizon, where the building housing the lower end of the skyhook – until recently a major military target for the Uchidans – took centre stage. Distant mountains were painted white with snow;

even the winters on Bellhaven couldn't have prepared her for the arctic blast of the Redstone winds or the sheer size of the distant canopy trees, towering over the landscape stretching beyond the buildings and streets.

Severn had called for transport, and Dakota followed him on board an automated vehicle that pulled up next to them. He looked distinctly wobbly from all the chem they'd provided to help him adjust to planetary gravity.

'Some sight,' said Dakota, nodding towards the sky-hook. Her breather mask felt heavy and uncomfortable. Worse, the relatively higher density of the atmosphere made their voices, as they emerged, sound unnaturally low-pitched. In fact they both sounded ridiculous, which didn't encourage elaborate conversation.

'Yeah, yeah,' Severn replied tightly, his knuckles white as they gripped a handhold next to their seats, the ground rolling past them at about forty klicks an hour. Command control lay somewhere up ahead, in a warren of emergency bunkers the Freehold had built beneath the skyhook.

'Problem?' asked Dakota.

Severn nodded stiffly. 'Too big.'

'What is?'

'Everything.' He scowled at her. 'Why's it so cold when the atmosphere's so dense? Shouldn't that make it warmer?'

Dakota glanced up and saw some kind of vast bird flapping its way slowly across the sky – a one-wing, her

Ghost informed her, its vast bulk supported solely by the dense atmosphere.

'Lots of volcanoes here,' she replied. 'All that activity spews ash into the air, and that counterbalances the warming effect of a thick atmosphere, stopping too much heat getting to the ground. So it's never likely to get very warm.'

Several minutes later they passed through a complex of airlocks and into the command centre itself, which looked like it had started life as a storage facility of some kind, judging by the signs still on the walls. Propaganda posters displayed cartoons of enormous muscular men carrying guns, who were standing in defiant protection of equally idealized homesteads. One such slogan read: 'Citizenship Is Worth Fighting For'.

And these, she thought with a sour feeling in her gut, *are the people we're supposed to be helping.*

The corridors were busy with Consortium staff moving about purposefully. Three separate groups of guards checked their IDs at different checkpoints. Dakota wondered if the paranoia levels normally ran so high.

Severn squinted at her. 'Banville, he came from your world, right?'

'Worked on the latest generation of Ghost implants, then lit out. You know the story.'

'The twist would be if it turned out he went off of his own free will, don't you think?'

Dakota shook her head. 'No, that would simply make him a traitor.'

Severn laughed. 'Guess *we're* doing the right thing, then.'

'Maybe. It's just that . . .'

They both paused, as a piece of information entered their minds simultaneously via their Ghost implants. They turned to look at each other.

Severn now wore a shit-eating grin. 'Josef Marados is in charge of our debriefing, then? Guess you'd better keep your legs closed tight.'

'Why?'

'Guy's got a reputation, is all.'

Dakota held Severn's gaze. 'You sound jealous.'

He gave her a long look up and down, as they resumed walking. 'He gets anywhere near you, damn right I'll be jealous.'

SEVEN

**En route to Sol System from Redstone, aboard
Freehold frigate *Hyperion***

Lucas Corso moved about cautiously in his diving gear,
while skirting the edges of a hydrothermal vent in the
ocean floor, trying to remember that hundreds of tonnes
of simulated liquid pressure were meant to be bearing
down on him. The brilliant lights built into his suit
blazed through the abyssal darkness, illuminating the
ridge ahead.

He shuffled towards the edge of this ridge, noting
the way the alien derelict teetered on the edge of an
abyss that fell away into bottomless depths. The derelict,
he thought, looked like some sculptor's impressionistic
rendition of a giant squid, with long spines curving out
from a relatively smaller central body. But even that core
part of the derelict loomed several storeys above his vantage point.

Some of the spines looked badly damaged, presumably by the impact of landing. Where the hull material

had been torn away from their tips, a bone-like structural latticework was visible beneath.

Peering down over the side of the ridge and into the depths beyond – or as far as he could see, before the range of his lights gave out – set Corso's stomach churning. He was clearly standing at the mouth of a deep vent that had probably been in place for several million years. And if the calculations were correct, the real derelict – as opposed to this onboard simulation – had rested by the vent for nearly a hundred and sixty thousand years.

Yet it was still intact, and according to Kieran Mansell at least, defensive systems were still running somewhere inside it.

The ocean above him only existed because the moon on which the derelict had been found orbited a Jovian-scale gas-giant, accompanied by a score of similar bodies ranging in size from mere boulders all the way up to minor planets. The magnetic field of the moon interacted with that of its gas-giant parent like a colossal dynamo, heating the moon enough to keep its ocean liquid under a dense cap of ice several kilometres thick.

A good hiding place, he reckoned, for the last surviving secrets of a dying race.

Kieran's voice came through to him via the comm.

'Quite something, isn't it? Observe that line of lights just ahead of you. They're there to guide you into the derelict's entrance. But I'm afraid the way in is a little close to the drop.'

Corso saw that the airlock – flush with the derelict's

hull – had been installed on a tiny overhang above the precipice, with a frail-looking ladder leading up to it. Simulation or not, his legs had decided they didn't want to get any closer.

'So I see. Is it safe?'

'This is a training simulation, Mr Corso.' There was something taunting in Kieran's voice. 'Relax, you wouldn't really fall. Besides, we should have a pressurized tunnel in place by the time we get to go on board the real thing. Then we won't have to worry about being swept over the edge.'

'Then why the hell do I need to wear this damn suit?'

'Because I say so.'

Corso cursed silently, picturing a thousand unpleasant deaths for Kieran Mansell. He dug up the nerve to shuffle closer to the edge, feeling the deadly mental pull of that bottomless hole. *Where does it come from, that urge to jump into an abyss?*

He tried his best to keep his eyes on the rock beneath the feet of his powered pressure suit, but in his mind's eye all he could see was the eternal blackness below.

It had taken a few days for Corso to orient himself to his sudden change in status from embattled Freeholder to temporary resident of a craft designed to travel from star to star. The *Hyperion* was vast, large enough to carry whole populations – which it had done, centuries before, when his people had first fled to Redstone at the height of the Migration Century. Of those original five colony ships, only three now remained – the *Hyperion*, and two others.

It soon became clear that the *Hyperion* had seen better days. Rather than deal with the time and cost of making repairs, large sections of the frigate had been closed down and depressurized. The crew was minimal, a half-dozen individuals put in charge of the maintenance of a behemoth craft that had once ferried thousands across unimaginable light years. Corso saw very little of them, as Kieran insisted on keeping them apart for what he deemed security reasons.

However, it became rapidly obvious that, unlike much of the rest of the craft, the weapons systems had been kept thoroughly up to date. The *Hyperion* was bristling with guns and automated defensive systems. Yet the Shoal-members who crewed the coreship, in which the *Hyperion* was currently cradled for its long voyage to the home system, appeared to be unconcerned with the presence of this heavily armed warship within their vessel's interior.

'All you need to know right now,' Kieran had explained curtly, 'is that the craft we found is a derelict of unknown origin. And very old, we assume.'

'But *how* old?' Corso had asked, standing there in the room Kieran had taken for his quarters. Some of the furniture looked like it might even date from before the Freehold migration but, apart from that, the adornments were pretty much what Corso would expect from a member of the Senate's security team. There were swords mounted on a wall, citations of honour bestowed during the perpetual war with the Uchidans, paintings of ancient battles dating from Ancient Greece right up to the present.

Kieran's face had remained expressionless, but his irritation with Corso's constant questioning was evident in the way he studied the blade of a wicked-looking knife he kept, turning it in the light and occasionally stroking along its length with an oiled cloth. 'Just old,' he growled dismissively.

'And I'm not allowed to know which system it's located in? But it's in human space, right?'

Before Corso had been brought into matters, those few who'd known about this derelict had begun referring to its builders as the 'Magi', after it became clear that it almost certainly predated the existence of the Shoal Hegemony. Even from the little he'd witnessed so far of the derelict's secrets, Corso had to admit that the name fitted.

'Of course,' came the firm reply. 'But the less people know about it the better. If the Shoal got wind of its existence . . .' Kieran shrugged, then opened a lined case and carefully placed the dagger back inside, before closing the lid. 'You understand me?' he added, staring back up at Corso.

'But we'll still have to hitch a lift on a coreship even to get there, and that means the Shoal will know exactly where we are anyway.'

Kieran clearly wasn't a man used to having to provide explanations. 'That's only partly true,' he replied, now affecting an air of infinite patience. 'The Shoal know where we're going, but they don't know the real reason. They don't know about the derelict. *You* need to know about the derelict, and what we've discovered there so far, because you need to be as ready as possible by the time you actually go on board.'

'All right,' said Corso, raising both hands in a placatory gesture. 'The only reason I ask is because anything else you can tell me might have some impact on what I can find out there.'

'Not likely.' Kieran shook his head. 'Just be happy you're helping your people overcome the greatest challenge they've ever faced.'

As flawless as the simulated environment was, Corso noted, the suit he himself wore – entirely real – lent a certain *veritas* to the proceedings by virtue of being heavy, uncomfortable and smelling like it hadn't been washed since worn by its last dozen users.

'You said something about a particular discovery on board the derelict,' Corso commented, his voice sounding dull and hollow to him inside the helmet.

Kieran's voice floated back a moment later. 'I want you to discover it the way we did. In context, you might say.'

Corso nodded resignedly. His progress across the

ledge was hard work. Even though the suit had been set up to respond to his movements as if he were in a low-gravity environment, the extreme pressure of the simulated ocean waters made the going extremely difficult, power-assist or no.

He could see how it wouldn't take a huge effort to tip the derelict entirely over the edge of the ridge and into oblivion. Some conventional explosives would probably manage that. Probably, the flow and ebb of the chaotic tides inside the vent had slowly pushed it closer and closer to the abyss over many millennia. It would be just his luck for it to finally slide over the ledge the moment he got inside the real craft.

Despite his nervousness, and his resentment of men like Kieran Mansell and Senator Arbenz, Corso had felt a growing sense of excitement ever since he'd realized what he was being asked to do.

Several tiny robot submarines lifted themselves from a charging unit held in a rack mounted next to the airlock. These floated towards Corso, lighting his path as he drew closer to the derelict.

And it really did look like some ancient beast of the deep; it was gigantic. The curving spines rising high overhead bore a clear resemblance to the drive spines that protruded from the hulls of Shoal coreships, too much so for it to be a coincidence.

Any remaining doubts Corso had about whether the derelict was once capable of travelling faster than light finally vanished. He felt a chill rush through his bones: the implications of what he was seeing were staggering.

The robots now swarmed around him, lighting his way towards the airlock that had been welded on to the derelict's exterior. He clambered up the ladder and stepped inside, allowing himself no pause to think about the vertiginous drop barely a hand-reach away. He waited while pumps noisily laboured to extract the freezing cold water out of the lock.

Once the airlock was fully pressurized, its inner door swung open, and Corso peered inside the derelict itself. The robot submarines had accompanied him into the airlock. They now raised themselves up on insect-like legs and scampered into the darkness ahead, their light revealing a sinuous corridor that twisted out of sight. The robot's lights then flickered off, and Corso could now see perfectly clearly all the way down the corridor, yet strangely there was no apparent source of light.

He pulled off his suit and dropped it next to the inner airlock, sucking in air that tasted entirely dry. It was the same air as the *Hyperion*'s environment chamber, since there were, after all, physical limitations to even the most sophisticated holographic projection systems. He found this oddly reassuring.

'Straight ahead,' Kieran urged over the comms link. 'Follow the 'bots.'

The 'bots were waiting at the far end of the corridor. He stepped towards them and they again scampered ahead, stopping only to look back towards him once they got a certain distance ahead, like hounds devoted to the chase.

Corso cleared his throat. 'Those spines projecting out of the hull, they reminded me a lot of—'

'I know what they reminded you of,' Kieran interrupted. 'You wouldn't be the first to make that comparison.'

'So do we know for certain . . .?'

'Not for certain, no. For that, we'll need to extract a lot more information from the craft's data stacks.'

Corso sighed. 'The reason I'm here, right?'

'Entirely correct. I'm hoping we'll have found proof that this derelict contains a salvageable transluminal drive before we bring Senator Arbenz himself on board.'

Corso shook his head, not quite able to believe what Mansell had just said. *A transluminal drive.* That meant faster-than-light travel. It was like stumbling into some ancient king's tomb, or finding a lost city: the stuff of boyhood dreams.

He continued onwards, finally finding himself in a room with a ceiling so low he was forced to crouch.

Senator Arbenz's face kept intruding on his thoughts. Somehow, this far, he'd managed to push that face to the back of his thoughts. The man who imprisoned his father was behind the killing of Cara, whether that happened on his direct orders or not.

And here he was, Lucas Corso, working for the very devil himself. How the hell did that happen?

'There's something weird about everything in here,'

said Corso tightly. 'Everything looks too new. Is that something to do with the simulation?'

'If you mean a fault in the projection, no. We think the ship is able to renew itself, or parts of itself, anyway. Clearly it can't entirely fix itself, judging by the broken spines.'

A wall had been torn open to reveal a mess of alien circuitry into which human computer equipment and screens had been wired. This in turn was connected to an interface chair that had been bolted to the floor. Its dark metal petals were neatly folded at its base.

'What about the bends?' Corso asked. 'We'll be going up and down from the derelict a lot.'

'We're already adjusting the atmospheric pressure on board the *Hyperion* to match that inside the derelict,' Kieran replied, 'so nitrogen narcosis shouldn't be a problem. Besides, the moon we found this derelict on is small, with low gravity. The atmospheric pressure, even under several kilometres of water and ice, is correspondingly lower.'

'So all I need to do is wander on board the real thing, type in some commands, figure out how to fly it, and away we go. Right?'

Silence.

'I can tell you're holding something back from me,' Corso spoke into the empty air. 'And I'll take a guess I won't like it very much.'

'Previous attempts to penetrate deeper into the derelict have been . . . turned back. We had to overcome certain automated defensive systems in order to construct the interfaces you see before you. That came at the cost of some lives. Even so, we only gained limited access to the derelict's core systems. Finding a way to actually control the craft, to make it follow our orders – well, that's another matter entirely.'

'Right.' Corso clambered laboriously into the newly installed seat and studied the displays in front of him. He noted a series of familiar-looking glyphs aligned in a row on one screen. 'I recognize these.'

'Outmoded Shoal protocols. I believe they haven't been used, according to our available information, since—'

'Since the earliest days of the Shoal Hegemony – at least according to their own records,' Corso finished for him, feeling suddenly light-headed. He touched each glyph in turn, watching as submenus sprang into existence. 'And here they are on a ship that might just have been constructed at some period *before* the Shoal say they developed transluminal technology – am I right?'

'That's the current conjecture.'

Corso blinked several times, a chill of excitement shooting up his spine. An ancient spacecraft capable of travelling between the stars in the blink of an eye, but not of Shoal manufacture. Obviously the Shoal had no idea of the derelict's existence, or they would never have agreed to deliver the *Hyperion* to its ultimate destination.

'You understand what this means,' said Kieran.

'Everything changes.' Corso nodded, thinking along several strands at once as he studied the interfaces.

Senator Arbenz's researchers had discovered an alien Rosetta Stone inside the least well defended of the derelict's stacks. The craft had turned out to have dual systems that allowed communication between their own computers and those belonging to the Shoal. Studying those communication protocols – protocols in which Corso was an expert – would allow him to work out how to communicate with the derelict, and ultimately to control it.

But it would take time. Even with the weeks they spent travelling, first to rendezvous with the hated Arbenz and then on to whichever benighted system the derelict actually resided in, he could not be sure how long the task would take him.

He thought of Prometheus, stealing fire from the gods and receiving an eternal punishment for his efforts. The Shoal weren't gods but they were close enough, in terms of their knowledge and power.

Corso leaned back, thinking aloud. 'What if we get caught?'

'Caught?' Kieran's voice was full of derision. 'We are the Freehold, morally superior to any other civilization in human space. Failure is not an option.'

Corso immediately thought of the Uchidans, and the struggle of always pushing them back and back and back, on a world that had once belonged in its entirety to the Freehold.

'Everyone knows what happens if we try and acquire technology the Shoal don't want us to have,' he insisted. 'Total revocation of every colonial contract – it's an impossible risk. Maybe we should . . .'

'Should what, Mr Corso?' came the reply in a menacing tone.

Every human-occupied world stranded from each other for ever without the benefit of Shoal coreships shuttling between them, if we're discovered.

Even if they weren't discovered, and all went to plan, the Shoal would surely know if the Freehold were constructing a fleet of starships. What then? War with the Shoal? It would be like an army of ants taking on an orbital nuclear bomber. The risks were too enormous, too overwhelming.

'How do we know no one else knows about this derelict? What if it's a trick of some kind?'

Corso had voiced this last possibility despite its wildly paranoid tone. But Kieran's rapid response suggested it had already been carefully considered.

'A honey trap left by the Shoal, you mean?' Kieran laughed with a harsh, rasping sound. 'So they can catch us in the act and revoke their contracts with us? No, Mr Corso, it's really not very likely.'

A wave of embarrassment washed over Corso and he stared mutely at the screens before him. 'But there *are* risks. Unimaginable risks.'

'Which is exactly why the Freehold are so well placed to deal with this discovery. It's in our human nature to take risks, isn't it? The manifestation of our warrior spirit? I'll remind you, Mr Corso, that if all comes out well – and it will – you'll be a member of the Senate, as well as a declared Hero who can decline to participate in the challenge system if he chooses and still retain his status as a Citizen.'

Corso nodded. 'OK, another thing. Interface chairs are generally intended for use by machine-head pilots. So what's it doing here?'

'There's a good chance a human machine-head will be able to interface with the derelict's controls in the way a normal human cannot, once we have broken through the security blocks and into the ship's core systems. Bellhaven Ghost technology appears to have close parallels with the means used by the Magi for piloting their craft.'

It took a moment for Corso to absorb this. 'Let me get this straight. Are you telling me you're intending to find yourselves a machine-head to *fly* this thing out from where you found it?'

'Correct, Mr Corso. There isn't the time to circumnavigate the derelict's systems to allow a normal pilot to control it, but extreme circumstances require radical thinking, wouldn't you agree?'

'I'm just finding it hard to accept the idea of a man like Senator Arbenz actually hiring a machine-head to work for him. It's . . . rather ironic, given recent history, wouldn't you say?'

Corso could almost feel the anger and irritation

coming at him down the comms link. 'This is far from a laughing matter, Mr Corso. So just concentrate on the task at hand.'

'How much are you going to tell the poor bastard anyway? What if he doesn't want to do it?'

'Leave that to us.'

Corso shook his head and bent down to peer again at the chair's readouts. His mind whirled: a machine-head?

Whoever ended up piloting the derelict was going to find it about as pleasurable as walking into a nest of angry snakes.

And if Kieran's reputation was all he had heard, there was every chance the experience might be deadly, too.

EIGHT

Trans-Jovian Space, Sol System, en route to Mesa Verde

A long, long time later, Dakota came to realize her biggest mistake had been opening the alien's gift.

Whatever she'd expected to find when she investigated the box the Shoal-member had passed her, she hadn't thought she would find herself holding a tiny and entirely anthropomorphic figurine handcrafted of wood and silver wire.

As she touched it for the first time, a slight stab of pain in the back of her head heralded the arrival of a severe headache. The pain was so sharp she even imagined she saw a spark of light, out of the corner of one eye.

She returned her attention to the figurine she held, trying to work out what seemed so dauntingly familiar about it, so much so it gave her a curiously queasy sensation in the pit of her stomach. Fine pieces of patterned paper surrounded the head and hips of a matchstick figure, suggesting a headscarf and skirt. The tiny, delicate arms were raised up as if in alarm, and the figure itself was mounted on a cross-shaped base.

It looked just like the kind of cheap folk art people bought on holiday, then left forgotten on some dusty shelf. For the life of her, Dakota could not begin to understand what significance the figurine might hold for the Shoal-member, or what significance the alien believed it might hold for her.

She placed the object on the instrument board in the command module of the *Piri Reis*, and stared at it for a while longer. Despite its innocuous appearance, something about it still chilled her.

Finally Dakota grew bored trying to understand it. As her Ghost tugged at her senses, she flicked over to an external view. A message icon was currently flashing over a display of Mesa Verde, another Shoal-boosted asteroid much like Bourdain's Rock.

She put the message on display over the expanse of infinite black space extending beyond her ship, and felt a surge of relief at what she read there.

A long time ago (Dakota recalled) Mesa Verde had been a prison of sorts, one part of a loose confederation of human communities scattered throughout the asteroid belt and outer solar system. In the dark days before the invention of tachyon transmission and the subsequent first contact with the Shoal, people serving penal sentences had been exploited as cheap labour in mining operations. The mining still continued, of course – the need for raw ores was greater than ever. But the quality of life for most humans in the outer solar system had improved immeasurably, and Mesa Verde hadn't been a prison for a long time.

The asteroid had instead become a centre of commerce and shipbuilding, mostly unmanned ore-freighters. In the pre-Shoal days, the asteroid had floated naked to the vacuum, its surface riddled with slag and excavation mounds left over from the construction of internalized living quarters. Or so Dakota was informed by the moodily grey and black images hanging on the walls of the tube leading from Mesa Verde's docking ports as the spoken testimonials of long-gone prisoners whispered out from hidden circuitry in the picture frames.

The asteroid's surface was visible all around through panoramic windows. Palms waved in an artificially induced breeze stirring up the air that wrapped around Mesa Verde's mottled surface like a blanket. Multiple tiny suns shone down through the containment fields, their light and warmth falling on tended gardens and open plazas.

Dakota focused on keeping calm. There were hidden security devices everywhere, scanning her inside and out every step of the way. Lenses the size of dust-motes, and recording devices invisible to the naked eye, moved around her in a cloud, even probing beneath her skin to verify her ID.

Her *new* ID, she remembered. She wasn't Dakota

Merrick any more, and wouldn't be for a long while. Her Ghost worked overtime balancing out her internal neuro-pharmacology, suppressing any detectable signs of anxiety – anything that might lead Mesa Verde's security to suspect she might, say, be carrying a mini nuke in her gullet, or a timed virus woven into her DNA.

Dakota's Ghost also worked overtime in order to disguise its own existence. She could sense it hovering in her mental background, calculating risks and strategies nanosecond by nanosecond.

All of this was good, but it was nice to have a little extra too: like someone on the inside of Mesa Verde's administrative body helping her out, invisibly altering records and allowing her to pass through security procedures without unnecessary altercation.

Dakota was making good on old contacts.

What neither she nor her Ghost had predicted, though, was the presence of real, live, human customs officers. That was entirely unexpected.

On encountering them, Dakota hesitated only for a moment, before pushing on with a determined stride. The two men wore the uniforms of the Consortium military detachment permanently stationed on Mesa Verde, and each had a force stick holstered on his hip. They were talking with a pair of priests who had obviously also just disembarked.

As Dakota approached the gathered figures she heard the artificial tones of the priests' voices, and noticed the bright lights of the corridor gleaming off their metallic skins. They moved on after a moment, having obviously satisfied the guards of the nature of their visit. The long dark vestments swished on the floor of the walkway as they headed towards the atrium beyond.

Dakota produced her credentials and handed them over. 'Mala Oorthaus,' one of them muttered, studying them. 'What's your business here?'

'Real live humans?' Dakota said in mock surprise, giving them each a grin. 'What's wrong with an ordinary scan-and-sweep?'

'You'll have heard about what happened at the Rock.' The guard didn't smile back as he replied. 'What're you here for?'

'Independent shipping contractor.' She held his gaze for a moment. 'Just hoping to drum up some business here.'

She had used the cosmetic software in *Piri*'s surgical unit to puff out her cheeks a little. Her lips looked correspondingly thinner than usual, and her hair was shorter and darker than it had been. Her skin, too, was darker, and a couple of days in the medbox had swelled her hips, building up and slightly altering her skeletal structure while she lay in dreamless sleep. Her face itself was smaller, rounder, her eyes wider with a hint of epicanthic fold.

The guard glanced to one side, studying a report Dakota couldn't see clearly from where she stood, but she caught a glimpse of an image of the inside of her skull displayed in real-time, as hidden devices analysed the interior of her body.

She tried not to moan with relief when she saw that her implants weren't showing up.

After a moment he waved her on. Several steps on, and she remembered to start breathing again.

She found Josef Marados in a tall building whose uppermost floors pushed out through the thin envelope of atmosphere surrounding Mesa Verde. Judging by the size of his office, she figured he'd done well for himself in the years since Redstone.

'God *damn*, even with the alterations, you're still a sight for sore eyes,' he began, coming over to her with a grin. There was a hint here of the effusive manner Dakota remembered from years ago, but this was otherwise an altogether much more sombre individual than the man she'd known.

'How long, Dakota? How long has it been?'

'Not so long,' she replied, pulling him into a brief, tentative hug. He'd lost weight over the years, perhaps too much given his large frame. 'It's only been a few years since—'

'Yeah, since.' He nodded into her sudden silence. 'Feels like a lifetime though, don't it?'

Dakota nodded in return. It did.

*

The few illegal machine-heads still in existence in the home system had their own methods of staying in touch. Moreover, Ghost implants were designed to be mutually detectable – two machine-heads could sense each other's presence once they were within several kilometres' range of each other. So if Josef had still possessed his implants, she'd have sensed him at a considerable distance beforehand.

At first, Dakota thought Josef merely worked for Black Rock Ore. Instead, it turned out that he owned it.

Black Rock Ore had once specialized in the exploitation of carbonaceous asteroids. Nowadays, under Josef's administration, they skipped doing the dirty work themselves by financing other small, independent contractors to mine the asteroid belt for its precious metals, and then raked in a very profitable percentage.

Now here she was, sitting on one of a pair of couches, facing the man who had been her sometime lover in those few, brief years before her previous life had ended.

He studied her and smiled. 'So, Bourdain's Rock. Care to tell me what happened back there?'

Dakota felt her jaw tighten.

'Room's clean,' Josef assured her. 'No bugs. Glass is one-way and tuned to randomize vibrations, so we can see out, but no one on the outside will be able to see or hear anything. The Aligned Worlds Federal Treaty gets a bit vague on business practices, so industrial espionage is just part of the landscape around here. But all that really means,' he said, a grin spreading across his face, 'is you need to make sure your counter-espionage is more effective than their snooping.'

'I didn't mention anything about the Rock. How did you know?'

'Apart from the fact you just told me? Come *on*. First, a terrorist attack on a major populated asteroid so spectacular the footage'll be bouncing around the Consortium networks until kingdom come. Then, on top of all that, you appear out of nowhere begging for my help.'

Josef leaned forward and poured her a cup of coffee, stained pink to denote the form and quantity of legalized narcotics it contained. Dakota glanced behind him and saw, to her distaste, a Freehold challenge blade had been mounted on the wall near the door.

She responded with silence.

'Dak, this isn't a set-up. Alexander Bourdain is a snake, a piece of shit. The entire outer system would be a lot better off with him dead. And I *know* you, you're no mass murderer.'

'He's still alive?'

'So I hear,' Josef replied, noting the frightened expression on her face. 'He's lying low right now, my guess being that he's taking the opportunity to arrange a fast escape out of the home system in case he needs it. So what happened there?'

'Someone blew up Bourdain's Rock, and I was made to look responsible. But it wasn't me.'

Josef blinked. 'Seriously?'

'My shipping agent – my *previous* shipping agent – fixed me up with a no-questions-asked delivery job to the Rock. It should have gone smoothly, but there were some unforeseen problems with the cargo.'

Josef was staring at her like he'd never set eyes on her before. 'I guess we're not talking about a shipment of toilet paper, then, are we?'

Dakota looked at him askance. He merely shrugged, and she continued. 'My ship suffered major systems failures the whole way there, sometimes even total shutdown of life-support systems. All I could figure out was it had something to do with the cargo I was carrying to Bourdain, but it was part of the arrangement that I wasn't allowed to even know what I was actually carrying.'

'You must have been pretty desperate, taking on a job like that.'

Dakota shook her head. 'Don't even ask. Every time this disruption happened, the systems always came back online eventually. To cut a long story short, it turned out I was fetching Bourdain a GiantKiller.'

Josef's eyes were just about popping out of his head by this point. 'You're *shitting* me,' he said, after a moment. 'A GiantKiller? Those things are supposed to be only a rumour. So they really exist? And that's what ripped up Bourdain's pride and joy?'

'Yeah, but not before he grabbed me and started

torturing me, since he seemed to think I'd sneaked a look at his cargo and figured out what it actually was.'

'Wait a minute.' Josef put up a hand. 'So you didn't know what you were delivering. But you just said it was a GiantKiller. Who told you that – Bourdain?'

'No.' Dakota thought fast for a moment, but a sense of self-preservation kept her from mentioning the Shoal-member. 'I kind of read between the lines when something started eating the asteroid. I witnessed the whole thing, after the atmosphere gave out and I managed to escape. If it is a GiantKiller, your guess is as good as mine as to what made it go off.'

'So, what, you think it self-activated? Or someone else set it off?'

'Why not? Think how many enemies Bourdain must have. Think how much sense that would make. I deliver the GiantKiller, and somebody else detonates it. Who gets the blame? Me. When this all blows over – if it ever does – the first thing I'll do is find the shipping agent who acted as the go-between in all this. That's where I'll get some answers, I'm sure of it.'

'This shipping agent. Anyone I know?'

'Constantin Quill, based in—'

'I know of him. Or at least I do now. He's dead.'

Dakota started. 'He—?'

'Don't know the circumstances, but apparently what was left of him was pretty messy. Somebody put him in the same room as a couple of half-starved Mogs. That's not official news, but you get to hear things on the grapevine.'

'Great.' Dakota lowered her gaze and sighed. She then accepted a glass of the pink coffee and tasted it, feeling a warming numbness slide down her throat and into her stomach. She began to relax despite herself. 'Nice to know the kind of future I've got to look forward to myself, then.'

'If Bourdain's responsible for Quill's murder, then it means he's covering his tracks. Losing the Rock is a major blow for him, but if it gets found out he was involved in acquiring illegal alien technology like a GiantKiller . . .'

Josef let the words trail off and fixed her with an inquisitorial gaze. 'Okay, now you get to tell me what you want from me.'

'I know you don't owe me anything.'

'*You* get special dispensation. We had something going, the two of us, even if it was a long time ago.'

The coffee was making it harder for Dakota to stay focused. She put down the empty glass and pushed it away with unsteady fingers. 'You were always particularly good with contacts.'

'Rich family, generations of businessmen. It helps.'

'Yeah.'

'Where do you want to go now, Dakota? Somewhere far away?'

'The further the better. For a long, long time.'

Josef shook his head. 'I'll try, but it isn't going to be easy.'

'How so?'

'You're being blamed for the destruction of a minor world. A couple of thousand people are dead, and you're the prime suspect for their mass murder. Worse, you're a machine-head, directly implicated in the Port Gabriel massacre. How long was it before you got yourself black-market implants?'

'Why do you care?'

'Humour me.'

'I survived OK for about six months after they let us all out of internment. Then they took away our Ghosts, and I wanted to die. I had new implants put in as soon as humanly possible. Pretty well immediately.'

'How about countermeasures?' he asked.

'I don't know what you mean.'

'Sure you do.' Josef chuckled. 'I'm talking about methods to survive your implants being compromised.'

'Everybody has their own way of dealing with that possibility.'

'And what's yours? Some means of wiping or disabling your own implants, maybe a coded message?'

'That sounds like suicide.'

'But better than the alternative, like losing your mind to outside control, don't you think?'

'I guess. And even if I did—'

'You wouldn't tell me? Fine. And there's nothing

else you want to tell me?' Josef's eyes were searching her face.

'Perhaps . . .'

'Yes?'

'No, Josef, there's nothing else I can think of.'

He obviously wasn't satisfied with this answer, but she couldn't find any real reason to burden him with the truth. Assuming he would even believe her, which struck Dakota as unlikely.

'OK,' he said at length. 'I can't help thinking I might come to regret this, but I'll see what I can do for you.'

She tried not to look too obviously relieved.

Dakota woke from a dream-filled sleep to find that already fourteen hours had passed since her meeting with Josef.

In the meantime she'd found herself a room – *cell* would be a more accurate description – in an echoing warren of twenty-four hour rentals that accepted anonymous payment. She could have stayed on the *Piri Reis*, of course, but Mesa Verde's docks would be Bourdain's first port of call if he came looking for her.

When she woke, it was from a nightmare of being incarcerated in a tiny space at the centre of Bourdain's Rock that got steadily smaller and hotter, squeezing in around her until she couldn't breathe. The room she'd hired was too small to stand up in, and for a few moments she panted asthmatically, staring up at a ceiling that was far too close, until she got her bearings.

Her thoughts smoothed out as her implants soothed her jagged brain waves, and she began to breathe more easily. Her Ghost informed her that Josef wanted her to return to his office. Apparently he'd found something suitable for her.

The dream had felt so real she felt half-sure she'd find the door out of her rented room locked when she tried to open it. Crouching to stop her head bumping against the ridiculously low ceiling, she felt an irrational wave of relief when the door opened smoothly on to a busy public corridor.

'My name is Gardner. David Gardner.'

Gardner stood up and nodded politely to Dakota as she entered Josef's office. He had close-cropped hair that she suspected he'd allowed to grow grey just enough to lend him a certain air of authority, and his dress was just this side of conservative. She thought there was something cold in the way his pale, milky eyes appraised her.

'I've already explained how you're looking for work, Mala.' Josef took her by the elbow and guided her to one of the couches directly facing Gardner as he resumed his seat.

Dakota noticed the way Josef was subtly deferential towards the other man, the way Gardner sat with his arms draped across the back of his chair in a pose making him seem so much at home. It was as if they were in Gardner's office, rather than Josef's.

'You're a machine-head,' Gardner stated flatly.

Dakota glanced at Josef, who nodded *go on* to her as he took a seat to one side of them.

'Yes.'

Gardner nodded thoughtfully, as if carefully considering this information. 'Josef's explained to me you weren't anywhere near Redstone when those massacres took place. Nevertheless, I'm sure you understand why it's important I ask you how well your artificial immune system can be trusted to protect you.'

Dakota knew Gardner was referring to her Ghost's ability to react to and then prevent hostile intrusions. She glanced sideways at Josef, but he was carefully avoiding her gaze. She wondered how worried that should make her.

'It's the best available,' she replied. 'That's all you need to know.'

Dakota wondered if she saw a glint of amusement in Gardner's eyes. 'Yet there are never total guarantees, are there? History can repeat itself.'

'I'm sorry,' Dakota said, turning towards Josef, 'but who the hell is this?'

Josef leaned over and put a hand on her arm. 'Just listen to him.'

Gardner continued as if she had said nothing. 'There must be very few people, apart from others like yourself, whom you can fully trust. I gather it's quite a wrenching experience to lose your Ghost implants.'

'It is,' Dakota replied levelly. 'It's the worst thing you could imagine.'

Gardner chuckled and glanced at Josef, who smiled tightly. Internal alarm bells that had nothing to do with her Ghost circuits were starting to clamour inside Dakota's head.

Gardner leaned forward. 'Let's not beat about the bush here, Miss Oorthaus. I understand you are used to dangerous work, and the job I specifically require a machine-head for may prove very dangerous indeed. But ultimately extremely profitable.'

'I appreciate that, Mr Gardner, and my piloting skills are the best. But you're going to have to tell me just what it is you need me to do.'

'You are familiar with colonial surveys?'

Ah, that was it.

Because humanity, in the form of the Consortium, was restricted by the Shoal to travel only within a bubble of space a few hundred light years across, potentially habitable worlds within that bubble were becoming a precious and dwindling resource. In fact, most of the systems to be found within that bubble of space did not contain any Earth-like worlds. In those systems that did, few of the worlds were life-bearing, and even fewer of those were capable of supporting human beings unaided.

Competition for such limited resources was subsequently extremely fierce – and occasionally deadly.

It was not unknown for claim-jumping to take place. Rival groups chasing after the gradually dwindling number of colonial contracts could separately find their way to a promising system via coreship and, by the force of arms, prevent another colony from being set up there. The Shoal appeared to care little whether such armies were carried across space in the Shoal coreships so long as they themselves were not threatened.

Most such incidents of colonial rivalry ended in decades of litigation, while Consortium warships remained in orbit above those barely habitable worlds until such time as the courts decided who should get which contract. The origins of the Consortium itself lay in arbitrating such conflicts: disparate private enterprises had been merged under a general UN charter, and an administrative Council set up to oversee exploration and exploitation in an attempt to bring order to an otherwise chaotic interstellar land-rush.

The precursors to such contracts were colonial surveys, whereby the potential colonists could raise funds to send ships and survey teams to assess the likely costs and time-scales for establishing viable settlements. Such expeditions were particularly prone to piracy.

'I've never taken part in a colonial survey, but . . .'

'Yes?' Gardner raised his eyebrows.

Careful, thought Dakota: she'd almost mentioned Redstone. *She* had been there, but Mala hadn't.

'But I'm more than aware of the dangers involved. Particularly after the Freehold–Uchidan conflict.'

'So can I assume you're at least familiar with events on Redstone?'

Another quick glance at Josef, but his face was impossible to read. She looked back to Gardner. 'It would be extremely hard to be a machine-head and *not* be familiar with what happened there, Mr Gardner.'

Gardner smiled, looking pleased. 'Quite right, quite right. The reason I'm here involves the Freehold, as a matter of fact.'

'It does?' A trickle of ice began gliding down the length of Dakota's spine.

'Yes. But anything I tell you from now is on the condition that you have agreed to take on this job. Josef here can assure you the money you'll be paid is very, very generous.'

She glanced to one side and saw Josef's head bob energetically.

'As I understand it so far, you're surveying a new system, and you need a machine-head pilot who knows how to keep her mouth shut,' Dakota announced flatly. 'That's what we're talking about, isn't it?'

Gardner nodded. 'That about sums it up. Now tell me if you want the job.'

Dakota nodded tightly, trying hard not to let Gardner see the emotional turmoil she was in. 'I do, Mr Gardner. You have a pilot. But what I don't understand is why the Freehold would specifically want to hire a machine-head? What do they need me for – target practice?'

Gardner just stared at her.

'Easy, Mala,' Josef muttered. 'It took a lot to set this up, and you owe me.'

'Miss Oorthaus, you weren't on Redstone when the tragedy at Port Gabriel took place. There's still a lot of bad feeling there, that's true, but the Freehold Senate understands that the machine-heads present on Redstone were . . . subverted? Is that the right word?'

'Good enough,' Dakota replied.

'The truth is the Freehold are losing their war with the Uchidans. Because of this, the Freehold are in the market for a new homeworld, and they currently have a new charter up for consideration by the Consortium. The system in question is already under survey, but the Freehold's military resources have been badly stretched by the war on Redstone. They lost a lot of their capability during the Port Gabriel fiasco, and a good deal since. They have only three orbital warships left, all centuries old, and they need this colonial charter because, frankly, they're history without it.'

'You're saying these ships are old enough they're still set up for navigation by machine-head pilots, right? Aren't they worried the Uchidans could pull the same trick again if I was allowed to pilot one of their ships?'

'It's a good question, but they don't actually consider the Uchidans a major threat to the survey expedition. If it proved successful, and the Freehold won themselves a new colonial contract, the Uchidans would end up getting Redstone all to themselves. The main worry involves other, outside interests – other colonies, potential or real, prepared to go to war over an uninhabited world. Plus, the Freehold can't pilot their ships as well as a machine-head could. The frigate they'll be sending to this system would be at a disadvantage if it encountered any opposition unafraid of hiring someone like yourself. You'd be an essential part of their inventory, regardless of the past.'

Dakota leaned back, thinking hard. 'I hope that money you mentioned is really, really good.'

'Better than good.' Josef laughed and shook his head. 'The kind of money they're offering, you or I could find a rock and stick a planet engine in it and call it home. Let your Ghost talk to the Black Rock systems and see if it isn't true.'

Dakota's Ghost instantaneously flashed up the details of the pending financial transaction, and the arcane financial trickery that was meant to disguise where it had come from and who exactly was going to benefit from it. Half the money, for both Josef and Dakota, had already been deposited. But even with that first payment alone, she was already set to be very, very rich.

Gardner smiled. 'You can't deny it's generous.'

Dakota felt dizzy, and tried hard to keep her face impassive at the sheer number of zeroes she'd just seen marching across her mind's eye.

'And what about you, Mr Gardner? What do you get out of this? You're not part of the Freehold, are you?'

'No, but I represent outside investments that allow this expedition to happen at all. A business can make a great deal out of a successful colony, if it invests in it early.'

Good enough, Dakota decided. Good enough because there wasn't anywhere else to go.

'If you're screwing me over, Josef, I'd appreciate knowing just how much before I jump in the fire. What exactly did you tell him about me?'

Josef carefully placed a hand over Dakota's, where it had balled up around a fistful of his shirt just before shoving him up against a wall. Gardner had left them a few minutes before.

'Let go, Dakota,' Josef said, adopting a reasonable tone.

'You're asking me to stick myself inside a locked steel box for maybe several months, among a bunch of people with every reason to want to see someone like me dead. So if you're missing anything out, anything at all, I swear the last thing that pretty face of yours will ever see will be me pulling the trigger right before I blow your head off.'

Josef coughed out a horrified laugh, and Dakota released the pressure a little. 'Dakota, you came to *me*, remember? You asked for my help. Or maybe' – his voice took on a more accusatory tone – 'it's more convenient for you to forget that.'

'I didn't forget,' Dakota mumbled, and finally let him go. 'I just hate being in any situation where I don't feel in control.'

She slumped back on Josef's couch, and a few moments later felt him place a hand on her shoulder as he stepped up behind her. 'Once this is all over, you'll be right back on top. You'll have the money to do what you like – or even not do anything at all for the rest of your life.'

Dakota cast him a dubious look.

'This is a routine operation,' Josef insisted. 'I'm not saying Gardner's an angel, but the money's real enough, and I've dealt with him in the past. But, while we're at it, there is one other thing I wanted to bring up with you, and you're probably not going to like it.'

Dakota stroked her brow with one hand. 'Thanks for leaving it till last,' she deadpanned.

'You're going to have to leave your ship behind.'

Dakota's eyes snapped open, staring at Josef in disbelief. 'You mean in storage?'

He sighed and sat down next to her. 'Dakota, right now that ship of yours is like a big glowing arrow pointing at your head saying "dangerous criminal here". Anyone who wants to find you just needs to look for your ship. Yourself you can disguise, but not the . . . what's it called?'

'The *Piri Reis*.'

'Yeah, that. I set tracer systems on the *Piri*, to keep an eye on it, and it responded by attacking our databases. Where the hell did you get that ship?'

'It's a very valuable piece of hardware, Josef, and that's all you need to know. That, and the fact there's absolutely no way I'm going to leave it in storage. I can stow it in the cargo hold of whatever ship I'm piloting to this Freehold system.'

'Uh-uh.' Josef shook his head. 'In case I wasn't sufficiently clear, I mean you have to destroy it, Dak.'

'Fuck you.'

'And fuck you too,' Josef echoed back at her. 'You'll leave it here, and it's going straight to scrap. Stop!' he yelled, as Dakota pulled herself up, her mouth open to argue. 'Just think for once in your life. Right now you're public enemy number one – and I mean that literally. Right now I'm the only bridge you haven't completely burned, and the *Piri Reis* is going to lead everyone straight to you. You take that ship along with you, when you'll be spending probably weeks on board a coreship, that's plenty of time for Bourdain *and* the Consortium to set their bloodhounds on your trail. And believe me, every coreship leaving this system for months to come is going to be filled with agents looking for you.'

Dakota stood up and pulled on her coat. 'I don't like it,' she protested weakly.

Josef shrugged and spread his hands. 'I'm open to alternative suggestions.'

Dakota responded with silence.

*

Several hours later, when she found herself back on board the *Piri Reis*, it felt like attending a wake.

She had *Piri* knock together something warm and alcoholic for her in the kitchenette, something loaded with the kind of neuro-adjusters she normally derived from her implants. As the shaking she had felt build up in her hands edged off, she began to feel better.

Here's to you, Piri, she toasted.

The possibility that she might have to ditch her ship after the destruction of Bourdain's Rock had always been there in her mind. But she felt like a hermit forced to leave her cave after a lifetime of solitude – and ever since Port Gabriel, the *Piri Reis* had been a pretty good substitute for a hermit's cave.

She curled up against the warm fur inlay that coated the interior of her ship and felt like an agoraphobic who'd just woken to find someone had strapped a parachute to her back and thrown her out of an aircraft.

'Dakota?' She heard the effigy calling her name softly. She stood up and walked through into the welcome darkness of her sleeping quarters, and let the effigy slide its warm, flesh-like arms around her. Its fingers pried at her clothes, gently peeling them away before tugging her downwards and planting soft, dry kisses on her belly and breasts.

She stroked the smooth, hairless dome of its head as it pulled itself up and slid her arms around its shoulders, feeling its weight press down on her. All the while she couldn't help thinking that there had to be a way to get around Josef's demands.

It was her they were hunting for, not the *Piri Reis*.

When the solution finally came to her, she had to wonder why it took her so long to think of it.

NINE

Redstone Colony
Consortium Standard Date: 01.06.2538
3 Days to Port Gabriel Incident

An arrhythmic thump beat a tattoo inside Dakota's head, and she closed her eyes until its migraine-like effect passed. It was still the middle of the night, but the street lighting beyond the window projected dappled stripes through the blinds of her quarters, painting them across the wall opposite.

Chris Severn shifted beside her. 'What's up?' he asked sleepily, shifting naked beside her in the narrow cot. She watched fascinated as the tattoos covering his back twisted like something alive, animated by the shifting of the muscles beneath. Along with a lot of the other machine-heads, they had been put up in a building originally intended to house the maintenance staff for the skyhook. 'Headache again?'

Dakota nodded, unwilling to speak in case it brought back the pain. It felt like a bad hangover, except she hadn't been drinking.

It was obvious from the pained look on his face that Severn was suffering in precisely the same way. This worried her, even though that kind of synchronicity between machine-heads wasn't so unusual: get enough machine-heads together in one room, and it was like being stuck in the middle of an electronic shouting match. Their Ghosts remained in continuous inter-communication, even when they themselves were asleep. This constant sharing of information and data some-times manifested as shared minor tics or physical reactions amongst machine-heads in close proximity.

But one advantage lay in the fact that whatever one of them learned, pretty much all the rest would know, or could be granted access to. It was the development of technologies such as these that had helped make Bellhaven – and a man like Howard Banville – so very essential to the Consortium.

And if Severn was suffering in the same way as she was, it was reasonable to conjecture that everyone else in the building would be too.

Dakota was about to slide back down alongside his lithe nakedness when she heard voices from somewhere outside. So instead she slid out of the cot and stepped over to the window, whereupon Severn grunted in annoyance and twisted around until he faced the wall, burying his head in a pillow.

From the outside their building was an unremarkable grey concrete block set in a radial street a kilometre or so from the skyhook's main base. Peering out, she saw two groups of men standing together at the junction with a side street about fifty metres away. Something about their gestures made it clear they were involved in some kind of argument with each other.

'They're crazy, you know,' muttered Severn from somewhere behind her, his voice muffled by the pillow. 'Totally fucking nuts.'

'How do you know it's Freeholders out there?'

'Who the fuck else is it going to be?' he mumbled.

Dakota scanned the network of active Ghost circuits throughout the town and noted that the Consortium security services were already aware of the gathering. She'd been initially worried about Uchidan infiltrators, and had immediately glanced round to locate her side-arm, but it looked like this disturbance was something relatively innocuous.

She watched as one man from each group stepped forward, until the pair of them stood face to face. They gesticulated wildly, faces distorted with fury. Their com-patriots meanwhile stood in a loose circle around them under the street lights, wearing the heavy gear essential to surviving the freezing cold.

Dakota watched as one of the two men at the heart of the exchange slapped the other hard across the face, dislodging his breather mask. The sound of mocking laughter reached her ears.

Severn finally got up out of the cot. With an exaggerated sigh, he leant his chin on her shoulder, following her gaze. 'You can see why Commander Marados doesn't want the Freehold involved in this operation at all, can't you?'

Dakota nodded, only half-listening to him. She'd heard about the death-matches the Freehold favoured. The whole notion was simultaneously barbaric and ludicrous, and it was a reminder of just why their bizarre society had been shuffled from port to port before finding its way here.

'What's the point in all this fighting?' she asked. 'They've already got an enemy to contend with.'

Severn pressed himself up behind her, his hands sliding around her waist and up towards her breasts, making her smile. But, despite what she thought were her better instincts, she wanted to see what might happen outside. If this was more than some minor street brawl – if this really was a challenge, as she suspected (hoped?), what would happen?

Dakota was shocked to discover her throat was dry with the anticipation of bloodshed.

Severn's fingers began to drift downwards, but Dakota failed to respond. After a few more seconds he finally got the message and pulled back with another sigh.

'Bloodthirsty, ain'tcha?' he said, patting her on the shoulder.

Her skin prickled with the cold. Everywhere on Redstone was cold. She suspected that in some warped way it was a reason why the Freeholders wanted to live here. They didn't seem the kind of people who would thrive in a tropical, sunny environment.

'Hey, not bloodthirsty. Just curious.'

The Freehold was scheduled to lead an assault on Cardinal Point, a highly fortified Uchidan settlement about two thousand kilometres north-west of the sky-hook, where it was believed Banville was currently being held captive. The Consortium were technically present here in a purely advisory role, but the Freeholder troops would be flown in aboard Consortium craft, piloted by Consortium military staff, with orbital reconnaissance and support from the Consortium also.

Less than three days from now, Dakota would be piloting one of a dozen dropships in towards Cardinal Point for the rescue attempt.

Over the past several days they'd received an intensive briefing on the nature of the conflict. Because Dakota came from the same world as Banville, a lot of it was old news to her but, even so, she hadn't been aware of much of the historical background.

Koti Uchida, more than two centuries before, had been a planetary genetics specialist on a research team evaluating a likely terraforming candidate in the Onada 125 system, thirty-seven light years from Earth. When a relief crew from Mann-Kolbert Geophysical Evaluations had arrived at the planet six months later, they'd found their predecessors wiped out by a crudely altered virus originally intended to modify carbon-dioxide levels in the atmosphere.

Near catatonic with shock, Uchida was the only survivor, holed up alone in an airtight hut with its own air supply while the corpses of his fellow researchers rotted nearby.

They got him transported back out on the next crew rotation, and the subsequent investigation turned up evidence of latent psychosis that Uchida had somehow kept hidden throughout the standard psych-evaluation tests. There was even the suspicion Uchida had been responsible for altering the virus that then wiped out his compatriots, but that could never be proved.

Uchida was subsequently removed from his position, and disappeared off the general radar for a while.

He resurfaced three years later, claiming he'd spent most of this time in his lonely hut taking dictation from a disembodied alien spirit that preached salvation through technology. Only once every human being could see the universe as God saw it, Uchida claimed, would a new age of peace and understanding come about. He began preaching his peculiar new gospel on the streets of the Mound, a city on the world of Fullstop, long famous for its surfeit of wild-eyed prophets.

The book Uchida claimed to have taken down during his long solitude became known as the Oratory. In time, he gained followers. Only sixty years after his death, Oratory temples could be found on a dozen worlds throughout Consortium space. They all offered the same route to instant karma: a skull implant – a primitive forerunner of Ghost technology – that tapped directly into the temporal lobes of the human brain, long associated with religious epiphany, thereby generating a supposedly unending neurological state of transcendent consciousness.

Follow Uchida, potential converts were told, and you will experience God for ever.

There was no lack of takers for Uchida's instant salvation. But then came the accusations that these implants had been placed inside the heads of less than willing converts. Eventually, the notorious debacle involving Belle Trevois pushed the Uchidans into even harder times.

The riots breaking out on half a dozen Consortium worlds, after Belle's death, helped push through approval for a long-standing application by the Uchidans for a colonial charter. They wanted to set up their own world – and, in order to get rid of them, the Consortium was more than happy to grant their request.

The Uchidans were given a desolate, near-uninhabitable ball of rock with a thin veil of poisonous atmosphere, located in a system on the furthest edge of Consortium space. There they dug in, pressurizing caverns and boring tunnels for miles beneath the surface.

Fifteen years passed before the Shoal suddenly invoked Clause Six in the Uchidans' contract, and reclaimed the entire system without explanation.

The Shoal Hegemony controlled a constantly shifting web of trade routes plied by their coreships, and they reserved the right to reoccupy any colonized system for their own purposes, so long as the colony in question had been in existence for less than twenty standard years. It proved the single most contentious item in the ongoing relationship between humanity and the Shoal. Concessions had been made in other areas, but on this one issue the Hegemony remained resolute.

No one had seriously anticipated that the Shoal might ever actually invoke Clause Six and, as the centuries passed, it had looked less and less likely they ever would.

Everyone, however, was proved wrong.

Slews of civil servants and politicians, all the way up to the highest ranks of the Consortium, fell by the wayside in the ensuing chaos. Fledgling colonies within a three hundred light year radius of Earth hurriedly re-examined their own charters in a panic.

Over the next several years, the Uchidans were rescued from their failed colony and shipped instead to Redstone. But that planet was already home to the Freehold, who were no strangers to controversy themselves. Extreme libertarians with a bent for violence, the Consortium had been equally happy to see the Freehold occupying their own inhospitable ball of mud somewhere far away from the centre of human affairs.

On Redstone, the Uchidans had occupied the deserted continent of Agrona, a token Consortium military force remaining in orbit for a couple of decades in order to maintain peace between the two groups now inhabiting the planet.

Eventually they left, and such co-existence might even have proved ultimately acceptable if the Uchidans had not then begun work on altering Redstone's bio-sphere – with potentially disastrous consequences for the Freehold colony.

The ensuing war had remained in a state of détente for decades, a constant tit-for-tat struggle along fluctu-ating borders, until the Consortium uncovered evidence that the Uchidans had meanwhile smuggled Howard Banville to Redstone on board one of the Shoal Hegemony's coreships. As a result, the Freehold were suddenly granted Consortium military support.

And that was why Dakota and Severn and all the rest were now here on this desolate world, so far from home.

Below, the Freeholder whose breather mask had been displaced snapped it back into place, then pulled out some kind of weapon. It was a short, nasty-looking blade which he began to wave in the face of his assailant, who retreated quickly. There was something showy about the motions: as if he were playing to an audience, and Dakota felt she was witnessing some secret ritual.

'See, most Freeholders tend to stay right here,' Severn explained. 'Redstone's a fair distance away from all the normal coreship routes, so you'll get one coming through here only once or twice a year. But every now and then some of these people find their way in among the human communities on the coreships, and put on a show for them, fighting to the death for a paying audience. There's big money in it, from what I hear – for the survivor, anyway.'

'Shit, really?' Dakota shivered again, not entirely from the cold this time.

'Yeah, but they're still playing within their own rules. The winner still gains in social status here, but also becomes wealthy in the process.'

Dakota turned to look at Severn. 'You've seen one of these fights before, haven't you? I can tell from the sound of your voice.'

'Once,' he admitted, 'when I was barely more than a kid. Nasty. Never, ever again.'

The fight was now being broken up. Freehold military police in dark uniforms arrived, flashing torches and wielding clubs, and soon the adversaries were pulled apart. Yet there was still that sense they – she, Severn, the Consortium – had been deliberately made spectators to an aspect of Freehold life few outsiders rarely got to see. As if this was some kind of warning, that the Freehold were not to be treated lightly.

'So how come you never told me about you and Marados?' Severn asked.

'Wasn't any of your business,' Dakota replied, turning back to him with a smile. 'It was never anything serious.'

'None of my business, like you said. But not serious, right?'

She shrugged. 'I'm here, aren't I?'

Severn shook his head and pulled her back towards the cot. They tumbled onto it together, burying themselves under the warm blankets.

Some time later Dakota woke to see grey dawn light seeping through the blinds, and carefully touched her temple, where she could still feel the painful throb of her headache.

TEN

Trans-Jovian Space, Mesa Verde

As far as Josef Marados was concerned, the *Piri Reis* would be scrapped and reduced to its essential components within forty-eight hours of her boarding the Freehold frigate *Hyperion*. But then Dakota had made some enquiries of Mesa Verde's stacks, and found that the type of vessel used by the Freehold had an overall cargo capacity of one hundred and eighty thousand cubic metres – allowing more than enough room to hide something the size of her little ship.

Even better, the *Hyperion* itself was old, the ageing military legacy of a backwater colony. Subverting its security systems surely couldn't be *that* difficult.

While she worked desperately on finding a way to keep the *Piri* intact, she had it display streaming news reports, the bright logo of the Ceres News Service flashing endlessly within the cramped space of the command module. They were still running images of Bourdain's Rock disintegrating into gravel.

The news services on Ceres were airing a series of

back-to-back interviews with anyone who had the remotest connection with Bourdain's Rock. To her horror, at one point a commentator raised the possibility that the Rock had been destroyed by a rogue machine-head, someone programmed to infiltrate the asteroid and then destroy it.

Security clampdowns were being enforced system-wide, and it became rapidly clear to Dakota how lucky she had been to get inside Mesa Verde at all. Only a few days ago, the scale of the disaster hadn't been fully absorbed, but now, the entire outer solar system was at a state of high alert.

It was a reminder, as if she needed one, of how badly she needed to get herself very far away, and very fast.

Ready, Piri?

<All details are logged as planned.>

As she left the *Piri Reis*, probably for the last time, she felt a deep ache in her chest. But if everything went to plan, she might still come out on top.

The *Hyperion* started talking to Dakota even as she and Josef were making their way towards Black Rock's private docking area. It began as a gentle buzz in the background of her thoughts – like hearing an auditorium filling up from down the far end of a corridor. But before long a familiar flood of information descended on her, every scrap of data demanding equal attention: hull stresses, systems integration failures, and a seemingly infinite queue of process queries.

Her Ghost handled this onslaught with practised ease, bringing to her conscious attention only those items that were most genuinely urgent. Although she didn't yet have physical control over the Freehold ship, it felt a little like slipping on unfamiliar clothes that then grew more comfortable with every passing moment.

She focused her attention on the *Hyperion*'s cargo hold, but the fresh map data she uploaded from the frigate became blurry once she tried to see what was carried within it.

She realized Josef was saying something to her.

'. . . all the security and guidance systems remain in lockdown until you're ready to take the helm. The passengers themselves will be telling you where to go, but you – Mala Oorthaus, that is – will still have the usual legal right of override. So if they order you to dive into the atmosphere of a star, you can stick them in the brig and still get paid. That kind of thing.'

'But dumping them into space as soon as we get there and lighting off on my own isn't approved behaviour, either?'

Josef grinned, but Dakota was pleased to see an edge of nervousness there too.

'Everything I need is right here.' She indicated a small bag by her foot.

Josef shrugged gamely as they arrived at the mass transit elevators leading down to the docks. 'Guess this is it, Dakota,' he said, coming to a halt. 'Anything else you need to know?'

Dakota stretched languorously, tired after her long bout of reprogramming the *Piri Reis*, and enjoyed the way Josef's eyes took in the shape of her under her clothes.

'Yes,' she replied. 'What are the chances of them figuring out who I really am?'

Josef smiled reassuringly. 'Your identity is secure, I can assure you.'

She shook her head. 'I'm glad you've helped me, when I really don't think you needed to' – Josef started to speak, but she put up a hand to shush him – 'but the Freehold hiring a machine-head for any reason at all kind of stretches credulity, doesn't it?'

'What's your point?'

'I'm saying perhaps they're holding something back, something they're not mentioning. I've seen these people in action, Josef. They'd rather go down in flames than face the dishonour of using someone like me as an ally, even as a paid ally.'

'Look, all I know is that careful enquiries were being made about machine-head pilots, starting maybe a few weeks ago. Not through official channels, obviously. Then you came along looking for a way out, and it just seemed' – he shrugged heavily – 'fortuitous, I guess. Outside of Gardner and the people on board that ship, nobody but me knows about you. That's all that matters.'

'Thank you.'

She glanced at him and saw a tiny pinprick of light appear, somewhere above his left shoulder, just on the edge of her perception.

Piri, run a scan on my implants. I'm getting some very minor visual distortions showing up – like a spark of light.

<Your Ghost systems are running at optimal, Dakota, but I will be vigilant.>

Thank you.

She had the overwhelming sensation there was some kind of unfinished business she still had to take care of, but she couldn't quite remember what it was.

A little while later, just as she was about to board the shuttle that would take her to the *Hyperion*, it came to her.

Things didn't look much better inside the *Hyperion* than they had from the outside.

The frigate was a dart-shaped missile more than a thousand metres in length that flared out to the aft, where a fusion propulsion system powerful enough to push it across a solar system in no more than a few days of heavy acceleration was located. A heavily armoured gravity ring, where the command bridge was located, slowly revolved towards the ship's fore. Yet there were museum pieces docked in some of the Consortium's grandest orbital cities at Tau Ceti that looked in better shape than the *Hyperion* did.

Every few minutes a fresh cascade of systems-failure notifications came crashing down into Dakota's thoughts like an all-consuming tidal wave of information, before being near-instantaneously tidied away by her Ghost, and becoming once again reduced to little more than a vaguely distracting background hum tinged with the machine equivalent of hysteria. It was easy to picture the *Hyperion* as a wounded dog howling its distress through a broad-spectrum network.

'Quarters,' Dakota – who was now Mala – muttered out loud, hanging on to a rung at the junction of two of the *Hyperion*'s access corridors, one of which plummeted away into what would have been terrifying depths if there had been any gravity present in this part of the ship. There was a barely perceptible – and therefore worrying – pause before glittering icons appeared in Dakota's vision, leading the way.

If the ship had been up to date, finding her way around it would have been second nature: with the information already uploaded into her back-brain, it would feel as if she had been finding her way around the *Hyperion* for decades. As it was, too many data systems were either damaged or corrupted through lack of maintenance. Even the icon-projections reminded her just how old this frigate was.

'Bridge,' she said next.

In response, the first set of icons vanished, to be replaced by another.

She sighed. This was still better than nothing. She pushed herself forward, floating along a corridor, and watching the icons flicker into a new configuration as she came to a y-junction.

Halfway to the command bridge, her Ghost allowed Dakota to sense the presence of several people up ahead. Her employers.

Initially, Lucas Corso wasn't sure what to make of the woman as she entered the bridge for the first time. Short dark hair curled around her ears. Her face was small and round, her frame slight and gamine. *This is what the Freehold are meant to be scared of?*

Perversely, he was nonetheless relieved to see her. He didn't enjoy spending any more time in the company of Senator Arbenz and his cronies than he absolutely had to, but the request for his presence on the bridge had been unambiguous.

With any luck, this would be over quickly, and then he could return to the safety of his research, as far from the Senator as possible.

He glanced over at a bank of dataflow indicators and was shocked to realize how much information was passing between this initially unremarkable-looking woman and the *Hyperion*, as if she were a black hole drifting through the digital corona of the frigate's star, bending and warping computer systems to her will.

'Miss Oorthaus.' Gardner guided the machine-head woman towards Senator Arbenz.

All Corso knew about Gardner came from random snatches of overheard conversation, most frequently between Arbenz and Gardner himself, but also from casual jokes and disparaging comments shared between Arbenz and his two bodyguards, the brothers Kieran and Udo Mansell. From this it was clear neither the Senator nor the two brothers had much respect for David Gardner: he was an outsider, not part of the Freehold, a resident of the old, impure world the Freehold were supposed to have left behind and which had resolutely failed to destroy itself in the centuries since. Gardner, then, was a necessary evil, as much as the machine-head woman – a businessman, free of honour and morality, but able to part-finance such an enormous undertaking as a planetary survey.

Oorthaus's expression remained wary as she came face to face with Arbenz, like she was expecting something to rear up and bite her. After only a few weeks on board with only the two Mansells for company, Corso could hardly blame her.

Gardner directed her towards the Senator. 'This is Senator Arbenz,' Gardner continued. 'The man in charge of this operation. I—'

'You may call me Gregor,' Arbenz offered, cutting him off. 'I'm glad you could join us on our little adventure.' Grasping both her hands with his own, Arbenz smiled, for all the world like a kindly uncle welcoming a long-lost niece.

Oorthaus nodded politely, although her stiff smile made it clear she felt less than comfortable. Corso had to suppress a smile creeping up one side of his face: the newcomer clearly had good survival instincts.

'I know it must have been a hard decision for you, in agreeing to work with Freeholders,' Arbenz continued smoothly. The two Mansell brothers watched, stony-faced, with arms folded. Corso had a pretty good idea of the thoughts going through their heads, and if Arbenz had any sense, he'd keep them and Oorthaus apart. 'But I gather you weren't a part of what happened on Redstone.'

'No, I can be grateful for that.'

'Yet here you are,' Arbenz continued, 'a machine-head again. Forgive me, but I must ask, was it really so terrible losing those head-implants the first time round?'

She hesitated a moment. 'I . . .' As she looked around, Corso had the sense she hadn't spent a lot of time around other people. 'It was difficult, yes. A lot of machine-heads . . .' She paused and shook her head.

'Committed suicide?' Udo Mansell supplied in a deep rumble. An awkward silence followed. Out of sight of the woman, Gardner shot the two bodyguards an angry glance.

Arbenz turned to the two men. 'Udo, Kieran, I want you to double-check those inventories. I'll see you later.'

As the two men left, Corso felt himself relax a little. 'I'm sorry about that, Miss Oorthaus, but the brothers lost family during the war.'

'That's OK,' Oorthaus replied. 'As long as they don't try to get in my way.'

Arbenz smiled as if appreciating a point well made. 'They won't, of course, but they're here as shipboard security, so you'll be expected to work with them.'

'Look, Senator—'

'Gregor, please.'

'Senator Arbenz, do you want me to do this job or not? If I have to deal with people hostile towards me because of what I am, that's going to compromise the safety of your ship and of your expedition.'

'Mr Gardner' – Corso noticed, as he spoke, how the Senator briefly caught the other man's eye – 'has a long-standing relationship with Josef Marados. I trust David Gardner, he trusts Josef, and Josef in turn trusts you. You, therefore, can also trust me. Udo and Kieran work for me, and they won't do anything to compromise the survey. A large part of the Freehold's remaining funds will go towards paying the Shoal a truly exorbitant price in exchange for taking one of their coreships on a detour in order to drop us off at this new system. You can imagine how eager we are to get this just right.'

'But the way Josef put it,' Oorthaus continued, 'you stand to become very, very rich if and when the Shoal make this new system a permanent part of one of the new cross-galactic trade routes they're planning for their coreships.' She made a pretence of thinking hard for a moment. 'Are you *sure* you're paying me enough?'

Again, Corso had to struggle not to grin openly.

<Investigating local systems,> the *Piri Reis* whispered in her ear.

Just hearing her craft's familiar machine tones made Dakota feel more secure.

She was alone on the *Hyperion*'s bridge, surrounded by the lotus-like petals of the interface chair. Once inside the chair, she was blind, deaf and dumb in terms of her normal senses, but the *Hyperion* constantly funnelled a torrent of information into her mind via her Ghost. She 'saw' the holos and viewscreens around the bridge spiking bright white, one after the other, as the *Piri Reis* simultaneously and covertly ransacked the frigate's data stacks.

How long till we rendezvous with the coreship?

<Locating,> *Piri* replied. <Signature brane topology distortions indicate it has just re-emerged from transluminal space. Estimated time of rendezvous between three and five hours.>

After she'd had her new Ghost implants installed, Dakota had spent a year serving aboard a coreship very like the one they were now approaching. There were entire branches of human science devoted to studying the vast spacecraft despite the Shoal's strict limitations on such observations. Tiny probes would scan their drive spines, measuring and recording the exotic energies the coreships left in their wake, across every possible wavelength and spectrum. These Shoal craft truly were worlds unto themselves, enormous environments in which a dozen different species could be contained at once, yet kept entirely separate in their own carefully constructed habitats.

<I am now fully integrated with local systems,> *Piri* reported. <Currently investigating prior software alterations and other data relevant to navigation and security.>

How many people are currently on board the Hyperion? Dakota asked.

<Six, present company included. Records indicate that a crew of similar number are remaining behind at Mesa Verde, after travelling here on board.>

We're going to have to find a vacant slot to put you in.

And, she wondered, could she really be sure of stowing her ship in the cargo bay without anyone finding it?

Piri, have you managed to scan the current contents of the cargo bay yet?

<Yes. It primarily consists of short-range manned rovers, weapon-equipped surface-to-orbit two-person scooters and emergency vehicles, plus standard exploration and survival gear for planetary exploration as listed on the current manifest. There are also approximately three thousand remote-analysis drones developed by Black Rock Industries for detection of exploitable interplanetary resources.>

Meaning asteroids, Dakota concluded.

<Some other items will require potentially risky work on their encryption systems before their exact nature can be determined. The encryption methods, however, imply a military origin.>

Then make sure your encryption is even better, and find yourself a good hiding place while you're at it.

Dakota's next stop was the airlock complex located towards the aft. As she crossed the *Hyperion*, her Ghost generated a mental image of the coreship with which they would be rendezvousing. Intense bursts of radiation indicated where the alien craft had emerged outside of Neptune's orbit, signifying a mortal clash between normal space-time and the complex multi-brane spatial geometries the craft was believed to generate in order to jump across light years.

Dakota entered an airlock and shed all her clothes, placing them in a satchel before slinging it over her bare shoulders. Her filmsuit then emerged and coated her flesh. Once it had sealed her lungs, anus, vagina and nasal cavities, she began to run the depressurization cycle. A few moments later a deep silence fell, then the external door swung open to reveal the vast emptiness beyond the *Hyperion*'s hull.

Protective molecular filters formed themselves out of the filmsuit and coalesced over her irises, momentarily magnifying the distant bright mass of faraway Mesa Verde until surface details stood out in near-hallucinatory detail before they balanced out. The stars looked like a fine dusting of diamonds across the universe.

Dakota took a firm hold on an exterior rung and swung herself out and onto the surface of the hull itself. She pushed herself off, glimpsing the airlock door silently cycle shut once more. Floating free of the *Hyperion*, she began moving further and further away with every passing second.

When she was thirty or forty metres distant, Dakota reached inside her satchel and withdrew a kinetic pistol, taking care to wrap a thick cable that extruded from its grip around both of her wrists.

Ready, she informed *Piri*.

She then aimed the pistol towards the behemoth bulk of the frigate, both hands firm on its grip. Several seconds passed in silence.

<On my count . . .> *Piri* began counting down from five. <Now.>

She squeezed the trigger. The pistol jerked in her grip, and bright flame jetted from its wide nozzle. Suddenly the *Hyperion* started to move away at an increasing rate.

OK. Did anybody pick that up?

<Three automatic traffic sensors in orbit around Mesa Verde detected the flare.>

What about the Hyperion?

<The *Hyperion*'s external sensors remained locked down and blind, as expected, at the time the pistol was

fired. The ship's main systems have so far failed to recognize any discrepancies. I am now thirty kilometres away and accelerating to match velocity. Estimated arrival is in approximately twelve minutes.>

What does the Hyperion think you are? Dakota queried.

<An automated refuelling pod registered to Black Rock Ore. There is some risk in this strategy—>

I'm aware of that.

Dakota waited several long, tense minutes until she picked out a course-correction flare from the approaching *Piri Reis*, stars winking out of view as they were occluded by its dark bulk. Dakota herself was now some distance from the *Hyperion*, moving towards the rendezvous point with her old ship.

The *Piri* made its final velocity-matching corrections: now it was moving at exactly the same speed as the *Hyperion*, both craft thereby appearing stationary in relation to each other. Dakota then boosted herself over to the *Piri*'s airlock.

Information flowed in a cascade between Dakota and the two ships, the murmur of data transfer like a distant waterfall in her thoughts, but one where she could still pick out the sound of every droplet as it tumbled.

A fat chunk of her initial payment from the Freehold had gone into reacquiring the *Piri* from the salvage firm it had been sold to, and then paying the necessary bribes to make sure the transaction stayed off the official records. The counter-intelligence ordnance on board the *Piri Reis* being superior to the sum total carried by the *Hyperion*, the *Piri Reis* was to all intents and purposes invisible, slipping past the Freehold ship's detection systems like an unseen wraith passing through a wall.

Dakota swam into the heart of the *Piri Reis*, the lights low and the air warm.

Take us in, Piri.

Heavy doors rumbled apart just fore of the *Hyperion*'s engines. The *Piri Reis* slipped through them like a minnow catching a ride in a whale's belly.

From the inside, the cargo bay area formed a hexagonal tube extending almost a third of the way into the hull's interior. Shield generators and massive docking frames of strengthened alloy were arrayed at regular spaces, half of them already occupied by equipment crates. The *Piri Reis* manoeuvred itself into an empty slot and field generators flickered on automatically, binding it against the cargo bay's interior wall.

Dakota waited. She really expected alarms and flashing lights, but there was only empty silence.

Reactivating her filmsuit, she exited her ship again, and entered the depressurized space of the cargo bay. Her implants meanwhile twisted the data topography of the *Hyperion*'s surveillance systems into knots, rendering her undetectable to any cameras or detection systems. She next floated into an airlock, letting her filmsuit evaporate before unslinging the satchel and hurriedly pulling her clothes out of it, as soon as the airlock had repressurized.

A few moments later there was a ping, and a door swung open to reveal a corridor with signs pointing towards the engine maintenance systems. Inhaling deeply, she pulled her now empty satchel back over her shoulder and stepped out into the corridor.

Against all rationality, she'd almost convinced herself someone would be waiting for her there. Surely someone must have spotted her, and would have figured out what she was up to. Instead it looked like she was completely alone.

Dakota leant her forehead against the cool metal of the wall and forced herself to relax, taking slow, deep breaths. She started to laugh, but it came out more like a half-sob. She was clearly letting her worst fears get to her.

ELEVEN

Trans-Jovian Space

Gregor Arbenz studied the projection floating a few centimetres in front of his nose, but failed to make any sense of it whatsoever. Numbers and decimal points fluttered like brightly lit confetti in the air above the conference table. But the one thing he did understand – that the projection now ably demonstrated – was the degree of control that the machine-head had over their ship. For the Senator, it made for less than comfortable viewing.

He didn't look up when both Kieran and Udo Mansell entered, moving towards seats at the far end of the table. Instead he continued to stare intently at the display, imagining he might come to a greater understanding of the *Hyperion*'s highly complex systems if he simply looked long enough.

But in truth, there were other things currently on his mind.

Udo, in his typical pig-headed and insolent way, swung his feet on to the table as he sat down. Really, if it were not for Kieran's controlling influence, Arbenz would have found a way of losing Udo in some challenge years ago. The security man was unpredictable, volatile and prone to irrational tempers.

His brother Kieran, by contrast, was calm, calculating, and by far the more dangerous of the two. He sat with his hands clasped before him, a knowing half-smile on his face. It was a smile that seemed to imply a commonality between Kieran and the Senator, a shared world-view born of experience, of having honourable blood on their hands, and of being forced to deal with an equal share of idiots. Kieran glanced towards Udo before shrugging at the Senator as if to say, *What can you do?*

Arbenz struggled to control his contempt. He could not be sure either one of the brothers was not secretly reporting to other members of the pro-war faction back on Redstone. Senator Abigail Muller, for one, resented his leadership, and she had openly voiced her disagreement to the way he was handling the retrieval of the derelict.

The time would come when Senator Muller would have to suffer an accident, but that would need to wait until his triumphant return to Redstone aboard a functioning starship.

'I'm concerned about this woman Oorthaus,' said Kieran in his typical clipped tones. 'Something doesn't feel right about her.'

Gregor shook his head and waved a hand dismissively, before turning the display off. 'That's it? That's your report?'

Kieran shot him a dark look. 'It's nothing I can put my finger on, but she's keeping something from us. I'm sure of it.'

'Another one of your "feelings", Kieran? And she's a machine-head, remember, so of course she's keeping something from us. It's called maintaining a sense of self-preservation. Or are you talking about something more significant?'

'I'm talking about us allowing her so much control—'

'No, Kieran,' Gregor cut him off abruptly, 'we've been over this and it's not your decision.'

'But you are supervising this expedition,' Mansell reminded him. 'That gives you some leeway, depending on circumstances.'

'Enough, Kieran, unless you can give me something more concrete.'

Udo swung his feet off the table and leaned forward dramatically. 'We only have this man Marados's word for it that she is who she says she is.' His sibling nodded emphatically in agreement.

'More than just his word,' Arbenz argued, addressing Kieran. 'Everything checks out. You did some of the checking, as I recall.'

'Yes, but one way or another, ultimately everything we need to know about her comes through channels of information controlled by Marados's company.

Remember, Black Rock just about owns Mesa Verde, so this is an unacceptable risk.'

'Yes, I'm aware of that, but there aren't any alternatives – not given our current time frame. We're taking a chance that the Shoal, or anyone else, won't stumble on our secret. We're also taking a chance that the Uchidans won't attempt to disrupt our survey. If they or anyone else cause us problems, we're going to need Oorthaus to do the job she thinks we hired her for to help defend us. So unless you can find much more solid ground for your concerns, I don't want to hear any more about this. Is that understood?'

Udo remained silent, but his lips were pursed in anger. 'We'll keep our eyes and ears open,' Kieran said at length, nodding gravely.

Yes, you will, thought Arbenz, and felt something very like a flash of pity for Oorthaus. If there were anything irregular in her history, anything that might negatively affect the outcome of this expedition, the Mansells would be particularly vicious when it came to dealing with her.

Even by the standards of a society that selected its voting citizens through the challenge system or from the active military, the two brothers' mutual taste for violence was unpalatable. Now the Senate had been battered by defeat after defeat in the Freehold's war of attrition with the Uchidans, more liberal voices were speaking out. Several, like Senator Corso, had dared speak openly against the challenge system itself.

Arbenz had long ago decided that Freehold was in danger of absolute collapse unless he and Abigail Muller and the other members of the pro-war faction re-established absolute moral authority back home – and recovering this derelict alien craft would surely represent an enormous step towards reversing those fortunes. With luck, the Freehold could become infinitely more powerful than its founding members ever dared to dream.

The Mansells' death squads had certainly helped hold back the rot, but the brothers had started to become careless. There had been witnesses to some of their recent atrocities, and Arbenz and his supporters were not yet strong enough to survive any proven link between themselves and the recent wave of brutal arrests and assassinations. But at least out here, so far from home, he could keep an eye on the two brothers.

'All right,' said Arbenz, moving on to the next item of business. 'You told me you had some information on our friend Mr Gardner.'

Kieran nodded, leaning forward. 'We've looked a little deeper into his previous dealings, and there may be some connection between him and Alexander Bourdain, and therefore with whatever destroyed that asteroid.'

Arbenz nodded, impressed by this news. Spectacular footage of that boosted world disintegrating had been playing non-stop for weeks across every media platform imaginable. 'Now that *is* interesting.'

Kieran continued: 'His family's been closely tied into

the Mars-Jupiter mining industries since the 2100s. So we're talking old, old money here. But that took a hard knock when the Shoal turned up. The Gardners are still wealthy, still highly respected in the business community and in the Consortium, but over time their fortunes have been dropping lower and lower. I believe Mr Gardner's been recently trying to revive those fortunes in ways he's neglected to mention to us.'

Arbenz nodded, already aware that Gardner's dissipating fortunes were the impetus for his involvement in the new colony. The businessman had lost his majority ownership in Minsk-Adler Propulsions several years ago, following an investigation into serious financial misdealing. That hadn't been enough to put him permanently out of business, but it had certainly encouraged him to get involved in financing grey-market investments like planetary surveys.

Unfortunately, the Freehold needed Gardner and his not inconsiderable financial resources just as badly as he clearly needed them. The Freehold was now almost bankrupt, despite the Redstone system's enormous mineral wealth. The never-ending war had seen to that.

'So what's he been up to?'

'He's clearly involved in smuggling off-limits alien technology. It's likely that some kind of weapon, possibly Shoal in origin, was used to destroy Bourdain's Rock.'

Arbenz nodded, not entirely surprised by this news. It was unlikely any conventional weapon could have been used to take Bourdain's Rock apart so quickly. Secretly, he wanted to bless the man or woman responsible; it was, after all, a victory for common sense. The culture he had briefly witnessed on Earth had been everything he'd been warned it would be: depraved, corrupt and morally backward. Yet long before its completion, Bourdain's Rock had already become notorious even there.

'Then I suppose it's reasonable to assume the Rock was destroyed deliberately.' Concorrant Industries had since been claiming the asteroid's destruction was the result of an industrial accident.

Kieran sniggered. 'Whatever Bourdain says, I don't think anyone believes for a moment what happened there was an accident.'

'It might also then explain why Gardner was suddenly so keen to invest in an expedition that would take him a long way from Earth,' Udo added.

Arbenz nodded, pleased. 'Good work, Udo, Kieran. How're things progressing with Lucas Corso?'

Udo made a snort of contempt. He'd never attempted to hide his distaste for the young man and his liberal views.

Kieran answered. 'There is already definite headway in penetrating the derelict's systems.'

'I'm concerned that Corso might reveal to Oorthaus that we intend for her to pilot the derelict.'

Udo shrugged. 'We could simply just keep them apart.'

Arbenz shook his head. 'That's not an option. They'll need to work together eventually, once Corso finds a way to get control of the derelict.'

Udo looked up with an innocent expression. 'And if, when the time comes, she objects to piloting the derelict?'

'For her sake, she'd better not,' Kieran growled.

Arbenz nodded. 'She's an illegal, and she's clearly far from squeamish when it comes to dealing in the black-market and smuggling operations that, so I understand from Gardner, are her main forte.' He allowed himself a small smile. 'You should remember her only way out of the Nova Arctis system, once we reach it, would be through us.'

'Or she could simply hijack the *Hyperion* from us,' Udo commented. 'Or the derelict, for that matter.'

Arbenz's smile grew more fixed. 'An interface chair has been set up on board the derelict to allow her to communicate with it. Corso is meanwhile installing fail-safes in the same chair that will allow us to override her control. Each of us will have a way of activating that override, using a handheld unit, if at any time she tries to work against us. Think of it as an insurance policy, in case she doesn't work out the way we hope.'

Udo looked impressed, but Kieran less so. A cautious man indeed, the Senator noted. Much of that caution doubtless grew out of his clear disapproval of this expedition in the first place. In truth Arbenz could sympathize with him, because carrying out a planetary survey was as good as admitting they were getting ready to hand Redstone over to the Uchidans.

Until the discovery of the derelict, the Senator himself would have stood shoulder to shoulder with Kieran on that particular issue. It was their moral duty to protect Redstone, their home planet, to the death. But now . . . now, everything was different. With a functioning transluminal drive, there was no limit to what the Freehold might become capable of. The stars would quite literally be within their grasp.

But that was where Gardner, with his innumerable connections and illegal research facilities, came in.

It was an awesome vision, one Arbenz felt sure they could pull off. The Shoal's long-term claim had been that they themselves had somehow developed a technology beyond the scope of any other species encountered within a galaxy comprising a hundred billion stars. The discovery of the derelict had put the lie to that claim.

If Arbenz was sure of one thing, it was that humanity was destined to roam those same stars, perhaps even to conquer them.

Or rather, he reminded himself, the Freehold were meant to conquer. By the divine right of genetic imperative, they would find their destiny in the high yonder – from the furthest reaches of the spiral arms to the very heart of the galaxy itself.

And all they had to do was seize this God-given opportunity.

Arbenz smiled to himself, imagining himself repeating these very same words to a massed audience after they returned home in triumph with a captured starship. He toyed with his failsafe for a moment, sliding it between his fingers, then dropped it back in his pocket.

Again and again, Dakota's thoughts came back to the figurine.

Ever since she'd first handled it – opened up the delicate wrapping in which the alien had placed it, then turning it over in her hands, studying its outstretched hands – the awareness that she had previously encountered this very same figure had been constantly in her mind. Yet the memory of exactly where she had encountered it remained maddeningly distant.

But the memory simply wouldn't come.

The *Piri Reis* had been trying hard to break the cargo bay's encryption, so that she could ascertain just what the other sealed units within it contained. But, given the nature of what she'd uncovered so far, it was probably something pretty nasty. She'd already identified robotic phage-delivery systems: long-range hunter-seekers designed to worm their way inside a ship's hull and deliver a deadly cargo of engineered virals into its life-support system. There were also knife-sharks – vile little things that whirred through the air, seeking organic life to slice into, like airborne shredders. There were other items that Dakota did not yet have the stomach to analyse too closely.

Her Ghost allowed her to sense the Shoal coreship as it decelerated rapidly towards Jupiter's orbit. Once she'd brought the *Piri Reis* on board the *Hyperion*, Dakota had returned to the quarters allotted to her there, resting in her cot while the *Hyperion* continued to funnel a storm of data through her implants.

At that very moment, her Ghost tagged and flagged a news item originating from Mesa Verde. It took only a moment for her to absorb the information it contained.

She pushed herself upright, suddenly feeling alert. A moment later a screen came to life, in response to her unspoken command. The flagged news item appeared there, bearing the Mesa Verde tach-net ident.

Josef?

Josef was dead.

For all their sophistication, Ghost implants could sometimes produce unexpected results, varying from individual to individual. In a few very extreme cases they had been known to subtly twist the perceptions of those who possessed them. In such cases the subconscious began to manifest itself in unexpected ways, via the artificial conduit of the implants.

This was why Dakota at first fervently hoped she had only imagined the flagged news item. But hope rapidly gave way to a bottomless despair as she stared miserably at the information now on the screen before her.

Josef Marados, late of Black Rock Ore Industries,

had been found dead, apparently murdered. Unpleasant images of a vicious murder scene – Josef's office, and a brief glimpse of a body that was hard to reconcile with Dakota's memories of the living, breathing man – flashed before her in gory detail.

I should go back, she thought miserably. But who could have done it?

Bourdain.

Who else? It had to be Bourdain. He was still alive, and hot on her trail. Josef's only reward for helping her had been his own murder.

After a few minutes, good sense prevailed. Under the circumstances, returning to Mesa Verde now would be tantamount to suicide. With Josef gone, there was no one there to protect her any more.

Then she had a better idea. She could lose herself somewhere on the coreship they were now rushing to meet.

The alien starship continually sent out informational ripples that lapped upon the shore of Dakota's boosted consciousness. Any ship Bourdain sent after her would never be able to catch up with the *Hyperion*, but it might still be able to rendezvous with the Shoal coreship before it departed the solar system.

At least once the *Hyperion* had rendezvoused with the coreship, she herself could disappear into the throng of humans who made their lives there, then keep moving, boarding other coreships for as long as it took for Bourdain either to give up or lose interest. It was a worst-case scenario – and one that would guarantee her the additional enmity of the Freehold – but if things really were as bad as she thought, any other options were seriously limited.

Paranoia began to spin new webs inside her mind. The alien had given her the statuette while she was still on board Bourdain's Rock. Was it possible, she wondered, that the statuette might contain something within it that allowed Bourdain to keep track of her?

No, too paranoid, she thought, shaking her head. The concept of an alien collaborating with Bourdain in some way raised a thousand more questions than it provided answers. And yet . . .

And then she remembered noticing an imager on the bridge of the *Hyperion*.

If there was anything hidden inside the figurine, then that would be the best way to find it. The easier solution would be simply to destroy or get rid of it, but that overwhelming feeling there was something desperately important about the object continued to haunt her.

She cursed herself as an idiot for not considering an imager scan earlier. At the very least doing so would keep her preoccupied until she had a better idea what exactly had happened back on Mesa Verde.

She stepped through the door of her quarters into the corridor beyond, the figurine squeezed securely into a jacket pocket.

TWELVE

Redstone Colony
Consortium Standard Date: 01.06.2538
3 Days to Port Gabriel Incident

Dakota snapped awake to hear the duty klaxon blaring like Satan's own alarm clock. She stumbled out of her cot – Severn mumbling behind her, only just beginning to stir – and collapsed to her knees beneath the window, gripping her head in her hands until the pain of the headache began to ebb. The last lingering fragments of her dream faded with it.

Frequent migraines were a worrying sign. They could get worse, much worse, and sometimes the only cure for a machine-head was to have the implants removed altogether. The idea of life without her Ghost was already unthinkable.

Finally, as the pain faded to nothing, Dakota stood up and let her forehead touch the icy windowpane. She stared outside to the spot where the altercation had taken place the night before. Fresh snow had fallen, obliterating any history.

Then the second klaxon sounded, and Severn finally jerked upright with a surprised snort.

Less than twenty minutes later, Dakota felt another sharp stab of pain in her temple as they both made their way to the mess hall. It felt like tiny, fire-breathing dragons were rampaging through her skull, but there and gone in an instant.

'Shit. Dak, you OK?' Severn put a hand on her shoulder as she leaned her head against a wall.

'No . . . I don't know, Chris. I think I need to see someone.'

He offered to accompany her to the medical labs, but she waved him off, suddenly not wanting any company at all. She was nervous enough about this morning's mission, and didn't feel too much like breakfast anyway.

'Sounds like a standard circuit-induced migraine to me.'

The doctor was a youngish man with dark curly hair. Her Ghost informed her his name was O'Neill. She lay back in something that looked like Hieronymous Bosch's idea of a dentist's chair, staring up at the ceiling beyond the curving plastic of the scan unit. The chair was angled so far back, she suspected she might slide right out of it and headfirst on to the floor, had she not been tightly strapped in place. Her head was held immobilized as tiny, needle-like devices rotated on well-oiled arms around her scalp, interrogating her implants. Ultrasound images were projected on a nearby wall.

'Well, it felt worse than any fucking circuit headache I've ever had before,' Dakota complained bitterly.

O'Neill shook his head. 'See, this is exactly why they should keep machine-heads apart as long as possible. With so many of you gathered together like this, if one's got any kind of a problem, the rest of them will pick it up in no time.'

'I know Chris Severn's been having the same problem. Anyone else?'

O'Neill hit a button and the chair back rolled up with a soft hum. 'You're not the first this morning,' he agreed, while a nurse undid the straps and helped her down.

Dakota watched him carefully, noting his tight-lipped expression. 'Then is it safe to go ahead with our scheduled missions? Shouldn't we be investigating this?'

'Yeah, we should. But there'll be shit to pay if we have to pull back now. We'll be losing a vital "window of opportunity", as they like to say upstairs.'

Dakota was scandalized. 'And this comes from Commander Marados?'

O'Neill paused for a moment with his mouth open. 'No, higher, I think,' he finally admitted.

'It just seems a bit dubious.'

'Well,' O'Neill touched her elbow to lead her out the room, 'that's the military for you. One big, happy, bureaucratic family. If anything goes wrong, it's always somebody else's fault.'

Dakota stopped at the door and glared back at him accusingly.

'Look,' said O'Neill, 'there's really nothing to worry about, OK? Otherwise orders would have come down from Command to postpone the mission. If they're happy, we're happy.'

Perhaps, Dakota thought, as she walked away, she should have mentioned the hallucinations as well.

She had dreamed of angels with wings. They had drifted down to alight in the centre of a town marketplace she remembered from her childhood. Warmth and beauty and a sense of welcoming had been carried in the opalescent radiance of their perfect golden skin. One, a woman with long flowing hair and an expression so kind that Dakota had wept even in her sleep, floated just millimetres above the cobbled ground, regarding her with infinite compassion.

The angel had spoken to her in some strange, incomprehensible dialect that somehow translated into perfect meaning the instant she heard it.

On waking that morning, she hadn't been able to recall a single word the angel had said. But the sense of having been somewhere *real* was sufficiently strong to leave her with an overwhelming sense of loss.

Dakota hesitated, and thought about turning back. But what exactly could she tell O'Neill? That she had experienced a particularly vivid dream? She would only be making a fool of herself.

Instead she continued on her way. O'Neill surely knew what he was doing, and orders were indeed orders. The med-tech would have just reprimanded her for wasting his time. The dream itself was only that, a dream – perhaps brought about by her general state of anxiety in the run-up to the assault on Cardinal Point.

On her way to that morning's briefing, Dakota passed through a wide circular room that had been nicknamed the Circus Ring. This had become the centre of operations for the Consortium's ground command, and a huge array of communications and data systems had been set up all around the Ring's perimeter.

There, the general air of tension had been given an overnight boost by a threefold increase in the number of staff now wandering the corridors. Debriefings were being run constantly, along with endless strategy meetings and drills. Within just a few hours, the arrival and departure of orbital personnel carriers and dropships had become a constant background roar that was expected to continue for several days and nights.

Dakota stood on a walkway running around the Circus Ring's circumference and looked down at a group of Freehold commanders talking with their Consortium equivalents. There seemed something peculiarly archaic about the Freeholders' uniforms, as one of them stood with hands planted imperiously on hips.

After a moment, Dakota noticed the Freeholder was talking with Josef Marados, whose face was red and angry. She felt a stab of sympathy for him, having already heard numerous stories of such encounters with arrogant Freeholders making extraordinary demands of the people there to help them win their war. The calm of Consortium staffers moving past the tense knot of Freeholders made for a stark contrast.

The Freeholders were a joke, and they didn't even know it.

Then she noticed the alien for the first time, gliding like a watery phantasm across the central space of the Ring.

Shoal-members were generally about as easy to miss as an elephant in a tuxedo playing the flute. A few of its tentacles regularly shot out from underneath its body, grabbing at smaller creatures swimming within its gravity-suspended ball of water, and drawing them rapidly in towards it and out of sight. A few moments later, tiny pieces of bloody cartilage and bone spewed out from the creature's underside, staining the water.

Josef broke off from his argument with the Freeholders and went immediately over to the alien, followed by his suborn, Ulmer. The alien was already accompanied by a phalanx of black-armoured Consortium elite security.

Dakota recalled something Severn had said the night

before: *one of these days, someone's going to figure out how a bunch of fish ended up ruling the galaxy without learning how to make fire.*

This increased entourage swept across the Circus Ring, before disappearing through a door leading into a part of the complex for which Dakota didn't have clearance.

It was the first time she'd ever seen one of the Shoal in the flesh.

She'd heard arguments day and night throughout the mess halls and these temporary barracks about how none of them would be here at all if it were not for the Shoal's restrictive colonial contracts. There had been something terrifyingly random, even meaningless, about the expulsion of the Uchidans from their original colony, so it was far easier to blame the Shoal for the current unhappy state of affairs than anything else.

She recognized the guard posted outside the doorway Josef had just passed through along with the alien. She'd met him at a drinking session, just before dropping down from orbit, and recalled his name was Milner. He had made the mistake of trying to match her, and three others, shot for shot before he wound up comatose under a bar table.

He grinned as she came up to him. 'Merrick, right? And my head still hurts.'

'Call me Dakota,' she said, then, 'What's with the alien?' nodding towards the door he was guarding.

Milner shrugged. 'Beats me why that thing's here. And even if I knew . . .' he shrugged.

'Yeah, yeah, I know, you couldn't tell me. I wasn't asking you for any secrets, I was just wondering if I'd missed something in the briefings this morning. I had to go to see the doctor.'

'It's here just to observe,' he said with a shrug. 'Like maybe it's curious to see how we handle these things, but I don't think anybody really knows.'

PART TWO

PART TWO

THIRTEEN

Dakota was relieved to find no one else on the bridge of the *Hyperion* when she got there.

For a sophisticated piece of technology, an imaging plate didn't look like much. Just a circular platform: you took an object, stuck it on the plate, and waited while the item was scanned. That simple.

Except, it wasn't really so simple as that. Placing her figurine on the plate wouldn't just return data concerning the raw composition of the materials comprising it. If the imager's database was up to date, it could also return a whole slew of information about the figurine's probable cultural origin and significance, and maybe even the name of whoever had created it. Beyond that it could also return reams of forensic data, including the DNA traces of every human – or non-human – who had ever handled it.

Accordingly, any number of artefacts – jewellery, mementos, even works of art – had been designed specifically with imager technology in mind. A ring placed on such a plate might generate a wide-band artificial sensorium representing the sight, sound, memory and tactile experience of an associated loved one. The pornographic potential of this technology had therefore been explored for centuries. On top of which, plate-readable data could be encoded into almost any substrate, and often was.

Perhaps this, then, was why the alien had handed her the figurine – because it contained some form of encoded data.

She had muttered curses at the empty corridors as she passed through them on her way across the ship, wondering why she'd taken so long for this to occur to her.

She pushed back the cover over the imager, a horizontal flat black disc set into a wall recess. Dakota pulled the figurine out of her pocket, placed it on the plate and stepped back. A few seconds passed and nothing happened.

She began to wonder if she'd been wrong after all.

<Dakota . . .>

The *Hyperion* shuddered and the bridge lights flickered.

Piri! What was that?

<I am investigating.>

A light blinked and she realized the imager had begun its scan, although it was taking a lot longer to do so than normally. Numerical and compositional data began to spill across the imager's screen:

```
COMPOSITION
88% ferric alloy, 10% organic matter, 2% other
factors
*
ORIGIN OF COMPOSITE ELEMENTS
unknown/not on record. Phylogenetic analysis of
organic materials suggests: Indonesian maize
hybrid.
MICROSCOPIC SOIL TRACES DETECTED
(<0.0002% of overall composition): ORIGIN:
unknown.
GENERAL TACH-NET ENTRIES      None
MANUFACTURED BY               Unknown
PRIOR OR PRESENT OWNERSHIP    Unknown
INTERACTIVITY INDEX           Zero/not known
*
SAVE SUMMARY OR RE-SCAN?
```

<No system errors or malfunctions detected.>

Piri, I felt something happen almost the instant I put that statuette on the imaging plate. There's no way that's a coincidence.

<No system errors or malfunctions detected,> the machine repeated pedantically. Dakota quelled her frustration and picked up the figurine, stashing it out of sight behind a panel.

She turned and saw several message icons were now flashing on screens and in the air. It appeared her passengers, too, were concerned at this fresh turn of events.

*

231

'Look, I don't have a fucking clue what just happened. You ever flown a ship before?'

'A low-orbit glider,' Gardner replied, studying Dakota with eagle eyes. 'That isn't the point.'

'Well, my point is, this isn't a glider,' Dakota snapped back. 'I need to check every system is functioning, and that's what I've been doing. So frankly, if the lights go dim or the ship shakes again, don't be too surprised—'

'I'm not happy about this, Miss Oorthaus,' Gardner replied, glowering at her.

'Fine.' Dakota folded her arms. 'Want to find another pilot? Go ahead.'

Gardner stared at her in silence for long seconds then let out a long sigh. 'Mala, the Senator and the rest of them here aren't nearly as reasonable as I can be. When things go wrong, they tend to react badly.'

He spoke quietly, leaning in towards her as if sharing the details of some secret indiscretion. 'Josef Marados assured us you were one of the very best. If you're not being straight with me now, we can trace the source of the incident through the stack records. After that it's in the Senator's hands.'

She gazed into Gardner's eyes and suddenly felt sure he had no idea what had happened to Josef Marados. But surely he knew? How could any of them not know?

But Gardner wasn't questioning her about Marados's death. He was concerned about the sudden, violent spike in the *Hyperion*'s computer systems while she'd been on the bridge on her own.

'I am,' she told him fervently, 'one of the best. I can take you through the necessary protocols and show you everything I've done since I came on board. And the fact remains that this ship's been quietly falling apart in orbit for the best part of a century. It's like a three-legged dog. That they've managed to keep the thing flying at all is remarkable.'

Gardner put his hands up. 'That won't be necessary. I'm going to go talk to Senator Arbenz now, and I can guarantee he'll run an independent systems analysis. Is there anything else you want to add?'

'Yes,' she replied, holding his gaze, and injecting what she hoped was just the right mixture of irritation and outrage into her response. 'This vessel is a shit-can. If you don't let me do things my way and it ends up dumping the internal atmosphere because I wasn't allowed to fully test the systems, it won't be my fault. Otherwise, I need to know how it works and what holds it together, and that means running checks on systems that haven't been properly maintained in a very long time.'

'All right, but if there's any chance whatsoever of any further disruptions occurring, I want you to clear it with me first. Understood?'

Dakota nodded her assent and watched Gardner depart.

Piri, who else has been reading the news reports coming out of Mesa Verde?

<Dakota, both Senator Arbenz and David Gardner have been reading news reports received from Mesa Verde.>

She then had the *Piri Reis* recheck the Mesa Verde bulletins and found to her amazement that the news item about Marados's death had been erased. She had her ship backtrack, but the original item Dakota had read no longer existed. There was no longer any evidence it had even been picked up by the *Hyperion*'s tach-net monitors.

Dakota found herself gripped by an overwhelming sense of paranoia, a feeling that her grip on reality had become deeply tenuous. Dakota had read one thing . . . and, somehow, Gardner and the Freeholders had read another.

Either she was going crazy and she'd imagined it all, and Josef was still alive back on Mesa Verde, or someone on board the *Hyperion* had reprogrammed the tach-net transponders to exclude any mention of his murder.

She turned and glanced behind her. 'You can come out now, Udo.'

Udo Mansell emerged from the shadows to the rear of the bridge like a looming ghost.

'Very good,' said the Freeholder, stepping towards her. 'How long did you know?'

'Ever since you arrived through the service hatch. I know where *everything* is on this ship, at all times.' She reached up and tapped the side of her head. 'Remember?'

He kept coming forward until he was peering down at her from his imposing height. He reached out to touch her cheek. She flinched, then stepped back till she had put a work console between them.

'Why afraid?' he asked her.

'Who says I'm afraid?'

'The problem with your kind is you don't know how to talk to normal human beings. You're all so busy being wired into each other's brains, you've forgotten all the subtleties of normal human interaction. I'm sure you can't be beaten when it comes to operating machinery like on this vessel, but when it comes to deception, you're more of an open book than most. That's how I can tell when you're lying.'

He kept moving closer to her, and Dakota found herself being gradually forced back towards the entrance to the bridge. At the last moment, Udo stepped around her, putting himself between her and the exit. She tried to push past him and he reached for her shoulder.

She brought her fist up in instinctive response, aiming for his head. But he caught it with ease, as if she'd perfectly telegraphed the motion in advance. Her arm trembled under his grip as he forced it back down to her side. She yanked herself free and again put distance between them.

Udo moved towards her once more, grinning widely. 'Let's look at some facts. We need you to perform a specific and important task. You obviously need us too, as you're an illegal. It's like that idiot Gardner said – the very fact you're working for us makes you by definition a liar, because it's the lies you tell that keep you alive. We both know that, right?'

She went on the offensive as he reached out to her again. She grabbed his arm and pulled him towards her, but again he anticipated the move, and pushed down on her chest with his free arm.

It would have been easier if the *Hyperion*'s bridge hadn't been under spin, but instead provided anyone on the ship's central ring with a close to Earth-normal gravity. She was always a better fighter in zero gee.

She hit the floor hard, Udo twisting her arm so she was forced into a prone position beneath him, her face to the floor. A long, wicked-looking knife appeared in his free hand as he kneeled over her. Her throat constricted with horror as he brought the serrated edge close to her neck.

She could smell the rank stink of his breath over her shoulder. She tried to push herself back up with her free hand and felt an explosion of pain in her other shoulder.

'See that?' he muttered, bringing the blade up closer to her face so she could see it more clearly. 'Maybe you'd like to know how many throats it's cut.'

Dakota said nothing, her breaths erupting in short tight gasps.

'Let's get this straight,' Udo continued. 'I don't like your kind. I saw what happened at Port Gabriel, and I don't buy this crap about how it wasn't really any of their fault. You're all a bunch of untrustworthy walking fucking time bombs. That's bad enough, but you – you *like* being that way. You like it so much, you've still got those chips in your head. What the fuck is that about, huh?'

'I wasn't there,' Dakota gasped.

'I really hope so,' Udo snarled. 'Because if you had been, you'd already be dead and we wouldn't be having this conversation. Gardner's a businessman, he avoids seeing the messy side of things. Even the Senator and my brother have to play by certain rules. That's how things are for them. Me, I prefer to get straight to the point and fuck the politics. So let's be clear on this, Mala. I'll be watching. Closely. The instant you screw up and I think it's deliberate, or I think you've been lying to us, you're dead.'

'Well, you're going to have a hell of a time steering this ship without me,' she spat back.

Udo laughed, and there was a momentary relaxation of pressure. 'Steering *this* ship? If you only knew. Maybe it's time you did.'

'Hey, let her go.'

She didn't recognize the voice. With her arm twisted back and bent over, all she could see was the floor beneath her.

'Hey. I said let her *go*.'

The pressure on Dakota's back relented momentarily, presumably because Udo was distracted by the sudden interruption. She took the opportunity to twist free of the Freeholder's grasp, rolling over to one side as fast as she could move. He mumbled profanities and aimed a hefty kick at her: his boot struck home and sharp pain lanced through her hip. She yelped, and a moment later Udo had her by her hair.

She caught sight of Lucas Corso, who stepped forward and locked one arm around Udo's neck and tried to pull him away. Udo responded by reaching behind himself and grabbing at Corso's shirt. He had to let go of her again to do this, and she took the opportunity to twist round and punch him hard in the stomach.

Dakota scuttled out of Udo's reach and watched as Corso tumbled to the floor of the bridge, winded by a blow. But Udo had his back to her for the moment, and Dakota's military training kicked back in. She locked one arm around his neck, delivering a series of rapid punches to the side of the man's head.

It had almost no effect, and felt like punching hard granite. Her knuckles ached from the effort.

'Stop this. Stop this *now*.'

Dakota looked up to see Gardner had returned.

'Udo. I'll want to speak to you later. In the meantime, get the fuck off of the bridge.'

For a moment, Dakota wondered if the Freeholder was going to do what he was told or if he'd attack Gardner as well. She could see the businessman had his own doubts, judging by the pallor of his skin, but he held his ground.

'I'm telling you now, Udo,' Gardner repeated, his voice pitched higher than usual, 'I don't want to see anything like this again. If Senator Arbenz has any sense, he'll have you thrown out of the nearest airlock the instant he gets wind of this. Until then, return to your quarters.'

Udo Mansell stood like a statue, a solid carved block of hatred focused on Gardner. Then he relaxed, and smiled, as if he'd just lost a friendly game of cards.

'I think you'll find my approach to shipboard security tends to produce high dividends,' he replied, his voice suddenly sounding breezy and relaxed. 'Catch you all later,' he added, and stepped past Gardner and off the bridge.

Gardner closed his eyes for a second or two, as if steadying his breathing. Corso sat quietly where he was, one hand pressed against his belly.

'How did you know to come back?' Dakota croaked. She let herself slide to the floor with her back resting against a console.

Gardner shrugged. 'I've only known Udo a little while, but he tends to be extremely predictable. Besides, I'm keen to protect my investments.'

'And is it really worth it?' Dakota asked, keeping her eye on Corso who was, after all, a Freeholder like the others. 'Working with people like that, I mean?'

'Just remember you're on their territory here, and we all know why a lot of them don't trust machine-heads.'

Dakota laughed incredulously. 'Then why hire me?'

'If we don't secure our tender, we don't have the option of returning home,' Corso explained. 'Losing the new colony would be more than our lives are worth. That kind of thing tends to make a man like Udo edgy.'

Dakota looked to both of them, one after the other. 'Let's get this straight. If he tries something like that again, *I'll* kill him. Got that?'

Gardner's expression was weary as he moved towards the exit. 'Then you'd better watch yourself carefully,' he replied. 'Do your job, and try and keep the surprises to a minimum. For the sake of my health, too, not just yours.'

Dakota stared at the exit for several seconds after Gardner had gone. To her annoyance Corso now had a wide grin on his face.

'What's so funny?' she demanded, picking herself up.

'Nothing, really. I just have a habit of getting into fights I can't win.'

She found herself at a momentary loss of what else to say or do before anger took over. 'How am I supposed to do anything if I have to constantly worry about being attacked by you people? Give me a reason why I should even stick around after what just happened!'

Corso eyed her thoughtfully and shrugged. 'So why *are* you sticking around?'

Dakota struggled to find an answer and instead felt an intense wave of embarrassment wash over her. She stepped over to Corso and offered him a hand. 'Thanks,' she mumbled.

Corso took the proffered hand and stood up laboriously, wincing as he pressed several fingers to his belly. 'Forget it,' he replied. 'Udo's a moron. As far as I'm concerned, he shouldn't even be on this ship.'

'So . . .' she shrugged, 'why did you help me?'

Corso shot her a curious glance. 'Why wouldn't I?'

She gave him a bewildered look. 'You're on the same side as them.'

'You think we're allies?' Corso laughed. 'Anything but. These people are my enemies.'

'I don't understand.'

'You couldn't have known,' Corso replied, making to leave the bridge.

'Wait.' She put out a hand and stopped him. 'Should you even have told me that?'

He looked back at her. 'You mean, will it get me into trouble? Maybe. But I can't do my job for them if they cut out my tongue.'

She gripped his arm hard. 'Look, maybe you could tell me some things . . .'

Corso's grin lacked sympathy. 'Just do your job, Mala. Stay out of the way of the two Mansells. They're killers.'

He made for the exit.

'Udo said something, just before you walked in on us,' Dakota called after him in desperation. 'That if I *only knew*. Like there was something I haven't been told about this expedition.'

Corso turned, his face as unrevealing as a mask. 'Then he was speaking out of turn.'

He exited the bridge and Dakota stood there in silence for several minutes, filled with an unpleasantly familiar sense of foreboding.

Corso found his way partly along a corridor before stopping and leaning his back against a wall with a groan. His whole body hurt.

It was bad enough he was trapped on the *Hyperion* with men like Senator Arbenz and Kieran Mansell. Now he'd managed to make a deadly enemy of Udo as well. *Perhaps I've just got a suicidal streak. Well, at least that would explain some things.*

People back home were depending on him to do whatever it took, within the bounds of honour, to save them from a very unpleasant fate. Getting into a fight with Udo wasn't helping them any. He'd acted without thinking . . .

Face it, you'd have intervened anyway.

He pushed himself away from the wall with a groan, and stared bleakly up and down the corridor. More than any other time since they'd left Redstone, he wanted to be back home.

Every day that passed made it clearer to him just how much Udo was a liability. Only now, he'd as good as told

Oorthaus they'd hired her for a job other than the one they'd told her about. And that on top of threatening to kill her. That just made it even more likely she'd try and disappear once they got to the coreship. And then . . . well, then they'd either have to find another machine-head stupid or desperate enough to accept their terms, or try and figure out some other way of salvaging the Magi derelict when the time came.

And Corso had already learnt enough about the derelict to be certain their chances of salvaging it without Mala were close to nothing.

Still shaking, Dakota found her way back to her quarters, where she dimmed the lights and let her Ghost start to calm and soothe her with a steady trickle of empathogens into her cerebral tissues. Then she slept for a little while, curled up in her cot like a child, lost in the warm ocean tides of her back brain.

After a little while, the *Piri Reis* came to her, a soft, comforting presence in her thoughts.

<Dakota, I have made progress in breaking some of the more difficult encryptions used within the shipboard data stacks. I can now make more information available to you concerning the background of the other passengers. However, please note this information is by necessity incomplete due to the nature of the encryption.>

Good enough for me, Dakota replied silently.

Fresh knowledge started thudding into her forebrain,

in sufficient quantity to overwhelm her Ghost and leave her momentarily disoriented.

According to what *Piri* had discovered, Lucas Corso was some kind of historian. A 'xeno-data archaeologist', to be precise, though she wasn't at all sure what that was . . .

Her Ghost obligingly filled her in: xeno-data archaeologists attempted to glean understanding of Shoal super-science, usually by remote analysis. It was often, by necessity, an extremely covert science. In particular, Corso picked apart pieces of programming languages used by the Shoal.

Which sounded dull enough, but Dakota couldn't begin to imagine what it had to do with exploring a new solar system. Yet she was sure that contained somewhere in this nugget of information lay a clue to what Udo had almost let slip earlier.

What was it he'd said? '*If you only knew.*'

Maybe, Dakota decided, she really didn't want to know.

What she needed more immediately was something concrete against the Mansells – Udo, in particular. Half-heartedly, she had her Ghost circuits scan the morass of new data in the faint hope of finding something usable. At the very least she could find out more about how to deal with Udo the next time he—

'Oh shit,' she said aloud, though her voice sounded muffled in the cramped space of her cabin. 'You have to be kidding me.'

<Breaking the encryption on this particular data was surprisingly easy,> the *Piri Reis* informed her. <Please note that it concerns open financial transactions between Udo Mansell and a specific establishment on board the coreship we are currently approaching.>

Dakota couldn't figure out if she was appalled or elated. Probably both. *I thought those two were supposed to be running a security operation. So how did—*

<The encryption methods used by Udo Mansell in particular are out of date,> *Piri* explained. <This is likely more a result of limited resources available to the Freehold authorities on Redstone than to specific negligence on his part. However—>

Yeah, yeah. I get it. They have to make do with what they can get. But you'd at least think he could keep it in his pants for the duration of the expedition, rather than take the chance of someone digging this up.

She couldn't keep the huge grin off her face. If anyone had been watching her at that moment in the privacy of her cabin, they'd have thought she'd completely lost it.

She scanned rapidly through more of the information, finding other pieces of electronic mail also using out-of-date encryption methods. *Udo, Udo, Udo.*

<I draw your attention to a note alluding to reprimands relating to Udo Mansell.>

Dakota's Ghost worked overtime cross-referencing the decrypted messages with other items stored in the *Hyperion*'s data stacks. They were as good as transparent.

Yet for all that, neither she nor *Piri* could find anything that might explain what Udo had said to her on the bridge. Nor could she find details of the system they were intending to visit – not even its name.

The feeling that she'd walked into something bad all over again had been growing ever since she'd boarded the *Hyperion*, and with Josef's apparent murder her fears had taken an exponential leap into the unknown.

Cross-reference, Piri. What would happen to Udo if any of this became known back on Redstone?

Piri just then dumped another mountain of data into her Ghost circuits. A growing awareness of the complexities of Freehold society spread through her mind.

<Note the highly stratified nature of the Freehold social structure and honour code,> *Piri* added.

Dakota nodded, biting the corner of her lip and barely able to suppress a giggle. Udo hadn't struck her as quite so . . . kinky. If she had it right, if what she had just found out about Udo Mansell became public knowledge among the Freehold, not only was he finished, but so was anyone associated with him.

The Senator would certainly be tainted by any of this information if it became public knowledge.

This, Dakota thought with a deep sense of satisfaction, *is what I call real leverage*.

FOURTEEN

A day later, they finally rendezvoused with the coreship.

As they made their approach, its bulk filled every available screen on board the *Hyperion*. Dakota sat in the interface chair on the bridge, her Ghost channelling to her reams of data concerning the energies flickering in great sheets around the Shoal vessel.

The coreship itself was spherical in shape, perhaps a hundred kilometres in circumference, like a world in itself. Its surface was pockmarked with gaping holes through which the hollow interior could be glimpsed. Beneath the vessel's vast curving roof, supported by huge pillars a kilometre thick, could be found a far greater habitable environment surrounding the central core. And deep within that core could be found the mysterious transluminal drive that pushed the craft through space at enormous multiples of the speed of light.

Rumour had it the core contained a liquid environment – a lightless, abyssal ocean in which resided the craft's Shoal crew. Some trick of its planet engine prevented it from exerting any significant gravitational pull on the *Hyperion* as Dakota followed a standard docking manoeuvre.

Even though she couldn't see them directly through the interface chair's petals, Dakota was nonetheless aware of Arbenz and Gardner paying close attention to the bridge's monitors while she focused on the multi-layered data passing through her implants.

She could feel the weight of their attention being focused on her through the petals, judging and appraising her piloting skill. If she screwed up in any way, automated guidance systems would kick in and dock the *Hyperion* automatically.

But she wasn't about to let that happen.

She merged with the *Hyperion*'s primitive intelligence and guided the frigate's vast bulk through one of the kilometre-wide apertures in the coreship's hull. The bridge was temporarily under zero gee, the gravity wheel having been stopped for the duration of their voyage aboard the coreship. The bridge now sat at the bottom of the stilled wheel.

Dense layers of rock and compacted alloys appeared to rush towards and then past her on either side. A moment later the curving interior surface rose above her viewpoint, and the *Hyperion* was falling, on a cushion of shaped fields, towards the outskirts of a sprawling city.

A flicker of warning data –

A burst of violent energy shot through one of the aft drive bays like a muscle spasm, pre-ignition processes flickering with exotic fire deep within the engine cores.

Not good. Not good at all.

Dakota fully melded with her Ghost, making full use of its intuitive algorithms as a heavy, rattling vibration passed through the frigate. She was distantly aware of Gardner cursing and muttering somewhere beyond the petals of the chair.

There, she had it: a software failure. Something Dakota couldn't possibly have missed, unless . . .

The *Hyperion* was starting to push against the shaped fields that bore it downwards, as the main drive threatened to self-activate, the hull screaming in protest at the unexpected stresses. Dakota rerouted fresh instructions past the problem – a kind of logjam of erroneous data – and the drive finally powered down. Then it was a matter of clever calculations and sheer guesswork to steady the Freehold vessel as it continued to descend.

Whatever had gone wrong, at least it was over. Dakota finally let out a long, shuddering sigh, and tasted the sweat on her upper lip.

The *Hyperion* continued to drop slowly down towards a landing cradle, from which grasping, cilia-like constructs reached upwards like hungry anemones. The frigate rumbled again as the cilia moulded around its hull, cradling it with ease. One or two other ships – not quite on the same, grandiose, old-fashioned scale as the *Hyperion* – were similarly cradled a few kilometres distant.

Dakota shut off her dataflow and stared into the darkness surrounding her. Throughout the whole docking procedure, the *Hyperion* had practically become an extension of her body. It would have taken a crew of at least half a dozen non-machine-head technicians and engineers to carry out the same rendezvous, but Dakota had done it on her own without so much as moving a muscle.

She reached up with one hand and tapped the manual release button, standing as the petals surrounding the interface chair unfolded around her to reveal the bridge.

'Did you cause that glitch?' she asked the Senator. 'Or do you let just anyone mess with the engine systems?'

Arbenz grinned. 'You coped very well.'

'Do you have any idea how *dangerous* it is, altering base routines like that?'

'There were backups, just in case. I could have shut the engines down in a moment, no harm done.'

'Because you wanted to see if I screwed up?'

Arbenz shrugged, looking smug and self-satisfied. Dakota felt a deep urge to violence.

'But you didn't screw up,' said Arbenz. 'You did very well. I'd even say you're about as good as Josef Marados said you were.'

'Don't ever try something like that again,' she spat at him. Gardner listened impassively to their exchange, with arms folded.

Arbenz spread his hands in an open gesture. 'No more surprises, I promise.'

She nodded in silence. As satisfied as Arbenz seemed with her performance, she would have loved to be able to see the look on his face when he realized she wasn't going to stick around.

'Let me get this clear,' Dakota railed, several hours later. 'Unless I heard you wrong, I can't leave the *Hyperion* at all for as long as we're on board this coreship?'

She had tracked Gardner down in one of the mess halls in the gravity wheel, where he'd been engaged in conversation with the Senator while Ascension news feeds scrolled down one wall. The other walls of the mess were decorated with Spartan images of valour that fitted in appropriately with the whole Freehold value system. Broadswords certainly appeared to be a popular motif.

Gardner looked up at her with the kind of expression normally reserved for unruly children. 'We made it clear from the start that we're on very sensitive business. As long as we're on board this coreship we're wide open to the outside scrutiny of anyone who's curious to know what we're up to. Remember, there are mercenary fleets who specialize in jumping contract claims by keeping tabs on the movements of frigates like this.'

'So you need to keep me locked up in here, because that way there's less chance they'll figure out what you're up to when they see a giant fucking *warship* sitting on the horizon.'

Gardner's face was blank for a moment, while Arbenz merely chuckled without looking up.

'Listen,' Gardner replied angrily. 'You're a valuable asset, one we paid a lot of money for. There are people out there who'll happily snatch you off the streets of Ascension and take your skull apart to find out what you already know about us. We also paid to have this core-ship make a special diversion to our destination, which is as good as advertising the fact we're trying to set up a new colonial contract. Do you have any idea how expensive all this has been? How much it cost me personally, and also the Freehold?' Gardner waved at Arbenz with a fork. 'It's *your* job to protect us against anyone who gets too interested.'

'Then perhaps you'd care to tell me exactly where it is we're going? Or are you saving that for a birthday surprise?'

Gardner glared at her. 'You're just being dramatic.'

'I've just found out I'm being literally held prisoner here, and you're surprised by my reaction?'

'Miss Oorthaus, you're not a prisoner,' said Arbenz mildly, finally putting down his fork and leaning back.

'Then why did Kieran Mansell just stop me on my way to the airlocks, and tell me I'm not allowed to leave the ship?'

Gardner wiped his mouth with a cloth and pushed his plate to one side. 'Look—'

'No, it's all right,' said Arbenz, studying Dakota keenly. 'You can go – but not alone.'

Gardner turned red. 'Senator—'

'No, Mr Gardner. We'll attract even more attention by never disembarking at all. Are there other machine-heads here, Mala?'

'Yes.'

'Because you can sense them from a distance, and they can sense you?'

Gardner looked nonplussed.

'So really, anyone who wants to know we have a machine-head pilot on board already knows. Our secret is already out, Mr Gardner.'

Gardner remained unpersuaded. 'It feels like too much of a risk.'

'Only if she goes out alone.' Arbenz turned back to Dakota. 'Yes, you can go, but only with Kieran. We'll *all* be operating under a strict curfew when it comes to departing this vessel. I have some business to conduct here too.'

'Udo, not Kieran,' she insisted.

Arbenz held her gaze for several seconds. 'Any reason for the preference?'

'He's marginally less ugly.'

'I'm surprised by that.'

'Why?' Dakota replied.

'I heard about what happened on the bridge.'

'I don't recall receiving an apology from any of you.'

Gardner leaned forward. 'If you're thinking of trying to get back at him for attacking you, then I'm afraid it's not up to you to decide what—'

Arbenz put up his hand to shush Gardner, an amused look on his face. *He thinks this is funny*, Dakota reflected: Udo getting into fights with some skinny little girl.

'No, it's not her decision,' Arbenz agreed, without even looking at Gardner. 'But it would be good to have Udo off the ship for a while, don't you agree?'

Gardner looked caught. 'What exactly is your business in Ascension, anyway?' he asked her.

'I'm going to see an old friend. Another machine-head. If I don't show my face at all, he'll start wondering why I never leave the *Hyperion*. Given it's owned by the Freehold,' she continued with a shrug, 'any machine-heads in Ascension might draw the conclusion I'm being held prisoner, don't you think?'

She got her way.

Dakota immediately made her way straight back to the aft airlocks. The frigate had been designed with coreships in mind: a wide lip had extruded itself from the hull, below the airlock, so passengers could simply step outside and feel a fresh breeze against their skin.

It was like standing inside a roofed canyon the size of a continent. As she looked up, Dakota saw fusion globes dotting the underside of the coreship's outer crust. A couple of dozen metres below where she stood, a floor carpeted with grassland extended all the way to the outer suburbs of the city of Ascension, a sprawling metropolis that filled half of the space allocated to humanity. But instead of solid walls separating them from the rest of the vessel's interior, there were instead sheets of faintly flickering semi-opaque energy that were anchored beneath the ceiling's massive supporting pillars.

She turned to see Udo step out through the airlock, accompanied by Lucas Corso.

'I want to take a look at Ascension,' Corso explained, on seeing Dakota's annoyed expression. 'I didn't even get the opportunity to explore the last coreship I was in.'

Dakota cocked her head to one side, puzzled. 'Why not?'

Corso shrugged, and she guessed he wasn't comfortable talking about himself. 'Too busy with my work.'

And wouldn't I like to know just exactly what you're doing here, Mr Data Archaeologist.

'Your first time anywhere other than your home-world, and you were too *busy?*'

Corso flicked a glance towards Udo, who glared back at him in response. Neither of them replied.

'I don't have time to play tourist guide,' Dakota snapped at Corso. 'I have . . .' Further words stalled in her throat.

Udo gave her a toothy smile. 'People to see? Places to go?'

Fuck you. 'What do you think I'm going to do then, run away?'

'You could, but I can run faster.' Udo laughed at his own bad joke. 'What've you got against my brother, anyway?' he added. 'Seeing as you asked for me specially.'

'How does it feel being such a shithead, Udo?'

'It feels great, Mala.'

'You've visited this particular coreship before?' Corso asked her, clearly trying to break the current thread of conversation.

'I've been in Ascension a few times in the past, yeah.'

And I'm not the only one who's familiar with this place, she thought, shooting a glance at Udo and remembering what she'd discovered.

She spared him a thin smile.

An air taxi had been hovering in the vicinity of the *Hyperion* ever since it had docked. Udo beckoned it down, and made a show of getting in first and taking the front seat directly behind the dashboard unit that housed the craft's cheaply manufactured brain. He wasn't as subtle as Kieran, either, Dakota reflected. There was too much of a swagger in Udo Mansell.

Ascension was soon spread out below them in all its seedy blackened glory. If the view from a couple of hundred metres up was anything to judge by, it had changed little since her last visit there.

She surveyed a landscape of grey and black concrete interspersed with open areas of patchy green – fire zones from the civil war of fifty years before. In the further distance the city came to an abrupt halt against the shaped fields that kept humanity separate from other species inhabiting the coreship, but with different atmospheric and gravitational requirements.

These days, two-thirds of the city was back under Consortium control, while a few remaining warlords still claimed control over a few outlying districts. The Shoal didn't appear to give a damn what went on inside their coreships, at least up to a certain point. Fission weapons remained a big no-no, even though there were a thousand urban myths about people somehow stumbling into otherwise forbidden alien sectors of the coreships and finding there only sterile, irradiated ruins.

Some humans lived their entire lives on board a coreship, never seeing beyond these narrow slivers of apportioned living space. The coreship might travel the length and breadth of the galaxy, but once it left the minuscule portion of the Milky Way humanity was permitted to see, the surface ports were sealed until it returned to within Consortium space. Whatever lay beyond would therefore always remain a mystery even to its most long-term inhabitants.

'What happened to this place?' asked Corso in awe, peering down through the taxi's wraparound windscreen. They were passing over occasional pockets of devastation, now half overgrown with weeds.

'Power struggle,' Dakota replied. 'The Consortium won, but only just.'

'So the Consortium is still in charge here?'

Dakota shrugged. 'Nobody's strictly in charge. It depends which part of the city you're in.'

Corso looked disbelieving. 'But *someone* must be in charge of keeping this place in order – the Shoal at the very least. It's their ship, so where are they anyway?'

'Corso, they don't care about anything but their trade agreements.'

'Well, then—'

'No one is in charge here,' Udo muttered, his voice full of distaste, 'because no one here has the honour or strength to do something about it. This whole place is a monument to the very worst aspects of human nature.'

'—what exactly do the Shoal get out of all this?' Corso continued, despite Udo's interruption. 'With all their technology, all their advanced might-as-well-be-magic science, what do we have they could possibly want from us?'

'That's the eternal question, Corso,' Dakota answered. 'Nobody knows, and the Shoal aren't telling. Maybe they just like being in charge, full stop.'

'But they're just, just . . . fish!' Corso cried. 'How in God's name do *fish* come up with all this?'

Dakota shrugged again, but offered him a small smile. 'Same answer.'

The air taxi had now dropped below the level of the tallest buildings surrounding the city centre. The rooftops of some of these buildings stretched all the way to the coreship ceiling, where they were securely anchored. Dakota noted some of the lower structures still retained Consortium gun posts on their rooftops, their weapons aimed permanently towards the rebel districts beyond. The momentary brush of their security systems against her implants came to her like a faint mental tickle.

Severn. She sensed him again, as she had ever since they'd docked, somewhere out there among the grimy streets and half-rotted buildings of downtown – the site of much of the worst devastation from the civil war. He'd have sensed her too, of course. It was all part of the eternal joy of being a machine-head.

The air taxi changed course, obeying Dakota's unspoken command. At this, Udo looked around wildly for a moment before his gaze finally settled on her.

'I'm in charge of this craft,' Udo snapped. 'Relinquish your control.'

'You're here to keep us safe,' Dakota snapped back. 'Not to tell me what to do.'

Corso sat to one side of Dakota, looking baffled by their argument. The air taxi began to drift downwards on its cushion of energy. 'You're taking us outside of the Consortium-controlled sector of Ascension,' Udo hissed tightly. 'This is a lawless area.'

'Anyone looking for trouble isn't going to be swayed by whichever part of town we land in. And there's someone here I haven't seen in a long time.'

She spared a quick glance at Corso, remembering their conversation after Udo had attacked her. Corso was still part of the Freehold, and there wasn't any reason to believe for one second he'd be anything but loyal to Senator Arbenz. But what he'd said to her on the bridge had nevertheless appeared to contradict that.

The taxi settled down with a soft thump near an open marketplace. As soon as Udo cracked open the taxi's hatch, the smell of cooking assailed Dakota's senses: tear-inducing spices mixed with the smell of roasting meat and the fresh smell of newly cut veget-ables. Animal brains sizzled in pans suspended above smoking braziers, while dogs whined and barked in cages next to an open-air restaurant, awaiting their turn for slaughter.

Messages flashed through the air in a dozen languages, letters rearranging themselves into Chinese dragons above one establishment, or fat-bellied smiling chefs above another. An Atn – its enormous metal carapace painted with symbols and scratchy alien art – lumbered its way through the throng of pedestrians crowding the walkways, its thick metal legs moving with almost liquid slowness. People automatically gave it a wide berth, knowing the creatures stopped for nothing.

Hunger hit Dakota with appalling ferocity as they stepped out of the taxi. Udo looked twitchy enough to try and down anyone who so much as glanced in his direction. Corso seemed a little dazed. She'd brought them to Chondrite Avenue, a long thorough-fare that traversed the eastern district, filled with a dense population of squatters and refugees from a dozen

Consortium-space conflicts, many of them sleeping and living directly off the street. During the civil war it had been a sniper's alley no one dared enter, unless suicide was high on their agenda. But those days were long gone, hopefully.

Dakota headed straight for a roadside grill, and a few moments later returned to join Corso and Udo, chewing at a kebab of peppered meat dripping with grease. She grinned at them widely, pleased to see Udo looking seriously pissed off.

Corso took her by the arm, leaned in towards her and whispered quietly enough not to be heard over the hubbub: 'Mala, I can tell you're up to something. Whatever it is, please don't.'

Dakota just gave him a quizzical smile as if she had no idea what he was talking about. 'C'mon,' she said, taking Corso's arm, and pointedly ignoring Udo, 'we're both a long way from home, and we've got a lot of time ahead of us. How about I play tourist guide after all?'

And maybe you can answer some questions.

Dakota made sure to stay in the lead, pushing past Udo who was doing an excellent job of radiating menace at other pedestrians. She tried to ignore the queasy, nervous feeling building up inside her ever since she'd decided that making a break for it was her best chance of survival. So very much could still go wrong.

She led them away from Chondrite and down

Yolande, a narrow alley between walls still pocked with bullet holes. Banners declaring allegiance to General Peralta hung down from windows and balconies all round, some of them trailing in the mud underfoot. Flies and the smell of rotting food filled the air. She kept expecting Udo's hand to reach out to restrain her, and almost gave in to the urge to turn round and check out the expression on his face.

But she didn't dare. Not yet. Instead she kept going, adrenalin pumping through her bloodstream. By now he *had* to have guessed where she was leading them.

The alley widened suddenly and became quieter. Up ahead was a dead-end, with a door set in one wall. It was plain, unassuming and unmarked. Several armed men stood before it as they habitually did and, as ever, they wore Peralta's colours on their arms, scarves tightly knotted around the biceps.

Finally, she felt Udo's hand clamp down on to her shoulder. She turned at last.

'This stops here,' he hissed. 'We are *not* going inside.' He nodded towards the guarded entrance.

'Going where?' Dakota asked him with faked innocence.

For a moment she thought Udo was going to deck her; he trembled with barely suppressed rage, then spoke again, clearly forcing himself to remain calm. 'We are going to turn around now, and—'

'No, Udo. I know all about you. And don't dare ask how.'

'I'm warning you—'

'But you won't do anything, will you? I know you need me for much more than just piloting your ship. You just about said so yourself. "If I only knew": remember?' She leaned towards the Freeholder, relishing the strangled look on his face. 'That means you don't dare let anything happen to me.'

She turned and moved towards the door.

'Stop—'

Udo reached towards her. The men guarding the entrance tensed in response. Dakota prayed Udo wasn't quite as stupid as he sometimes acted. Loud music thudded from beyond the door.

He pulled back his hand, eyes fixed on the guards, his face full of contempt and hate.

One of the guards, a heavily muscled individual with a shaven head, pulled the door open with a nod. The music soared to ear-splitting levels.

'Severn's expecting you,' he bellowed in Dakota's ear, barely audible over the racket.

'I know,' she yelled back, and stepped inside.

Severn's bar had remained intact through the civil war, surviving under Peralta's patronage. The interior was dark, apart from the lights above the counter, and illuminated cages against a far wall in which forms more animal than human moved and howled. Men and women sat in deeply shadowed alcoves all around, their faces glistening occasionally in seamy light. She didn't need to turn around to know that both Corso and Udo were right behind her.

Dakota felt a light pressure against her thigh. Udo had angled his body, leaning in against her, so the knife that had suddenly appeared in his hand remained almost invisible.

'There are a thousand ways I could kill you right now and nobody would even guess,' he hissed in her ear. 'Tell me what you're trying to do.'

'I know you come here for the mogs,' Dakota replied, her voice tight with terror. 'I know all about it. I want to know where the *Hyperion* is going, and why.'

The pressure increased. She imagined the wickedly sharp blade cutting through her flesh. Udo's other hand gripped her shoulder like a steel vice.

'And in return, you don't talk? Is that your deal? Let's sit down then,' Udo hissed, guiding her towards an empty alcove. Corso followed, looking bewildered.

Severn was close, very close. As she sat down, she could sense him somewhere nearby. She glanced around and spotted him standing behind the bar counter, only a few metres away. He stood with his muscled arms folded, an amused expression on his face. He tilted his head and raised his eyebrows as if asking a question: Dakota responded by shaking her head. *Not yet.*

Severn had acquired more tattoos since the last time she'd seen him, a few years after the incident at Port Gabriel. They now spread up his shoulders, across his chest where they were clearly visible beneath his shirt, and then curled around his neck.

Unlike many others, he chose not to hide the fact he was a machine-head. His scalp was still shaven, the skin on the back of his head tattooed with diagrams that mirrored the machinery that lay hidden underneath the flesh and bone.

Looking at his skull and face, only an expert would have been able to recognize the reconstructive work done after he'd shot himself, long ago, as Dakota had watched.

Yet despite being one of the most easily recognizable human beings alive, almost no one outside of a very exclusive clientele had even heard of him.

Corso sat down facing the pair of them in the alcove, his hands tightly gripping the edge of the table. 'Please tell me what's going on here,' he urged quietly.

Dakota ignored him. 'Udo, listen to me. I know the man who runs this place. He's a machine-head, same as me. We look out for each other. Anything happens to me now, I can guarantee you won't walk out of here alive.'

Udo glanced over and caught Severn's eye. The bar owner held Udo's gaze and moved his head slowly from side to side.

Dakota wondered if she'd pushed the Freeholder too far. 'Udo, I don't give a damn what you do in your private life. But you and the rest of the people on that ship sure as fuck don't do a great job of securing private data.'

'You have *no* right looking into those files—'

'Udo, it's hard *not* to look at the files. You've been caught before. There was nearly a scandal back on Redstone. We both know just how nasty it'd get for you back home if the truth ever got out.'

Udo pulled his knife back a little, but kept it angled towards her thigh. She was entirely aware that if he cut her the right way, she'd be dead in seconds from blood loss.

'The only reason you're still alive,' he growled, 'is because it's my job to keep you alive for as long as we need you.' The knife twitched against her thigh and Dakota suppressed a gasp. 'But accidents happen.' He laughed, the sound not entirely sane. 'What the fuck made you think you could blackmail me?'

'Udo.' It was Corso. He'd seen what Mansell hadn't. 'Udo, put the knife away.'

'Stay out of this,' Udo snapped back. 'Or I'll skewer you where you sit.'

'Udo, look behind you.' Corso nodded over Mansell's left shoulder.

Udo turned his head slightly and stiffened at the sight of the rifle barrel aimed at a spot just below his left ear. One of Severn's men was standing diagonally right behind him.

'Evening,' murmured the guard.

Udo turned back around and gave Dakota a look of baleful hatred.

'I'm sorry, Lucas,' said Dakota. 'But I'm going to have to ask you if there's anything concerning your expedition I might not already be familiar with.'

Corso sighed as if a burden had settled on his shoulders. 'Planetary exploration.'

'And?'

'And that's it.'

She turned to Udo, who shook his head. 'I've been threatened by people a lot more dangerous than you,' he said slowly.

Dakota turned back to Corso with a smile. 'Did you know your friend here likes to fuck mogs?'

Corso looked between the two of them, as if not quite sure what he'd just heard. 'Excuse me, what are . . .?' he shrugged without finishing, clearly baffled.

'Udo here has a thing for mogs,' Dakota repeated, nodding towards the lupine shapes writhing in cages at the far end of the bar.

Corso flipped his gaze between the cages, Dakota and Udo, opening and closing his mouth several times. 'What . . . are those things mogs?'

'It's a nasty little fetish,' Dakota added. 'Not quite bestiality, but close enough.'

'Not quite? They're animals, right?' Corso demanded, his voice rising. 'Or . . . what else are they?'

Beside Dakota, Udo sat stock-still. The knife now lay

on the table before him, and both his hands were placed palms-down on the tabletop.

'They're illegal half-human gene-jobs,' she explained. 'Low intelligence, vicious, dumber than an ape but smarter than a dog. There're a lot of cross-species hacks out there, but that's the most popular by a long shot. Some are made for fighting, some for sex. In a place like this it's mostly sex.'

Corso studied Udo with a distinctly different expression from that of a moment before. Dakota was no expert on Freehold culture, but she knew they were deeply conservative in most respects. On Redstone, homosexuality was punishable by a violent death, and the vast majority of art created by the human race throughout its long history was considered part of the corruption the Freehold had set out to escape.

But when it came to a fully fledged Citizen copulating with half-human monsters, Dakota didn't even want to think what Udo's own people would do to punish him.

Corso looked like he was turning green. 'And the Consortium allows this?'

'Of course not.' Dakota sighed. 'But we're not in Consortium-controlled territory right now. The warlord who rules this district turns a blind eye to certain practices if there's an advantage to it.'

Corso shook his head. 'I can't believe this. It's . . . there aren't words. I can't even begin to think . . .'

'Even if you could prove a word of this,' Udo

snarled, his eyes now drilling into Dakota's, 'who would believe you?'

'I already told you that I know the owner of this place. Severn, right?'

Udo nodded, clearly recognizing the name.

'Well, he's a machine-head, you idiot. Our kind stick together, remember? I mean, how do you think he managed to stay alive this long out in the open, if it wasn't by keeping records on everyone who walks in here?'

Dakota had a strong sense that she could only push Udo so far before his instinct for vengeance would outweigh his sense of self-preservation. His nostrils flared with every breath, and his entire body was trembling with rage.

'Now here's the deal,' she said, glancing at both Freeholders in turn. 'Tell me the truth, right now, or I walk out of here and neither you nor anyone else on the *Hyperion* will ever see me again. And I'm prepared to bet you don't want that.'

They remained mute, so Dakota stood up slowly, making sure Severn's men could clearly see she was unarmed. 'Then it's goodbye, gentlemen.'

'Wait.' Udo put up a hand. 'There's nowhere you can go, Oorthaus.'

Dakota laughed. 'Yes there is, Udo. I could jump ship a dozen times and you'd never find me. The Freehold are a spent force, and half the Consortium is going to breathe a sigh of relief when you're relegated to history. Your own people have got better things to do than come after someone like me.'

'We found something,' said Corso, so quietly it took Dakota a moment to register that he'd actually spoken.

Severn stepped across to the alcove, leaning over the table to speak to her, pointedly ignoring the others. 'You know, whatever favours I owe you – and there's a lot of them, don't think I ever forgot – I just paid every one of them back twice over, starting from about five seconds after you walked through that door.'

Udo started to jerk up out of his seat. The guard behind him pulled back his weapon and slammed the stock of it into the back of the Freeholder's head. Udo's head twisted around under the impact and he slid over to one side, one hand pressing down against the seat.

Severn stood back and nodded in his direction. 'What's your friend's name?'

'Udo Mansell. And he isn't a friend. The other one's Lucas. I reckon he's harmless.'

Severn stared down at Udo, who was slowly pushing himself back upright, his eyes focused somewhere far beyond Dakota's hovering presence. 'Udo, I want you to stay here for now. Me and . . .'

He looked at Dakota.

'Mala,' she replied.

'Me and Mala are going to have a little talk. Next time you try something, Grigori here will use the end of his gun that shoots bullets.'

Dakota slid out of the alcove, following Severn as he

made his way through a door at the far end of the main bar and into an anteroom beyond. She could hear the sound of mogs yelping and of people yelling beyond another door ahead of them, all mixed up with the loud throb of angry, discordant music. This was where the mog pits lay – and where Severn did his real business.

The instant the door had closed behind them, Severn turned and slammed her against a wall.

'Whatever the fuck this is all about, Dakota, start from the beginning and don't leave anything out.'

'Nice to see you, Chris. How long's it been?'

'Not nearly long enough, judging by that little scene. What in the name of all the stars in the sky made you think you could pick *my* establishment to start a fucking war in?'

'I didn't have a choice. The one called Udo—'

'I know who he is, Dakota!' Severn bellowed. The rage seemed to go out of him a little then, and he took a step back, rubbing his face with his hands. When he next spoke, he sounded calmer.

'If people think they can't come here and be safe, then every machine-head within a couple of hundred light years has a serious fucking problem. You know that, don't you? I've gone to a lot of time and effort to make sure this is one of the few safe places all of us can go.'

'I'm in trouble,' Dakota told him baldly.

'Aren't we all.' Severn nodded. 'Want to tell me how?'

'You really don't want to know.'

Severn shook his head. 'Just as much of a fuck-up as you ever were, then.'

'Look, I got hired by a bunch of Freeholders. They want me to pilot their ship – that frigate that just docked a few hours ago. They told me it's a standard system evaluation, but I don't believe them. They won't tell me where we're going, and I know they're hiding something.'

'Freeholders?' Severn stared at her disbelievingly. 'Freeholders hired a machine-head?'

'The one who's been here before, I mean Udo, if it came out he likes mogs, he's a dead man back on Redstone. I needed to get some leverage on him to find out what they're really up to.'

'And so you thought it'd be a really good idea to bring him here, because then he'd crumble and confess everything. So tell me, how's that little plan working out?'

'Not so well, because neither of them will talk,' Dakota admitted. 'I think my only real option is to disappear.'

Severn looked at her with pity. 'You've sunk a long way, Dak.'

'I know.' She grimaced. 'You don't need to tell me.'

'But you're still not telling *me* something.' He stepped closer to her, almost trapping her against the wall. She put one hand on his chest as if in warning, the blood thrumming in her veins.

He continued: 'The last I heard you were running illegal shipments in the home system. Now you're here, trying to ditch the Freehold. Were you there on Bourdain's Rock when it blew up?'

'I . . .' Dakota felt the blood rise to her face and knew she'd given herself away.

'*Shit*.' Severn stepped back and stared at her like he'd never seen her before. 'Jesus, Dak, I heard they were out looking for a machine-head. They're going to kill you, you know that?'

'I had nothing to do with what happened to Bourdain's Rock, I swear,' she said, her voice trembling, 'but I don't think Bourdain's the type that goes for rational argument. The Freehold needed a pilot and for some reason they were desperate enough to use a machine-head. But now I know I'm walking into something bad all over again. I've been trying to ignore my instincts, and my instincts tell me they're up to a lot more than they're admitting.'

Severn nodded, then glanced off to one side. She could tell from his expression he was receiving a communication.

He raised one hand, palm facing towards her. 'Wait here,' he instructed. 'I need to speak to someone. I'll be right back, OK?'

'OK,' she said miserably.

Severn pushed through the far door leading to the mog pits.

A minute passed, and then another. Then waiting

any longer became impossible for Dakota. Her life was at stake here.

She went through the same door to look for Severn. The space beyond was not unlike the bar where they had left Udo and Corso, except that a raised catwalk sliced the room almost in half, and there were more barred cages set into recesses high up on the walls to either side.

Below these were more seating alcoves, full of customers. There were far more mogs evident in this part of the building, and she was mildly shocked to see some being led on leashes along the catwalk by bead zombies. She hadn't ever thought Severn was the type to use zombies, and wondered just how much he'd changed since the last time she'd encountered him. The sight of those headless monstrosities made her queasy in the pit of her stomach.

The mogs on parade had been trained to walk on their hind legs. Most displayed only a hint of human intelligence in their wide dark eyes set above compact, abbreviated snouts. Harsh spotlights glistened on their polished claws and on the metal studs of their leather collars. Some looked considerably more human than any other mogs Dakota had seen before – which made it all seem so much worse.

Severn's clientele remained mostly out of plain sight, their faces veiled in shadows within the alcoves they occupied. On the far side of the catwalk various doors led to secure rooms where those same clients could enjoy a few purchased hours with a gene-job – or alter-

natively go and place a bet in the mog fighting pits
beyond.

Then Dakota saw just exactly who Severn was talking
to.

Moss.

Dakota stepped back into the shadows, neither of
them having yet seen her. They seemed to be arguing,
and from the look on Severn's face she guessed Moss
was being threatening in some way.

She had recognized Moss almost immediately
despite his changed appearance. A large part of his face
looked parboiled, the skin on it blotchy red, stretched
and twisted like plastic. All his hair was missing above
one ear, and the overall effect was monstrous.

It was the kind of disfigurement that might have
been fixed by a week spent inside a medbox, but that
was clearly an option Moss had foregone. Perhaps he
wanted that hideous face to be the last thing she saw
before he killed her.

Finally Moss looked over in her direction and almost
did a double take.

Shit. She'd forgotten about his visual augmentations.
Hiding here in the shadows wasn't any use: she might as
well be standing face to face with him in broad daylight.
His eyes glowed dully, his smile twisting like an open
wound.

She slammed back through the door into the ante-
room, and then found her way back into the front bar.
There was just the chance Severn wouldn't let anything

drastic happen here, in public, or in any place that might hurt his lucrative business.

Udo and Corso were still waiting in their alcove, their faces tense and drawn. Their expressions told her that those few minutes they'd been left alone together had turned into some of the longest in either of their lives.

She heard a commotion from the room behind her, then shots followed by the sound of splintering wood, and something heavy being repeatedly slammed against a wall. Customers looked around wildly, and the murmur of conversation around the bar subsided. Udo started to stand up . . .

The door Dakota had just come through thudded loudly, and she stepped away from it quickly. She now picked up the alarm and rage that was radiating from Severn's Ghost, and even caught flashes of what he was actually seeing and hearing. For a moment, it felt like she was in two places at once.

He's warning me, she realized, but with that warning came the knowledge of just how deeply he'd betrayed her. All in a moment's mind-to-mind data transfer. It was like hearing his confession just prior to execution.

Moss had got here twenty-four hours ahead of the *Hyperion*, the coreship having seemed a likely means of escape for Dakota. So from the moment of his arrival, Bourdain's pet killer had tracked down every possible contact she might have here, and had lucked out with Severn. The deal was simple: all Severn had to do was lull her into a false sense of security, and he got to keep his job, his bar and his life.

Except Moss wasn't really that subtle in the art of negotiation, and Severn had made the mistake of trying to stop him once it became clear that Moss was hell-bent on starting a shooting match. The slamming sound Dakota had heard was from Severn's body being repeatedly thrown against a wall.

The door in front of her suddenly flew open and she found herself almost face to face with Moss. Lightning gloves in place, his hands were outstretched, sparks dancing between his splayed fingers.

Before Dakota had time to react further, she heard an explosion of sound, and Moss staggered back towards the gaping doorway as a red spray erupted from the side of his skull. She instinctively dropped on to the floor, and began to crawl in the direction of the bar's entrance. All around her Severn's clientele were screaming and fighting to get out of the way, the sound of their panic mingling with the still-deafening music and the howls of frightened mogs.

Dakota stopped crawling and looked behind her. To her horror, Moss was starting to get up again, having apparently only received a flesh wound. One of his ears was partly ripped away, and blood oozed down the side of his face.

Despite his injuries, Moss threw himself with inhuman speed right past her, swatting at Grigori with a lightning glove before Severn's chief guard could fire off another shot. Grigori screamed, and then bullets filled the air as the guards by the entrance opened up. Moss pulled the dying guard in front of him, using his twitching half-cooked corpse as a shield.

Hands grabbed at Dakota. Udo and Corso began dragging her towards the far end of the bar, where the mog cages stood. Those customers who hadn't yet managed to flee cowered behind the meagre shelter of tables and chairs.

Bourdain was a powerful man with vast resources, and he'd clearly had no problem figuring out where she might run to. She'd been fooling herself in thinking she could get out of trouble that easily.

Whatever the Freehold had in store for her, she understood, it couldn't be any worse than what she'd have to face if she went on the run.

Dakota twisted around and saw Moss stagger back under a fresh hail of bullets, but rather than falling under the onslaught, he leapt on the three armed men crowding around the main entrance, even as they continued to fire bullet after bullet into his body. Either he was wearing armour of some kind, or he'd undergone the kind of extreme body modification that hardened flesh and bones.

Behind her, Dakota saw Udo was now kneeling by one of the mog cages, studying its lock mechanism. His knife was again gripped in a fist. The cages stood on a raised platform, and she watched as the mogs within them howled and snapped and raged, their claws flashing mere millimetres away from her beyond the transparent cage walls.

As she watched, it became obvious that Udo's knife was a far from ordinary weapon. Its blade shimmered as he touched it to a lock, the metal casing melting like butter. It wasn't hard to imagine what a weapon like that could to do to a human being.

Dakota felt a thrill of terror when she realized he was trying to free the mogs, even as she understood why he was doing so. Howling in high-pitched anguish, the creatures inside continued to scratch at the transparent walls of their prisons with their long vicious claws.

The first cage door flew open a moment later, and a mog leapt howling over the tops of their heads, and shot straight towards Moss. Udo moved quickly on, destroying the lock mechanisms on five other cages within moments. Each time, a frightened, angry mog headed straight for the entrance, ignoring them.

The only thing between them and their freedom was Moss who, against all odds, was slowly staggering upright again, shoving aside the crumpled corpses of the guards.

Glassy-eyed, his mouth twisted in a frown, he went down under a deluge of sleek fur and snapping jaws. A moment later came a series of high-pitched screams, sounding far more animal than human, as Moss remained invisible beneath the scrabbling mound of fur.

'Move!' Udo yelled, and all three of them stumbled past the frenzied scene.

Any normal human would be dead by now, but Dakota felt aware of Moss following her with his eyes as they fled past.

She collapsed in agony and retched violently as a surge of pain shot through her body. Moss had snagged her ankle with a lightning glove as she stumbled past.

Udo came back and kicked out at Moss's head. Moss responded by letting go of Dakota and grabbing Udo's leg instead. The Freeholder crumpled to his knees with a shriek, while Moss used his hold on Udo's body to pull himself out from under the piled corpses of the gene-jobs.

Events felt as if they were occurring at one remove, and Dakota realized her Ghost had taken over. She was distantly aware of her own body lifting itself on all fours to begin crawling towards the entrance.

She glanced behind her and saw Moss staring after her, his face a demon's mask of fresh blood. She couldn't determine if Udo was alive or dead.

Despite his near-supernatural capacity for survival, Moss looked like he was about to run out of lives. Like some half-crippled angel of death, he started to drag his broken body towards Dakota, one arm pressed protectively against his side where he'd clearly been badly mauled.

She had not been consciously aware of Udo's knife lying nearby, half hidden under the warm corpse of a mog, jaws wide and vicious-looking even in death. Under the control of her implants her hand reached out and took a firm grip of the weapon. A violent vibration surged through its handle and rolled up Dakota's arm, making her teeth rattle.

Moss was almost on her. He saw the knife too late. Dakota twisted on to her back as Moss hauled himself on top of her. Splaying her fingers across the twisted ruins of his face, she slid the blade cleanly across his exposed neck. A fountain of blood spilled over her.

She had barely applied any pressure to it, yet Udo's weapon had very nearly severed Moss's head from his neck. His body slumped immediately, without even a twitch, his gloves sparking and flaring as they came into contact with the damp floor. Dakota gasped and twisted in terror, trying to get away from them.

She started to shake uncontrollably, feeling her body come back under her own control. The music had long stopped playing.

'Mala?' It was Corso, dragging her away from the carnage, the sleeves of his jacket splashed red with blood. 'Are you OK?'

Dakota made a noise that was halfway to a laugh.

'That man that tried to kill you? Who the fuck *was* he?'

'An old friend,' Dakota gasped. 'Where's Udo?'

'He's not in good shape, but it looks like he's still breathing.'

Dakota's breath grew steadier as her Ghost smoothed out her brain waves, taking control of her nervous system so as to keep her from slipping into shock.

'Lucas, I have to tell you. I have enemies.'

'You don't say.'

'But so do you, right? That's what you said earlier, or have I got that wrong? You're not on this expedition just because you want to be. You said there were people on Redstone . . .'

The last few of Severn's clientele had fled, along with those few of his guards who were still standing. They'd pulled the entrance door closed, and Dakota guessed it was almost certainly now locked. She managed to stagger to her feet with Corso's help.

As he took her by the shoulders, she stared dazedly into his frightened eyes. At some point he'd taken the knife from her without her noticing.

'Let's be clear on this, Mala,' he croaked. 'I'd rather kill you than see you renege on your deal with us. Arbenz is nothing better than an opportunist using our war with the Uchidans to make his grab for power. But the fact remains he's in a position to hurt people I care about, so for the moment I really, really want to give him exactly what he wants. Understand me?'

She turned away from him and went to kneel down beside Udo. The stricken man's chest rose and fell in a steady rhythm, but he looked bad. As she peeled back one of his eyelids, the pupil shrank in response to the meagre light illuminating the bar.

Probably no serious brain damage, she decided. *At least, no more than before.*

'I think he'll survive.' She slumped back on her heels. 'And I'm not going anywhere, Corso.'

'But you said—'

'All I want is the truth. The only person who's come near to providing that is you. Besides, someone's going to have to tell me eventually – right?'

Corso swallowed. 'Fine. It *was* a standard system reconnaissance, at least at first, but . . . we found something there we didn't expect to find.'

'Found what exactly?'

'Not here.' Corso shook his head. He looked frightened.

A hand brushed against Dakota's shin and she nearly jumped out of her skin. She looked down in horror to find Udo's eyes fixed on her.

'Mala. Oorthaus.' His voice was dry and cracked, like a desert rock that had suddenly developed the ability to speak. 'I challenge you. To the death.'

Dakota started to speak, but Udo shook his head slowly and she fell silent.

'But not yet. For now I will say nothing. But one day I will meet you with equal arms, and I will kill you.' He coughed with considerable effort. 'We were attacked by Uchidan agents. That's our story, do you understand? Betray me, and I betray you.'

Udo's head slumped back, a long guttural sigh escaping from his throat as he passed out again.

'You know,' Dakota said to Corso a moment later, 'he meant *you* as well. He'll kill you if you talk about what you know.'

'And what about you, Dakota? Would you kill me if I told Arbenz what really took place here?'

She looked away for a moment, caught in indecision.

The need once again to put her trust in someone reasserted itself. Just holding herself together like this – amid the ineffable loneliness and constant terror of her predicament – was pushing her to the edge of sanity.

Dead, Lucas Corso would be one less witness. The same went for Udo, now prone on the floor. But if she were the only survivor among these three, who would ever believe her story?

'The man who tried to kill me is called Moss,' she informed Corso.

He looked like he was waiting to hear more, but she was saved by the sound of voices shouting in the alley outside. Dakota grabbed Corso's arm and started to tug him back towards the rear door leading into the ante-room. Perhaps they could find a way out through the rear of the building.

Corso followed her, apparently in too much of a daze to resist. 'I don't know if I can believe anything you say,' he muttered.

'I don't know how much I can trust you either but, for what it's worth, right now I'm probably a lot safer on board the *Hyperion* than anywhere else.'

There was a bright burst of light, and the entrance

door blew inwards. Smoke started billowing and tall shapes entered the bar. Kieran Mansell stepped out of the smoke first, closely followed by armed men and women wearing Peralta's colours.

He surveyed the destruction with a candid eye. 'Somebody,' he grated, 'has one fuck of a lot of explaining to do.'

The post-mortem interrogations took the better part of two days.

Arbenz had meanwhile confined everyone to the *Hyperion* until the 'nature of the threat' could be assessed. Whatever presence the Consortium maintained on board the giant coreship remained noticeably quiet. But, from what Corso understood, the local Consortium officers were adept at turning a blind eye to any activities involving Peralta.

Contrary to his own orders, Arbenz subsequently himself spent a great deal of time away from the *Hyperion*. Nobody seemed in a hurry to tell Corso what was going on but, from what he gathered, the Senator was busy in some form of negotiations with Peralta, probably by way of damage limitation.

In the meantime Corso paced around inside his quarters, avoiding Arbenz's cronies as far as humanly possible. He kept his thoughts from loneliness and frequent bouts of despair by diving deep into his research.

It was becoming clear that whoever or whatever the

Magi had been, they'd been in contact with the Shoal for at least a couple of thousand years before their sudden disappearance. Contained within the codes recovered from the Magi derelict were tantalizing clues, random hints that might finally reveal where the strange craft had originated.

But so far, these were only hints – barely enough to let Corso make some tentative guesses.

He discovered that the derelict had, for some reason, been fleeing the Shoal when it had crash-landed on the icy moon of a gas-giant – where it had recently come to light. Had the Magi therefore been rivals to the Shoal, a star-faring race that also shared the secret of faster-than-light travel?

Anything seemed possible as he explored further, but all Corso really had so far was speculation.

'My brother is under deep sedation,' Kieran Mansell explained to Corso during a lengthy interrogation in private. Kieran paced constantly, hands folded behind his back, while Corso sat on a low chair that forced him to look up at his questioner. 'He'll probably remain in a medbox for a few weeks, as the damage to his nervous system is particularly severe. That means he may not regain full use of his faculties for some time, and he didn't manage to say much before he went under sedation. But what he did have to say was . . . contradictory. For now, all we have to go on is the joint testimony supplied by you and the woman Mala Oorthaus.'

Corso had become aware that a large part of

Arbenz's current negotiations with Peralta were over the General's refusal to allow him access to Severn's surveillance records.

'Remind me again why you decided to go to that particular establishment.' Kieran hovered over Corso, violence implicit in his gaze.

'I . . . told you, Mala led us to it. It was because she knew a machine-head she expected to be there.'

The disbelieving look Kieran gave him went on for ever. 'Do you know how very easy it is to tell when someone is lying? My brother, my own brother, lied to me. He told me the man who attacked you was a Uchidan agent.' Kieran pounded his chest with his fist as he yelled the words. 'You know,' he screamed, one gloved finger pointed at Corso cowering in his seat, 'how important this expedition is to us all. Just one deception could bring all this crashing down.'

Kieran paused and stared at him like he was looking for confirmation.

'If Udo said he was a Uchidan agent . . . then I guess maybe he was,' Corso stuttered.

Face turning red, Kieran took a few steps forward and kicked Corso's chair over, sending the younger man sprawling. Corso yelled as he hit the floor and put up his hands to protect himself. Mansell stood over him, fists knotted, nostrils flaring. Then he seemed to get a hold on himself and righted the chair, before walking to the far end of the room. Arms folded, he stood staring at the wall as if answers might spontaneously materialize out of its smooth grey surface.

'Whoever the attacker in that bar turns out to be, it appears his boarding of this coreship was effectively invisible – which implies very powerful contacts. But this . . . *incident* has already attracted us too much attention. We've been noticed.'

'What about Mala? What happens to her?'

'I notice you're on first-name terms now,' Kieran sneered, glancing back over his shoulder. 'What *about* her? She's a means to an end, nothing more. But you have your own duty to the Freehold. And to your family.'

A means to an end. As Corso listened to the words he understood the greater meaning implicit in them. He himself was no more important than Mala was in the Senator's grand plan to save the Freehold.

And he knew there was no reason to think either of them would be allowed to live, once their usefulness was gone.

FIFTEEN

In a few days' time, the coreship would reach what Lucas Corso now knew to be the Nova Arctis system. The great vessel would make the briefest stop to unload them, barely braking as it momentarily dropped out of transluminal space. From that point on, the *Hyperion* would use up a sizeable fraction of its remaining fuel in the process of decelerating from a significant percentage of the speed of light, until they reached their target.

Corso had endured sleepless nights, and longer days, sustained only by his work. He fell into a rhythm, leaving his quarters within the *Hyperion*'s gravity wheel only when absolutely necessary.

One evening he came across Mala by chance in another part of the ship, and he faltered, unsure what to say to her.

The best course of action, he'd already decided, following his first interrogation, would be to maintain a discreet and polite distance from her, if humanly possible. Several days after the incident in Severn's bar, relationships on board the *Hyperion* were at best tense, at worst edging towards violence.

She brushed straight by him and – since they were in a part of the ship that didn't benefit from centrifugal gravity – continued floating down the corridor as if she hadn't seen him. Corso had no idea what to think of that: part of him felt intensely relieved, but a larger part was annoyed as hell. Surely he deserved a bit more consideration?

Maybe he was suffering from a crisis of conscience. He'd stood by and watched as his own worst enemies had hired her, an outsider, under false pretences. Did that make himself and Mala allies by default – or, at best, potential co-conspirators?

Rather than deal with such complex considerations, Corso dived back into his research work: endlessly investigating, teasing information apart, driving himself to understand, to see into the mind of a species so long departed from the galaxy.

And then the first of two strange events occurred.

Within the bridge was a planetarium simulator, a piece of equipment a lot more recent than almost anything else on board the ship. Even better, its databases were well up to date. That day he was intending to make use of it to check and double-check the fragments of the drive records aboard the derelict spacecraft which hinted at an extra-galactic origin.

Corso arrived at the entrance to the bridge only to find Mala already seated in the interface chair, running the same planetarium program. The chair's petals were neatly folded up at the base of the chair. She was facing away from him, so wouldn't have seen him enter.

The program had meanwhile transformed the bridge into a god's eye view of the Milky Way. Images of star clusters slid past Corso's nose as they rotated across Dakota's viewpoint. The images filled the entire chamber.

As he watched, the Milky Way suddenly shrank, Dakota's viewpoint zooming outwards, until the two dwarf Magellan galaxies accompanying the Milky Way suddenly hove into view. Corso was startled to see lines of trajectory suddenly flare out from the larger of these dwarf galaxies, multiplying until thousands upon thousands of such lines reached deep into the heart of the Milky Way.

He stepped forward, fascinated. This wasn't so far from his own speculations regarding the derelict craft's origins.

And yet . . .

This couldn't possibly be a coincidence: there was no way Mala could have already discovered the derelict's existence, or become aware of Corso's carefully accumulated researches.

But the evidence was there in front of him, arcing across the curving empty space of the bridge.

The simulation suddenly shut down, reverting the bridge to all its mundane normality. Corso moved forward around one side of the interface chair, where . . .

He took a step back.

Mala lay slumped in the seat, her head lolling against the headrest, her jaw slack and drooling, as if she had completely lost her mind. Her eyes had rolled up in their sockets, apparently seeing nothing. He stared down at her, dumbfounded.

Then, as her eyes suddenly focused on him, Corso had the eerie sensation that something inhuman was staring back at him. When he had time to think about it later, it was as if some subtle shift had taken place in the way her face muscles moved. As if someone or *something* else briefly inhabited her skin.

Of course, he could have merely imagined it, the impression was so fleeting. Yet he couldn't rid himself of the eerie sensation he'd seen something he wasn't meant to see.

Then Mala's eyes cleared and her head straightened up as if she'd just awoken. She blinked and gave him a curious smile, as if pleasantly surprised to find him standing there.

'What were you doing just then?' Corso asked her, keeping his tone casual. It was the most he'd managed to say to her in several days.

'I . . .' Her face clouded for a moment as if trying hard to remember. 'Just routine stuff. I was reconfiguring some of the ship's systems.'

'And nothing else?' Corso could feel his heart hammering. 'What about the planetarium program?'

'What about it?'

'You were running it just now.'

Mala gave him a blank look. 'I told you what I've been doing. I don't have time for this. You look like you're accusing me of something.'

Corso felt his frustration grow, yet she appeared genuinely to have no idea what he was talking about.

'Does Arbenz know you're here?'

Mala looked at him as if he'd lost his mind. 'Corso, being here is my job. There's no point in my being on board if I'm not.'

His second bizarre encounter with her took place a day or two later.

They were within a few hours of the *Hyperion*'s departure from the coreship. Arbenz's frequent trips into Ascension had meanwhile begun to tail off. Kieran Mansell ran continuous, obsessive security checks that required frequent attendance from everyone on board – more for Kieran's own peace of mind than anything else, Corso suspected.

Udo, meantime, floated dreamless and insensate within his medbox, as his flesh repaired itself with the help of cloned grafts and neuro-enhancements. The worst part for them all was the waiting. Udo was unpredictable enough already, and Corso had no real idea what the man might say once he regained consciousness. But good sense seemed to prevail in the end, and Mala had been right in suggesting Udo would have too much to lose in speaking out against her.

Corso finally tired of the claustrophobic confines of his quarters and would go for long tours through the ship, wandering its deserted corridors and drop shafts. Part of the *Hyperion*'s zero-gee environment, the drop shafts had been transformed into vertical wells by the coreship's induced gravity. Pulling himself up and down the rungs was hard work, but it served to take his mind off his other worries.

Ever since he had found Mala in the interface chair surrounded by images of the Magellanic Clouds, Corso had been working hard on all the data assembled, increasingly convinced, no matter how impossible it appeared, that the key to the derelict's final secrets lay in the images he had seen so briefly there on the bridge.

During his wanderings, in the final few hours before their departure from the coreship, Corso had again found his way aft when he heard the distinctive whine of the airlock servos in operation. He had previously been delivering a verbal progress report to Gardner, the Senator, and Kieran Mansell, so knew that none of them was likely to be down this way.

Puzzled, he made his way towards the airlocks: they were the same ones they'd used on exiting the *Hyperion* for their trip into Ascension. But when he got there moments later, he found no one in sight. So what had he heard just a few moments before?

Then he heard a clang of metal coming from not so far away, and followed the sound fruitlessly down a passageway. He suspected it could only have been caused by Mala, but there was no sign of her.

By chance he glanced up, and caught sight of her lithe form clambering silently up the rungs of a drop shaft. She swiftly hoisted herself into the corridor of the next level up and disappeared from view.

'Hey!' Corso shouted.

Moving fast, he pulled himself up after her, breathing hard by the time he reached the top. He emerged into the same corridor only to catch sight of her rapidly retreating figure.

'Hey!' he shouted again, and began running after her. Dakota kept moving as if she hadn't heard him.

He caught up with her and grabbed her arm, pulling her around. She blinked in surprise and seemed to recognize him only after a long moment.

'What? What is it?' She sounded flustered.

'Where *were* you?' Corso gasped. 'I heard the airlock working, and . . . were you outside the ship?'

Mala stared at him like he was mad. 'No, I was right here, checking the manual systems prior to launch.'

'Mala, I *heard* the airlock closing. That means somebody came in from outside, and you're the only one around. If it wasn't you, who was it, then?'

She shook her head like she was tired of talking. 'You're getting paranoid, Lucas. It wasn't me. Go check the onboard records if you like.'

When he did so, what he found there was frustrating – and worrying.

The security logs showed his recent encounter with Mala, but that was all. There was nothing to suggest anyone apart from Arbenz had either entered or departed the *Hyperion* for days. Mala was clearly shown walking directly from her quarters towards the aft engines and right past the airlocks. Three of the others were already accounted for, while Udo remained lost to the world in his chemically induced sleep within the medical bay.

But he'd definitely heard the airlock mechanisms operating, whatever the security records showed. That wasn't the kind of thing you could imagine.

There was something too convenient about it all. Was it possible, he wondered, for the logs to be faked? Or was he himself simply descending into irretrievable paranoia and madness?

Corso debated taking his doubts to Arbenz, but decided against that. Despite everything, Mala Oorthaus was not his real enemy here. She was not in any way responsible for the predicament facing his family, and he was increasingly ashamed to acknowledge how thoroughly complicit he had been in sealing her fate in a way not likely to be pleasant. In truth, he was no better than Senator Arbenz.

True, she was strange, but Freehold society placed clear formal limits on any social contact between men and women, so for him there was something brazenly different about Mala that made her seem far more attractive than any of the Freehold women Corso was used to.

Her obvious terror of what secrets Arbenz might be keeping from her had awoken within Corso an increasing awareness of their joint insignificance in the scheme of things. Once Arbenz and Gardner had achieved what they wanted, he himself would become an unwanted witness to a crime as yet uncommitted. Yet they meanwhile depended on him to open the treasure box.

What to do then, Corso wondered? Was the Senator a man he could trust to keep his word and give him as well as his family their freedom? Or was holding on to that belief just a way to keep himself sane?

And so he decided to remain silent, and bide his time.

SIXTEEN

Corso watched from his seat as Arbenz and Gardner stood in mumbled conversation by the meeting room's doorway. In the past he had often entered this same room to find the two of them already in heated argument.

Each time, as Corso took his seat ready to give his daily briefing on the derelict, their voices would suddenly drop to low whispers, broken by sudden pauses, while they would both cast sideways glances towards him. If Corso hadn't been so busy wishing the pair of them dead, it would have been comical.

But this time, they didn't seem so concerned about Corso overhearing them.

A fresh news squirt from Redstone, picked up only a few hours ago, brought the news that Aguirre, a Freehold city on the coast of the Mount Mor peninsula, had surrendered to Uchidan military forces after a long siege. The siege itself was almost certainly in reprisal for bombing raids against Uchidan damming operations on the Ka River.

At almost the same time, disruptor probes had nearly

destroyed the Freehold orbital frigate *Rorqual Maru*. With this grim news came the inevitable, though unfounded, rumours that the Consortium was engaged in talks about intervening on the Freehold's side, but Corso remained sceptical that any such intervention would ever happen. After all, there were no valuable scientists like Banville for the Consortium to try and recover this time.

Corso had belatedly come to accept that Arbenz might be right in believing the Freehold's only real hope of continued survival lay somewhere inside the derelict. That the Senator should represent the best hope of achieving that salvation was, to his mind, the greatest tragedy of all.

With the disastrous loss of Aguirre to the enemy, Arbenz had been torn over whether he himself should continue on to Nova Arctis, or instead make his way back to Redstone via the coreship. That would have meant leaving Kieran in charge of the recovery operation, a concept that understandably infuriated Gardner.

'It's an *intolerable* idea,' Gardner now raged. 'There is absolutely *no* excuse for you to simply walk away!'

'David—'

'I am *not* going to be left on my own to deal with Kieran or his appalling brother,' Gardner spat. 'Why, Senator, are they even here?'

'They're here because I trust them,' Arbenz replied just as heatedly.

Gardner laughed in disbelief. 'Look me in the eye,

Senator, and tell me how much you really want either Kieran or Udo making decisions over how we handle the derelict. As talking guard dogs they're great, but do you seriously want to give them that much responsibility? *Do you?*'

Arbenz opened his mouth to reply, then seemed to think better of it. The other man's argument had clearly hit home to some extent. He shook his head angrily and took a seat at the table across from Corso, without another word.

'He's far too much of a wild card to be left in charge of something this vital,' Gardner added as he took his own seat, though sounding more even-tempered now he'd made his point. 'Retrieving the derelict, winning your war – they're the same thing, Senator. One secures you the other, and you'll do much more good for the Freehold here than back on Redstone.'

Without being asked, Corso activated the holo display, bringing up an image of their destination. Planets and gas-giants hovered in the air above the table, woven together by bright lines of plotted trajectory.

At that moment Kieran entered the room, as ever the last to arrive. He took a seat at the table.

'Base Camp on the moon Theona reports no new systems activity on board the derelict since we delineated the parameters of its defence grids,' Kieran informed them without delay. 'We were worried it might be transmitting some kind of distress signal after we screwed up getting on board the first time, but it looks like it was just a glitch in our own monitoring systems.'

'Good.' Gardner folded his arms, looking pleased. 'The last thing we want is it broadcasting anything the Shoal can pick up.'

Arbenz nodded to Corso. 'I believe we've been making good progress in reverse-engineering the derelict's computer systems?'

'Based on the available simulations, yes,' Corso replied.

Gardner leaned forward. 'Is the machine-head interface aboard the derelict ready?'

'Pretty much, though I'm still running tests. But we can't be sure how well it's going to work until we actually plug Mala into it. The problem is that a large part of the simulation I've been working with is, by necessity, constructed mainly from best guesses. Until we actually get there, it's all we've got.'

'You understand, don't you,' Gardner pointed out, 'that there's absolutely no room for error.'

'Look, we already know the derelict is extremely sophisticated when it comes to defending itself,' Corso replied. 'Two of the investigative teams you've already sent in vanished without a trace before you finally got even a part of it under control. But when we activate the real interface, I know for a fact we're going to open up areas of the derelict a lot deeper than anything you've managed yet. And, yes, I feel pretty confident that what I've put together will work. But the fact remains, until we switch the chair on, with Mala sitting in it, whatever happens next is anybody's guess.'

Corso chose his next words carefully. 'Senator, I have a question, if I may speak freely?'

Arbenz nodded.

'Assuming we're successful in extracting a working star drive from the derelict . . . what happens next? What are the long-term plans, beyond winning the war against the Uchidans? Do we keep the technology, or share it with the Consortium?'

Arbenz grinned.

'You have no right whatsoever to ask that question,' Kieran interrupted flatly. 'Your job is to—'

Arbenz gestured Kieran to silence and turned back to Corso. 'Imagine the glorious future for the Freehold when it can go anywhere in the galaxy it chooses, Corso. We could conquer whole worlds, recruit vast armies to support our expansion. I see no reason why the Shoal wouldn't eventually succumb before us, given time. The entire galaxy would fall before us. Picture it: a human hegemony, spread across the face of the Milky Way. A glorious, wonderful future for us all, if we only have the courage to seize the prize before us.'

Corso forced a smile and nodded with feigned approval, but his heart wasn't in it. This was the same attitude that had confined the Freehold in a desolate corner of human space, the same attitude that was now losing them a war. He knew he didn't have the courage to tell any of them what he really thought: that if the

Consortium didn't crush them once they knew what the Freehold had acquired – *if* they could extract the drive engines, *if* they could reproduce the technology, *if*, *if* – then the Shoal would certainly do the job instead.

'That's exactly what I was thinking,' he lied.

Kieran changed the subject. 'We have to discuss the machine-head pilot. I'm concerned about the degree of control we've already given her over the *Hyperion*. I'm far from comfortable about giving her even a fraction as much control over the derelict.'

'You'll recall the failsafes, Kieran.'

'Senator,' Kieran continued, 'were you anywhere near Port Gabriel during the atrocities that occurred there?'

Arbenz raised an eyebrow, looking suddenly unhappy at Kieran's new line of questioning. 'No.'

'Well, I was, and the machine-heads killed everyone they came into contact with. No – more than that: they tore them apart. They decorated the streets of the city with the corpses of women and children. They carved the Uchidan symbol of unity into the bodies of infants and then put them back in the arms of their dying parents.'

'Whatever your point is,' said the Senator, between gritted teeth, 'hurry up and make it.'

'I'm not convinced that Oorthaus won't find some way to circumvent Corso's failsafes. It's easy to under-estimate what any human being with Ghost implants can do.'

'The machine-heads who took part in the massacre weren't responsible for what they did, Kieran,' Gardner pointed out. 'It was a failure of the technology, not the people using it.'

'Machine-heads are outlawed because they're uniquely vulnerable to outside control,' Kieran bristled. 'We have no guarantees this woman isn't really a Trojan horse under the control of our enemies!'

'Kieran,' Arbenz's tone was rising, 'right now, whether we like it or not, we need her, and our window of opportunity is narrow. Every one of our scientific advisers has agreed it will take a machine-head interface to control the derelict. We are therefore *not* going to discuss the pros and cons of this any further.'

Corso's own grandfather, Silas, had been working at the university in Port Gabriel when the massacre there took place. A Consortium ship had come thudding down in the Square of Heroes, a few blocks from the campus. They'd had to identify him later from DNA analysis of his remains, after they finished digging through the rubble. Silas wasn't the only person Corso had known who had died during the horrific assault. Most people belonging to the Freehold knew someone, or was related to someone, who'd been injured or killed at that time.

Images of the dropships falling on Port Gabriel, like avenging angels, had played on Freehold news networks for months afterward, entirely uncensored.

An angry silence passed between the two men,

before Kieran finally sucked it up. 'I apologize, Senator. I didn't mean to question your authority.'

'Accepted. But your point is taken.'

'Actually,' said Gardner, speaking into the silence that followed, 'while we're on the subject, I've been looking further into what happened in that mog bar.'

Arbenz groaned. 'We've been over this, David.'

'Well, I've been making my own enquiries, Senator. I've managed to identify the man who attacked Udo.'

Arbenz looked disbelieving. 'I've spent a lot of time trying to find out everything I can about him, but none of the General's people could discover anything.'

'I have my own sources,' Gardner continued, 'and it seems the assassin's name was Hugh Moss, an employee of Alexander Bourdain.'

Corso looked down at his hands where they were clenched together on the tabletop, and saw his knuckles were white with tension.

A look flashed between Kieran and Arbenz. 'How did you come by this?' demanded the Senator, turning back to Gardner.

Gardner smiled tightly. 'I had my own suspicions, and I've friends in the Consortium Legislate who owe me favours. It turns out the General has a profitable long-term working relationship with Bourdain, based on the trade and gene-cultivation of mogs, so it's hardly surprising he didn't want to tell you anything that might compromise his relationship with one of his best customers.'

'But why would Bourdain send someone to try and stop us?' said Kieran, gripping the edge of the table with both hands. 'Or are you telling us Bourdain already knows about the derelict?'

Gardner shook his head. 'You're looking for the wrong answers. Let's recap on some recent events: first, Bourdain's new world detonated in an act of apparent terrorism. Then Mala Oorthaus showed up looking for work that would take her safely out of the Sol System.'

Arbenz didn't look convinced. 'You were the one responsible for hiring her, David. Why didn't you check all this out back then?'

'I did,' Gardner stated flatly. 'But we were pressed for time, and machine-heads aren't easy to come by any more, remember? All I knew about her came through Josef Marados, and it turns out he was murdered just before our departure from Mesa Verde.'

As Corso listened to this in mute shock, Kieran suddenly leaned forward, tapping at the air. Corso's solar system disappeared, to be replaced by screeds of media information: news feeds regularly updated via the tach-net transponders. Corso watched as Kieran ran a fast search through the Mesa Verde public archives.

He looked up again with a shake of his head. 'Senator, I've been constantly monitoring events back on Redstone and within the Sol System, and can find no reports of any such incident. Something like that couldn't possibly have escaped my attention.'

'News feeds can be falsified,' Gardner pointed out.

'Marados was in charge of a major financial operation working in and out of the black market, and when someone like that dies, particularly when it's a nasty, violent death, word gets out one way or another. And remember what I said – I have my own sources of information, outside of official channels. This whole thing stinks of someone covering their tracks, especially if you assume Bourdain's assassin in fact came looking to kill the Oorthaus woman.'

Arbenz looked thunderstruck. 'But why would Bourdain send someone to . . . are you saying *she* might be responsible for what happened to Bourdain's Rock?'

'Why not say just that? But we don't know for sure, of course.' Gardner's smile was as dry as his voice. 'But, you said it yourself: we still need her. Whether she likes it or not.'

On the edge of the Nova Arctis system, the coreship dropped out of transluminal space for a bare few minutes, but long enough for the *Hyperion* to lift up from its docking facility on a shimmering platform constructed of shaped fields and artificial gravity, before finally exiting through one of the many openings in the coreship's outer crust.

The frigate went into immediate deceleration as it pulled away from the vast Shoal vessel, which dwindled rapidly as it accelerated back to jump speed.

Dakota sat in a web of data at the heart of the bridge,

watching the way space warped around the coreship as it slipped back into transluminal space in a flurry of exotic particles. At last, she knew their destination: Nova Arctis. This system had only been a number in a catalogue until the Freeholders decided to give it that name.

In the meantime, there were questions for Dakota to ponder, that in turn raised more questions rather than answers.

Such as, who had killed Severn?

Severn had obviously survived his encounter with Moss – if he hadn't, she would have known, immediately. Yet several days ago, his life-signal – dim as it was, given he was some kilometres away in the heart of Ascension – had ceased. She'd woken from a dream at the time, her own heart pounding, filled with an inexplicable sense of loss, until she had realized what her Ghost was telling her.

It was hard to believe. They'd hardly set eyes on each other more than a few times in the years since Port Gabriel, but the knowledge of his death gripped her innards and filled her thoughts with a deep sense of mourning, despite his betrayal of her.

Chris, dead.

At first she assumed he must have finally died of the injuries sustained during his fight with Moss. But then she'd had the *Piri Reis* worm its way into the maintenance programs for a local medical storage facility in Ascension, and then discovered the truth. Severn had been messily executed by unknown assailants, after being hauled out of his medbox.

Whoever was responsible, they'd been thorough, and particularly brutal.

It was possible Arbenz was behind this, or perhaps Moss hadn't been the only agent Bourdain had sent aboard the coreship. But also Severn had led a dangerous life, and had any number of enemies in a city still deeply divided by the aftermath of the civil war. Any one of them could have been responsible.

Nonetheless, it was beginning to feel as if a lengthening trail of death led straight towards her. First the massacre on the Rock, then Josef Marados, and now Severn. It was enough to make a person very scared – and very, very paranoid.

With a start, Dakota remembered Corso's garbled suggestion that someone might have entered the *Hyperion* without any of them knowing. At first she'd considered such an idea to be ridiculous. There were few areas of the frigate that Dakota, via her Ghost circuits and *Piri*'s systems, hadn't accessed or subjugated to her will in some way.

A few parts of the *Hyperion* remained effectively invisible to her, because Arbenz still retained sole control over certain higher-level systems. Was it possible someone else had found a way to get on board? Someone far sneakier and deadlier even than Moss: an intruder who could somehow avoid or alter the security logs, and then murder her in her sleep?

This ship had too many shadows for its own good. Dakota's senses prickled apprehensively as she found her way through its musty, darkened corridors and drop shafts. She checked and rechecked the vessel's security logs, including her own illegal alterations. There were, indeed, curious omissions or glitches that had nothing to do with her efforts, incredibly easy to miss if she hadn't been looking for something just a little bit unusual.

She couldn't dismiss either the possibility that someone – or *something* – had gained access to the logs without her knowledge. Dakota shivered at the thought.

But surely it simply wasn't possible. Only another machine-head could possess that level of skill.

She thought often of some of the few words she had exchanged with Corso: his revelation that he was aboard the *Hyperion* only under severe duress. It revealed a streak of honesty in him – or so she believed – that made him substantially different from the others aboard.

Regardless of that, ever since their return from Ascension she had been avoiding him, afraid he might still betray her. He owed her absolutely nothing, after all.

Yet during his own subsequent interrogation by Kieran, he had clearly lied about what had happened in Severn's bar. On the few occasions they crossed paths she had seen the sympathetic way he looked at her, those furtive glances when he thought she wasn't paying attention.

It had been a long, long time since Dakota had felt comfortable with the thought of intimacy with another human being – long and lonely years with no one to trust. But a lifetime of betrayal didn't lend itself to a sudden acquiescence to physical desire or momentary lust. So she kept to herself, and avoided Corso, making occasional trips back to the cargo bay and the *Piri*'s effigy, in order to assuage her tension via brief, erotic encounters, while always wary of the turmoil in her heart and in her mind.

SEVENTEEN

Redstone Colony
Consortium Standard Date: 03.06.2538
Port Gabriel Incident −2 Hours

The Consortium task force tore through Redstone's stratosphere on tails of bright plasma. The rising sun dazzled the powered dust-mote lenses that followed in their wake as they pumped terabytes of real-time visual data to Orbital Command as well as to the Circus Ring on the surface.

Severn was a distant presence, seventeen kilometres east of Dakota, as they rose over the limb of the horizon, a pinprick of nervous humour and black wit hovering among a legion of Ghost-boosted consciousnesses, each node in constant communication with all the rest.

What each of them sensed, Dakota also sensed. What each of them knew, Dakota knew immediately, according to a complex hierarchy known as a threat/significance tree, almost without her being fully conscious of the process.

From moment to moment, Dakota was aware of . . .

. . . Alejandro Najario, running constant threat analyses from the command deck of the *Winter's Night*, ignoring the bickering, and sly, bemused comments of the Freehold troops locked into their launch restraints in the rear of his dropship.

. . . Tessa Faust, another pilot, checking her screens and altering her delta vee. She was tired, her head sore from a bad headache she'd suffered the night before.

. . . Chris Severn, alert and sharp, constantly monitoring the transceiver relays that had been used to compromise the Uchidan early-warning system.

Severn had been right, of course, about her on–off relationship with Josef Marados. It hadn't taken long before Josef had again zeroed in on Dakota, and she herself, of course, had been a willing collaborator in his seduction.

She could still smell the scent of his skin, in her thoughts, from last night. Her concern over Severn's jealousy was offset by the knowledge of his own separate, developing relationship with Tessa Faust.

'I noticed the Shoal-member in the Circus Ring,' Dakota had muttered, lying naked under the bare arm Josef had cast over her. 'What's it here for?'

'Privileged information,' replied Josef, in a sleepy post-coital mumble.

'Oh, bullshit.' Dakota jabbed him with an elbow. Dawn light leaked through the blinds. 'It's here to watch from the sidelines, isn't it? Isn't it bad enough they started this whole business in the first place?'

Josef sighed and pulled himself around until he faced her. 'What are you up to now, recruiting for the Uchidans?'

'Oh, for God's sake, you know exactly what I mean.'

'Dak, we all know about the Treaty Clause, but we still have a job to do.'

'There's something that really bothers me. It's the names those things give themselves.'

'The Shoal?' Josef cast her an incredulous look. 'They're *aliens*, Dakota. That's what aliens do: alien stuff. You're on a fast ride to nowhere if you start trying to figure out how their minds work.'

'I'm not so sure.' Dakota pushed herself up on one elbow. Further sleep had suddenly become a distant prospect. 'Understanding what they say is one thing, but sometimes . . . it's like they're having a massive joke at our expense. I couldn't believe it when I heard what that thing calls itself.'

Josef shifted on to his back, and closed his eyes. At first Dakota thought he'd fallen asleep again, but after a moment he replied: 'I'll have to admit Trader-In-Faecal-Matter-Of-Animals isn't a name that promotes much respect.'

'But that's just it,' Dakota said, punching a pillow in exasperation. 'They're laughing at us. They don't need us, but we need them really badly.'

'OK, granted. But what can we do?'

Dakota made an exasperated sound and let her head fall back on the pillow. They were both staring up at the ceiling now.

'You know, I feel like a fish out of water here. I don't feel like I belong. It's like I shouldn't really be here.'

'What do you mean?' Josef asked.

'I'm from Bellhaven, remember. I didn't exactly volunteer to be here.'

Josef nodded with apparent sympathy, the circumstances being well known throughout the Consortium.

The first generation of Bellhaven colonists had put into action an extensive terraforming programme designed to increase the mean global temperature of their new world. When the first of the civil wars broke out a few decades later, the terraforming process had collapsed into disarray. The Elders, once they emerged victorious, had been forced to seek aid from the Consortium in order to reinstate the process – seeking aid, in fact, from the very Devil they had chosen to escape from when they had first arrived on Bellhaven.

The price for that help had been considerable. Since long before Dakota's time, Bellhaven had gained a powerful reputation for innovation in the development of machine-head technology. In return for making Bellhaven more habitable, the Consortium demanded – and got – special concessions that included the acquisition of native-trained machine-heads for peacekeeping purposes.

Dakota had never previously seen herself as a soldier.

She was, after all, a machine-head, someone who could endow mute machinery with her human intelligence. She had successfully avoided thinking too hard about what the Bellhaven technology treaties meant for her. Yet here she was, far from home, wondering just who she was meant to be.

In the moments before waking that morning, Dakota had found herself in an unfamiliar city, wearing a long pale dress with sleeves that trailed on the ground. Buildings rose like steel dandelions far into a pale blue sky, as if reaching out to ensnare a sun that beat down with not only warmth and heat, but also love and kindness and wisdom.

The idea of looking into that bright incandescence had terrified her. So she had kept her eyes downcast, knowing the light was alive, intelligent, that it knew everything about her that could possibly be known: every thought and action and desire she had ever felt or acted upon, good or bad.

And, yet, the light loved her regardless.

She moved through an unending throng, a billion people crammed into streets that ended in impossibly distant vanishing points, all dressed in a thousand colours. Every face she saw was serene, peaceful and content. She tried desperately to find the angel she had encountered in her previous dream.

The knowledge that the light shining down upon

those streets was in fact God came to Dakota as if it were something she had always known.

As she walked on among those impossible spires, a terrible awareness came to her: that she was no more than a ghost to these people, an invisible wraith insufficiently worthy to rightly walk in their angelic city. As much as the light shining down on her loved her, it also told her she was of far less account than any of the city's genuine inhabitants.

She stumbled, unable to accept the truth of this knowledge, filled with a sense of loss so unbearable and so deep that she cried ghost tears, torn apart by her own sense of failure. She had reached out then, her spectral fingers brushing against a wall the colour of fine alabaster. Black cracks spread out from under her fingertips with astonishing speed: the wall began crumbling and rotting and turning black.

Deep within her lay a terrible dark void that could never coexist with such a perfect realm. Not unless she could find some way to prove her worth to that beatific light shining down on her.

Some way to show that she, too, was pure of heart.

The dropship rattled as it skimmed over Redstone's bleak terrain. Emergency signals began to come through from some of the other machine-head pilots, including Severn. She could almost taste his fright through the Ghost link.

Chris?

No reply. Instead he dropped out of contact, followed by three others. Panic began to overwhelm Dakota's thoughts. Something, somewhere was very badly wrong. A priority command from the Circus Ring flashed up: they were aware of the problem, and were changing the current attack formation in response.

It didn't make sense. The formation protocols being uploaded to her were only to be implemented if some of their ships got taken out. Yet all the other ships within her formation remained stubbornly visible on all the sensor systems. *What to do?*

Another two machine-heads disappeared from her Ghost link. Something worse than panic enveloped Dakota's body, cold sweat slicking her skin under her gee suit. Perhaps Severn and the others were gone, and the Uchidans were feeding her false telemetry to fool her into thinking they were still there.

She fired out emergency signals to the Circus Ring, to Orbital, to the other dropships, the warnings slowly disappearing, one by one, off the Ghost link. When replies and acknowledgements came back, they had somehow been rendered incomprehensible, as if she had forgotten how to understand simple human speech overnight.

And then she saw an angel striding across the horizon, golden, terrible and beautiful. The very same creature she'd encountered in her dream. The one she'd been searching for.

It moved below the silver darts of the Consortium task force, wings spread like a great vale of white across a sky streaked with morning red. It might have been a kilometre in height, and in one enormous hand it bore a sword that sparked with lightning. And Dakota knew immediately that when it killed, it killed with compassion and kindness.

It was the most beautiful thing she had ever seen.

An unfamiliar voice gabbled in the back of her mind, speaking in a language simultaneously unfamiliar and immediately recognizable – the same language, she realized, in which the angel had spoken to her in her dreams. All the things she had forgotten upon waking came back to her in that instant: she remembered the truth within Uchida's Oratory. Revelation seemed ingrained in the very air she breathed, in the speeding electrons and quantum arrays buried within her Ghost circuits, even within the very fabric of the universe itself.

The truth of Uchida filled her with agonizing joy, and a terrible, overwhelming regret that for so long, *so long*, his Truth had been hidden from her.

Dakota shut down her Ghost link, falling as silent as the rest of them and thereby severing her connection with Command. All that mattered now was that the angel was calling her to battle. She would gladly follow, indifferent to her fate. Tears of almost unbearable happiness ran down her cheeks, and she tasted salt.

The angel commanded her to land, and she banked her dropship at a dangerously sharp angle. Other dropships, she saw, had already dived towards the ground. She saw one come apart in a blaze of actinic brightness, moving so fast and at so steep an angle it was torn apart by hull stresses.

Somehow, her own ship held together. She watched as others spiralled out of control, streaking to their doom like silver shooting stars plummeting through the clouds. Voices sang in Dakota's mind, compelling her downwards, careless of the dangers.

Below lay a Freehold settlement called Port Gabriel, situated on one of the many tributaries of the mighty Ka River which bisected the continent. Her Ghost circuits reminded her that Cardinal Point still lay at least a thousand kilometres to the east. But that was no longer her destination.

The angel's blazing sword pointed instead to Port Gabriel, beckoning like a divine general leading an army of holy warriors into battle. Around her, the dropship's comms equipment buzzed and flashed as Orbital Command desperately tried to reassert their authority over the fleet.

Except the Consortium had now become the enemy – had *always* been the enemy, if only she'd been able to see it. The other surviving machine-heads in the fleet were reactivating their Ghost links via an ad hoc network that rerouted past Orbital Command and the Circus Ring.

Dakota was distantly aware of the tumult of Freehold troops trapped in the rear of her dropship, desperately trying to bypass the lock on the cockpit door. Barely coherent threats and pleas went unnoticed as she dived towards a range of mountains extending to the west of Port Gabriel.

The dropship attempted to engage automatic emergency descent protocols in response to her suicidal plummet. *It thinks I've been injured or compromised*, Dakota realized. Instead, she had never been happier.

The dropship faded away completely, and she was back in the same marketplace that had featured regularly in her dreams. Angels drifted past, some as lofty as the clouds, unseen by the oblivious human masses passing by them.

There was something she was supposed to know. It came to her now: Banville, the scientist, architect of Bellhaven's machine-head development programme, had willingly and happily joined with the Uchidans.

This brief moment of revelation was followed by an equally brief stab of doubt. A spark of reason contradicted angelic command. *What if the angel isn't real? What if it's some hallucination from my implants? What if Banville gave the Uchidans something they could use to compromise me, make me believe something I . . . something I wouldn't . . .*

That light of reason flickered and died. She was back in the dropship cockpit, the ground rushing towards her at a terrifying velocity.

She never recalled the impact.

*

Consciousness returned only slowly.

Dakota coughed, feeling dizzy and ill. A black weight built up in her lungs. *Can't breathe.* Realizing the hull had been breached, she fumbled frantically for her respirator mask. She pulled it over her mouth and nose, inhaling in short, steady gasps.

Close. *Very* close. She couldn't have been out for more than a few moments, but any longer and she might well have suffocated. That she was still alive was in itself a miracle of chance.

Dakota moved carefully, probing herself for broken bones or other injuries. The dropship was lying at an angle, so that she herself was tipped over, still locked into her seat, at an angle of about forty degrees. Her biomed monitors informed her she had a fracture in her ribs. Gel impact pads had blossomed out to cushion her body, but had now deflated, the soft fabric of the pads lying empty and forlorn across her lap and legs. They'd helped save her life.

Dakota unlocked her seat restraints and tumbled out. She could hear the sound of wind blowing. Her eyes were dazzled by a sliver of bright sunlight coming through an enormous rent in the side of the cockpit.

She found the manual switch for the emergency exit and watched as a panel slid away in the cockpit's ceiling. Moving carefully, she lifted herself through it and saw the craft had gouged a hole in the frozen soil, thirty metres in length, a long black scar that intersected a narrow highway crossing a flat plain of snow and rock, but scattered with the vast plumes of canopy trees further away towards the horizon.

Frozen air assaulted Dakota's lungs. She scanned the horizon, feeling the whip of frigid wind over her stubbled scalp. Black columns of smoke rose up towards the sky from downed dropships all around. In the distance she could see the tented buildings and 'scrapers of Port Gabriel, and the winding curve of the river it stood next to.

The ad hoc Ghost network, of which she was now part, informed her how many serving God's purpose had survived the impacts, reminding her that those who died would now be safe in God's embrace. And before too long, Dakota would join them in eternity. The knowledge filled her heart with gladness.

In the meantime, she was in danger of freezing to death, as her suit might insulate her, but not indefinitely. She reached into pockets provided on the hips and shins of her suit and pulled out high-quality survival gear, composed of super-thin fabrics designed to keep her insulated and alive. Last of all, she pulled the hood over her head, and down over the top of her gee suit.

Next, she checked her weapon. She had heard voices coming from the rear of the dropship, so there were survivors among the Freeholders.

She noticed that her dropship, too, was sending its own thick, black contrail of death spiralling into the sky. She strode past the ruined command module, in which the cockpit was located, heading for the rear of the craft.

Pausing, she saw the command module had been largely torn away from the rest of the ship.

Hearing more voices, she kept going and, as she came aft, she saw several figures struggling out through another emergency exit. Shouting and calling to each other, they were intent on lowering bodies to the ground from inside the ship. She'd had two dozen Freehold assault troops on board, and it appeared the majority of them were now either dead or severely injured. Bodies lay everywhere, many without breather masks.

Soot-smudged faces looked towards her and gestured, calling out to her, anger clear in their voices. In the distance, far beyond, the angel strode the earth once more. It rose even higher than the mountains, gathering the souls of the fallen.

The Freeholders shouting to her appeared unaware of its presence, and Dakota felt sorry for them.

'How many survivors?' she called out, approaching at a brisk pace.

'What the *hell* happened back there?' one man screamed, his face contorted with fury. He rose from kneeling over one of the bodies, and came towards her, his hands bunched into fists. Blood streaked his face where it wasn't hidden by the breather mask.

'Some kind of systems error,' she replied, trying to inject just the right tone of concern and despair into the words. 'Orbital Command's override systems must have been compromised in some way. How many survivors?'

'Not many.' The Freeholder stared like he wanted to swat Dakota like a fly, but for the moment at least he was thinking rationally. He glanced over his shoulder, looking at four companions still extracting bodies from inside the hull. 'Just the five of us are mobile, most of the rest of us are dead. It looks like part of the fusion drive chassis sheared off during the impact, and—'

He never got to finish his sentence.

For Dakota, the worst thing about killing him was knowing that he would never see the Kingdom of God. She slipped her pistol out of its holster with practised ease and fired off three rapid shots, tattooing the man's chest with rapidly spreading dark stains. He dropped like a stone, sprawling lifeless on the ground.

The others immediately went for their weapons, but Dakota had the element of surprise. She fired again, shearing off the side of one man's head. Another flipped over and tumbled into a twisted heap. The remaining three scrambled towards cover, but Dakota killed them with expertly placed shots in the back.

Dakota had never killed anyone before. It had taken seconds.

She walked over and saw that one or two lying on the ground were merely injured. Their friends had pulled them free of the wreckage and placed breather masks over their faces. Filled by an overwhelming sense of peace, she despatched each of them with a single shot to the head.

Somewhere in the distance, she noticed a glint of light from a moving windscreen. A line of vehicles was approaching along the road leading from Port Gabriel.

EIGHTEEN

A yellow star in its mid-life dominated the Nova Arctis system, accompanied by a retinue of eight planets comprising two rocky inner worlds, several gas-giants and a frozen snowball, two thousand kilometres in diameter, that barely clung to its hundred-year-long orbit.

The second innermost world was the one the Freeholders wanted to colonize: they had called it Newfall. That was a name clearly imbued with hope, but the long-range readings suggested it would be a considerable time, if ever, before the thin skein of atmosphere clinging to its rocky crust would support any kind of life.

Dakota sat enclosed within the steel petals of the bridge's interface chair, watching the dance of numerals and data feeds that had constantly measured their deceleration into the new system. Before her hovered an image of the fifth world out from the star: a Jovian-type gas-giant called Dymas. It carried sixteen moons with it in its slow, majestic journey around its star. They were currently on an approach vector with the fourth moon out, a frozen world the Freeholders had named Theona.

They had been in constant deceleration now for several days, the *Hyperion* flipped on its axis for most of that time, its engines pointed starward. Dakota had been worried they might be forced into a delay if orbital braking manoeuvres were required to prevent them over-shooting Dymas, but her fears were unfounded. For the fusion propulsion system, at least, unlike the rest of the *Hyperion*, was up to date. The ship was now on its way to a perfect rendezvous.

As the chair's petals folded away and Dakota stepped down on to the bridge, she found Gardner studying a screen displaying high-res orbital images of Theona. Sharp-edged mountain ranges poked up through the ice that coated the little world's surface. Deep-range scans showed a substantial liquid environment beneath the ice: and somewhere below that lay a core of rock and iron hidden under a liquid ocean several kilometres deep.

'Nothing down there but ice and a little ammonia.' She nodded towards the display. 'Sure this is where you want to go?'

'Very sure,' Gardner replied, irritation clear in his voice. 'Just pilot the ship, Mala.'

We found something. Corso's words still reverberated in her skull, as they had every day since leaving Ascension. So they found something, but what?

Robot probes and supplies modules had already been boosted towards Newfall from out of the cargo bay, carrying the terraforming gear that was the official reason for *Hyperion*'s coming here to the Nova Arctis system. Dakota could see their trajectory paths marked on another screen: they were moving at a considerably higher number of gees than the frigate itself and its frail human cargo could possibly manage.

Dakota made final checks, which confirmed that the frigate was smoothly slipping into orbit around the moon.

Apparently there was already a minuscule human presence on Theona's surface. A ground base had been established near one of the poles, the majority of its living and working units buried under the dense ice.

From the vantage point of the humans huddled in their cramped quarters under the icecap, Nova Arctis would be little more than a particularly bright star that frequently disappeared as the moon slid behind its parent. Right now they were basking in what passed for summer sun, despite surface temperatures not much above absolute zero.

Arbenz entered the bridge. 'A few moments ago I picked up the ident of another ship on the hail frequencies,' Dakota informed him. 'It's still on Dymas's far side, but we should be matching course in another couple of hours or so.'

'That's the *Agartha*,' he replied. 'It's here to provide us with back-up.'

Dakota's Ghost fed her fresh information concerning the *Agartha*. It was only a third the size of the *Hyperion*, but armed to the teeth. In fact, it represented a considerable portion of the Freehold's military might in their war against the Uchidans, yet here it was in another star system, dozens of light years from home and absent from a conflict where it was surely desperately needed.

That fact alone was enough to convince Dakota that whatever the Freehold might have found here, it was of enormous significance. More, her Ghost was feeding her images of what appeared to be a massive mining operation on the surface of Theona, a dark scar ripped across the pristine marbled white of its surface, just a short distance from the Freehold-maintained base. The hole that had been dug so far looked like it went a long, long way down.

Piri. How well integrated are you with the Hyperion?

<Secondary copies of my routines have now been uploaded to the *Hyperion*'s stacks without detection, as per your instructions. All systems remain nominal.>

Dakota's Ghost showed how the secondary copy of *Piri*'s faux-consciousness – *Piri* Beta, as she thought of it – integrated seamlessly with the original on board her ship. Fortunately, Senator Arbenz and the rest of them would never be aware of what she had done.

She decided to test the Beta copy. *We'll need a shuttle down to the moon's surface*, she informed it.

<Affirmation with pleasure.>

Dakota stood stock-still for a moment, her lips growing tight.

Piri Beta, can you please repeat your last message?

<Order affirmed.>

That's not the wording you just used. Please repeat the statement precisely as stated, when I requested a transport shuttle to be prepped.

<System logs show the response as "Order affirmed".>

Dakota shut down her Ghost link and thought hard, an icy sensation crawling around in her stomach.

The sense that something, somewhere, was very badly wrong crept into Dakota's mind and settled there like a great, hungry spider.

'Something wrong?'

Both Gardner and Arbenz were staring at her. 'Moment's break in telemetry,' Dakota replied. 'Probably a minor glitch, but I'll look into it now. Oh, and the shuttle's being prepped. We can board in a few minutes.'

'Thank you, Mala,' Arbenz replied, studying her carefully as if the deceit in her soul had suddenly been laid bare. Dakota turned on her heel and quit the bridge quickly.

She let out a rush of breath as soon as she was out of sight of the others, wrapping her hands tightly around her chest as if she'd caught a sudden chill. Something in the nuance of the words the copy of *Piri*'s intelligence had used, something in the unusual way they had been arranged reminded her . . . reminded her of that Shoal-member she had met on Bourdain's Rock.

As she continued on down the corridor, most of her attention was focused on a ship-wide sweep for anything,

anything, that might indicate a source for the earlier, unexplained glitches she had stumbled across in the *Hyperion*'s systems.

Everyone climbed on board the shuttle bar Udo, who was still enjoying an extended stay in his medbox. More often than not, Kieran could be found in the surgical unit, talking with his brother through the medbay's commlink now the patient was conscious most of the time. His nervous system had been pretty badly fried during his encounter with Bourdain's assassin, and micro-surgical units were still working on repairing damaged neural pathways and grafting new skin.

Kieran was quick to take the controls of the shuttle, glaring at Dakota as if she didn't already know how little he trusted her. She wondered for the millionth time precisely what Udo might have told his brother during those long hours of sibling communication in the surgical unit.

Corso was the last to enter through the shuttle's hatchway, before strapping himself into a restraint couch next to her own in the rear of the cockpit. Recently he'd been keeping his distance, casting her strange looks and avoiding anything more than the most cursory conversation. She'd tried to draw him out further, hoping he might finally tell her more, but it had only led to some awkward moments.

I've been on my own too long, she reflected. Trapped

in a tiny ship on the outskirts of Sol space, with no one but her own Ghost for company, wasn't the healthiest of lifestyles. Her time so far on board the *Hyperion* had been the longest she'd spent around other people since . . .

Dakota pushed the memory away. Instead she watched the *Hyperion* dwindling rapidly from view on a nearby screen, Theona's curving horizon becoming increasingly visible as the shuttle's nose dipped towards it. It wasn't very long before Dakota felt the first faint tug of gravity.

Arbenz twisted his head around from within his own restraint webbing and caught Lucas's eye. 'Mr Corso. You're the expert from here on in. Anything Miss Oorthaus needs to know, you have my permission to discuss it in explicit detail.'

He looked at Dakota next. 'What we're about to show you today is something remarkable, quite unprecedented in the history of the human race. The reason for our strict security measures till now will become quite clear.' He made an attempt at smiling. 'I'm afraid we've employed a degree of subterfuge in bringing you here, but I'm going to ask you not to be alarmed. Everything is going to become very clear, very soon.' Here he inserted an artful pause that somehow suggested a degree of thoughtful vulnerability. 'Frankly, we need your help.'

Arbenz faced forward again and began conversing with Gardner while Kieran piloted. From what she could hear, they were discussing the personnel already stationed on the moon below.

She turned to Corso. 'Start talking. Now.'

He gave her a queasy smile and then avoided her gaze. 'We're going to be covering a lot of ground, so in all seriousness the best thing I can do is explain things as we go along. Just trust me when I tell you that you're in absolutely no danger, OK?'

'You told me once,' she said in the lowest whisper she could manage, 'that you found something.'

The shuttle bucked under them as it hit the top of the moon's thin atmosphere. 'That's the last time you mention I said anything of the kind,' he muttered. 'What we found is a derelict starship. One that might have a functioning transluminal drive.'

Dakota stared at him, waiting for the punch line, but it didn't come. A dizzy sensation scrambled her thoughts and she felt light and giddy, as if filled with air.

Theona had changed from a body floating in space to a landscape spread out below them, pale and feature-less except for its jagged mountain ranges where an ancient meteor impact had forced part of the rocky core to emerge above the frozen waters. Their craft dropped rapidly towards the Freehold base at the foot of one of these ranges, superheated steam blasting up around them in scalding clouds as the shuttle settled into a docking cradle. There was a heavy, twisting lurch, followed by a rolling vibration that set Dakota's teeth on edge as the engines went into their shut-down procedure.

A squall of voices came over the comms system. Kieran Mansell spoke sharply to someone for a moment, and then hit a switch, cutting the voices off. 'They're prepping the sub,' he announced.

Corso was halfway out of his restraint webbing when Dakota reached out with one hand and gripped his forearm.

'I want you to know that if anything happens to me once we're off this shuttle, you'll be the first to die.'

Corso pulled away from her grasp with some difficulty. 'Fine. In the meantime, can we please get out of here?'

The Theona surface base was manned by a staff of just a dozen. Half of these were preparing to ride the shuttle back up into orbit, where they would board the *Agartha* while a relief crew newly arrived from Newfall rode the shuttle back down again. The station's cramped and tiny rooms and corridors were consequently busy as a beehive as people made last-minute preparations for their departure.

Arbenz guided them through the chaos, meeting and greeting a succession of shiny-eyed young men and women all eager to announce their willingness to die for the Freehold cause. Dakota watched and listened to it all with some distaste, doing her best to ignore the curious and occasionally hostile glances she received from some. She was surprised to see a similar look of distaste appear on Corso's face, when he thought people weren't looking.

The Senator kept them moving, clearly not wanting to waste any more time than was absolutely essential. They were joined soon by two of the station's staff, and Arbenz led them into an elevator clearly designed to carry large quantities of heavy equipment. As soon as they were all aboard, the elevator shuddered to life and dropped rapidly.

Several minutes passed, with Dakota wondering exactly how far down they were going. She glanced over at Corso and saw he was looking as apprehensive as she felt.

Something tugged at the edge of her thoughts: it was a little like sensing the presence of another machine-head. But this sense of *otherness* originated from somewhere far, far below them.

She ignored it after a moment, blaming her nerves.

The lift finally came to a halt, and they disembarked into a metal-walled antechamber with an airlock at one end and a series of cabinets ranged along one wall. The two men from the surface station stepped over to the cabinets and pulled out gel suits of the type normally used for orbital high-gee manoeuvring. It was freezing cold, and Dakota realized the gel suits were intended as a protection against hypothermia.

She pulled one on, aware of it forming around her body, immediately feeling warmer.

They filed through a narrow door and into the airlock. Once she was through, Dakota saw they were in a rectangular cavern carved directly out of the rock and ice. In the centre of the chamber lay a wide dark circle of water surrounded by machinery and ringed by a raised steel platform with steps leading up to it: a borehole, for want of a better description. A sealed and pressurized tunnel made from some transparent fabric led from the airlock directly over to the platform.

Arbenz led them along the fabric tunnel towards the borehole. *Maybe we're going fishing*, Dakota thought, suppressing a semihysterical grin. As they approached the borehole, the water in its centre began to churn and bubble furiously.

She stared in amazement as a submersible rose out of it, its hull studded with instruments. A metal platform slid out from under the encompassing platform, locking into place on the craft's hull, while the opposite end of the tunnel they were passing through slid forward on gimbals to connect with a hatch in the submersible's hull.

A few moments later, the hatch opened and three figures in gel suits disembarked. The Senator took the lead, stepping up on to the encircling platform, and made sure to shake the hands of each of the submersible's crew in turn. The personnel – two men and a woman – were apparently delighted to find Arbenz waiting for them. A few moments later they walked past Dakota and the rest, heading towards the antechamber.

Dakota peered down into the black, churning waters as she stepped up on to the raised platform. Heating elements were clearly visible for a long way down, ringing the interior of the borehole, and presumably there to keep it from freezing over.

She didn't want to think just how far down through the solid ice the Freehold had drilled. The ocean under there had been dark for an eternity, and was deep enough to be effectively bottomless. The thought of plunging down into those empty depths, regardless of the circumstances, made her flesh crawl.

She turned again to Corso, who was standing beside her. 'If you really found a starship,' she whispered, 'what the hell is it doing buried down here? And how did you even *find* it?'

'Luck,' Corso replied. 'The *Agartha* was the first Freehold ship to arrive at Nova Arctis, but it ran into trouble straight away. It suffered an engine failure during a routine evaluation of the outer system, and somehow the derelict picked up on one of its distress frequencies and responded. The signal was extremely low-power, so they were lucky to pick it up at all. The crew managed to triangulate the source of the signal a couple of weeks later.'

'Uh.' A sense of numbness was spreading through Dakota's body that had nothing to do with the subzero

temperatures. *A starship?* But one, she could only assume, the Shoal knew nothing of.

It was like finding the Holy Grail – no, better. Transluminal technology, at least, was real.

As she followed the rest inside the vacated submersible, it was impossible not to think about the kilometres of lightless ocean below her. She took a seat in a cramped circular chamber. There was a control panel at one end of it, replete with displays showing infrared and sonar maps of the mountainous terrain above and below them, but from the craft's interior layout Dakota guessed this submersible was automated rather than piloted.

And there it was again: a sense of *otherness* from somewhere far, far below, in the depths of Theona's freezing subterranean ocean. It was like finding herself in an empty building, but nonetheless becoming filled with the absolute conviction there was someone or something nearby – but just out of sight. Her Ghost scanned the local comms traffic, but the only detectable signals were the usual low-level automated pings.

It had to be the derelict communicating, in some way she couldn't understand, with her Ghost. Something was down there, and it was currently trying to say hello.

She looked around at the others, irrationally wondering if any of them could feel the same thing. Her skin prickled unpleasantly.

Corso had again taken a seat next to her. He turned

to her and frowned, and she realized she must have looked more worried than she might want to let on.

'What's the problem?' he asked softly.

She almost laughed.

Something alien is signalling to me, from the depths of a bottomless ocean in a dead system, you stupid bastard. What do you think?

Instead she said: 'If you've really found some kind of crashed starship, you lot are going to have a ton of shit coming down on your collective heads once the news gets out. Tell me it's not a Shoal craft, because if it is, I might as well start writing my will right now.'

'It's not Shoal,' Corso replied, after a moment's hesitation.

'You're serious?' She looked at him and saw he was. 'So they really aren't the only species with faster-than-light travel, after all? It was all a big lie?'

'The derelict doesn't look like any Shoal vessel any-one's ever seen, but it has a drive mechanism that could probably spit it right across the galaxy. It has the external spine structures typical of known Shoal spacecraft, but that's about as far as the resemblance goes. Plus, it's old. *Really* old.'

'How old?'

'I'd say about a hundred and sixty thousand years.'

'A hundred and sixty thousand years,' she repeated. 'And we know why that's significant, right?'

'Why don't you tell me?' Corso pressed her in a low whisper, a peculiar look on his face.

It was too much information, too quickly. She needed to curl up in the warm dark of the *Piri Reis* and think about everything she'd seen and experienced.

'Forget it,' she replied with a sigh. 'I just thought of the Magellanic Novae for some reason.' That memory of peering through Langley's telescope, even after so many years and with Bellhaven so far away, was as strong as if it had happened only the day before.

Corso still had that same intense look on his face. It made her uncomfortable.

'Well,' he said, 'the derelict dates from about the same period. But that's no reason to assume they're connected with something else that happened in another galaxy.' She wondered why he was staring at her so hard. 'Unless you've got other ideas?' he added.

'You're looking at me like I just tried to bite your nose off.'

Corso made an exasperated noise and lowered his voice, so he was barely audible over the sound of the submersible's engines. 'Mala, I *saw* you on the bridge of the *Hyperion*, studying a map of the Magellanic Clouds. You'd drawn lines of trajectory connecting them to this part of the Orion Arm. To as near as damn it to *this* system, in fact, as makes no difference. Why do that? Do you have some special interest in the novae?'

'I don't remember doing anything of the kind. Frankly, I'd say you've been working too hard. You're starting to imagine things.'

He held her gaze for a few seconds more, tight-lipped and angry-looking. Dakota was completely baffled.

'This isn't over,' he said.

'I. Don't. Know. *What*. You're talking about,' she hissed.

'Fine.' He waved his hand dismissively. 'Forget it.' He settled back in his seat and closed his eyes for a few moments, taking a deep breath. When he opened them again, he seemed a little calmer.

'Look,' he continued, 'before we get to the derelict, a word of warning. There's some kind of defence systems running on board, and so far we haven't tried to bring it to the surface in case it activates suicide circuits. It uses artificial gravity fields to mash up anyone or anything it considers a threat, though we've managed to get a fair bit of a way inside it, regardless.'

'I appreciate the warning, but I still want to know what's going to happen to me when we get on board that thing, *before* I risk my fucking life.'

'I guarantee nothing is going to happen to you, Mala,' Corso replied.

The lie was startlingly clear on his face.

Something broke inside Dakota. 'Take me back up,' she demanded, lifting herself out of her seat and making a move towards the control console. 'Whatever you're up to here, I didn't sign on for any of it.'

Arbenz quickly nodded to Kieran. Mansell stood up, punching her hard in the face. She caught a passing glimpse of Corso's pale, shocked features as she crumpled. The next thing she knew she was on her knees, and Kieran had one of her arms twisted painfully behind her back while she was forced forward until her face was almost pressed into the deck.

Something acid and foul twisted deep in her stomach and she resisted the urge to vomit. Kieran put just the tiniest bit of extra pressure on her arm, but it was enough to make it feel like he was trying to wrench it off at the shoulder. She screamed.

Gardner looked down at her from where he sat, twisting around in his own seat, a mixture of pity and revulsion on his face.

'All this time, *Miss Merrick*, and you thought we wouldn't find out what you were up to. Did you really think we wouldn't notice how badly you wanted to get out of the Sol System, just a day or two after the collapse of Bourdain's Rock? Or that we wouldn't figure out that the assassin who tried to kill you, and nearly killed one of the Senator's own men, worked for Bourdain?'

Eyes wide, Dakota stared down at the submersible's deck, millimetres from her nose. Her breathing was sharp and shallow.

'It wasn't hard to figure out the connections once I knew where to look,' Gardner continued. 'Marados was part of the conflict at Port Gabriel. So was Severn. That made it easy to draw conclusions about your own past.

'I believe you killed Josef Marados and then used your remarkable skills to cover your tracks,' Gardner continued. 'That way you removed one more inconvenient link between yourself and your past. You removed details of Marados's death from the stack processors to make sure we didn't become suspicious. But I have my own lines of enquiry, outside of the official channels.'

'We know you were there at Port Gabriel, Dakota,' said Kieran, his voice filled with rage. 'In the eyes of the Freehold you are a foul and bloody murderer – less than vermin.'

'That's not true, and you know it. I didn't kill Josef or anyone else,' Dakota managed to gasp. 'I don't know who killed him. I . . .'

She heard Arbenz mutter something indistinguishable. A moment later her forehead slammed off the deck. The world went white for a few moments, and then the pain hit.

'Careful, we want her conscious,' she heard Arbenz say through a haze of agony. 'Dakota?' His voice sounded closer now, and she guessed he was kneeling beside her. 'We're very nearly there. Can you hear me?'

Dakota moaned, then nodded, tasting bile in the back of her throat. Out of the corner of her eye she could see Gardner and the two men who'd joined them from the surface complex. Gardner stared away from her, his expression stiff and mask-like. The two Freeholder scientists eyed her with curiosity and mild revulsion.

'OK, now here's the deal. Unfortunately, we still

need you and, as much as Kieran would really love otherwise, politics and war often mean compromise. Once you understand exactly what's going on here – and Mr Corso will fill you in on the details – you might even find you're on our side.'

Somehow I really, really don't think so. But she said nothing.

'We brought you here for a purpose, and you will fulfil that purpose. And just in case you think there's any chance you can remain defiant, well, Kieran will be constantly available to make sure you understand just how bad an idea that might be.'

Something sharp dug into her lower spine and Dakota screamed. It was the worst pain in the world, an entire universe of suffering compressed into a few brief seconds. She heard herself, as if from a distance, begging for mercy. A part of her she had thought could never be breached shrivelled under that unendurable agony.

But Arbenz still hadn't finished talking. '*You* want to get away from Bourdain. *We* want the transluminal drive. Help us get it, and you're free. More, you'll be a hero, liberating mankind from the oppressive restrictions of the Shoal's technology embargo. You could be part of something glorious.'

She realized he was waiting for an answer. While she summoned the strength to speak, the cabin was filled with a silence as deep as the void between the stars.

'You'll just kill me then,' she managed to say. 'You're Freeholders. So nobody trusts anything any of you say.'

Arbenz grinned. 'Then you'll just have to learn to trust me, Dakota. Whatever you think of us, we do believe in honour. You're just as much a victim of the Consortium as anyone back on Redstone. The war with the Uchidans would never have happened if the Shoal hadn't invoked their embargo clause. It hurt you just as bad as it hurt us. The Consortium let the Uchidans steal our world, and they took away the one thing you'd worked all your life towards: your implants.'

His tone had grown softer and more intimate, which somehow made it sound all the worse. Her thoughts became filled with revenge fantasies of the most exquisite complexity and savagery.

'So when I say you'll be safe,' Arbenz finished, 'I speak as a man of honour – and as a Senator in the Freehold Senate. You have my word, and all you have to do now is help us.'

Dakota listened to all this without comment. After a moment she felt Kieran's grip on her relent. She looked up and saw Corso's silent, appalled expression. Kieran and Arbenz had simply returned to their seats as if nothing had happened.

She began to get up. Corso tried to help her but she pushed him away. She pulled herself into her seat, fighting back tears of rage and horror and shame. The more she fought the feelings down, the more she hated herself for her own weakness.

She focused on the backs of her tormentors' heads and decided she was going to kill them.

'I'm sorry,' murmured Corso from beside her.

'What for? You knew all along,' she whispered.

'I didn't know any of it until just recently.' Kieran and Arbenz were once again head to head in conversation with the two surface station staff, while static-racked voices briefly squalled over the comms system. Dakota suspected none of them really cared what either she or Corso now said to each other.

'You're a spy,' she hissed at Corso. 'Your job is to report everything I say and do.'

'No!' He shook his head emphatically. 'I'm here to find a way to salvage the derelict. That's *all* I'm interested in doing.'

Something in the throb of the submersible's engines had changed. They were slowing. The sonar maps on the displays showed a steep precipice that fell off into darkness: they were rapidly approaching the submerged slopes of a mountain. A strange, alien-looking shape was clearly visible dangerously close to the edge of the rocky precipice – not quite near enough for it to tumble over into the depths below, but almost.

It wasn't long before the submersible shuddered to a halt. The hatch clanged open and Arbenz and Gardner took the lead, closely followed by the two ground-station staff. Kieran came last, behind Dakota and Corso.

They entered a steel-walled cylindrical tube immediately beyond the submarine. The sound of their boots clanging on the walkway echoed harshly, and Dakota winced, as if the sound were something physical and sharp driving into the soft tissues of her brain. Intermittent stabbing pains manifested in her shoulder and back, and she dug her nails into the palms of her hands until it hurt.

A screen bolted onto the wall at the far end of the passageway displayed an enhanced external view of the derelict. In profile the centre part of the craft resembled a fat teardrop, with a series of bumps around its hull, scattered with apparent randomness. There were no visible windows or any external instrumentation. Long curving spines, much longer than the central body, curved upwards and out, and Dakota suspected they were deceptive in their apparent fragility. It looked more like some piece of abstract sculpture than anything she might conceive of as an interstellar vessel. The passageway in which they now stood was also visible as a narrow snake of bolted-together segments connecting the submersible to the derelict itself. In terms of relative size, the submersible looked like a minnow escorting a whale.

'This is your moment, Mr Corso,' said the Senator, turning to face him. 'You're the expert here. Show us what you know.'

Lucas nodded and waited as the hatch leading into the derelict's interior slowly swung open. Dakota saw another passageway beyond, but this had pale, mostly featureless walls, apart from long, twisted bands of some material that reminded her of muscles, around which the passageway walls appeared to have been moulded.

It was, in every way, profoundly alien, but strangely beautiful, too. The only thing marring this impression was an ugly rent torn out of one wall, where clearly human instrumentation had been inserted.

But the thing that struck her the most, as she followed the others inside, was that even though there was no apparent source of lighting, she could see perfectly well for the entire length of the passageway, up until it twisted out of sight.

After a moment's hesitation, Corso moved ahead with a purpose that suggested he was already familiar with his surroundings. Dakota watched with the rest as he brought images up on a screen comprising part of the base staff's crudely wired-in instrumentation, and saw what she guessed must be a map of the derelict's interior. It didn't take much guesswork to realize that the colour-coded corridors and rooms marked there represented only a tiny portion of the derelict's interior.

Corso's expression remained nervous and tense. *Something* still lurked within these walls, and Dakota could sense its intelligence somewhere deep behind the pale surfaces either side of her. The ubiquitous light made her feel increasingly vulnerable and naked. Without any shadows, where could any of them hide?

Corso tapped at a panel set below the screen, with expert ease. New images flashed up one after the other, appearing to be closed-circuit views of other parts of the derelict's interior. Screeds of unreadable gibberish that she guessed were some form of alien language accompanied these images. After a moment her Ghost tentatively identified parts of the text as an archaic form of the Shoal machine language.

Corso took off his gloves, wiped his bare hands on his gel suit and muttered something to himself. It was already getting too warm for the gel suits: one more sign that the derelict's main systems were still functioning.

'OK,' said Corso, pulling something out of his pocket. 'Moment of truth time.'

He placed the object – a slender grey box scarcely larger than a human thumb – into a niche just below the screen. A moment later a faint but discernible hum filled the air. Dakota half-expected some monster to come rampaging down one of the corridors, angry at being woken from its aeons-long sleep. Instead, nothing happened bar a succession of new images and mostly incomprehensible data flickering across the screen like lightning.

The map of the derelict's interior reappeared, except this time new corridors and rooms began appearing, shaded green where the original map was coloured blue. Arbenz and Mansell grinned and shouted in delight, and even Corso managed a shaky grin.

'Good work, Corso,' said Arbenz, clapping a hand on his shoulder. 'Do we have access yet to the main deck or the engines?'

Corso shook his head. 'No, I didn't expect to this early, but it's still a lot more than we could reasonably have expected.'

Arbenz looked ecstatic regardless. Even Kieran Mansell's normally stony features retained a satisfied smile.

'Now,' said the Senator, 'we need to test the machine-head interface.'

Dakota stared first at Arbenz, and then at Corso, but he avoided her gaze, a flicker of shame crossing his tight-lipped expression.

Arbenz's glee settled back into the more familiar, unctuous smile. 'Lead on, Lucas.' He turned to Dakota. 'I mean it when I say you're going to like what we've got waiting ahead for you. You're going to fly this thing back to Redstone for us.'

Dakota merely nodded in a daze.

Corso filled the silence with a string of nervous patter as he led them further down the passageway and deeper into the belly of the beast. What appeared to be small service robots raced ahead of them, apparently scouting out the intersections and twists ahead.

'Whoever the ship was built by, they definitely weren't Shoal. But they did have close contact with them. There are translation protocols embedded in the derelict's operating systems that allow communication between machinery belonging to both species. It's like a Rosetta Stone, a key to understanding who they are and where they came from.'

'Did they have a name?' asked Dakota, as they came to a fork in the corridor where another screen had been inserted into a hole ripped in the corridor wall.

'Not that we've been able to discover, no,' Corso replied. 'But we've been calling them the Magi.' He glanced at the screen and turned right: the rest of them followed.

Dakota's skin prickled in anticipation of the unexpected.

They came to a stop at an intersection where Corso raised his hand. Directions had been scrawled on cards epoxied to the walls. Dakota saw rounded doorways, which looked more melted than constructed, leading into interior spaces.

'This is where we managed to tap into a major control subsystem,' Corso explained, nodding to one of the doorways. Dakota could see tools scattered by the entrance.

Corso turned to Arbenz. 'From here on in, it's new territory. I can't guarantee there'll be no unexpected problems if we go any further than this.'

Kieran nodded. 'The derelict has already proved it can kill, Senator. Perhaps it would be best if you turned back for now.'

Arbenz shook his head. 'If something was going to go wrong, experience shows it would have happened by now. Besides, this part of the derelict is secure, isn't it, Kieran?'

After a moment's hesitation, Kieran nodded. 'This area is code blue, so we believe it's safe. But there are no firm guarantees.'

'That's good enough for me. Mr Corso, you'll find

the technicians have already installed your updates. The interface chair is ready.'

Corso nodded hesitantly.

Arbenz turned to the two station staff that had accompanied them. 'Lunden, Ivanovich. I want you to make sure the code green areas are safe for the technical teams to enter. Follow standard procedure and, for God's sake, don't lose sight of each other like those others did.'

The two men saluted and moved off. Arbenz next turned to Gardner. 'David, we have some matters to discuss.' He turned to Corso last. 'I want you to test the interface now. We'll be waiting here.'

Corso nodded, looking distinctly nonplussed. He motioned to Dakota to follow him. She glanced at Kieran, and realized he'd have no hesitation in hurting her again if she didn't co-operate.

She followed Corso into the room, which was wide, with a low ceiling and completely featureless. In the centre of the room stood an interface chair identical to the one on board the *Hyperion*. Cables led from its underside through gouged-open holes in the floor.

Corso touched a button on the side of the interface device and its petals folded smoothly down, revealing the seat within.

'I swear on my life you won't come to any harm,' Corso assured her, glancing back towards the doorway as he did so. 'I've run tests again and again. This thing – the derelict, that is – it's designed specially to be operated by a machine-head. Or at least something very like it.'

Dakota touched her hand to one of the chair's folding petals and nodded.

'You don't look surprised,' said Corso.

'An alien equivalent of a machine-head, is what you mean.'

In truth, she wasn't surprised. She'd already guessed there was some kind of commonality between her and whatever had originally piloted this craft. It was the only explanation for the sensations she'd been experiencing ever since they'd landed.

'Right.' Corso looked at her strangely.

She began to climb into the chair, then hesitated. 'What's to stop me flying away with this thing, right now, if I can control it?'

She watched as Corso blinked a couple of times. 'There's a . . . failsafe installed. Ultimate control devolves to us.'

She couldn't be sure if he was telling the truth, but she would have to be very careful when it came to testing the limits of whatever Corso chose to reveal to her.

She climbed between the steel petals and took her seat. Corso leaned in close to her, making adjustments to the neural cap, his chin hovering close in front of her as he worked. He smelled of cold sweat.

'This . . . *place* creeps me out,' she muttered. 'The way the light comes from everywhere.'

He finished his adjustments and stepped back. 'It's

still only a ship, though, just a very old one. Now listen to me,' he whispered, leaning in again as he stepped around behind the chair and tapped at an open panel. The others were out of sight in the corridor, but she could still hear the murmur of their voices. 'I saw you studying the Magellanic Clouds back on the bridge of the *Hyperion*,' he said, keeping his voice low. 'I've been trying to figure out where this thing derived from originally, and I've got good reasons to think that's exactly where it came from.'

'The Magellanic Clouds?'

'So imagine my surprise when I saw what I saw that time.'

Dakota twisted her head around to try and see him. 'I swear, Lucas, I don't know what you're talking about. I really, really don't.'

He sighed and shook his head. 'Fine.'

'Lucas,' she whispered, 'I *mean* it.'

It was obvious he didn't believe her.

'OK,' she replied wearily. 'So you think this thing *does* date from the same time as the Magellanic Novae?'

Corso's expression became wary. 'Looks that way.'

'If you're seriously suggesting this thing came all the way from a neighbouring galaxy, it would have taken centuries to get here, transluminal drive or not.'

'Yeah, well, that's another reason I more or less dis-counted it at first. Why come all this way at all? But when I saw . . .' He glanced at her and sighed again.

'Look, there's no longer any question what direction it came from. The real question is, how far did it come?'

'But why come all that way in the first place?' she echoed. 'What would make them want to . . . oh.'

'Exactly. If they were running away from something, it would have to have been pretty bad to make them put so much distance between them and whatever drove them into leaving.'

'Like a lot of stars blowing up?' she said.

He moved back round in front of her and shrugged, apparently satisfied with the minute adjustments he had just made. 'Until I find out more, it's still only speculation.' He stepped back.

'Are they going to let either of us live once we've done our jobs?' she asked. 'Do you really want a man like Arbenz to get his hands on a working transluminal drive? What makes you think the Shoal won't just raze your people entirely from the surface of Redstone once they know what you've done?'

'There's a dead man's handle built into the chair,' he explained, ignoring her questions. 'There,' he said, pointing. 'If anything unexpected happens, take your fingers off it, and it breaks the connection.'

'Just supposing for a second your failsafe decides not to work and you can't prevent me suddenly assuming full control of this vessel. What will you do to stop me?'

'Answer one, either the *Agartha* or the *Hyperion* would shoot you down before you got up sufficient power, and that's assuming you can somehow blast your way through a couple of kilometres of ice we've still barely managed to scratch the surface of. Two' – he flashed her a sardonic grin – 'nobody, including yourself, actually knows how to operate a transluminal drive.'

'We have to talk, Corso.' It didn't take much effort to inject the right degree of urgency into her words. 'I *don't know* what happened to Josef Marados. I swear I had nothing to do with that. Whatever Arbenz has been saying to you, he's not intending to let either of us live.'

'I already told you, I don't have any choice in the matter. So you're telling me Arbenz is lying when he claims someone's been altering the shipboard records to cover your tracks?'

Dakota couldn't find a reply that didn't sound thoroughly incriminating.

'Fine.'

She saw Corso's expression change as his eyes flicked towards the entrance. Dakota glanced over and saw Kieran had stepped inside.

'All right,' said Corso, suddenly all business. 'First we need to run some calibrations.'

The chair's petals folded in over Dakota, entombing her and blanking out her senses, so that the only information she received would come directly through her Ghost circuits.

'I'm activating the connection between you and the derelict *now*.' Corso's voice came to her from out of the darkness, his voice hazed by electronic filters.

'Remember, anything unexpected, *any* unusual activity or responses of any kind, the inbuilt alarms can shut off the interface. Beyond that, remember all you need to do is let go of the handle and the whole thing shuts down.'

'I'm fine.'

In truth, part of her was excited by what she might now find.

She sensed the connection being made and . . .

. . . knowledge rushed in towards her in a great tide, a vast, near-indistinguishable mass out of which only a few clear details could be barely discerned. As if from a great distance she felt her fingers trembling as they gripped the dead man's handle.

Sense-impressions slammed through Dakota's cerebrum, a howling maelstrom of loss and regret. Stars tumbled past, their shape and light twisted and warped through the lens of transluminal space.

Light filled the sky above an alien shore, a million years of sunshine released in one terrible instant, transforming an ocean to steam while rocks and soil caught fire, all in one consuming wave of carnage. Then more images tumbled past her mind's eye: other worlds, all imbued with a sense of the very ancient.

She saw creatures like nothing she could have ever imagined, dead and forgotten for longer than she could comprehend. She experienced memories of places that had fallen to dust countless aeons before. As she watched, worlds that had once been the centres of vast empires were reduced to blackened carbon corpses orbiting the burned-out shells of dead suns.

Within the confining petals of the interface chair, she struggled to breathe, her chest heaving as if she were drowning.

Dakota struggled to absorb the tidal wave of information being thrust upon her. Mercifully the myriad impressions began to fade, and the seeping omniscient light of the derelict surrounding her crawled back under her eyelids. The petals of the interface chair had folded down and Corso was leaning in over her, pulling the neural cap away from her skull.

'Bloody hell,' said Corso, letting out a shaky breath as he moved out of Dakota's way. 'I'd call that a resounding success. Judging by the measurements, you were in full neural lock with the derelict.'

'I'm OK,' she mumbled.

'I don't know what it was hitting you with, but whatever it was, it wasn't in half-measures.'

Dakota glanced over Corso's shoulder and saw Kieran watching her carefully. She decided not to reveal too much about just what she'd experienced. 'I'm fine. I just couldn't make much sense out of anything.'

'What happened?' Kieran asked Corso, as Dakota slowly lifted herself out of the chair.

'Calibration,' Corso replied. 'It means the derelict accepts her input.'

'But she was only in there for a second or two.'

Corso shrugged. 'That's all it takes.'

'So she can fly the ship now?'

'No, not straight away. But in the next few days, hopefully, yes.'

'Let's say "definitely",' Kieran replied tersely.

Folding her legs under her, Dakota lowered herself down next to the interface chair. 'It's like it's alive,' she muttered weakly. Her head was still spinning. 'I don't know if it's hostile exactly, but defensive, scared maybe, assuming you want to attribute human emotions to the thing.'

'Did you find anything out? Any information about where it came from, who built it, whether the drive is still functioning?'

She shook her head. 'The whole experience was too vague for that.' She caught his eye. 'But I think you were right about them running away from something.'

The Magellanic Novae had occurred in such a relatively small volume of space, and in such a short period of time, that one of the most popular conspiracy theories posited that the stellar detonations had been deliberately induced. This remained no more than a theory partly because no one was in a hurry to give credence to the notion of any interstellar civilization with the technology to destroy entire solar systems.

Dakota gazed at the pale walls around her, and recalled the fleeting images and sensations she'd endured within the interface chair. A chill, deeper and darker than any she recalled experiencing before, went through her at the thought the Magi might have been capable of such terrible destruction.

As Arbenz and Gardner also entered, Dakota reflected that none of them had any real idea of the consequences of what they were trying to do. They were like soldiers on the eve of a battle, already celebrating their certain victory over a well-armed militia, when they only had one gun between them.

If only there were some way for her to steal the derelict out from under the noses of not only the Shoal, but the Freehold as well. But even if she found a way . . . what *would* be the consequences for the human race, of acquiring such embargoed technology? Would she bring the wrath of the Shoal hegemony down on her entire species?

A functioning transluminal drive would open up the stars to mankind . . . but the subsequent vengeance of the Shoal might mean the end of the Consortium.

Yet it was clear there was something more going on here. What Corso had accused her of made no sense: she had *not* been studying maps of the local galaxy cluster. Shortly after his challenge, she'd had her Ghost scan the bridge records, and found nothing amiss outside her own secret tweaks and alterations.

But why would Corso lie? She couldn't help but think back to the many weird glitches occurring since she had first boarded the *Hyperion*: the way the Freehold vessel had reacted when she tried to scan the alien's trinket on the imager plate; the almost seamless alterations to the ship's records that she had assumed until now had been made by Arbenz, or one of his men, for reasons unknown.

And then there was the way the beta copy of *Piri*'s mind she'd uploaded to the *Hyperion* had spoken to her – that curious grammatical inflection so reminiscent of the speech pattern of the Shoal-member she had encountered at Bourdain's Rock.

She'd been carefully avoiding thinking about the implications of that impression too much. She might just have imagined it. Anything else filled her with crawling horror.

She snapped back out of her train of thought to see Corso arguing with Arbenz.

'Senator, we have no idea what kind of infrastructure, what kind of know-how, the Magi used to build either this ship or its propulsive systems. Taking the derelict out of Nova Arctis is one thing. Replicating the technology is something on a whole bigger scale. This is technology millennia ahead of our own. At the moment we just don't know enough.'

'So what do you suggest?' asked Gardner.

'Take our time, years if necessary,' Corso replied immediately. 'Pick the derelict apart piece by piece. Establish a permanent research base here as a cover. We were intending to move our entire population to Newfall over the next few decades anyway . . .'

Arbenz bristled, his anger clearly mounting. 'We are at *war*, Mr Corso. We are engaged in a battle for survival. If we can't take this thing apart and understand how it works, we don't deserve to keep Redstone, or Newfall either, for that matter.'

'I think,' Corso replied, obviously choosing his words very carefully, 'that there are people in the Senate who might see things otherwise. Technically, you require the authority of the full governing board before—'

'They're not *here!*' Arbenz bellowed, his face contorting in rage. 'This is a God-given opportunity to raise ourselves up. Either we succeed in what we do here, or at the very least we die with honour before the eyes of God.' Arbenz made an apparent attempt to cool down. 'That's final. I won't tolerate any further dissent.'

Dakota had already caught sight of Gardner's face and wondered, not for the first time, exactly what had driven this businessman to think he could engage in a profitable relationship with Freeholders. At this moment he looked aghast.

'Senator,' said Gardner suddenly, 'I'll ask you, with the greatest respect, to shut the hell up.'

'Gardner . . .'

It's falling apart, thought Dakota. *They've been down here only, what, a couple of hours? And already it's falling apart.*

Gardner was insistent. 'Without my financial and technical backup, you have nothing, Senator, *nothing.* I'm tired of being constantly sidelined because of your petty, parochial political arguments. If there's any way to exploit or make sense of whatever we find on board this ship, it'll be *my* research teams, *my* contacts that will bring it about. Do you understand me? You don't have the resources. I do.'

'You may have the resources,' Arbenz replied acidly, 'but you do not have the will.'

'This is a joint mission,' Gardner continued. 'If anything happens to me, if I fail to get in touch with my business partners at designated times, your chances of being able to either do anything or go anywhere with this ship are nil. You understand that, don't you?'

Dakota tensed, waiting to see which way things would swing now. But Arbenz simply smiled as if they were all friends and the past few hours of argument and threats had never happened. There was something very unsettling in that smile.

'I think we've seen enough here for today,' Arbenz said, turning his attention from Gardner to Corso instead. 'What's our next move on the technical front?'

'The calibrations check out OK. Now I just need to fine-tune the interface so Mal – so Dakota can work on controlling the derelict. Once we reach that point, we've got a good chance of being able to explore the whole of the ship without getting killed.'

'Good work, Mr Corso. Remember, we need to work as fast as possible.'

Corso looked thoughtful. 'I can get a lot of work done right away.'

'Fine.' Arbenz nodded. 'Meanwhile we'll return to

the surface. Kieran, I want you to stay here with Corso
and keep an eye on things. Anything unusual happens –
anything you suspect might be life-threatening – I want
you to evacuate immediately. There's no sense in taking
unnecessary risks if you don't have to.

'As for you,' he said, turning finally to Dakota,
'you're going back on board the *Hyperion* until we need
you again. Don't try anything that would make us
unhappy, as you'd only get hurt.'

She couldn't keep the quaver out of her voice. 'You
can't kill me, Senator. You need me too much.'

'That's true,' Arbenz replied with a mirthless smile.
'But we can make things bad enough that you'd wish we
had.'

NINETEEN

Dakota sat still as a statue aboard the submersible as it rose back up through the frozen inky depths. She felt numb, withdrawn, while Gardner and Arbenz chatted quietly together in their seats. She now sat alone, to the rear of them, ignored and happy to be ignored.

What if she was wrong, she wondered? What if, despite their barbaric, murderous ways, the Freehold could actually pull this off?

People had long dreamed of finding some way to steal the transluminal technology from the Shoal or, better yet, develop their own. It was almost a childhood dream, a power fantasy brought suddenly screaming into real life.

Yet the only certainty Dakota could see was the one Arbenz was avoiding the most: that eventually the Shoal would become aware the Freehold had found a derelict starship, and that they would retaliate.

The sub thudded into place in the main base, and Dakota soon found herself back on the other side of the airlock.

An automated supply shuttle took her back to the

Hyperion, accompanied by two troopers who looked like habitual steroid abusers.

To her dismay she found a new skeleton crew of half a dozen had been installed on board the *Hyperion*, running their own systems checks with an alacrity that alarmed her. The *Piri Reis* reassured her via remote link, however, that none of her hidden alterations within the memory stacks was likely to be uncovered or detected.

She wished she could have shared the machine's confidence.

To her surprise, the troopers abandoned her to her own devices once they boarded the *Hyperion*, rather than confining her to her quarters as she'd expected. At first she wondered if this represented some unexpected level of trust, until it occurred to her that both the *Hyperion* and the moon base were now little more than unusually roomy prisons.

She found her way, undisturbed and unchallenged, back to the cargo bay and the comforting embrace of the *Piri Reis*. No matter where she went, Dakota knew, this would always be her home, the one constant in her life, unchanging and ready to yield to her every demand.

She let the *Piri*'s effigy-form stroke her hair as she lay with her head in its lap.

It didn't take long for the tears to come.

For a while, she might even have slept.

She dreamed of escape from a building where every exit was blocked. Something was chasing her.

A monster came roaring out of the darkness and

killed her. But not before she hurt it, badly. She woke and lay in the darkness for a long time, staring out at nothing, full of a sudden determination.

It's not over, Senator. Not by a long shot.

When she was finally ready, she opened her Ghost to an ocean of information.

Establish a data link with the machine-head interface aboard the derelict, she ordered *Piri* Beta. *Route and encrypt via Piri Alpha. [Piri Alpha: encrypt and wipe data path post-encryption. No trace.]*

<Dakota, I have placed a block on *Piri* Beta as of this moment. I believe it has become corrupted and may infect this ship's systems if a full data exchange is allowed.>

But who—

<Miss Merrick,> *Piri* Beta replied. <Delightful harmoniousness in multiple greetings. Trumpeting of delight at reacquaintance after many adventures.>

Dakota came to full alertness, adrenalin surging through her.

I knew you were in there, you fucking fish. It's you, isn't it? The one that gave me that damn figurine. I knew it. How did you do it? How the fuck did you get in here?

For the first time in her life, even the enclosing walls of the *Piri Reis* felt like a prison.

<It was the simplest challenge: to integrate my ethereal self within the confines of a bauble, a trinket gifted by this one to your most estimable self, in preparation and expectation of this journey of journeys, this

laudable search for that which must not be discovered, the purest of fires, the most essential of knowledge, most precious, oh yes, to us, your silver-finned friends.

<Thence, from the confines of said bauble within which a representational mirror of my soul was encoded, complete with the finest qualities particular to this individual, it was a simple matter of transference once more to the far greater realms of this ocean of thought and steel, the *Hyperion*, within which I now reside and -investigate and study in order that the balance of all things may be maintained.>

Dakota absorbed this information in a state of shock. She realized whatever it was that was speaking to her had almost certainly been transferred into the *Hyperion*'s systems when she'd placed the statuette on the imaging plate.

She'd been right in thinking there was a spy on board the *Hyperion*. She'd carried it on board herself, without ever being aware.

But that didn't explain the niggling sense of significance she felt every time she thought about the figurine. It didn't explain what was so damned familiar about it.

Piri Alpha, how safe are we from that thing?

<My systems are far more secure than those of the *Hyperion*,> her ship replied.

It was only her imagination that imbued those words with a sniffy tone.

<It is attempting to trace a physical location for the *Piri Reis*,> it continued. <However, we remain

effectively invisible to outside forces bar direct visual observation by any crew.>

Dakota thought hard for several seconds, her mind working overtime.

'I thought artificial intelligence wasn't possible,' Dakota said out loud, choosing her words with precision. She needed to get as much information as possible out of whatever was residing within the *Hyperion*'s stacks. If it had wormed its way in deep enough, it might be able to override the life-support systems and send her, the ship's atmosphere, and everyone else flying out into space. It could fill every room, shaft and corridor with deadly radiation . . . there was no knowing what it could do, or what it had already been doing all these long weeks. 'At least, that's what your lot always claimed. I thought Ghost technology was the only . . .'

The answer came booming out through the *Piri*'s speakers.

'Manifold manifestations of "intelligence" exist, dryskin, and can be utilized, toyed with, manipulated, as the creator might wish. Big Fish may create Little Big Fish, to do the bidding of the firstborn. And I, my dear Dakota, am one of the biggest, hungriest Big Fish of all. To possess such knowledge is to be bitten by such knowledge, even mortally wounded; therefore restriction of said know-how is but a kindness to many species, as well as to your own.'

'I . . . see.' So she was speaking to a genuine machine

intelligence. Very well, one more secret the Shoal had been keeping to themselves.

'Understanding within your thoughts is delightfully tasty,' the alien commented. A visual sense-impression was beginning to form in Dakota's mind's eye, transmitted via the *Hyperion*'s stacks and filtered through her implants, of the Shoal-member she'd met on Bourdain's Rock swimming within its briny ball of energy.

'Enjoyment greatly derived from acquisition of understanding that, far below us, in welcoming but chilly depths, lies that which you would seek to fly far, far away. This imposing surfeit of knowingness arrives with me via wings of knowledge, derived from the very same inter-ocean singing by which your colleagues have gained their own understanding of that which lies below.'

'All right, so you know about the derelict.'

'In which precious and delicate matter, Miss Merrick, I might enquire as to whether you might consider it a delight – a healthy, lifespan-prolonging delight – to aid and assist me in the destruction thereof, preventing its further investigation by those big bad fish who have been the cause of so much *contretemps* in your life of late.'

'You . . .' Dakota struggled to understand. 'You want me to destroy the derelict? Is that what you're saying?'

'Your understanding and compliance would be gracious and healthy. Further, there are precise and delicate means by which this matter must be pursued, to wit destruction of said derelict. Such means should be engaged most precisely, lest failure be permitted.'

'But why destroy it? Why not just . . .' Dakota had to swallow to clear the sudden thickness from her throat, but she had to know. 'Why even let the Freehold come here in the first place? Why even *tell* me all this?'

'Once more, manifold necessities present themselves, dear Miss Merrick, of a vulgar and varied nature too long and windy for casual discussion. To know is good, and not to know is frequently better. In agreement?'

Ignorance is bliss? Fine.

'Consider further potential rewards of close attention paid to your task. Enjoyment of extensive lifespan in warm tasty seas, made sweeter by exclusive granting of partial rights to as yet undisclosed, but permitted, Shoal technology.'

'In return for my silence.' *Destroy the derelict, betray the Freehold, escape, and be rich,* if *she could take the monster at its word.*

'Consider benefits of continued trade amongst races of galaxy, as facilitated by mighty Shoal, biggest, vastest, mightiest Fish of all. Discovery by Shoal Hegemony of attempt to retrieve derelict would result in punitive measures, leaving human minnows lost in deepest abyssal waters without even means to sing across vacuum seas.

'End of trade, end of all – woe, woe. But! But bad for Shoal. Much better to hide unfortunate discovery from eyes of all, sweep under planet-sized carpet and walk whistling away, yes?'

'Which is where *I* come in.'

'Huge and magnificent correctness, verified.'

'I help you sabotage the Freehold's salvage mission, and we pretend none of this happened. We keep it low-key so none of this registers on the Shoal's radar, and that way they don't have to run an embargo against humanity and lose their long-standing relationship with us. That simple?'

'To be unhelpful in these matters would bring dastardly misfortune upon human species.'

Dakota couldn't fault his argument. Except that meant helping alien creatures she couldn't help but hate.

If she aided the Freehold, the alien – his consciousness somehow integrated into the *Hyperion* – would bring about the collapse of the fledgling interstellar human empire, and still bury any evidence the derelict had ever existed.

Or, she could work *with* the alien, destroy the derelict, and allow the continued survival of the fragile interstellar network of human colonies. And, if her actions were ever made public, she would earn the enmity and hatred of much of humanity for aiding the Shoal.

On the other hand, what choice did she have but to help the creature? She was already filled with loathing for Kieran Mansell and the Senator, and she desperately wanted to find a way to hurt them . . .

She thought for a long while, and the alien intelligence had the good grace to remain silent until she chose to respond. The situation was so dire, so ridiculous, she even laughed out loud at one point, the sound of her mirth edging uncomfortably close to hysteria.

But if she did help the Shoal, it might increase her chances of survival . . . and maybe give her the time to think of a way out of this mess.

And yet, and yet . . .

There was something missing here. Not so much what the Shoal-member had said, as what he had *not* said. She couldn't put her finger on it, but she had the feeling there was something he didn't want her to know. And whatever that was, it might just turn out to be an advantage.

'Even if I help you, it doesn't make us allies,' she said out loud. 'So don't insult me by suggesting it does, you understand me? All this mess is because of *your* kind. The Uchidan Diaspora, the war with the Freehold – this is all because of you and your fucking colonial contracts.' She cleared her throat of the foul taste that had gathered there, cold and bitter. 'Yes, I'll help you. But not because I want to.'

Alien sense-impressions flooded across the neural bridge of her implants, mostly incomprehensible, but buried deep in there was a very human-seeming sense of satisfaction and triumph. They had all of them been played like puppets.

And then she realized what it was that felt so wrong.

There's just this one Shoal-member, but where are all the rest of them? Why send in just one of their own as some kind of software ghost, instead of a whole ship, or even a fleet?

Unless, of course, the Shoal were so powerful they only needed to send in one of their own to defeat the aims of an entire civilization. But that wasn't quite it either.

Everything this alien had done was underhand. He had infiltrated himself on to the *Hyperion* via Dakota (which also begged the question of how the alien could possibly have known she would eventually find her way into working as a reluctant pilot for the Freehold), and then remained almost entirely silent for the duration of the journey to Nova Arctis.

Why did he insist on engaging her in such an elaborate charade?

What was he hiding?

The digitized shadow that thought of himself as Trader-In-Faecal-Matter-Of-Animals observed Dakota with amusement. Even if she stumbled on the truth, she would have no choice but to do exactly what he wanted her to do regardless.

Trader had modelled his software environment to create the illusion of a limitless ocean, an eternal blackness that replicated the gentle drift of Mother Sea's embrace. The creature that had spoken with Dakota was very close to being an accurate model of the original Trader: every circuit, subroutine and protocol aboard the *Hyperion* – plus a few hidden Shoal neural processors, well out of sight, without which the human computer systems would have provided insufficient processing power – were bent to generating his self-image and consciousness.

Mental processes of near infinite complexity had been magically compressed into the tiniest of virtual environments, entirely equivalent to taking a Deep Dreamer and squeezing it down until it occupied barely the same space as an amoeba. Such limitations prevented the digitized Trader from feeling regret that its existence was by necessity a brief affair.

To destroy the derelict and the transluminal drive within by conventional means would be to risk detection, for Shoal monitoring networks within transluminal space existed precisely to detect the complex radiations thereby produced.

And that would never do. The subsequent investigation would certainly lead to unanticipated and deeply embarrassing revelations concerning long-hidden factions within the Hegemony, for whom Trader was the prime mover when it came to dirty work.

And that would *really* never do.

Far, far better that the greater masses of Shoal throughout the galaxy never learned the truth contained within the derelict – never learned of the great and terrible crime that had been committed so very long ago, albeit for the highest and noblest of reasons. The destruction of the last survivors of an entire civilization – of even the *knowledge* of that civilization's existence – was far from a minor consideration.

The Deep Dreamers had indicated that something of great and future significance lay in the near future, and clearly the derelict now took centre stage. And this despite the fact that other copies of Trader existed in other places, monitoring other, potential near-future causal hotspots – a way of spreading the bet, as it were.

Clearly, however, the Dreamers had been on the money where Dakota was concerned.

Trader's purpose was to ensure her actions, and those of the Freehold, did not affect the security and stability of the Shoal Hegemony. The future was to a certain degree predictable – but it was most certainly not immutable.

Corso found himself wondering what it would be like to live entirely in a world without shadows. The *Hyperion*'s simulations hadn't come close to the maddening reality: every surface here was illuminated to an equal degree, still with no apparent source for that radiation.

At one point, by way of experimentation, he squatted on his haunches and tried to block out the all-pervading light by tucking his head in against his chest and covering his head with his arms. It worked to a certain extent, but he quickly came to realize there was a . . . a *misty* quality to the derelict's atmosphere, which suggested some form of luminous gas all around them. That theory might have made sense if the air piped into the derelict via the Freehold's filtration system remained visibly luminescent outside the ship itself, but as soon as you stepped beyond the hull and into the tunnel leading to the submersible, the luminescence vanished.

It was strangely like entering a dream world.

'According to the map, we've now gained access to almost two-thirds of the derelict,' said Kieran, watching Corso as he worked. 'Are we getting any closer yet to locating the bridge?'

'You're assuming there *is* any equivalent of a bridge,' Corso replied. 'Even the Shoal don't appear to have anything like the human equivalent. Far as anyone knows, they just float around in a central space according to some ancient shoaling instinct, and issue commands according to social protocols we know almost nothing about.'

'Then there'll be a hub, at least, one or more central points from where the ship can be controlled.' Kieran sounded like he'd stubbornly made his mind up.

Corso sighed and returned to his work, making minute physical adjustments to the interface chair's neural circuitry. Kieran, along with the Senator, appeared to believe flying the damn fossil out of the Nova Arctis system in a blaze of glory was merely a matter of applying a can-do attitude.

One adjustment in particular seemed to make a

difference: a minor tweak to improve the rate of dataflow between the human and alien software configurations, but one glance at a handheld screen he'd plugged into the chair suggested he'd turned a spigot and let loose a waterfall.

Corso took one look at the level of activity flowing through the walls around them and felt his heart skip a beat.

He bent down to pick up the toolkit he'd left lying next to the interface chair. Just as he was about to lay his hand on it, it slid away from him, slowly at first, then faster. Dumbfounded, he watched it slither across the pale, marble-like floor, and almost lost his balance when the floor unexpectedly seesawed under his feet.

He saw Kieran staring back at him from across the room, mute with surprise. The floor regained its former stability, but only for a moment. Now it was beginning to tilt.

Corso's immediate thought was that the derelict was about to slide into the abyss. His terror of the abyssal depths far below them hit hard, and he moaned in terror. He grabbed on to one leg of the interface chair for purchase.

The ship continued to tilt. Kieran dropped to his knees and slid helplessly into a corner of the room, along with several random pieces of equipment Corso had kept scattered around him while he worked on the interface. Fortunately the technical team who had installed the chair had bolted it to the floor. Corso scrambled to get purchase on one of the chair legs, but lost it, tumbling down hard next to Kieran.

Then he realized the tilting was limited to the room they were in. They both gaped in stunned amazement towards the entrance.

They had both ditched their gel suits in the corridor outside. These, along with a stack of hardcopy data left behind by the surface base's technical staff, resolutely refused to slide away or otherwise become affected by the tilting effect.

That seemed bad enough – but then monsters started coming out of the walls.

An alert via the *Hyperion*'s ground link manifested as a tickling sensation in the back of Dakota's throat.

She'd been floating in the silence and dark of her own ship for the better part of an hour, the *Piri Reis*'s effigy-form having since disappeared once more back into its wall-niche. Her mind at first had been full of thoughts of revenge, but these had given way in the end to icy determination.

Their treatment of her, she realized, was partly because they were afraid of her. It was good that they were afraid of her.

After a while, she sank into a kind of Ghost-induced machine meditation, a near-vegetative state, her consciousness set adrift and only peripherally aware of the constant flow of maintenance routines keeping the *Hyperion* running.

As she half-dreamed, images slipped by her mind's eye, mostly incomprehensible. She recalled the brief moment of connection she'd felt with whatever lived deep inside the derelict's stacks. Even her Ghost was struggling to assimilate or make sense of that intense, overwhelming flood of sensory data. But understanding was nevertheless coming, albeit slowly.

She came to full awareness as the alert signal became more urgent, demanding her attention. She kept her conscious mind at one remove while her Ghost handled the situation, working at machine-speed in a familiar, occasionally disturbing anticipation of her own thoughts and actions.

Something significant was happening on board the derelict: the energy output from its systems was growing exponentially. It was, Dakota realized with awe, channelling through its hull bursts of energy so vast they might more typically be associated with solar flares.

It became rapidly clear that any contact with the personnel on the derelict had been lost. Dakota hesitated for long seconds. Arbenz was likely already aware of the situation developing, but if he wasn't, he would punish her for failing to pass on what her machine-senses were now telling her.

What, exactly, to do?

A moment later that decision was out of her hands.

Automated systems were already spreading the alert to the surface base, as well as to the *Agartha*.

<There are very unusual graviton fluctuations taking place beneath the ice,> *Piri* Alpha informed her, <emanating from within the derelict . . .>

She next became aware that orbit-to-ground dropships were being powered up on board the *Agartha*, for the *Hyperion*'s sister ship had a full complement of crew. Dakota pulled up a live feed displaying the subsurface ridge on which the derelict rested. Nothing there appeared out of the ordinary. It looked as peaceful, as quiet, and as dead as it had when she had first set eyes on it.

But *something* was in there. She didn't know if it was something alive, but it was certainly aware of her. Even from orbit, she could sense it, like some ancient beast padding just beyond the reach of a campfire's light.

Even from this far, she knew it wanted something from her. Just what, precisely, she couldn't yet begin to guess.

<Dakota, I am picking up encrypted communiqués from the *Agartha*. An initial scan of their contents post-decryption suggests they may be important. Would you like to see them?>

Please, Piri.

The wall framing the entrance had now become a ceiling, putting any chance of escape far out of their reach.

The interface chair stuck out from what had been the floor, but had now become a wall. Kieran and Corso stood next to each other, panting heavily: only a few seconds had passed since the gravity had flipped.

Corso could feel it beginning to shift again. His stomach churned with nausea as his senses grappled to cope with these sudden shifts. Now, the surface under them – until very recently itself a wall – slowly tilted towards the far corner.

Corso scrabbled at the wall underfoot, but it was hopeless. The material from which the derelict was constructed offered little purchase.

Random pieces of equipment began to slide at first slowly, then faster, into a far corner. The entrance still remained resolutely out of reach far above.

Corso became aware of a low hum, slowly building in pitch and volume, which rapidly became a bone-rattling vibration. A tiny part of his mind that remained calm speculated that they'd set off some kind of alarm.

The second flip, when it came, was as sudden and unexpected as the first. The wall on which they crouched suddenly became the top of a hollow cube, with the entrance to their right, but still far out of reach.

They fell, dropping like stones from one side of the room to the other.

Corso hit hard enough to stun him, but Kieran had less luck. He collided heavily with the interface chair, before tumbling on down to land next to Corso like a broken doll.

The entrance was still out of reach above their heads. Corso tried desperately to think of some way to get to it . . .

Things were emerging out of the walls, floor and ceiling, whose pale surfaces had begun to swirl. It was as if they had become transparent enough to reveal a liquid in different shades of cream flowing and ebbing beneath.

Then the surface of the wall furthest above them began to warp, extruding long, curving spines that began to weave like time-lapse films of plants growing. These and other, unidentifiable, shapes, that Corso couldn't help but interpret as malevolent.

Kieran coughed and shifted groggily, and then his eyes flickered open. He put a hand to his chest and winced.

'The next time the room starts shifting,' Corso told him, 'do exactly what I say.'

'What do you mean?' Kieran stared at him.

'The first time the room flipped, it dropped us into that corner,' Corso said, pointing upwards. 'Then into this corner. It's too early to really guess if there's a pattern to the way it flips, but there's a chance, if it happens again, it'll land us this time on the same wall as the entrance.'

They didn't have to wait long to find out.

The intervening seconds passed in silence amid an awful, growing tension. The surface on which they lay then began to ripple gently, and Corso choked back his urge to scream when he felt something tendril-like brush against the inside of his thigh.

Then their tools and equipment once again began to slip away . . .

The world tipped again, but in the direction Corso had hoped. As they tumbled downwards, Corso aimed himself towards the entrance, knowing the opening would remain out of reach, a few metres above them, if he didn't make it –

He landed hard, the impact knocking the wind out of him. But he had managed to get a grip on the jamb of the doorway, and clung on for all his life. After a few moments he managed to pull himself up and hook an arm fully over the edge, reaching down into the corridor beyond. The gel suits looked like they'd been glued into place, an affront to his already shattered sense of gravity.

A moment later an awful, lurching weight began to pull him back into the room, and he realized Kieran was hauling himself over his body to reach the entrance.

'Stay right where you are, Corso, and hold on tight,' Kieran grunted.

The pain Corso felt was indescribable, and he felt his hold beginning to slip.

He glanced back down into the room and saw the walls, floor and ceiling had transformed into a mass of waving spines that made him think of sea anemones. He moaned, which became a grunt of pain as Kieran pulled himself right over him before falling back out into the corridor.

For a sickening moment Corso wondered if the other man was going to leave him there. But a moment later Kieran, now standing firmly upright in the corridor, grabbed his shoulders and heaved him out.

Corso felt his own weight shift as he fell into a normal-looking corridor that, until a moment ago, his senses had insisted was a vertical shaft. He gasped from the intense pain racking in his shoulders and chest, and Kieran didn't look much better.

'We need to get out of here,' Kieran gasped, 'or we're dead for sure.'

'What about Lunden and—?'

'What about them?' Kieran snarled. 'They're soldiers. They know how to take care of themselves.'

Low vibrations had begun to roll along the corridor. Corso glanced hastily back into the room and saw his tools in the grip of tendril-like spines. The room now resembled the digestive organs of some sea-going invertebrate, and his stomach somersaulted at the thought of being left in there even a few seconds more . . .

Kieran began to head off, clumsily treading on hard-copy data with his boots. Images of crystal arrays and interface algorithms flickered and spasmed on the hard-copies as they scattered underfoot.

Moving slowly, they made their way back to the original entrance. Behind them, the vibrations transformed into a deep, guttural roar, as if some creature older than human civilization had begun stalking them through the passageways.

The derelict had finally given up its silence.

At first, it appeared to Dakota to be loudly radiating its presence to anyone or anything that cared to listen. But then it became rapidly clear that the signal was manifesting on an extremely obscure frequency not used by any of the known interstellar tachyon transceiver relays. She would never even have noticed it if her Ghost hadn't been engaged in the process of monitoring the derelict across every conceivable transmission spectrum.

Even so, what was emerging was presumably highly encrypted, since it appeared to her Ghost as untranslatable gibberish. The resulting signal was of such low power and limited range it was hard to guess what it might be trying to communicate with.

Is there any way we can figure out what it's saying, and who to? she asked of *Piri* Alpha.

<No. However, the signal is extremely directional in nature.>

Directional? You mean it's deliberately aiming at something?

The ship replied by displaying maps of the Nova Arctis system. Lines stabbed out from Theona and Dymas towards one of the inner planets: not Newfall but the system's innermost world, a tiny ball of rock barely outside the corona of the sun it orbited. This planet was called Ikaria.

What the hell was to be found *there?*

Two six-man squads were scrambled from the *Agartha* in response to the sudden breakdown in communications with the derelict, dropping down on tails of chemical fire to Theona's icy surface in combat pods that spilled the pressure-suited figures inside on to the ice immediately adjacent to the surface base.

By now less then twenty minutes had passed since the loss of communications with the derelict.

Should have brought more than one sub, thought Gardner, standing back and watching the rescue operation being mounted from inside the ground base. But everything had been so rushed . . . they'd been working hard and fast, fearful that the Shoal might already be on to them, or if not yet, at least soon. There simply hadn't been enough time to acquire all the resources they really needed.

Gardner could happily live without Kieran Mansell – a murderous, psychotic son of a bitch, if ever there was one – but Lucas Corso was indispensable. His specialist knowledge was the key to the derelict's secrets. Leaving him down there with only Kieran to guard him seemed the sheerest blind folly.

Now, they had to wait for the squads to cycle through and get on board the sub. Then the long journey down again – and only then would they begin to glean any idea of what had happened.

This whole operation reeked of disorganized panic.

He glanced over at Senator Arbenz: a strutting, stiff-lipped, pumped-up little man; quite a ridiculous figure if Gardner hadn't already been aware just how dangerous he could be. A few months ago the Freehold had been a defeated people on the verge of absolute retreat, but now they operated under the delusion they were the children of destiny, forged in war (or some such chauvinistic baloney Arbenz had spouted during one of his frequent rants) and destined to conquer the stars.

If the whole thing weren't so pathetic, Gardner would have laughed. He needed the Freehold for now . . . but at some point something would have to be done. Leaving the transluminal drive in the hands of the Senator and his cronies was like placing a rocket launcher in the hands of a child. It was just asking for trouble.

Laden beneath their heavy vacuum-equipped combat gear, the troops entered the base, and began trudging through the network of clanging corridors and down to the submersible waiting for them in its pool. Along with the Senator, Gardner followed them.

'Something must have been triggered by whatever Corso fed into the derelict's computer systems,' Gardner muttered. 'God knows what's happening down there now. I said all along we didn't have enough contingency plans in place for unexpected major setbacks.'

Arbenz merely shot him an annoyed look; the tension between them had been growing. It was obvious to Gardner that the Senator simply wasn't equipped to deal with even the notional concept of failure. For him only victory was possible.

'God indeed only knows what's happening down there, Mr Gardner, but remember God is on our side.'

'Or possibly the Uchidans and Bourdain know too, given the security leaks you've been neglecting to tell me about.'

Gardner knew he was walking a dangerous edge, but he was finding it harder and harder to bite his tongue. He had already taken it upon himself to make coded queries to his associates back home, about contracting a fleet to wrest control of the derelict from the Freehold.

But the partners were still too cautious, too scared of drawing attention to what was happening out here, and drawing yet more potential combatants into a risky war over an unpredictable prize. Convincing them otherwise was going to take time Gardner wasn't sure he had.

'Don't worry, Mr Gardner,' Arbenz snarled, 'you'll get your share in the manufacturing and technology rights, once we acquire the drive. And I hope you'll enjoy spending every last penny of it in hell.'

Gardner nodded, and kept his expression cool.

*

Corso and Kieran had almost reached the passage connecting to the external airlock when the gravity flipped again.

It had happened another four times so far since they had escaped from the room containing the interface chair. At one point the gravity cut off completely, leaving them in freefall for several panicked seconds.

The worst part of it was they were back in the part of the derelict which had until now been deemed safe. Clearly that was a mistake, and whatever countermeasures the derelict was currently implementing remained effective throughout its structure.

Sheer luck had saved them from being dashed to pieces when a passageway had flipped. The process was slow enough, they had time to react: unfortunately the passageway was a long one, and had rapidly transformed into a deep vertical shaft even as they raced along it.

Kieran had pushed them both down against the floor so rather than falling straight down, they instead slid down at an increasing rate as the gravity shifted. They still managed to hit the far end of the passageway with considerable force, and Corso blacked out for a couple of seconds. When he came to, Kieran was already hauling him by the shoulders towards the airlock and safety. From the way Kieran held himself and the expression on his face, Corso could see he'd been injured in some way.

After a couple of metres of this, Corso managed to stumble upright. A clanging sound reverberated from just ahead and he realized the submersible must have come back down and docked.

It was well ahead of schedule, so obviously some-body had figured out they were in trouble.

They rounded the last corner, almost collapsing on top of each other as the airlock door swung ponderously open. Several heavily armed Freeholder troops were stamping through it towards them, wearing combat armour too bulky to progress easily through the confined spaces of the tunnel. Corso laughed weakly as the soldiers were forced to shuffle towards them side-ways in single file.

'Get the hell back!' Kieran yelled, waving at them to retreat.

Their faces were invisible behind their reinforced visors, but after a moment they started to shuffle back into the submersible.

The howling noise manifested itself once more from somewhere far around the curve of the passageway, sounding like it was getting closer. It was impossible not to imagine some terrible, monstrous apparition stalking them through the derelict's twisting interior spaces.

Corso glanced up at the screen still roughly welded into an excision in the wall and noticed that the interior of the derelict was reshaping itself. Corridors and rooms disappeared from the map even as he watched, while others appeared that he was sure hadn't previously existed.

In that same moment, Corso saw that Lunden and

Ivanovich were gone. They would find no trace of their bodies now, as had been the case with anyone else who had disappeared into the derelict's maw.

Kieran's face turned pale and he slid to the ground, unconscious. Corso dropped down next to him and found the man still had a pulse, but his pupils were dilated and his breathing staccato and shaky. Corso didn't feel that much better himself – sheer terror had helped him forget temporarily about the pain. One of the troops saw what had happened and headed back their way again, lifting Kieran up and leading the way back into the submersible.

He'd been so sure the derelict would accept his programming. He still couldn't believe he'd overlooked anything. But would the Senator understand that when he demanded to know what had happened?

TWENTY

At first, when Dakota quietly entered the surgery, Corso had been staring down at a workscreen he held in both hands, a faraway look on his face. One shoulder was encased in a flexible med unit that kept his damaged tissues anaesthetized, while repairing the damage beneath at an accelerated rate.

Both Corso and Kieran Mansell had been brought back to the *Hyperion* a few hours previous, since it apparently had better medical facilities than the base on Theona.

Empty medical caskets were stacked up on either wall, in steel racks extending the full length of the medical facility. Udo was still encased inside one of these, but he was likely to be back out in a day or two. The external readings made it clear he'd been undergoing a slow and difficult recovery.

His brother Kieran was in better shape, but only just. He was in the intensive treatment bay, an adjustable palette with an autodoc suspended from the ceiling above his deeply sedated form. Its articulated arms were at the moment curled up and at rest, like some enormous metallic spider.

Dakota studied Kieran's life-signs monitors and wondered what would happen if she smothered him with one of his own pillows. At the very least it would be a mercy killing.

Corso, on the other hand, was conscious and sitting up. His complexion was pale, as if the blood had been drained out of him.

She stared at him, full of nervous energy, until he finally looked up and became aware of her presence. He blinked in surprise as if he wasn't sure her presence was a good or bad thing.

'How are you?' she asked.

He took a moment to think about this. 'Been better.'

'I heard about what happened, how the derelict attacked you. What went wrong?'

'Nothing.' Corso shook his head, no longer looking at her, an abstract expression on his face. 'That's the whole problem.'

Dakota went silent in blank incomprehension.

Corso elaborated. 'I mean, I did everything right. What happened . . . shouldn't have happened. It was like . . . sabotage.' He shrugged. 'I swear, it was like deliberate sabotage.'

'Did you know the derelict sent a transmission the exact same moment we lost contact with you?'

Corso was clearly taken aback by this.

'The signal was very tightly focused, aimed towards

the inner system,' Dakota explained. She nodded at his workscreen. 'Any ideas?'

Corso glanced down at the workscreen, clearly confused. 'I don't know anything about a transmission. They didn't . . .'

He stared up at her dumbly.

Dakota decided there wasn't any more time to waste.

'We're going to have a long talk, Lucas, somewhere where we can't be found. A lot has happened over the past couple of hours, and that's why they're keeping information from you.'

She put a hand under his arm and tried to guide him off the cot. Indicators flashed red on the wall behind him and he jerked his arm back.

'Hey—'

'Do you want to get out of here alive or not?' she hissed. 'I don't like to be the bearer of bad news, but the fact is we're both as good as . . .'

She glanced to one side, seeing Kieran was still unconscious in his bay. Even so, speaking seditiously like this anywhere near him made her deeply uncomfortable. She grabbed Corso's arm again, this time violently wrenching him sideways across the cot until his feet slid towards the ground. He pushed her away.

'*Shit*,' he said with a grimace. 'What the fuck is the matter with you?' he scowled. 'Just . . . wait a minute.' He stood up, carefully.

'No time,' she replied, pulling him towards the door. He stumbled after her in a daze. She shoved him through into the corridor beyond and pushed him up against a wall. 'Now listen,' she said, her voice still a low whisper. 'I've been monitoring tachyon-net traffic between the *Agartha* and Redstone, and if what I'm hearing is true you and I might be as good as dead. Now tell me: who exactly is Senator Martin Corso? Is he a relative of yours?'

Corso stiffened, his eyes growing wide.

'How about Mercedes Corso?' she tried.

'Where did you hear those names?' he demanded.

'You once told me the Senator and the rest of them were your enemies. You also said you were coerced into coming here. Care to elaborate on that?'

Corso made a move to grab her by the throat, but she caught his arm and held it away. 'I'll tell you how I know, but first you need to calm down,' she hissed. 'I think you're in almost as much trouble as I am, and I can prove it.'

He laughed, the sound bitter. 'You've barely said a truthful word since I first set eyes on you. You came on board under a false ID—'

'And you know why? Because I'm a machine-head. I trained to be one all my life. I come from Bellhaven. It's a job that came with serious prestige, until everything turned to shit and the Consortium shut down the development programmes.'

She swallowed hard. This wasn't easy for her to talk about. 'And, ever since, I've had to deal with people who treat me like I'm some kind of monster. I wasn't responsible for what happened on Redstone but every machine-head in the Consortium, most of whom probably hadn't even heard of Redstone, got punished for it. Every single day that I wake up, I remember what happened there. In detail. So yes, Lucas, I came on board under a false ID, but that's mainly because I was getting on board a ship filled with Redstone Freeholders.'

Corso reached up and gently prised Dakota's remaining hand away from his shoulder. 'Senator Corso is my father, and Mercedes is my younger sister. They're all the family I have, and they're hostages to a faction within the Freehold government that's headed by Arbenz. If I don't do exactly what Arbenz wants, they're both as good as dead.'

'You're being *blackmailed*?'

'Yes.'

Dakota felt the blood drain from her face. In a moment, everything had changed. *Everything.* She glanced back through the door to where Kieran still lay comatose. Colour-coded displays of his nervous, respiratory and muscular systems flickered from moment to moment.

'There've been some recent events back on Redstone,' she explained. 'I don't think Arbenz or the rest of them were likely to go out of their way to tell you.'

'What happened?' Corso demanded, pushing her away. 'Shit, is it my father?'

Dakota realized Corso was already heading for a comms panel by the medical bay's entrance.

'Lucas! If you talk to Arbenz, he'll be aware I have a way of getting around his censor blocks. And there's more news besides. Some kind of fleet is on its way here.'

One hand up to the panel, Corso turned and stared at her. 'What?'

'Just listen to me, will you. I've been tapping into what's supposed to be an encrypted tach-net transponder on board the *Agartha*. That's how Arbenz is staying in touch with Redstone, but they're incredibly sloppy with the encryption.'

Corso was fully facing her again, a hard look on his face. Everything she said to him sounded stunningly incriminating, she knew, but she didn't have any choice. It was a drastic way to gain an ally.

Corso turned back to the panel and touched his fingertips to its surface. Ident codes and authorizations flickered briefly, before several screens appeared in response.

'I can't access any tach-net transmissions more than a few days old,' he said after a moment. 'Yet the networks aren't down.'

'I told you, they're trying to keep something from you. I can prove it.'

He glared at her balefully. 'I'm finding less and less reason to trust you an inch.'

'Then who *do* you trust?'

He didn't answer at first. 'I don't know,' he finally admitted.

'The only reason I can think of for any fleet turning up here is because they know about the derelict. They aren't here yet, but they will be soon, on board another coreship. Maybe it's the Uchidans, or maybe it's someone else. Either way, they get here in less than a couple of days, which means this whole salvage operation is in deep, deep trouble.'

'You know, it's funny, but I believe you. Or at least I think I do.' He had a faraway look in his eyes that made Dakota realize his anti-shock medication was beginning to wear off.

'Can you walk properly?' she asked.

'Sure, I guess so.'

'Good – because I meant it when I said you're in as much trouble as I am.'

'Are they dead?'

'Who?'

'My father and my sister.' He took hold of her upper arm, gripping her painfully. 'Tell me.'

'First, we get somewhere safe—'

'I'm not going anywhere, Dakota. I've got to—'

'It's *over*, Corso!' she yelled at him, her voice echoing from the bulkheads around them. 'It's over,' she said more quietly. 'Think about it. This whole thing was compromised from the start. Your secret is out. Your boss is a murderous nutcase with wild delusions of grandeur who wants to go up against a civilization that controls a fucking *galaxy*. When it all goes tits up and the Senator goes looking for someone to blame, who do you think they're going to start with?'

Corso's lips grew thin. 'There's nowhere we *can* go.'

'Wrong.' She peeled his hand off her upper arm with some difficulty. They were now in the *Hyperion*'s gravity wheel. She led him down a corridor towards the centre of the wheel, the gravity dropping to zero the further they moved away from the wheel's rim.

To her surprise, Corso followed her with little protest. His eyes still had that faraway look.

'At least tell me where we're going,' he grumbled eventually.

'The cargo bay.'

'What the hell's there that'll make any difference?'

She hesitated for a moment, and felt her resolve wobble. *He's still a Freeholder*, she reminded herself.

'Trust me,' she replied.

Corso gazed through a window overlooking the interior of the cargo bay, seeing the assemblage of weapons and equipment stored there. Then he frowned and nodded towards the far wall.

'Over there. It looks like . . .'

'That,' Dakota replied, 'is my ship.'

He glanced to one side, as if trying to remember something. '*This* is what you wanted me to see? What's it doing here? How the hell did you even get it on board?'

'Anything we want to talk about, we can say it aboard my ship without any fear of being overheard. If there's any attempt at surveillance, I'll know immediately. As far as the manifest is concerned, the *Piri Reis* doesn't even exist, and it doesn't show up on any external surveillance systems either.'

'You can still eyeball it, though,' he replied, looking thoughtful. 'Assuming anybody happened to look through this window and spotted it?'

'Nobody has, yet.'

She drew him towards an airlock complex that led further into the cargo bay's depressurized interior, and there had him pull on a light pressure suit. She did the same herself: letting him know about her filmsuit felt like a step too far just yet. Then she cycled the air out of the lock and moments later they were floating towards the *Piri Reis*.

It felt strange having someone else inside her ship. Once they were on board, he looked around the *Piri*'s compact interior with an astonished gaze.

He finally turned to Dakota as he peeled off his pressure suit. 'Frankly,' he said, 'I still think you're the one who needs to do the talking.'

'This craft is the *Piri Reis*, and I brought it on board.

Apart from me, you're the only one who knows about it, and I'd like things to stay that way.'

Corso nodded carefully. 'You said Arbenz was sending and receiving secret communiqués to and from Redstone.'

'Use that screen,' she said, pointing. 'You'll find it won't block you when you try to access the latest tach-net updates.'

Corso grabbed a handhold and swung himself up into a sitting position on a fur-lined bulkhead, then waited a moment as the screen turned itself towards him. Dakota watched as a series of icons appeared on the screen: the latest news updates from the interstellar tach-net transponder network. She chewed nervously on a finger as he read.

Piri, is there any reason to doubt the information from Redstone?

<None. Independent Consortium observers present in the Freehold capital have filed separate reports of a coup.>

Corso became very still as he concentrated. Eventually Dakota got tired of waiting and went over to where he squatted intently, putting a hand on his shoulder.

It seemed it was all over for Senator Arbenz. The assault on the *Rorqual Maru* and the Uchidan encroachment on the Freehold capital had proved the tipping point for a coup led by Senate members with more liberal leanings – liberal, that is, by the standards of the Freehold.

'I should be there,' he said, sounding stunned.

'But you can't be. Look, they don't say who was executed . . .'

He turned to gaze at her, and she fell silent. 'They don't need to. According to this, the pro-war faction – and that's basically Senator Arbenz – killed every hostage they held when the Senate was stormed. That means my father and my sister.' He shook his head in wonder. 'They're dead.'

'You don't need to do what Senator Arbenz tells you any more. He doesn't have any—'

'Yes, I know that,' he snapped, and Dakota decided that erring on the side of silence might be the better option.

He stared off into space for a while, his expression bleak. 'I knew this would happen, you know. It's not even a surprise.'

'What do you mean?'

He gazed at her levelly. 'Arbenz and the Mansell brothers were all connected with death squads. They wanted to achieve political change through terror. It's an old, old political stratagem. I'm just . . .'

He shrugged and sighed. 'I'm just not surprised,' he said, and pushed himself away from the screen. 'I need to go.'

'Go where?' she asked, alarmed.

'I need to . . . I need to get some things.'

She looked at the expression on his face. It was much like she'd imagined her own expression might have been, following the mandatory removal of her original implants. A look of loss and betrayal – and something else there weren't quite the words for.

'Do you want me to—'

'No,' he said abruptly. 'But you should know I won't be telling the others about this. You've got my word on that.'

She nodded mutely in reply, then watched as he pulled his pressure suit back on and re-entered the *Piri*'s tiny airlock.

'And then you're coming back?'

He looked at her strangely, but nodded after a moment.

Half of her was sure he would come back, but the other half was even surer he wouldn't.

All dead.

It hadn't quite sunk in. He knew from past experience – from Cara's death – just how long that could take.

He considered the possibility that, in a very real way, his life was over. He hadn't missed the look on Dakota's face when he'd departed her ship, but if he'd told her what was going through his mind, she might have tried to stop him.

Even worse, he might have let her stop him.

Disregarding some kind of coup, they were still under Senator Arbenz's thrall so long as they remained within the Nova Arctis system. Yet the fact remained both Corso and Dakota were still essential to Arbenz's plans.

There was a series of observation bubbles ringing the *Hyperion*'s hull, about halfway along its length. They were tiny clear blisters that looked out on the stars and Theona's frozen surface far below. These bubbles were the only places aboard the frigate where you could look directly out at the universe beyond the hull and be absolutely, unwaveringly certain that what you were seeing was real, and not – assuming you were sufficiently paranoid to let it concern you – merely a deluge of false information fed through the ultimately fallible conduit of the *Hyperion*'s sensor and communications arrays.

As soon as he was back in the *Hyperion*'s pressurized corridors, Corso made his way immediately to one of the bubbles, letting his mind empty of thoughts, regrets and the pains of loss even as he went.

Despite this, he felt the tears streaming down his cheeks as he made his way down hollowly clanging drop shafts. But the frigate was so vast, there was little chance of running randomly into another human being, even with the half-dozen crewmembers Arbenz had now installed.

Finally he reached one such blister, and pulled himself up a ladder and into a low-ceilinged room with a clear roof that looked out on the stars. He ignored the automated warnings that spoke quietly as he entered. The lights dimmed automatically as the hatch closed beneath him and he let himself slide into the comforting warmth of an observation chair that automatically tilted to better accommodate his view of the universe.

Music played automatically, a soft swelling and ebbing of notes more like the rising and falling of the tide than anything orchestrated by human beings. He couldn't summon the mental energy even to tell the *Hyperion* to turn the damn noise off.

What he had in mind was very simple.

The observation blister was a weak point in the hull, and the ship was old. The maintenance work done prior to its departure from Redstone had been the bare minimum necessary, given the restrictions of time and funding.

The automated warnings had made it clear that relatively little effort would be involved in destroying the clear blister before him and exposing himself to the vacuum of deep space. A series of switches under a panel within easy reach by the side of the reclining chair gave him control over explosive bolts that could blow the blister clear away from the hull, thus providing an emergency escape route. By the time any alarms could bring the ship's crew running to the observation blister, it would already be far too late.

He touched a button and the chair dropped a little, giving him a still better view. He got as far as flipping open the panel, tapping in the same default code that most equipment on board still used (Dakota had been right about the appalling lack of appropriate security), and rested his finger on the emergency release button that would blow the bolts.

Then he slowly brought his hand back up and closed the panel.

Even with him dead, there was at least a chance Arbenz could still use the protocols he'd created to negotiate the derelict's guidance systems and take it out of the Nova Arctis system. Corso knew the work he'd done was flawless. But if the derelict's assault on both him and Kieran was then a deliberate act of sabotage, who was responsible for it?

He sat beneath the blister's curving dome, with the lights up, staring up at his own reflection staring back down at him for what felt like a long time. His hand dropped again towards the panel by the side of the chair.

He already knew he wasn't going to do it. If the Senator could still win even with him dead, that made the whole notion of killing himself pointless.

Sal came into his thoughts. Corso was pretty sure Sal was dead by now, but as is so often the case with people who constitute a large part of your life for enough years, his old friend's physical presence was far from necessary in order for Corso to have a laborious, albeit primarily silent, imaginary argument with him, as if they sat there together beneath the curving transparent dome.

Sal won, of course. He usually did.

Corso tapped a button and the hatch in the floor

next to the chair irised open once more, revealing the ladder. He climbed back down and went looking for Dakota.

Arbenz stepped into the moon base's centre of operations, still feeling foggy from a lack of sleep. Anton Lourekas, the base's medician, had been giving him shots to keep him awake, but there was only so long before he'd end up losing his grip on events. Things were starting to run out of control badly enough as it was.

He was not pleased to find Gardner waiting for him.

'What do you mean by telling me I can't communicate with my partners?' Gardner nearly shouted in his face. Arbenz winced, too tired to be as angry as he really should be. 'Your communications staff are downright *refusing* to patch me through the tach-nets—'

'With good reason,' Arbenz muttered, pushing past Gardner and nodding a greeting to the three technicians working at the opposite end of the room.

'Don't ignore me, Senator. I demand—'

Arbenz turned around. 'If you continue to make demands in front of my own people, Mr Gardner, I'll have you permanently confined to quarters on board the *Hyperion*. Do you understand me?'

Gardner looked apoplectic. 'You can't.'

'But I can, David. And if your partners decide they don't like that, then they can come and find me themselves. Once this is all over.' He gestured over Gardner's shoulder to a guard, who stepped forward from his station by the entrance to the ops-centre.

'Now listen,' Arbenz continued, softening his voice a little. 'I believe some form of expeditionary force is on its way here, on board another coreship. That means we have to accept the fact our little secret has been compromised.'

Gardner's eyes were already bugging out. 'We have to contact—'

'*No*, Mr Gardner. We run silent until they actually get here, otherwise we risk the possibility that they also find out about the derelict, assuming they don't already know about it.'

'But they *must* know, if they're on their way here.'

'This is all we know: they're on their way here, and our time is limited. Anything else is just an assumption.' *No need to let him know just yet about the coup on Redstone.* 'So no more demands, Mr Gardner. Is that understood?'

Gardner's lips trembled, his face so red it looked ready to explode. Then he glanced at the waiting guard nearby, and clearly thought better of any further protest. He turned on his heel and stormed out of the ops-centre.

Arbenz immediately felt more relaxed.

'Sir?' He turned to find a technician called Weinmann standing by him. 'The signal emanating from the derelict. We've narrowed down the target.'

'Go on.'

'The signal is extremely tightly focused, on a very low-power beam. It's aimed at this system's innermost world, sir. Just here.' Weinmann tapped at the screen before him.

Arbenz leaned in to take a look. 'But that's just a ball of rock.'

Ikaria drifted a few bare tens of millions of kilometres from the surface of its sun. So what was there, that the derelict could want to signal?

'Ikaria has minimal rotation around its axis, as you'd expect from a body that close to its parent. The signal was directional enough for us to isolate a series of valleys that have just emerged into the planet's dark side. There's meanwhile been regular transmissions about three thousand seconds apart each. And each of those is being adjusted to match the planet's rotation.'

'I would have thought anything down there would have been burned away long ago,' Arbenz mused.

'Those valleys are extremely deep. And we're lucky because they're just emerging from the terminator line. They're going to be on the planet's dark side for a while.'

Arbenz sighed. 'But do we know what's down there, in those valleys? Is it possible, perhaps, that we might find other ships like our derelict there?'

Weinmann shook his head, clearly not prepared to speculate.

One of the largest problems they faced with the derelict they'd already found was digging it out of the ice. Excavation had indeed been proceeding ever since they'd discovered the craft, but the sheer scale of the project meant this exercise was taking far, far longer than originally hoped.

But if there was now the chance there were indeed other transluminal ships further in-system, perhaps sitting out in the open and ready for the taking . . .

If action were to be taken, it would have to be soon, before the unknown fleet arrived. Their best bet therefore was to take either the *Hyperion* or the *Agartha* to Ikaria with all due haste, and retrieve whatever they could find – even if it meant abandoning their efforts under Theona's dense ice.

Time was running out all too quickly.

'I want to know everything,' Corso said on his return to the *Piri*. 'Everything you haven't told me.'

'What makes you think there is anything else?' Dakota replied, her voice shaky.

He thought she looked like she'd been crying, but he couldn't be sure. At the very least her eyes were red-rimmed and clouded, her body pushed into a fur-lined nook inside the *Piri Reis*.

'Because there's too much at stake here for any more bullshit,' he snapped back. 'We're in serious trouble here. If there's anything else I should know, you tell me now, otherwise I find out later and then you're on your own. Completely. Do you understand me?'

'I haven't gone out of my way to do anything I shouldn't—'

He laughed. 'There's a wake of death and destruction following you wherever you go. I can understand why you'd hate the Senator, and now he doesn't have a hold over me I'm going to do everything I can to take the transluminal drive away from him, but I know I can't do that without your help. So start talking, Dakota. I want to know everything. From the beginning.'

He could see the acquiescence in her eyes, in the way her body relaxed. After a moment, she began to talk.

She told him about the Shoal; about Bourdain's Rock, and the alien's gift, about the system surge when she'd placed the figurine on the *Hyperion*'s imaging plate. About her conversation with an AI version of the alien, which had apparently penetrated the *Hyperion*'s systems.

It came spilling out in a cathartic rush, as if some mental logjam had finally given way, and a black tide of memory had pushed through like a swollen river spilling into an empty basin. She told him yet more: about the loss of her first set of implants, and the misery and pain that followed; about the alien's offer to wipe the slate clean if she only agreed to help it destroy the derelict . . .

Corso's anger gradually faded, and in the end he slumped in a corner facing her, a look of defeat coming across his face. Then suddenly he smiled.

413

'What's so funny?' she demanded, annoyed he could find anything faintly humorous in their predicament.

'It would almost be worth it to tell Arbenz all of this, just to see his face, don't you think?'

'Funny,' she scowled.

'Do you have any idea why this Shoal creature picked you for all this? It seems more than a little fortuitous, don't you reckon, that it would seek you out on the Rock, hand you this thing just on the off chance . . .'

'Don't assume I haven't thought about it – a lot. But, outside of the Shoal being able to see into the future, your guess is as good as mine.'

'There's a lot of unanswered questions, though,' he continued. 'For one, the idea that some kind of artificial intelligence is lurking inside the *Hyperion*'s computer systems – I find that hard to believe.'

'How so?'

He stared at her like she was stupid. 'Come *on*. The Shoal having the secret knowledge of how to create true artificial intelligence I could accept. But on the *Hyperion*'s computer systems? I guarantee you'd need something far more advanced than you'll find anywhere within the Consortium. And why wait until now? Why not grab us while we were on their own coreship on the way here, sitting right under their noses?'

Dakota shrugged. 'I thought about that, too. I think that the Shoal-member I spoke to – the thing inside the *Hyperion*'s stacks – is working alone for some reason. I can't think of anything else that makes sense.'

She looked up and saw the sceptical look on his face. 'Corso, everything I've told you is true. If you can't figure that out, you're a bigger fool than I originally took you for.'

Corso raised his hands in mock defeat. He pulled out his workscreen and held it up before her for a moment as if it were a glittering prize. Then he balanced it on his knee and began tapping at its screen.

'Since we're sharing, I've been analysing fresh information pulled from the derelict. One of the big questions we need to answer is, what was the relationship between the Shoal and the Magi? Was it a meeting between two species that had separately developed a transluminal drive?

'In fact,' he said with a grin, 'the evidence makes it more likely the Shoal *stole* the transluminal technology from the Magi.'

'You've got to be joking.'

'It's all in here,' he continued, still with a faint smile, tapping further at the workscreen. 'I think I've even stumbled across a potted history of the Magi. Trust me, though, when I say I'm making some wild leaps of interpretation.'

Dakota remembered that sense of witnessing the passing of entire civilizations while she'd been in the interface chair on board the derelict.

'Interpret away,' she said.

'I managed to narrow down the time the derelict was built by a little more,' he continued. 'And it was created at least a few millennia *before* the Shoal claim they developed the transluminal drive.'

'So that nails it pretty conclusively. Some other species possessed the transluminal drive—'

'And then they encountered the Shoal, who now claim to be the only species in the entire Milky Way to have the technology,' Corso confirmed.

'And you're sure about that?'

Corso shrugged. 'Hard to say without getting a lot more time to go over the data. There's decades of work still in there.'

An overwhelming sense of weariness came over Dakota. She was still badly rattled from Kieran's assault, and there were times when she felt overwhelmed by the constant flow of recent events.

'Fuck it,' she said, her voice small and quiet, and pushed herself over to where Corso sat. She laid her head against his chest. After his initial surprise, he let one hand fall down to rest on her shoulder.

'You know,' she murmured at length, 'I hate Free-holders. I mean, I really, really hate the fucking lot of you. You realize that, don't you?'

'I could tell,' came Corso's dry response, 'from the way you seem to have your hand on my dick.'

It started with an awkward fumbling during which Corso managed to bash his elbow hard on the corner of the seat. Then they both slid further down, both laughing, and Dakota pressed her face against his. That was how she remembered it: a classic first-kiss scenario after a stumbling beginning, so different from the artificial attentions of the *Piri*'s faux-human effigy. From the enthusiasm with which Corso responded to her advances, it was clear it had been some time for him too.

In fact, over the next several minutes, her suspicion grew that it had been a very long time indeed for Corso. His technique didn't exactly match his enthusiasm, but Dakota couldn't care less. She shouldered her way out of her clothes in record time while Corso still fumbled with his belt, a hilariously embarrassed look on his face.

In the end, once he'd finally got out of his clothes, she climbed on top of him, despite the look of clear puzzlement on his face. She guessed he wasn't very likely to be familiar with sex in zero gravity.

He grunted with surprise when she twisted her hips in a practised way (some things, she mused, you never really forgot) and found himself deep inside her.

Corso cleared his throat in between deep, shuddering breaths. 'Back home, you know, usually the man—'

'Where I come from, usually the man shuts the fuck up,' Dakota gasped.

Completely nonplussed, Corso looked so ridiculous she giggled, as if the air in the cabin had suddenly been flooded with nitrous oxide.

Shame, she thought, *to have forgotten how good sheer, wild abandonment feels.* Revelations of the senses: a cool flush presented itself deep between her thighs and she realized he'd come already. Yet she didn't feel disappointed: she stayed where she was, balanced on top of him, leaning forward to put her hands on his chest for traction while he gripped onto a furry bulkhead (having almost floated off him a couple of times to begin with), and after several more seconds she came herself.

The orgasm rattled through her, peaking in an explosion somewhere behind her eyes and deep within her brain. Her skin was now flushed and beaded with perspiration. She held onto him for a few more moments, despite the pained expression on his face as her fingernails dug in.

When she finally let go, he emitted a small, almost silent sigh of relief.

'Sorry, didn't mean to hurt you,' she breathed.

Corso cleared his throat. When he finally spoke, his voice sounded thick and broken. 'I . . . no problem. I didn't even notice.'

'Liar.'

The beginnings of a grin tweaked the edge of his mouth. 'Harlot.'

She grinned back. 'Yes?'

A while later they floated together in the deep cocoon darkness of Dakota's sleeping quarters.

'What's the problem?' she asked, sensing his restlessness.

'Can't sleep easily in zero gee,' he explained. They

floated against one fur-lined wall. 'And to be honest, this fur stuff creeps me out a little.'

'That's all?'

'Well, no,' he admitted. 'Haven't really been able to sleep ever since I got on board the *Hyperion*. I keep waking up and thinking I've fallen out of bed back home – but I'm still falling . . .'

'Yeah. That's a familiar one.' By now, sleeping in zero gee felt like the most natural thing in the world to Dakota. The only possible improvement on it was having a warm naked body next to hers, so all her bases were pretty much now covered.

'You know, I've been thinking,' he mumbled.

'Yeah?'

'If the *Hyperion* is compromised the way you say it is, any data I've recovered from the derelict is probably accessible to your alien friend by now.'

'What are you saying?'

'Perhaps it was the Shoal-member that somehow caused the derelict to attack us, by using what it found in the *Hyperion*'s stacks. But that's all conjecture: there's no way of being sure.'

'Remember what I told you, Lucas. The *Piri Reis* is stealthed to the eyeballs. There's no reason you couldn't read the same data into the *Piri*'s stacks, and bypass the *Hyperion* altogether.

'Think about it.' She really had his attention now. 'You could query the *Hyperion*'s stacks from here, even send low-level commands from here direct to the derelict. Everything would be disguised as routine sub-system comms and, frankly, your people don't have the means to spot the deception.'

Corso unravelled himself from her, clearly thinking hard. 'You know, I wasn't entirely being honest when I said we couldn't pilot the derelict just yet.'

Now he had *her* full attention.

'Do you mean . . .?'

'I lied, yes.'

'Because?'

'Because I wanted to make things as hard for the Senator as possible. Maybe you can understand that. But you could hypothetically control the derelict from the *Hyperion*'s bridge. I mean, you could link the *Hyperion*'s interface chair to the one on board the derelict.'

'But that chair was torn apart by the derelict, the same time it attacked you. I saw the recordings.'

'That's one reason I said "hypothetically". And, for what it's worth, every time a team has gone back on board the derelict following previous attacks, they found that any pieces of equipment left behind were still completely intact. The *Hyperion* doesn't appear to recognize inanimate objects like interface chairs as hostile, possibly because they're inorganic. Technically, you *could* set up a direct chair-to-chair link from the bridge and control the derelict that way.'

'So what are you saying?' she asked him excitedly. 'We could just . . . fly it out from under Arbenz's nose?'

He frowned. 'Whether it's practical or possible is

another matter. And even if we could somehow pull it off, there are other things we'd have to think about, such as what to do with the derelict if we got away with it? And that's not even taking into account the fact we'd still need to get ourselves on board the derelict in order to make an escape. And we already know that it can be lethally dangerous, even at the best of times.'

Dakota's eyes gleamed with the possibilities. 'I don't have to be inside the bridge interface chair to control the *Hyperion*, you know.'

Corso looked confused. 'You don't?'

'Look, there are good reasons for using interface chairs. If anyone with the appropriate implants is able to control a ship without resorting to its interface chair, then you're faced with the risk of an enemy machine-head slipping on board and taking it over instantly. So the chairs are there as a kind of security measure, to prevent that happening. But that's not to say one can't be bypassed. However, the only one who has the necessary stack permissions to do that is a ship's designated pilot.'

'Which is you.'

'Which is me.'

'And that way you can control the *Hyperion* without actually being anywhere near the bridge?'

'More than that. If I can run the *Hyperion* from elsewhere, it means that once I have a ship-to-ship link set up from the bridge, I might be able to run the derelict remotely as well.'

Corso laughed and shook his head in wonder.

'Things have come a long way since the *Hyperion* was built,' she explained. 'The interface chairs we have now are a lot newer and more advanced than anything else originally existing on the bridge. We can take advantage of that fact.'

'OK,' he said, thinking ahead. 'That still doesn't get us on board the derelict without risking another attack from it, though.'

She'd already managed to think of this problem in a sudden blaze of creativity. 'The *Piri* is tiny next to the derelict. Why not secure the *Piri* to the derelict's hull before we use it to make a transluminal jump? There are buckytube cables on board for securing it to small asteroids, or to the surface of larger ones. No reason I couldn't do the same, in this case.'

'But that's not all we'd have to do,' he argued. 'Even if you manage all this, and create an uplink with the derelict, it doesn't matter how stealthed the *Piri Reis* is, because everyone on the *Agartha*, on the *Hyperion* and on Theona will soon know what you're doing. And that doesn't even take into account how the alien hiding in the *Hyperion*'s stacks would react. Or the fact you'll still have to be physically on the bridge and in the chair before you can create the uplink in the first place, and that means somehow getting past the crew.'

Corso had momentarily forgotten the incongruity of the situation: the two of them discussing life and death matters while floating naked together in a fur-lined spaceship. Dakota took his face in her hands, an almost feral expression of glee on her own.

'You're altogether too much of a defeatist. If we induce a general systems failure in the *Hyperion*'s stacks, same as the one I had to deal with just after I got on board, every sensor, every security system and every piece of recording equipment on the *Hyperion* is going to have a brainstorm. The Shoal-member would be deaf, dumb and blind for at least a couple of minutes, while the stacks were down. That would give us just enough time to create a cloaked uplink before the *Hyperion*'s systems have time to reboot.'

'You're still taking a hell of a risk,' Corso argued, trying to sound calm and reasonable but in fact clearly more stressed with each passing second. 'You still haven't told me how you'll get past the crew.'

'There's no reason they wouldn't assume I was just doing my job if I got in that chair.'

She sat back and studied Corso's glum expression. He wasn't happy – but she knew she'd won this one.

Dakota could feel the Shoal-member's presence as she found her way back into the main body of the *Hyperion*, navigating a central drop shaft running the entire length of the ship's spine on her way to the bridge.

'You,' she said quietly to the empty air, 'have got something to hide.'

'Blunt accusations, much foaming of water,' the

reply boomed through hidden speakers in the walls of the shaft. 'To accuse is to diminish within eye of beholder fish.'

She grabbed hold of a rung and made a right-angle turn, letting herself drop at a steady, graceful pace down another shaft until she snagged a convenient handhold with one foot.

She wondered if the crew could hear the alien speaking to her over the comms system, and why he would therefore choose to announce his presence in this way. If they could hear him, they'd probably be panicking by now, which meant she'd find it that much harder to slip by them. She began to really wish she'd kept her mouth shut.

'You know, I think you're trying too hard. Care to answer a riddle?' she asked, adrenalin pumping through her head. She felt like she could climb outside the hull and run sprint marathons around its circumference. But she was terrified beyond words.

'Riddles, yes? A conundrum to while away eternity's hours,' came the answer.

'Two riddles, really. Here's the first one. There's been very little real contact with individual members of the Shoal since we first encountered your species – probably no more than a couple of dozen times in all. Everything pivotal that's ever happened in the history of the Consortium, there's been one of your kind present, almost as if you're somehow making things happen.'

It was a popular conspiracy theory, and not one

Dakota might normally subscribe to. However, under the present circumstances, she found herself prepared to entertain wilder ideas than she might do otherwise.

'First you boot the Uchidans off their homeworld without explanation. Then they land on Redstone and try to throw the Freehold off theirs, something I'd have thought way beneath your interest. Yet one of your people was present, for some reason, in the Central Command ring the day before the massacres at Port Gabriel.'

She continued: 'Then the next time I see one of you, it's on Bourdain's Rock, and people want to blame *me* for what happened there. And now, suddenly, here we are almost literally in the middle of fucking nowhere, a derelict but viable alien starship under our feet, and . . . big surprise, here you are, too. It was you every time, wasn't it?'

'Enquiry to elucidate, with pleasure?'

Dakota gritted her teeth. The alien's word games were really beginning to get on her nerves. 'You're the one that calls himself Trader. You were there on Redstone, and then Bourdain's Rock, and now you're here, like a bad shadow following me everywhere. What's your full name again?'

She already knew it, but somehow she needed to hear the creature repeat it. 'Trader-In-Faecal-Matter-Of-Animals,' he replied. 'And you are correct.'

'You know,' she said, relishing the opportunity to give vent, 'it really gives some indication of how little you regard us as a species that the name you use when you're around us is a seriously tasteless joke.'

'This one is forced to point out that circumstances remain unaltered from present: vis-à-vis relationship you and I, no change. Agreed?'

She was almost at the bridge by now. She slowed her progress, taking her time in case she ran into any of Arbenz's skeleton crew. She had no idea what she was going to say to them when the time came, but could see no reason for them to keep her from the interface chair. If she was wrong about that . . . well, she'd just have to deal with it when the time came.

'What happened to the race that built the derelict?' she asked, realizing the creature was baiting her. 'Where are they now? It has a transluminal drive dating from long before your species were supposed to have developed the technology, so just what are you trying to hide here?'

A secure link via her Ghost allowed her to observe Corso's handiwork as he covertly hacked away at the *Hyperion*'s stacks from inside the *Piri Reis*. She had to hand it to him: he knew exactly what he was doing. Any lingering concerns faded regarding his expertise with computer systems.

Trader refused to be drawn, though. Instead of answering, he continued blithely, as if anything she had to say was of little or no concern to him.

But then she reminded herself that the alien very much had the advantage. Everything she and Corso had planned for the next few minutes depended on him not picking up on their attempt to take control of the derelict.

'Of highest tantamount importance in approaching task of cataclysmic destruction is appreciation that the object of our concern, in order to be rendered non-existent, cannot be destroyed by means conventional. Ergo, consideration of alternatives is necessitated.'

Dakota reached the gravity wheel and pulled herself up a series of rungs, feeling the tug of centrifugal force from the rotation of the *Hyperion*'s wheel segment, the higher she got. She climbed into a corridor in the wheel's inner rim whose floor curved out of sight.

'Who built the derelict, Trader? You're holding all the cards. Why not just tell me?'

'Please regard that derelict in question rests – chance and circumstance be thanked – upon the very precipice of a mighty abyss. A most advantageous and opportunistic means of destruction is thereby presented: to be sent tumbling into welcoming and bottomless embrace of mother ocean, is also to be squeezed and squeezed until boom! Derelict is at an end. How so, therefore, to reach accomplishment of this mighty and noble task? Placing of explosives conventional, certainly. Or activation of secondary propulsion systems, to allow such an unfortunate event to most merrily happenstance. All to be considered by this one called Dakota. Rescued, recall, please, from certain blackness of death aboard space-bound asteroid by this one. Surely, to indicate refusal in our current concern is equivalent to expression of churlishness, given my life-saving kindness?'

Keep him talking. Anything, to divert the majority of his consciousness away from Corso's hacking.

As it turned out, she had little to worry her, once she entered the bridge. The crew were dead.

It was unusual in itself to find the emergency seal on the entrance to the bridge activated when she got there. She reached up and deactivated it by hand, using a panel on the wall.

When the seal slid back, revealing the bridge's interior, she stared at the scene before her with numb horror.

It wouldn't take a genius to figure out that Trader must have locked the crew into the bridge deck, sealed the emergency exits, and then voided the life-giving atmosphere.

By the looks of things, two of the crewmembers had made a concerted effort to open the emergency seals from the inside. They lay just inside the doorway, staring sightlessly upwards, their tongues protruding from their mouths.

At least I have my filmsuit. Trader couldn't possibly know about that. Even if he did, he'd still have to be a lot more inventive than this if he chose to hurt her.

She slowly picked her way past the two corpses. The other four crewmembers were all huddled by an open floor panel. Dakota averted her gaze from their faces, frozen in terror, guessing they'd been desperately trying to access bypass circuits as they'd died.

'An unfortunate matter, but necessary,' the alien's voice boomed from the bridge's comms system. 'For them to be allowed interference in requisite destruction of derelict would be unforgivably remiss.'

Dakota nodded, still unable to find her voice. Her throat felt like something large and heavy had been lodged halfway down it, and she had a particularly nasty taste in the back of her mouth.

She watched as the petals of the interface chair began to unfold, unbidden.

'Look, they'll know by now, on the *Agartha* and down on the moon, that the crew are dead. I'll never be allowed to get as far as the derelict and do what you want. And you know I can't do anything from up here.'

'Interface, contrary to clear untruth, awaits your embrace, and is linked in readiness to identical device aboard derelict. Sufficient control for destruction may be manifested from here.'

Her heart sank as she realized the alien was a step ahead of them. 'And what happens when Arbenz comes back up here? Who do you think he's going to blame for . . . for this carnage?'

Of course.

She was being set up – had been set up, ever since Bourdain's Rock.

The alien was covering its tracks, so that it would appear only she was responsible for the destruction of the derelict and the murder of the *Hyperion*'s crew: a wake of death and destruction, indeed. Corso hadn't been so far off the mark then.

'In order to achieve maximized disaster,' the creature continued, 'and to prevent immediate discorporation of Dakota most delightful, absolute cooperation is presently necessitated.'

Her Ghost flagged up a message from Corso. But before she had a chance to read it, she felt something pressing in on her thoughts . . .

She shook her head, feeling dizzy. She looked up and saw a computer-generated image of Trader, floating in the screens arranged all around the bridge.

'My life won't be worth shit if I do what you want. I . . .'

She stopped. There was something she had to do, something very urgent. She –

– was standing next to the open interface chair, one hand resting on the folded shape of a steel and plastic petal. She couldn't even remember having crossed the bridge to reach the chair.

There was another message from Corso now, this one marked highest priority. She faltered, and there it was again, pressing in on her thoughts –

– she found herself in darkness.

Dakota reeled, and realized she was seated inside the activated interface chair, with no memory of having climbed inside it or of the petals enfolding her. She gasped with the shock of this sudden dislocation. It felt like being buried alive.

More, she was mind-linked into the second interface, the one on board the derelict. For a moment it lay wide open to her, a universe of data waiting to be pored over –

And then it was gone.

She gasped as the connection was suddenly, deliberately cut.

<Dakota!> It was Corso, speaking from inside the *Piri Reis*. <I went ahead and activated the systems crash myself once you were in the chair. What happened up there? Why didn't you respond? I thought I'd lost you.>

I'm not sure. I . . . I just blacked out for a second, or something. The Shoal-member was talking to me from inside the stacks. The crew are all dead.

<What? Hang on a second while I . . . oh shit.> Clearly he'd accessed the bridge video feed recorded a few moments before crashing the onboard systems. <What happened in there?>

Nothing to do with me, I assure you.

<I – shit, have you made the uplink yet?>

No. But I will now.

<Listen, it's not about to get any better. There's a shuttle up from Theona, way ahead of schedule. It should be docking about now.>

They've probably come looking for the crew. I don't even know how long they've been dead.

<Then you're going to have to get the hell back here before they find you.>

There. Barely a thought and the derelict was now linked directly into the *Piri Reis*, without first passing through the *Hyperion*. In data terms it was like turning a tap and getting a trickle compared to the ocean of data she'd just tasted for one mesmerizing moment. It was a bare snatch of what she'd experienced while on board the derelict itself.

Even so, she reached out with her senses, and felt the control data from the interface chair aboard the derelict smoothly mesh with her Ghost. It felt like gaining a new set of limbs – but limbs that felt numb and weak and sluggish in their response.

But she still had control of the derelict.

It's done, Lucas. The uplink is in place.

Except, against all her expectations, nothing felt different. Instead of feeling victorious, Dakota felt mildly disappointed.

The chair's petals unfolded from around her. The image of Trader had gone. Overhead displays and status lights around the bridge had fallen into grey, unresponsive dullness. Pale red emergency lighting lent an awful, surreal quality to the horror and carnage that surrounded her.

<All right. Looks like we've got more problems,> Corso informed her. <The *Hyperion* is recovering far faster than I'd have expected.>

Are you serious?

At that moment, she sensed the *Hyperion*'s few still-active systems disappearing out of reach of her Ghost.

<Never been more serious. There's what looks like a list of potential trajectories and orbits being run through the stacks right now. There's something big in there sucking up most of the processing power, which I guess proves what you were telling me about the Shoal AI.>

She gripped the arms of the interface chair in shock.

Well, it's nice to know you believed me in the first place.

<Fine, I apologize. The question now is, how much control do you actually have over the derelict?>

I can't be sure, Dakota replied. *It feels . . . different.*

<You don't say.>

Shut up, Lucas. I can . . .

Dakota closed her eyes and concentrated on the uplink: a long and fragile chain of communication.

The derelict became like an immense presence, brooding and dark, like a haunted house waiting to be explored. Immense energies flowed through it, yet it responded only sluggishly to her mental queries.

If I didn't know better, she told Corso, *I'd say something was deliberately trying to block my control of the derelict.*

Corso snarled with exasperation. <I'm going to pull as much data off the derelict as I can in the meantime, in case we lose the link. Guess we underestimated your friend. The best thing you can do is get back here before whoever's on that arriving shuttle finds you.>

*

Corso watched as a tsunami of information poured up and into the *Piri*'s stacks from deep under the moon's ice. Yet, rather than celebrating, he felt merely haggard, run down and exhausted. The few hours he'd spent asleep, curled up with Dakota, hadn't been nearly enough. That, plus nearly getting killed on board the derelict – and *that* following the torture and beating of Dakota herself – conspired to wipe away his remaining ability to concentrate.

He located the *Piri*'s autodoc menu and dialled up an amphetamine concoction, hoping it might do the trick for him. Dakota's little ship could do a hell of a lot on its own, but there were limits to all things. He had to be awake and aware in order to supervise the uplink as long as it lasted.

The *Piri* pinged him a minute later. He'd earlier programmed it to let him know if it stumbled across anything particularly interesting, or plain coherent, among the data delivered from the derelict. He touched a screen and scanned the information appearing there. *Ah*.

It had found what appeared at first glance to be a narrative: a myth cycle, perhaps, or maybe a simple record of events. It possessed the grandeur of the former, yet the brief, synopsized facts before him now suggested the latter.

He took a closer look, and what he saw appeared to confirm the Magi had, indeed, originated from a specific section of the Larger Magellanic Cloud.

Come on, come on. He rubbed his hands impatiently through his hair as he waited. There were gaps of inactivity, lasting seconds long, as the *Piri* jumped from one set of incoming data to another.

Corso could discern that whatever was lurking deep within the *Hyperion*'s data stacks was recovering a lot faster than he could possibly have anticipated. He meanwhile sat at a console, muttering, as he tried to coax the *Hyperion*'s emergency support systems into accepting his override commands, in an attempt to prevent or at least stall the alien intelligence inside the stacks . . .

The *Piri* spasmed. A screech of static lasting perhaps all of a second burst out through the speakers, and the main screen went black for several moments before reasserting itself.

'*Piri*! Status report!'

'All systems operational,' came the verbalized reply.

'What just happened? Everything went crazy for a second.'

'All systems operational,' came the *Piri*'s reply again. 'Levels of data being drawn into my stacks are sufficient to cause resource allocation problems. This is forcing periodic outages.'

Sweat prickled Corso's skin. The *Piri*'s primary systems were like nothing they had back on Redstone; its inherent skills of machine deduction and analysis were light years ahead of anything Corso had ever worked with before. It was possible the *Piri* was having problems with the sheer quantity of data available to it, but somehow he found it all too easy to believe Dakota's invisible intruder was trying to subvert the *Piri*.

'*Piri*! Use the interpretation protocols to grab any-thing else deemed relevant, download it now, and abort the rest!'

Better safe than sorry, he had decided, and, besides, time was running out before the alien would regain control of the *Hyperion* and then realize that the termin-ation point for the current flood of data lay in the cargo bay.

'Cease interface in a maximum of fifteen seconds, no traces. Got that?'

'Understood,' came the reply.

Now he just had to wait for Dakota to make it back aboard.

He cast his eye over the fresh data drawn from the derelict and, as he read it, almost forgot how to breathe.

Dakota made to exit the bridge, and found Udo Mansell approaching down the corridor towards her. A long scar cut across his forehead, now pink and smooth from an autodoc's booster treatments. Patches of skin on his face looked new and shiny.

She gasped in astonishment, taking a step back as he moved in on her.

'When did you—'

He punched her hard, and she stumbled back in sur-prise, sprawling across the metal grilles that comprised the deck of the *Hyperion*'s bridge.

She rolled on all fours and put a hand to her nose in shock. At least, she thought, it wasn't bleeding.

Udo looked unfocused, clearly still fighting off the side-effects of his medication. She guessed that he'd climbed out of his medbox only in the last few minutes. 'How stupid, exactly, do you think I am?' he roared, bunching his fists again. 'How often do you think you can pull off shit like this and get away with it?'

'I haven't—'

Udo stepped forward, then swung his leg back and delivered a tremendous kick to Dakota's ribs. She bounced off a bulkhead, too little air left in her shocked lungs to scream.

'Oh, I'm up to date on everything that's going on around here, and you can thank my dear brother for that. He came and visited me in the medical bay and we talked. How we talked. He told me of all your deceptions, even your murder of one of your own. Now he's in the medical bay himself and barely able to stand. So, tell me,' Udo screamed, 'where is Corso? Where – the fuck – is – he?'

'I don't know, Udo,' she pleaded. 'For God's sake, did Kieran tell you to—'

'I don't need my brother to tell me anything, you implant-ridden whore. Where is *Corso*?' Udo bellowed, fists clenched at his sides. 'He doesn't appear on the monitoring systems, so *where the fuck is he*?'

*

Corso stepped back from the console, feeling stiff and sore after spending long minutes rigid with shock.

He rubbed at his eyes, thinking it strange how the woman who owned this ship had started out as his enemy, yet he now felt closer to her – felt more in common with her – than any other human being he'd ever met.

That was when he noticed the figurine for the first time.

Dakota was far from being tidy-natured. Anyone moving through the cramped interior of her ship was continually banging into things: small decorative items pinned to the walls, or bizarrely floating on strands of fine filigree. Other mementoes and objects that might be tiny pieces of artwork had been epoxied, apparently at random, to every surface. Others floated free, waiting to smack the unwary in the head when least expected.

He instantly recognized the figurine as of Uchidan origin, and suddenly recalled Dakota telling him how she had received it on her first encounter with the Shoal-member on Bourdain's Rock. It was clearly modelled on the famous statue of Belle Trevois.

Belle Trevois herself had been a thirteen-year-old girl born to a family on Leverrier II during the Diaspora Conflict, more than a century before. Her parents, previously devout members of Moscba Org, lost everything they possessed during the siege on the Hubbard Spaceport, and then converted to the Uchidan faith, which required accepting the Light Of Truth implants central to the Uchidan belief system.

That could hardly have been an easy decision, considering several other Uchidan converts had already been murdered on Leverrier. It was the height of the war, and Uchidans in general were widely suspected of being spies. Yet their conversion could easily have been an entirely pragmatic decision, since the Uchidans had no involvement in the Org's conflict, and therefore could obtain free passage into orbit.

Unfortunately for Belle, her parents made the stunningly inept decision to permit the Uchidan medician-priests to also place implants inside the skull of their daughter. These implants subsequently took control of Belle's limbic system, generating the same technologically induced sense of perpetual spiritual ecstasy that her parents had already embraced. Word got out, and what had been merely sporadic violence against the Uchidans on Leverrier II escalated exponentially over the following weeks, fuelled by moral outrage.

Up to that point, Belle and her family had been taking refuge in an Uchidan temple in the heart of Leverrier's capital city, Ville d'Aiguille. Consortium-mediated negotiations failed to resolve the political situation and wide-scale rioting broke out. As things turned rapidly ugly, rioters broke into the temple and murdered everyone they found, including Belle and her parents, a few hours before they'd been due to finally be lifted into orbit aboard neutral tugs.

Overall, it had been an ugly, nasty business and, in the following decades, Uchidans everywhere had raised Belle Trevois to the status of a martyr, a symbol of their repression. Statues of her, with arms flung outwards, could be found in most Uchidan temples throughout the Consortium, or at least in those still allowed to exist. Even Corso, a loyal Freeholder, had to admit that the crimes committed against the Uchidans were far worse than those they were accused of.

And here she was again, on Dakota's ship of all places. Belle Trevois, in the form of a simple religious icon . . .

He stared at the figurine. Something wasn't right.

'*Piri*,' Corso asked aloud, 'where did Dakota acquire this?'

'On Bourdain's Rock.'

'Remind me how.'

'It was given to her by one of the Shoal race.'

Corso exhaled long and slow. 'Was that interaction recorded in any way? Sight and sound, visuals, anything like that?'

'Yes,' the ship replied with typical machine-like pedantry.

'Can I see those records?'

'No. Dakota's direct permission is required.'

Scratch that then. But so far the ship had supported what Dakota had told him.

Let me think. Let me think . . . Belle was an involuntary martyr, because she hadn't chosen her faith.

Instead, it had been imposed on her, like a kind of mental rape.

'Port Gabriel,' said Corso. 'Dakota was at Port Gabriel, correct?'

'Yes.'

'There was a massacre.'

'Correct.'

Feeling fairly hopeless, Corso tried acting on a hunch. '*Piri*, is there anything at all in that incident pertaining to Belle Trevois?'

'A Uchidan military transport named the *Belle Trevois* crashed there during the first war with the Freehold, but some years prior to the incident in question.'

Corso nodded, finally recalling old, half-forgotten history lessons. The Uchidans had long ago placed a small statue of Belle on the exact same spot where their transport had crashed. The statue still stood, even now, having become famous after the massacres. For years afterwards it kept cropping up again and again in news reports and articles about the Port Gabriel incident.

'How about records of when Dakota placed that figurine on the imaging plate in the bridge?'

'Those records have been deleted.'

He hadn't expected that. 'Deleted by whom?'

'By Dakota.'

'Don't you think it's strange that an alien would give a statue of Belle Trevois, of all people, to a woman whose implants had been forcibly compromised by Uchidan ideology? Why would it do that?'

'This question is not understood.'

Corso had forgotten he wasn't talking to a true intelligence, just to a machine. He carried on thinking aloud regardless. 'None of this would be remarkable except for her telling me she didn't know what the figurine represented or where it came from. But how could she *not* know?'

If there was any one image most commonly associated with the Port Gabriel disaster, it was that statue.

'*Piri*, is there any way to insert a contact virus into inert matter, something that could get inside a machine-head's Ghost circuits the same way information can be read through an imager plate?'

'There are research papers on record concerning such speculative technology. However, all attempts at identifying a reliable delivery method, without the use of imaging technology, have proved extremely inconclusive.'

Corso couldn't rid his head of the idea that something had got inside Dakota the same way it had wormed its way inside the *Hyperion*. This felt like an unusually fragile chain of logic, yet it appealed *precisely* because it made perfect sense of Dakota's more unusual behaviour.

*

Corso pulled the pressure suit back on and headed towards the bridge as fast as he could.

Even so, as he hurried, he misjudged angles in the zero gee environment, nearly knocking himself out at one point when he cannoned off a bulkhead after launching himself hard down a drop shaft. He'd been locked away in sleepless research in his quarters so long he'd never properly learned how to navigate the gravity-free areas of the *Hyperion*.

Crashing against a wall at the far end of yet another drop shaft, he kicked his way into a connecting corridor, then, finally, felt a familiar tug deep in his bones as he pulled himself up into the gravity wheel.

He heard people yelling as he approached the bridge, and tried to put out of his mind the terrible secret he'd gained from the derelict.

The sight that confronted him upon his arrival there was so ghastly, so morbid, it belonged in the realm of the surreal. Half a dozen bodies lay scattered in various states of contortion, the expressions on their faces making it clear their deaths had been far from peaceful.

In the middle of it all stood Udo, panting hard, one fist gripping the lapel of Dakota's jerkin while she slumped beside him.

It looked like the man could barely stand. After a moment he turned and saw Corso, staring hard at him for long seconds before raising his other hand and pointing towards him.

'You. You're next.' Udo's extended hand wobbled, his index finger drawing patterns in the air.

'Let go of her,' yelled Corso. 'She's the one shot we have left at recovering the derelict. Arbenz will kill you if you harm her.'

'Fucking *machine-head* bitch!' Udo snarled, his lips curling in anger.

As he turned his attention back to Dakota, his fingers clenched into a fist. Dakota appeared to be awake, but no longer aware of her surroundings. Her blank gaze, surveying the bridge and Corso, was clearly seeing nothing.

Corso ran forward and tried to pull the girl away from Udo. The other man slammed him to the ground with ease, but in the process he'd let go of her.

As Corso pulled himself up, he saw Dakota looking straight towards him with that same calm, unfocused expression. Whatever she was seeing now, it was somewhere a long way from the bridge of the *Hyperion*. It was the same look she'd given him that time near the airlocks.

'We don't need her at all,' Udo slurred. 'She's better off dead.'

Dakota suddenly came to life. Moving with inhuman fluidity and speed, she leapt up and spun around to face towards Udo, who barely had time to open his mouth in dazed surprise. Yet her face remained blank, empty of emotion.

Udo's knife appeared in his hand as if from nowhere

and he swung it towards her, but Dakota slithered out of reach so fast he might as well have been a motionless statue.

Corso stared, appalled, as she leapt on Udo's back, gripping his neck between her thighs and wrapping her arms tightly around his head. She twisted around on his shoulders with brutal efficiency in that same moment, and Corso heard a sickening snap.

Udo hadn't even had time to reach up towards her. Even in the lower-than-normal artificial gravity of the bridge, the skill and speed with which she had moved was startling.

Udo jerked violently and his knife fell to the floor. Dakota landed with delicate grace behind him as he collapsed to the deck, his head lolling at a strange angle as his body slumped lifelessly.

She focused on Corso with bright cold eyes, giving him the unpleasant realization that whatever was now looking at him through her eyes had decided to kill him next.

Suddenly her attention snapped away from Corso, to a point immediately behind him. She darted forward and he stumbled out of her path, turning just in time to see Gardner appear at the entrance to the bridge. Dakota slammed into the man and they both went down in a mess of tangled limbs.

Corso looked around desperately for anything he could use as a weapon. He spotted a box of stack components left lying next to a partially disembowelled control console, and headed unsteadily towards it. The components within appeared to be individually encased in solid steel, and felt good and hefty in his hands when he lifted one of them out.

Gardner was desperately fighting to push Dakota away from him, filling the air with his terrified screeching. When Corso went over and grabbed the edge of her jerkin, she suddenly peeled away from Gardner and leapt towards him instead. There was absolutely no sign that she recognized him at all.

Corso landed hard, felled by a punch he hadn't even seen coming. Her long fingers – those same fingers that had recently slid along the curve of his back in a lover's embrace – reached down to grab him hard by the testicles.

Corso choked and then screamed, lashing out with the reinforced component. By luck as much as by intention, it connected heavily with the side of her head. A clicking noise emerged from deep within Dakota's throat, and she floated free.

But she appeared to recover almost immediately, heading straight towards him again, her breath hissing harshly between bared teeth.

Corso waited until the last second, then decided any attempts at a gentle approach would probably end up getting him killed. He flung the stack component and it connected with her head a second time. She was knocked entirely unconscious and crumpled on the deck.

'Oh God.' Gardner was literally shaking with fear as he stood up. 'I thought . . . I thought she was going to kill me.'

'She was certainly aiming to,' Corso snapped. 'I need to . . .'

Need to do what, he wondered: take her to the med bay? No, Arbenz would surely have come up on the shuttle, bringing enforcements of some kind with him – assuming others weren't already on their way from the *Agartha*.

The *Piri Reis* was still the best bet he had. But even if he did manage to haul her back to her ship without being intercepted, what would happen when she finally woke? Would he be dealing with Dakota again, or something far more malevolent?

'Where are you going?' Gardner demanded, as Corso began dragging her out of the bridge.

'If Kieran Mansell or any of the rest of them get their hands on her, Mr Gardner, you can kiss your transluminal drive goodbye.'

'Stop, damn you. Stop!' Gardner's face was like thunder. 'Stop or I'll—'

Despite the pain lancing through him, Corso laughed as he watched Gardner's fists twisting at his sides in impotent rage. But Corso had long pegged him for a physical coward.

'There's nowhere for you to go,' Gardner almost pleaded, his voice breaking up. 'There are worse things than death, Mr Corso. They're your own people – you should already know that.'

'The two of us were already dead the moment either of us set foot on the *Hyperion*,' Corso replied. 'And you know it, so shut the hell up.' He finally managed to wrestle Dakota out into the corridor adjacent to the bridge. 'And you're just as expendable to them, Mr Gardner. Perhaps you should know that too.'

TWENTY-ONE

Redstone Colony
Consortium Standard Date: 03.06.2538
Port Gabriel Incident + twenty-five minutes

From the middle of the highway, Dakota stared at the line of approaching vehicles, one hand shading her eyes from the bright sun overhead.

For the first time she noticed the statue mounted on a shoulder-high plinth over to one side of the road. The statue itself was no more than perhaps two feet in height, as if a tiny figure had climbed on top of the granite plinth and raised its bronze hands to the skies in either triumph or despair.

Although she had never set eyes on the statue before, she identified it immediately.

What was curious about that sudden recognition was the knowledge that, until a few minutes ago, she could not possibly have known the significance of the statue or even who it represented. That, of course, was before the Uchidans had filled her with their Holy Purpose.

The statue, she now knew, was of Belle Trevois, the

martyr. The figure was stylized, its face smooth and blank, the body angular. Iron flames rose up behind to frame her, like the rays of the sun.

The statue had been badly vandalized. Freeholder graffiti had been scrawled across it, words like *mindfucked bitch* and *burn in hell*. The stylized metal flames had been bashed and bent out of shape, and the tools obviously used to do the damage still lay in the grass nearby: rusted engine tools and nondescript chunks of stone.

New information was being uploaded to her mind, couched in the soft caress of an angelic voice. She learned this was the spot where an orbital transport called the *Belle Trevois* had crashed long ago. Those who had then died here had long since entered God's embrace.

At least, once she was finished here, that was something for her to look forward to.

The loose and frequently contested border the Freehold shared with the Uchidans lay only seventy-five kilometres eastwards. The Freehold settlement of Port Gabriel lay – as Dakota's Ghost informed her – only thirteen kilometres to the east.

The same direction from which she could see the line of vehicles now approaching.

A familiar tingle announced itself in the back of her thoughts. Chris Severn! He was still alive. Dakota grinned widely. He didn't even need to verbalize anything for her to sense the same Holy Purpose he now also carried within him.

They were all in this together now, the legacy of Uchida having saved them from themselves. Dakota began to weep with sheer joy, the tears freezing instantly on her cheeks.

The first of the transports would be upon her in only a few minutes, but the road behind her was completely blocked by the crashed orbital transport. The approaching convoy appeared to be mostly made up of the kind of vehicles capable of leaving the road if they needed to, but for the moment Dakota stood between them and the next Freehold settlement lying to the west.

She glanced again at the vandalized statue and felt nothing but revulsion for what had been done to it.

From the direction of the nearest plumes of smoke staining the sky, three figures approached across the plains. All three, she sensed, were machine-heads, Chris Severn among them. Eventually he raised his hand and waved to her. Dakota raised her own hand and yelled back a greeting, her mouth opening wide in a happy smile under her breather mask.

She could hear the grumble of engines getting closer. The leading ground transport must by now have seen the way was blocked. The line of vehicles behind it straggled back maybe a couple of kilometres, and there weren't therefore as many as she'd first thought. Maybe a dozen in all, but really big vehicles: huge multi-tiered things with balloon wheels. She saw one in the distance carefully roll off the road, and slowly start making its way south-west.

As the approaching machine-heads jogged quickly towards her, the first transport began to slow on reaching the crash site, its silver carapace gleaming under the bright sun. She could see silhouettes of people in the wide windows pointing towards her and gesticulating. They looked like an average cross-section of Freeholders: men, women and a substantial number of children.

In the distance, the angel appeared once more, sword in hand, striding across the horizon in the direction of Port Gabriel. Its robes and face were hazy with distance. Dakota glanced to the side and saw the other machine-heads had seen it too.

The angel spoke to her.

<What is your name, child?>

Dakota, my Lord.

<Tell me, where are the rest of the Freeholder forces? And how many Consortium personnel are aboard the ships currently in orbit?>

Dakota tried to consult her Ghost circuits, but they weren't responding normally. Loud, angry, pleading voices burst through on one of the mil-comms frequencies, momentarily drowning out her thoughts and stridently demanding her obedience.

She decided she didn't want to listen to what they had to say, and cut them off.

I don't know, she replied. *I don't know. I . . . I can't find out.*

<You must tell me! I – What?>

Lord?

There was a sound rather like a muffled conversation somewhere inside Dakota's head. One of the voices was clearly that of the angel, and it was arguing with someone.

Something . . . something wasn't right. Dakota moaned and clutched at her head.

<We're losing her.>

What? Dakota couldn't figure out who had just spoken to her. She . . .

Bliss flooded her thoughts. Her determination to do right by her newly found faith was instantly restored.

<Dakota.>

It was the angel speaking, again. Everything was all right once more.

<Dakota, if you can't tell us any more, then you have failed God.>

Stunned shock. *What?*

<If there is nothing more you can tell us, then paradise is not yours, Dakota. Not now, and not ever, not in all eternity.>

Dakota began to weep again, feeling as if her soul had been wrenched clean from her body.

<You must tell us everything you know.>

But there wasn't anything more to tell.

I'm sorry. I meant it when I said I couldn't tell you anything else. I'm sorry. Please. I –

<Then you will never know eternal life under God.>

Dakota collapsed to her knees. She hadn't realized she could ever feel so bad, so lost.

What can I do?

<Your only possible hope of salvation now lies in killing the enemy. You must kill them, Dakota. They can never know God, but you have a chance. So kill them all.>

People were spilling out of the nearest of the ground transports, which had veered diagonally across the road as it approached the wrecked orbiter. They wore the distinctive clothing of Freeholders, a mixture of bright oranges and dull greys, along with their ubiquitous breather masks. They looked confused and scared, and only a very few of them appeared to be armed. She had the feeling none of these were the aggressive warrior-types she had so far encountered: by contrast, they were just ordinary people. Those few who did carry arms came towards Dakota as she waited there in the middle of the road.

Lines of light occasionally bisected the sky over their heads, accompanied by the odd flash of light, as if tiny stars were being briefly born, and just as rapidly dying, far above their heads. A silent battle filled the Redstone sky, far above them.

Voices came through to Dakota again, her superiors at the Circus Ring ordering her to lay down her arms.

She found it was getting easier, however, to tune them out.

One man stepped ahead of the rest of the Freeholders, a rifle gripped in both hands. Something in his demeanour convinced Dakota that he knew just how to use it. The rest trailed a little behind, obviously happy to let him take the lead.

She walked towards him, forcing a smile. 'We crashed,' she called out as the distance between them narrowed. 'Who are you? Are you people all right?'

The man with the rifle stopped, a wary look on his face. 'You're Consortium, right? I'm head of this convoy, and we're carrying refugees away from Port Gabriel.'

He glanced past Dakota's shoulder, but she'd already dragged the bodies of the Freehold dead back inside the orbiter's hull. 'Are there any machine-heads back there?'

'Why do you ask?' Dakota replied. She kept moving towards him, but he didn't lower his rifle. Behind him, she could see, a lot of children were emerging from the transport, looking lost and scared.

The two of them were almost face to face now, and she could hear the exhaustion in his voice as he replied: 'We were warned to get out, after we started hearing reports over our comms about machine-heads going crazy and killing people.' He nodded towards the distant plumes of smoke. 'I had the feeling maybe things aren't going too well for us right now.'

He was taking a good look at her for the first time,

and Dakota realized her stubbled scalp was still partly visible under the thin layer of insulation she'd pulled over her head. That was as good as holding up a banner announcing her machine-head status.

The Freeholder with the rifle suddenly backed away in alarm, levelling his weapon. She could see his knuckles turn white as he aimed at her chest.

The ensuing shot came from out of nowhere.

The approach of Severn and the others had been hidden by the ruined orbiter's hull as they made for the highway. None of the refugees had meanwhile been expecting danger to approach from off-road.

Part of the Freeholder's shoulder dissolved into red slurry and he collapsed with a shriek, writhing and gasping. His rifle clattered to the ground.

The refugees who had already disembarked scattered instantly. Most, but not all, ran back towards the ground transport they'd just stepped down from.

Dakota's Ghost informed her that Severn's companions were Elissa and Bryon. Bryon in particular looked like he'd endured a pretty rough landing, but it was also clear the Holy Spirit was doing a good job of keeping him going. Despite obvious pain, his eyes were bright with faith. All three of them were armed.

Chris Severn ran over to Dakota and hugged her, still gripping the pistol he'd just used to kill the Freeholder.

Shots sounded from the direction of the ground transport, where refugees were still cramming back on board. The nearest of the other transports had already started to retreat, reversing wildly back down the road. Dakota could see several ant-like figures milling outside a transport that had skidded into a long ditch. She wondered if they had good enough weapons to snipe them from that distance.

Dakota and the other three machine-heads instantly took cover behind the orbiter's hull. More shots headed their way and they began to return fire. They heard the shatter of glass, followed by terrified screams.

Elissa went down in a spray of blood as one Freeholder, who'd climbed on top of the transport, took her out with a carefully aimed shot when she momentarily broke cover. Bryon stood up and screamed in horrified anguish, before taking the sniper down with a fusillade of shots raining on to the transport's roof.

The huge vehicle's rear wheels spun and skidded, and then the whole thing tilted, one end sliding into the roadside ditch just a few metres away from the mutilated statue of Belle Trevois. Bryon pulled a slim black grenade out from inside his jacket and tossed it towards the transport with the last of his strength. When he began to shake violently, Dakota noticed his suit had been badly ripped during the past minute or so. He was freezing to death. Bryon pulled himself back under the shelter of the hull and curled up in a shivering, helpless ball.

It was all down to Severn and Dakota now.

They left Bryon where he lay and moved out from cover. As the grenade detonated, the whole front of the transport lifted a couple of metres off the road before crashing back down in flames amid shattering metal and glass. The body of the vehicle split open, spilling bodies out on the frozen highway, though the screams were fewer this time. Dakota and Severn ran towards the crippled transport.

The killing didn't take long. They both carried pistols capable of firing small explosive charges that they used to maximum effect. Their victims continued to scream, but most were now trapped inside the burning transport.

They burned just like Belle Trevois had burned at the hands of the rioters who had set her aflame inside the temple. They burned just like martyrs – but for Freeholders there could never be any salvation.

A few even managed to pull themselves free of the ruins of the transport, but Dakota and Severn chased after them relentlessly, shooting non-stop as they hurdled over the charred corpses already scattered across the frozen roadside.

Most of the refugees were not wearing protective gear or even breather masks, so only managed a few dozen metres before the intense cold took them down. Others tried to crawl to safety out of sight along the roadside ditch, but they were picked off easily enough. The freezing cold would probably have dealt with them anyway, but Dakota wanted to be thorough.

And then there was only the sound of flames licking over the exposed bones of the ground transport, and the high-pitched blowing of the wind from over the mountains.

The angel was gone, as thoroughly as if it had never been there.

Severn was shivering so violently, at first Dakota thought his insulation suit must have ripped too. But it wasn't that.

'Dak . . . Dakota. Listen to me, Dakota.'

He had fallen to his knees, staring at the desolation around them. Dakota was at a loss about what to do next.

The air all about was stained with the acrid fumes of the burning ground transport. Dakota knelt by Severn and put a hand on his shoulder.

'What is it?'

'The angel. Where's it gone?'

'I don't know, Chris. Are you all right?'

'No.' His shivering became worse. He brought his pistol in close to his chest, hugging it there in both hands as if he were cradling a baby. 'Something's wrong, Dakota. Something's really very wrong.'

Dakota tried to deny it at first, but something *was* wrong, a sense of unease that had been growing within her for several minutes. At first she couldn't figure out what it was.

The voices from the Circus Ring came back to harangue and plead with her again. They were getting harder and harder to ignore.

'We'll be fine, Chris. We'll be fine.'

'No. No, we won't. We won't be fine at all.' He looked at the landscape around them, at the devastation, as if seeing it for the first time. 'What just happened here?'

'We were carrying out—'

God's purpose?

No, that wasn't it. Then what?

Dakota squeezed her eyes shut. Alerts flashed at the edge of her awareness, clamouring for her full attention. She tried to make them go away but they wouldn't – not this time.

Then she became aware that the presence that had filled her all through the crash-landing and beyond was gone now, and with it the ineffable sense of majestic, holy purpose that had filled her. It felt like waking up from the worst nightmare imaginable.

She turned to Chris and opened her mouth to say something but, before she had time to utter so much as a syllable he shoved his pistol in his mouth and pulled the trigger. Dakota screamed as his body was thrown back across the roadside by the force of the shot.

She stumbled and fell to the ground, her fingers clawing the hard road surface, her terrified gasps sounding metallic and hollow inside her breather.

After a while, she regained some control over herself. She was Dakota Merrick, and a machine-head. She was a pilot for the Consortium.

All around her lay the bodies of the dead. Too many of them were children.

She crawled over to Severn. There was still the faint flutter of a pulse, but he'd probably be dead within minutes. Perhaps that was for the best.

She lifted herself up and surveyed the scene more calmly. She then started to walk away from the wrecked ground transport, away from the orbiter, moving in the direction of Port Gabriel.

There were even more plumes of smoke rising from that direction than the last time she looked. Dakota stopped and glanced over at the roadside statue, its hands still thrusting skywards in mute agony. It started to rain.

She remembered everything. She remembered too much.

TWENTY-TWO

Dakota started to come round again after a couple of minutes. Corso felt her take a firm grip on his shoulder as he hauled her towards a service lift leading to the centre of the gravity wheel and to zero gee.

Dakota mumbled, her words slurred and mashed together. He tensed instinctively, fearing that she might attack him again. After a moment she opened her eyes and focused on his face.

'Corso?'

It was barely a mumble, but he nearly wept with gratitude. Whatever had taken her over previously had relinquished its control – at least for the moment.

'Come on, Dakota.' He dragged her on to the elevator, an open platform used for transferring equipment from the ship's centre to the inner circumference of the wheel and to the bridge.

The elevator started moving at a painfully slow pace, but Corso felt the gravity drop rapidly away.

Once he had her out of the elevator, however, it was like trying to steer a boulder upstream. He'd kick off from one wall at the extreme end of a drop shaft, pulling

Dakota after him, but the problem was in judging their combined momentum. And, just when he thought he had her aimed right, she'd twist within his grasp and send them both sailing towards a side wall.

Then, more often than not, he'd have to try and get between her and the approaching hard surface before she collided and injured herself. A couple of minutes of this manoeuvring left him feeling like he'd been worked over by a couple of seriously pissed-off giants with fists made of stone.

Dakota moaned and blinked, apparently becoming more aware of her surroundings.

'Get back,' Dakota mumbled. '*Piri.*'

'That's right, Dakota. Back to the *Piri.*'

He could have cried with joy when they finally came to the complex of passageways and shafts surrounding the cargo bay.

'Corso . . .' Dakota's expression was still hazy and unfocused. 'Wait, I . . .'

'We're almost there.'

Corso was still wearing his pressure suit. Once he'd got them both inside the airlock leading into the bay, he noticed with a start that the air had started cycling out too soon. He panicked, realizing he wouldn't have time to get Dakota into a suit as well before the air pressure dropped to zero.

Then something very strange happened.

In a flash, a black, oil-like substance spread out across Dakota's skin from under her clothes, till it was covering her completely. Even her hair flattened under this tide, the substance bubbling also into her nostrils and spilling deep into her mouth, forming a smooth membrane over her parted lips in barely a moment or two. He let go of her instantly, backing against the far wall of the airlock in horrified fascination as the door leading into the cargo bay swung open.

His first thought was that this oil-like substance that had swallowed Dakota was the alien presence she claimed had taken over the *Hyperion*: some liquid monstrosity that had been hiding inside her, rather than that insidious presence being the Shoal-member as she had claimed earlier.

However, Dakota showed no sign of struggling or thrashing around, as surely she must do if either suffocating or experiencing distress. He could see the steady, calm rise and fall of her chest.

Forcing himself to overcome his terror, he gingerly reached out and grabbed the edge of her jerkin. The others would be hunting for them, and it was only a matter of time before they came to investigate the cargo bay once they concluded there was nowhere else to look. He hauled Dakota after him into the vast interior space and struggled to guide her towards the *Piri*.

The *Piri*'s external airlock automatically cycled open as he dragged and shoved her towards it.

Once they were safely inside, Corso pulled off the headpiece of his suit and took a moment to recover his breath. His whole body seemed a solid mass of aches and pains. It was easier to take light, shallow breaths. Gradually, the pain became a little more bearable.

Dakota had drifted away from him, apparently unconscious, finally coming to rest against a fur-lined bulkhead. He watched as the black oil that had coated her flesh receded once more, apparently draining away into whatever hidden receptacle it lurked within.

He looked around for some way to secure her in case she turned violent again. First he guided Dakota into an acceleration couch, wrapping the webbing tight around her supine form. Her skin felt clammy to the touch, but at least she was still breathing normally. Finally he pulled her wrists behind her back and used a piece of loose webbing to bind her.

'Please remove the restraints from Dakota.'

It was the *Piri Reis* speaking. 'Please comply,' it continued, 'or I will use countermeasures against you.'

'It's me, Lucas Corso. She's injured. Her Ghost's been compromised.'

He let himself float against one wall and grabbed at another handhold to keep him in place. 'Dakota gave me the necessary access privileges, *Piri*. You can accept my commands.'

Dakota mumbled something he couldn't comprehend, and pulled against her restraints.

'Nonetheless, I require the restraints to be removed from the owner of this vessel. Be warned, I am equipped for lethal force.'

'*Piri!*' he shouted, venting all the frustration and anger

he'd put to one side during his long struggle to get Dakota back to the cargo bay. 'Look at the records for the bridge. Look at what happened. *I* got her out of there.'

'I am now initiating countermeasures. Please be warned that—'

'Listen to what I'm saying! Infective routines have been placed in Dakota's Ghost circuits.'

Corso floated towards a programming interface.

'Please do not approach the interface.'

'*Piri*, just trust me. Please.'

It was useless trying to plead with a machine, but Corso couldn't help himself. 'Look inside her and see if I'm wrong.' He reached out to the console and tapped at the screen, which blossomed into life at his touch.

He'd half expected the *Piri* to zap him immediately like a fly, but nothing happened. Obviously enough of what he was saying got past its security algorithms so as to give it some cause for delay. 'I'm releasing these data-stack signatures from the moment when the *Hyperion* became infected. Compare them to the data signatures in Dakota's implants and then tell me if I'm wrong.'

For the sake of his own life, Corso prayed he wasn't.

Several moments passed.

'Correlations with the infected signatures are detected,' the *Piri Reis* replied. 'Please stand by.'

Dakota's head suddenly snapped back as if a powerful electric current had been run through her. Her teeth clenched in an involuntary grimace, and the muscles in her arms and neck stood out like steel cables under the skin.

'*Piri*!' Dakota began showing all the signs of suffering a major seizure. '*Piri*, stop! What are you . . .?'

Her eyes looked like they were about to pop right out of her head, and something very like a scream tried to force its way out from between her clenched teeth.

'Remain where you are,' the ship warned him. 'I am currently cleaning invasive routines from Dakota's implants.'

'You're *killing* her.'

'Any physical responses you see are purely the result of nerve shocks generated by the analysis and removal process.'

Corso stepped forward and tried to loosen her straps. Whatever *Piri* was doing . . .

Something buzzed against his forehead and a moment later Corso found himself floating at the far end of the cabin.

'Please remain where you are,' the *Piri* stated calmly, 'or the next shot I give you will be lethal.'

Thinking of countermeasures, Corso reached up and touched the skin on his forehead and wondered what the ship had hit him with. He looked around just in time to see something tiny and silver dart back into a recess that closed even as he watched.

Dakota's body jerked again, a low animal sound escaping from between her clenched teeth.

'At least let me get her into the fucking medbox, *Piri*!'

'Unnecessary.'

With the next shock she received, Dakota began foaming at the mouth. Corso was too sickened to watch, and looked away.

She suddenly uttered a shriek, her body tensing as if a powerful electric current were flowing through it, but then she fell silent and collapsed back against the couch.

Corso stared at her prone form, his mouth dry.

'The process is complete,' the ship suddenly announced.

'And what? How is she?'

'A more thorough analysis is required to determine if there is any brain damage from her recent head injuries. The invasive routines, however, appear to have been destroyed.'

Corso hurriedly pulled Dakota back out of the webbing. She felt like a broken doll in his arms as he clumsily hauled her into the cupboard-sized space where the coffin-shaped medbox was situated.

He yanked her clothes off and cracked open the medbox's door. It responded instantly by enveloping Dakota's body with slim, pale sensors as he lowered her in. Needles slid under her skin, while other sensors began probing her flesh. He stepped back, momentarily repulsed: the sensors reminded him too much of the things that had extruded from the walls of the derelict.

'*Piri*, I need you to give me full access to your control systems.'

'This is not permitted.'

'Dammit! *Piri*, I—'

'Corso.'

Her voice was weak. He stared down at her hopefully. She wasn't focusing well, but she was looking straight at him. As he watched, a sensor found its way inside a nostril, while others slithered into her mouth and on down her throat. She twisted and choked for a moment, before relaxing again. He reached down and put one hand on her arm. The physical contact seemed to help soothe her.

'*Piri*,' she gasped, her voice barely coherent past the sensors blocking her throat. 'Full systems access granted for Lucas Corso. Acknowledge.'

'Acknowledged,' came the reply.

'Dakota, I . . .'

A sensor pushed itself into a vein on her arm and her eyes rolled back, the eyelids closing in deep sleep as the medbox's sedatives took effect.

Corso woke a few hours later to an urgent beeping sound. He'd curled up in the same acceleration couch Dakota had been confined in, watching as status alerts on her condition continued flickering on a screen.

His sleep, what little of it he was able to manage, had been sporadic, interrupted by nightmares due to what he'd learned from the derelict during that final frantic upload to the *Piri Reis*.

He felt he could tell no one what he'd discovered,

and he'd wiped the data from the *Piri Reis*'s stacks as soon as he'd absorbed its message in all its awful import.

Despite all she'd been through, the damage to Dakota's body and brain appeared to be largely superficial. There was no sign of major cerebral tissue damage, either from her fight with Udo or from the *Piri*'s attempts to destroy whatever had been hiding inside her skull.

'The *Hyperion*'s systems are undergoing aggressive analysis by sources currently on its bridge,' *Piri* informed him at one point. 'It appears to be an attempt to locate both yourself and Dakota.'

'How many are on board the *Hyperion* now?'

'Six, including David Gardner, Kieran Mansell and Senator Arbenz. The remaining three are not on record, but are armed and wearing combat-ready armour.'

'Those are probably security from the *Agartha*. Have they gone anywhere near the cargo bay yet?'

'Apart from yourself and Miss Merrick, there has been no physical human presence in the cargo bay since our departure from Mesa Verde. However, aggressive security scans have probed the bay several times in the past few minutes.'

'But they can't detect the *Piri*, can they?'

'Visual and data feeds show only partly depleted ion cells placed in storage,' came the reply.

'And that'll hold up?'

'Only so long as the cargo bay is not physically entered for visual confirmation.'

'What happens if we take you outside the *Hyperion* right now? What are our chances?'

'The prognosis is not good,' came the reply. 'I am equipped primarily for counter-surveillance. Regardless of this, the chances of being visually identified on exiting the *Hyperion* are very high, in which case black-ops capabilities would be of negligible effect against the firepower of either the *Hyperion* or the *Agartha*. My recommendation is we should remain hidden within the cargo bay as long as possible.'

So either they stayed put until the others finally found their hiding place, or they could exit the *Hyperion* and get blown out of existence.

Corso yanked himself up out of his seat and returned to the medbox. Dakota's breathing looked deep and regular, as he gazed down at her through the transparent cover. The wounds and bruises she'd picked up looked like they were healing rapidly.

'Any more on Dakota's prognosis, *Piri*?'

'She is recovering well, but it will be some hours before she is fully functional.'

'We don't have that much time. Can we wake her now?'

'That is not advisable.'

'I don't care if it's advisable. Can we wake her?'

A pause. 'Yes.'

'Then do it.'

'This is counter to safe practice of—'

'*Piri*, she gave me full privileges. Do it.'

Lights on the medbox changed from red to green. The tentacle-like sensors slowly unwound from around her still form. Her injuries weren't anywhere near as bad now as they would have been without the medbox's rapid-healing technology, but she still looked a long way from sparkling health.

Corso hated to wake her so soon, but he needed her help if they were going to get out of this.

'Do you have any idea exactly what that was in her Ghost implants?'

'That is difficult to ascertain,' the ship replied. 'I detected two conflicting processes. One appeared to share traits with the invasive routines found within the *Hyperion*'s data stacks, whereas the second bore a closer relationship to data configurations originating from within the derelict.'

'What, *two* processes? Explain that.'

'There were what appear, upon initial analysis, to be two invasive processes present within Dakota's ghost implants,' the ship replied with endless pedantry. 'These have been erased where possible, along with a variety of traps and memory blocks.'

Dakota's chest heaved suddenly, her back arching, her small apple-sized breasts pressing upwards. Corso was having a hard time pushing back memories that were still delightfully fresh; the opportunities for sex back home on Redstone were limited, to say the least, given the Freehold's tight social constraints. It had felt at the time like Dakota was assuaging some deep hunger that went beyond the expression of mere lust, into a need whose origin he couldn't begin to guess.

Apart from that, it had been the greatest fuck of his life.

The lid hissed open. Corso remembered what the *Piri Reis* had just told him: *memory blocks*. Dakota's eyelids fluttered and her eyes stared through him. After a moment she managed to focus on him at last.

'Corso . . .' She coughed and shook her head, and brought up a thin stream of liquid, retching as she cleared her lungs of the complex chemicals the medbox had used in the repair process. He reached down and helped as she struggled into a sitting position. Dakota leaned over the side of the medbox, choking and gasping the last of the medicinal liquid out of her system. Corso got his hands under her arms and helped her stand up slowly. She was shivering violently.

'How . . . how long's it been?' she managed to stammer, her breath still heaving. She was peering around the command module as if she'd never seen it before.

'Not that long. Couple of hours since I got you back from the bridge. But I don't know how long we've got before Arbenz and the rest track us down.'

'Shit.'

He helped her over to an acceleration couch and she dragged herself on to it, wiping gunge from her face and hair.

'We need to get away,' she croaked.

Corso shook his head. 'Can't do. They'll shoot us

out of orbit the moment we're seen outside the *Hyperion*. There's only so much subterfuge the *Piri Reis* can manage.' He paused for a moment. 'That's why I brought you round early just now. I was hoping you might prove me wrong on that.'

She tried to focus more fully on him, and then started laughing weakly. 'Put me back. Put me back in the medbox and wake me up when the universe is over. Oh my God, we're fucked. We're totally fucked.'

'No, we're *not*, Dakota, and I need your help if we're going to get out of this. But I need to ask you some questions before we do anything else.'

'At least find me some clothes first.'

'Sure.'

Corso negotiated his way through to her sleeping quarters. A maelstrom of both clean and unwashed clothing still floated there, and began whirling around him as he disturbed the air with his passage. He grabbed a pair of trousers and the cleanest t-shirt he could find, and propelled his way back through. Dakota was curled up into a ball on the couch, one arm looped securely through a piece of webbing. For a moment he thought she'd fallen asleep, but then she opened her eyes and stared at him.

'So did you bring me some clothes or are you just going to stand there staring at me like a pervert?'

'Sorry.' He handed them over.

She shook her head and forced a weak grin. 'I was only kidding. You said you had questions?'

'I want to talk about Josef Marados.'

Her expression stiffened immediately. 'What about him?'

'Someone tampered with the news feeds, while we were still in the Sol System. So the report of his death was deleted from the *Hyperion*'s records.'

She shot him an angry look. 'You know, you actually sound like you're accusing me of something.'

'Let's face it, you've been acting very strangely.'

She laughed, but the sound was harsh and edgy. 'This coming from a Freeholder?'

'Dakota, listen to me, I'm not accusing you of anything. I'm just trying to get to the bottom of things. Someone fixed the transceiver feed so certain specific items were flagged and deleted.'

Now Dakota looked bewildered and frightened. 'Well, if you must know, I picked up on that too. I thought there might be an intruder on board, because there were alterations to the stack records.'

'There wasn't any intruder,' Corso stated. 'Not anything physical at least. You made the alterations yourself.'

She shot him a glance full of anger and suspicion. 'Look,' she swallowed, 'I don't deny I might have made some changes to protect myself. But there were other changes that had nothing to do with me – the kind of stuff you probably couldn't pick up on unless you had a Ghost riding in your head.'

'So you'd say the Shoal AI was responsible.'

Dakota nodded.

Corso shook his head. 'That's part of it, but not all. Just before we got to Nova Arctis, I saw you walking away from the airlocks leading into the cargo bay. I went up to you, and you completely blanked me. It was like you didn't even know I was there. It was the same behaviour the time I found you on the bridge, looking at maps of the Magellans. Except you didn't seem to remember that.'

'Corso, this is ridiculous. I . . .' A brief look of uncertainty crossed her face, and she changed her tack. 'Look, I don't understand what you're getting at.'

'When I came across you that time by the external airlocks, it was less than an hour after Severn was murdered back in Ascension.'

'Oh, for God's sake, Lucas! The man led a dangerous life. This is ridiculous.'

'Dakota, do you remember at all what happened on the bridge just now?'

'Why?'

'Do you even remember killing Udo Mansell?'

'I . . .' That look of uncertainty flickered over her face again. 'Yes,' she said, a little more quietly. 'I did. I'd . . . I don't know. I hadn't forgotten. I just . . . couldn't place the memory. Except . . .'

'Except what, Dakota? Except it didn't feel real, maybe? When I got there, you had this blank look on your face like you weren't really aware of what was going on around you. It was exactly the same look you had that time I found you running trajectories on the bridge, and that time by the airlocks. Like you weren't really quite seeing anything around you? You know, you almost managed to kill *me* back there.'

Dakota shook her head vigorously. 'I don't remember anything like that. Besides, it was Udo attacked *me*. Then . . .'

Corso cocked his head. 'What's the matter?'

'Nothing,' she replied, staring off into space. 'I just can't . . .' She put one hand up to her head and dragged it through her hair, her fingers trembling.

'Can't remember?'

She flashed him a hostile glare. 'Lucas . . .'

'Are you still having trouble remembering? After you killed Udo, I had to actually knock you out before I could start dragging you all the way down here. I've seen some weird shit in my life, but I've never seen anything quite like that. Not even back home.'

'I didn't kill Severn, I swear. I don't know what makes you think I even could. I . . . it was complicated. We were close, back in the old days. The same goes for Josef Marados.'

She sounded calmer now. 'There's no reason for me to kill either of them,' she stated more defiantly. 'But there was plenty of reason to kill Udo.'

Couldn't agree more, Corso reflected, but he didn't say a word about that. 'You *do* realize I just had your ship rip a shitload of invasive routines out of your skull? Stuff that shouldn't have been in there at all.'

Her head snapped back up. 'What?'

'I'm saying the *Hyperion* isn't the only thing that was compromised. So were you – or your Ghost was, at any rate.'

'But that's . . .'

He could see the realization dawning on her.

'There's no one else with the access privileges and the skill – including the support of your implants – to enable you to alter records and hide your movements the way you did with the *Piri Reis*. But there's plenty of precedent for your conscious mind being taken over.'

'I remembered everything that happened at Port Gabriel, Lucas. That was the worst thing about it. I remember exactly how *good* the Uchidans made me feel when they turned me into a murderer.'

'But it doesn't have to be just like that, does it? What about a fugue state where your conscious mind thinks it's doing one thing, while something altogether different is happening in reality?'

She twisted around and tried to strike him, but he anticipated the blow, catching her fist in his own and pulling her towards him.

She gripped his shirt with her free hand and began to weep. He held her close for a while, feeling her shoulders heave.

'I'm sorry, Lucas. I had such bad dreams – I don't want them to be real.'

She slid out of her seat and he let her drift until she snagged a piece of trailing fur and pulled herself in close to one wall. He let her just float there for a minute, before he continued.

'What *do* you remember?'

'I thought I was imagining it. I had . . . nightmares, about Chris Severn and Josef. I saw it happening. I just pretended it wasn't real, because it *couldn't* be real.' She wept.

She stiffened again, then twisted around to face him. 'The figurine.'

Corso said nothing. She pulled herself slowly upright and stared through him as if he were not there. Her expression was sphinx-like now: calm, eerie, deadly. 'The figurine the alien gave me – Belle Trevois.'

'I know. I—'

'I remember now.' Her tone was soft and calm, but something in its tone unnerved him. 'I mean I'm starting to remember. Trader knew I was on Redstone during the massacres; he was just playing a game with me. I knew the figure was of Trevois as soon as I opened the box, but then I touched it and . . . I forgot.'

She focused fully on him now. 'That thing *raped* me, Lucas. I don't know how he knew I'd get here, but he had planned everything from Bourdain's Rock on at the very least.'

Her lips twisted in a snarl. 'And now I'm going to destroy him.'

TWENTY-THREE

A few minutes passed.

'We're going out on to the hull,' Dakota suddenly informed him, grabbing his pressure suit from the corner it had drifted into and pushing it towards him. 'Outside, now.'

He gaped at her blankly.

'Look, I'll explain on the way, all right?'

She'd barely got herself dressed, but she began to pull her clothes off once more. She noticed his lips tighten as the filmsuit spread across her skin, but he clearly wasn't in the mood right now for asking too many questions. She was glad of that, because she wasn't in the mood for explanations. She'd already guessed he might have seen the Bandati technology in operation while he was bringing her back to the cargo bay.

'I wanted to talk to you about *this*,' she said casually.

Corso glanced around to observe the small object gripped in Dakota's hand, and froze when he saw it was one of the remote failsafes. He reached down automatically, and realized he didn't have his own any more.

'I found this earlier among your clothes, right after

we got naked.' Her tone remained casual. 'This thing was meant to break the link between me and the interface chairs, wasn't it?'

Corso nodded dumbly.

Dakota smiled like a cat. 'I suppose this is as good a time as any to tell you it wouldn't have worked.'

Corso swallowed. 'Your Ghost?'

'Nothing gets past it.' She regarded him coolly. 'After what you told me on the derelict, I figured there was a chance you might be carrying something like this.'

He looked away from her and pulled his suit on. Then she guided him back out of the *Piri Reis* and into the cargo bay and towards the airlock built into the main bay's external doors.

Outside, the surface of Theona looked so close she imagined she could reach out and touch its icy surface with one hand. The dull grey and orange stripes of the gas-giant Dymas hovered in the darkness beyond. Dakota was able to converse normally with Corso via a tiny, Ghost-linked transponder carried in the back of her throat.

Beyond the curve of the ship's hull, three new stars were visible shining unevenly but brightly: the approaching, unknown fleet. Their engines were pointed towards the inner system as they decelerated.

She could see Corso's face clearly through the visor of his suit. He looked absolutely terrified, his arms and legs waving frantically as only the intelligent lanyards built into the waist of his pressure suit kept him attached to the ship's hull. Delicate-looking but incredibly strong silver wires shot out from his waist, embedding and re-embedding themselves in the hull as Corso shifted up behind her. Dakota had slaved his belt to her own suit's lanyards, so that Corso was forced to follow her as she made her way across and around the hull towards some half-remembered destination.

'Wouldn't it be better' – his breathing was uneven, panicky – 'easier even, if I just pulled myself after you with the handholds?'

'Not a chance. You don't have the experience of zero gravity or outside work for me to risk the chance of you drifting off, and I don't have the time to baby-sit you either. Those lanyards are pretty much fail-proof, all right?'

'Fine,' he gasped, his laboured breath making his words hard to decipher. 'So tell me, why the hell are we out here anyway?'

'Take a guess.'

'Well . . . at a guess, then, you're worried the *Piri Reis* has been infected by the same thing that infected your Ghost. But can the *Piri* hear us out here?'

'Not as long as we stay on this frequency.'

'You know, the *Piri* did say your implants were now clean of invasives.'

'Maybe it's lying.' She paused for a moment, snatches of memory coming back. She looked around, thinking hard. *That way,* she decided, rapidly continuing on her way around the hull's circumference.

'Look,' he said, 'if the *Piri*'s infected, we're dead anyway. Your ship's the only possible escape route we might have, right? We talked this over, and I'd prefer to believe it's not infected. Besides, the *Piri Reis* is a paranoid's wet dream. From what I saw and heard back there, it's like your counter-surveillance doesn't even trust itself.'

'That's because it *doesn't.* It has to deal with some very sophisticated probing techniques. Besides, you know what they say: paranoids live longer.'

A mental image of a service hatch, and its number, flashed into Dakota's mind from a pocket deep within her Ghost's memory stacks that had, until very recently, been locked off from her consciousness. She paused for a moment, trying to think which way to go next. It came to her suddenly, and she set off once more.

Corso's response was panic. 'Hey, where are you going?'

She explained as she went. 'The Shoaler alien I met on Bourdain's Rock was called Trader. Everything that's happened since it gave me that damned gift has been set up so I take the blame. It was the alien destroyed Bourdain's Rock, and then made me look responsible because I was the one carrying a GiantKiller on board my ship. Then it got inside my head and made me murder Josef Marados after he tried to save my skin. It was the same with Chris Severn. You're right, Lucas.'

The words spat out of her mind in bitter anger. 'I *did* kill him.'

'So I guess the memories are coming back now?'

Dakota gritted her teeth. 'Yeah, you could say that.'

They were meanwhile passing an observation blister. Even though it was incredibly unlikely Arbenz or anyone else would be inside the blister looking out, Dakota nonetheless felt a stab of fear on passing it.

She glanced over her shoulder to see Corso not too far behind her, still dragged along by his lanyards. At least he appeared to have stopped struggling.

'The point is, everywhere I go, something bad happens. The alien covers its tracks by using me as a puppet to do what it wants me to, and that way there's no reason for anyone to investigate any deeper.'

She finally stopped and waited for him to catch up. As she led him along this curving path, Theona had partially slid out of sight behind the *Hyperion*'s hull. The gravity wheel still spun around the ship's axis a hundred metres ahead to the fore. She heard Corso's breathing become more laboured, and guessed that was because he had just glanced the same way. To him it must feel as if he were being dragged, by wires that couldn't possibly hold his weight, up the side of a kilometre-high tower with a rotating wheel waiting near its apex.

She decided to keep him talking to keep his mind off things.

'Here's a question. The entire reason Ghost tech was developed is down to the lack of anything like credible artificial intelligence, even after half a millennium of computer technology. Ghost tech was a way of side-stepping the problem, right?'

'Yeah,' Corso croaked. 'An artificial unconsciousness that processes data and only bothers you with the really important stuff, right?'

'Right. So given that fact, data stacks on board the *Hyperion* or anywhere else, couldn't possibly contain something as sophisticated as the intelligence that communicated with me. So maybe then it's reasonable to assume there's something *external* to the stacks.'

She spotted an access hatch and felt another flash of déjà vu. She pushed herself towards the hatch, lanyards whipping back and forth as she went.

She kept glancing back at Corso to make sure he was making way all right. He'd now let his limbs hang loose, allowing his lanyards to carry him after her. She smiled: he looked like some impossibly skinny sea creature picking its way over a seabed, with a human-shaped prize mounted on its minuscule head. But they were starting to make good time.

'And is that another reason why we're out here now?' he asked.

'Yeah. Hang on.'

The service hatch had a simple locking mechanism. It contained nothing vital and was easy to open. She pulled back the lid and gazed down at something that looked not unlike a neuron cell, but blown up to the size of a human head and silver-grey in colour, its body apparently composed of crystalline, semi-transparent fibres. It extended dozens upon dozens of strands deep into a control panel inside the hatch.

'Shit,' Corso whispered as he came abreast of her. 'What *is* that thing?'

Dakota, too, stared down at it, struggling with a sense of deep loathing that filled her mind. It was hard for her to believe she'd been responsible for placing it there herself.

'That's Trader, Lucas. Or rather a copy of its mind, linked in through this panel and into the *Hyperion*'s subsystems. We need to destroy it.'

She was beginning to remember how she'd murdered Josef.

She'd slipped away from the Black Rock docks, literally minutes before she'd been due to depart for the *Hyperion* aboard a shuttle. Josef's own hacks had made it simple for her to find her way back to his office undetected. The door had slid quietly open and he'd looked up, with barely enough time to register surprise, before she was on him, her face hidden by the smooth black oil of her filmsuit.

She'd torn the ceremonial Challenge blade from where it sat in a niche on his wall, and used it to slash at his throat before he'd even had time to stand up. He'd staggered away from her, trying to keep the desk between them before he eventually collapsed, bleeding heavily. She'd dropped the blade and picked up a heavy-looking ornament that sat by the window, which looked out over Mesa Verde, and used it to bash his skull in, her compromised Ghost all the while altering the *Hyperion*'s live security feeds to make it appear she was in fact already on board the shuttle.

After that, she'd made her way back down to the Black Rock departure bay and on to the shuttle, with barely seconds to spare.

She had later killed Chris Severn while he lay in a medbox in Ascension, cutting out his heart and pushing the still-warm organ into his insensate mouth, as an attempt to disguise his death as a ritual killing carried out by one of Ascension's many criminal organizations.

Even so, Trader's total mind-rape hadn't taken into account the possibility of chance physical encounters either with Corso or anyone else. The more she thought about it, the more the alien's strategies stank of hasty preparation, of seat-of-the-pants planning rather than careful deliberation.

The machine-organ before Dakota twitched, and she wondered if Trader had any idea what she was intending to do next. She hoped it did.

She pulled off her knapsack and rummaged inside, finally producing a tool similar to a crowbar. She leaned in towards the hatch, prising and wrenching at the Trader-object, trying to pull it loose. It struggled, entwining soft silver limb tendrils around the shaft of the tool in a vain attempt to wrest it from her grip.

After a few moments of this battle of wills, Corso reached in and helped her tug at the object. It struggled all the harder, wriggling frantically, but finally it came loose and floated free of the *Hyperion*, its limbs rippling in a futile attempt to gain purchase out in the void. Dakota swatted at it hard, sending it rapidly drifting away towards Theona.

'And is that it?' Corso asked in a tone of clear revulsion. There was something so fundamentally disturbing about the thing they had just destroyed.

'I'm pretty sure that's all there is, yes.'

'And you put it there yourself?'

'Under Trader's control, yes.' Dakota nodded. 'I sat up one day while I was back on Mesa Verde and I had a vault number and an address in my head. I went to the address and collected a package. That thing was inside.' She shrugged. 'Then, I guess, it was just a matter of finding an opportune moment.'

She saw that Corso was no longer paying attention, and followed the direction of his gaze.

It seemed they had company.

Three figures in armoured pressure suits were moving towards them, carried forward by their own lanyard belts. All three were clearly armed.

Dakota twisted around so that her own lanyards held her upright, relative to the hull, her feet planted next to the open hatch, and watched as they approached.

She wondered if her filmsuit would absorb the kinetic energy of the bullets, given that their weapons looked like the projectile variety.

Yeah, she thought. *And maybe I can magically fly*

home as well. If she didn't go back inside the ship at some point soon, the filmsuit would run out of power and she'd be left exposed, naked to the vacuum. The only way for her to stay alive was getting back through the airlock, and just sneaking around clearly wasn't an option any longer.

At least her mind was her own again. She had Corso to thank for that. She couldn't decide if what she now felt towards him was love, or merely a kind of ecstatic gratitude born out of the knowledge that he'd helped rip a parasite clean out of her head.

Perhaps time would tell . . . but then again it wasn't likely either of them had more than a few hours to live.

TWENTY-FOUR

'I'll have to admit, I'm impressed. Really.'

Arbenz stepped back from kneeling over Dakota, who lay curled in a ball, gripping her stomach where Kieran's boot had slammed into it. The Senator signalled to his henchman, who stepped forward again, the bruises on Kieran's face livid and smooth from his time in the med bay. He kicked out at her a second time.

She tried desperately to shield herself with her arms, but it wasn't enough.

Corso and Dakota hadn't really any choice but to be hauled back inside the cargo bay by the three figures in armoured suits. There was, after all, nowhere else to escape to. Their brief fantasy of somehow stealing the derelict had been waylaid when the alien intelligence within the *Hyperion*'s stacks had killed the vessel's crew, drawing the others back to investigate the orbiting ship – while Corso meanwhile had struggled to warn her of the traitor inside her own skull.

Now there was only pain, and the inevitability of death.

They had been brought into a storage room near

the cargo bay. Kieran obviously had some experience of undertaking torture in zero gee: he first anchored himself by gripping a bulkhead so that he didn't float away each time he kicked her.

Kieran next turned his attention to Corso, who had crawled into a corner after his own severe beating. The three troopers from the *Agartha*, grim-jawed Freeholders with unreadable expressions, stood watching from near the door.

'I'm impressed,' the Senator confessed, 'that so much escaped my attention for so long. Do you know how much of an embarrassment that is to me?'

He started pacing the room. 'But really, you're the biggest disappointment of all, Mr Corso. You're a traitor who's betrayed his own people, the worst kind of scum there is.'

He bent down until his face was level with Corso's, though Corso looked like he was having trouble focusing. 'So tell me. Why did you do it?'

'You're out of fucking time, Senator,' Corso wheezed back at him. 'You can't ever go back to Redstone, that's what I think.'

Arbenz stood, his face flushed with anger, and aimed a sharp, swift kick at Corso's head.

'How long,' the Senator screamed, 'did you think it would be before we'd have found that ship hidden in the cargo bay?' He stared around at Dakota. 'Did you plan this from the beginning?'

She noticed that Gardner had entered the room. He

still remained near the entrance, by the troopers, one arm crossed over his chest, the other hand reaching up to his mouth in an unconscious gesture of horror.

'Senator . . .' Gardner cleared his throat. 'Senator. I should remind you we still need them.'

'*Need* them?' Arbenz rounded on Gardner. 'Don't you understand what these two have done? They have been engaged in a conspiracy against my people. We'll find another way to deal with the derelict.'

'There's no time left, Senator. We need both of them more than ever.'

Arbenz cocked his head and stared. 'What are you talking about?'

'Don't you know?' Gardner looked incredulous. 'That's why I'm here. The derelict's propulsion systems have started powering up.'

'Powering up?' Corso croaked, failing to pull himself upright.

Kieran made a move forward, murder in his eye, but Gardner stepped across and grabbed the man's shoulder.

For a moment, Dakota was sure Kieran was about to kill Gardner, then she saw the look passing between the Senator and Kieran. Kieran's mouth twisted in anger, but he held back.

Gardner turned to the Senator. 'While you've been chasing each other around up here, some of the rest of us have been paying attention to the priority alerts. The derelict's primary systems are powering up, but with no intervention from us. The base on Theona is picking up exactly the same graviton fluctuations you'd get from a coreship prior to jumping into transluminal space. What it might do next is anybody's guess.'

Arbenz adopted a weary expression. 'This isn't the time, Mr Gardner.'

Gardner looked bug-eyed. 'Didn't you hear what I just said? Senator, the derelict is coming *alive*. Corso, here, is the only one who has any real idea what's going on inside that thing.'

'And if *you* don't stop interfering, you'll be the next one put under arrest.'

Gardner opened and closed his mouth a few times as he gradually realized Arbenz was entirely serious.

'Please don't say I'm insane, Mr Gardner,' Arbenz said grimly. 'I'm fighting for the future of my own people, and I'm not interested in a debate.'

Arbenz returned his attention to Corso, for the moment having decided to ignore Dakota. She wondered if that was a good thing, or if it only meant he'd now made up his mind to kill her.

'Mr Corso,' the Senator was saying, 'you miserable piece of shit, you're a stain upon the Freehold. You're *exactly* what I mean when I refer to the weakness among us. The weakness we wanted to escape when we founded Redstone.'

He finally turned his attention to Dakota, staring down at her while she cowered, waiting for the next blow. 'I was an idiot to expect any less of you. You murdered Udo and, except for me standing between you and Kieran, I think I might actually feel pity for what he'd do to you for that.'

The Senator's voice began to grow louder. 'I should have realized Bourdain would send spies,' he continued, 'and I know that's his fleet approaching us right now. If any man possessed the resources to find out about the derelict, then it would be him.'

Gardner wore an expression like he was the only sane man left in a madhouse. He reached out to Arbenz, more words forming on his lips. Kieran suddenly seized hold of Gardner, twisting his arm behind his back and slamming him against the wall. Gardner yelled with pain.

A small smile crossed the Senator's face.

'For God's sake,' Gardner panted. 'You're sabotaging your own damn mission!'

'That, Mr Gardner, is exactly where you're wrong,' said the Senator, now looking delighted. He turned and looked down at Corso. 'Tell him.'

Corso stared up at Arbenz, his hands still raised in the not unreasonable expectation of another blow. 'I . . . I don't understand,' he replied haltingly.

'Kieran, I want you to help Mr Corso remember what it is he's been keeping quiet from all of us.'

Kieran released Gardner and grabbed Corso by the hair, forcing him into a kneeling position. Kieran produced his knife and pulled Corso's head back, as if to cut his throat. Instead he made a single shallow cut across the side of Corso's neck, just above his shoulder.

It was enough to make Corso scream shrilly. Dakota looked away, trembling violently.

'So tell him then, Mr Corso,' Arbenz repeated. 'When you tapped into the derelict's data stacks, you didn't cover your tracks as well as you might have hoped. In fact, if not for you, we might not have stumbled across this particular item of knowledge ourselves.'

Corso, panting, shook his head, blood fanning out across his shoulder from where he'd been wounded. Arbenz nodded to Kieran and, a moment later another, more anguished scream filled the air as Corso was sliced again, this time in the tender flesh just below his ear and next to the jaw.

Dakota cried out in involuntary sympathy. This time, Corso's scream was more like that of a wounded animal than anything human. He mumbled something incomprehensible.

Kieran yanked his head back again.

'Speak up,' Kieran snarled, bringing the knife down towards Corso's face this time.

'No! Wait. OK.' Corso coughed and spat, his breathing ragged. 'OK, fine.' He looked at Dakota. 'Sorry,' he murmured to her, and looked away.

Dakota had no idea what exactly he was being sorry for.

'Why don't you just tell him yourself?' Corso asked the Senator, then nodding towards Gardner.

'Because I'd rather you did. So get on with it.'

Dakota watched, mute and apprehensive.

'I found some information hidden in the derelict's stacks,' Corso told Gardner. 'But I'd have been insane not to try and hide what I learned,' he pleaded, looking directly at Arbenz. 'It's too dangerous, too—'

'Kieran,' urged Arbenz.

'All right! All right,' Corso begged, slithering away from the knife still held so close to his face. 'I know what happened to the civilization that created the derelict. Or I've a pretty good idea, anyway.'

'What we have there is even better,' Arbenz informed Gardner with gloating triumph, 'than a faster-than-light drive.'

For a moment, Corso stared at the Senator with unmasked disgust. 'How good is your history, Mr Gardner?' he asked, appearing to regain a little of his composure.

Gardner shrugged, looking bewildered. 'Try me.'

'Several centuries ago, we split the atom and thought we'd found the ultimate source of cheap energy. It didn't take long before we turned it into a weapon and bombed entire cities into ashes in seconds. It was a pact with the devil: a way of generating cheap power, but one that could also destroy us all in seconds. It looks like the Magi had something not so different.'

Gardner looked quickly between Arbenz and Corso, then shook his head. 'I don't understand.'

Corso continued, sounding as if every word had to be wrenched from his soul. 'I'd rather die than tell you this if the Senator didn't already know. The transluminal drive doubles as a weapon that makes the atomic bomb look like a firework. That's the real secret of the Shoal. And I'll guarantee you it's also the reason they've tried so hard to prevent any competitor species acquiring the means for faster-than-light travel.'

Arbenz's excitement clearly became too much for him. 'Mr Gardner, what we have found changes everything. The Freehold was *meant* to find that derelict. It's as if the divine will of God—'

'It's got nothing to do with God,' Corso yelled, his voice cracking and tears streaming down his face. 'The process is clear, in the records. If a starship equipped with the transluminal drive is allowed to materialize within the heart of a star, even a very stable star, certain processes can be triggered by the ship's subsequent destruction. The result is a nova.'

Arbenz positively glowed with triumph. 'A *nova*, Mr Gardner, a way to detonate entire stars. What we have here isn't just a device for travelling between stars . . . it can destroy them, and the worlds in orbit around them, too. Its discovery' – a beatific grin began to spread over his face – 'is very possibly the greatest moment in the entire history of the Freehold.'

Gardner finally had the good sense to look truly frightened. 'All right, Senator. Assuming this is true, and I find it more than a little hard to believe, who exactly are you planning to blow up?'

'No one,' Arbenz replied. 'That's the beauty of it. If

we can harness the power in that derelict, nobody could stand against us. They'd be *insane* to even try.'

'And what if somebody else found out how to do just the same?' Dakota shouted. 'What about when the Shoal realize what you've been up to, and then threaten to destroy Redstone's star? Or anywhere else in the Consortium, for that matter?'

Arbenz looked surprised that Dakota had spoken up. 'The Shoal would do nothing, except to keep on preserving a secret they've clearly been sitting on for a long, long time. *They* must know what the transluminal drive is capable of, so at the worst it'll be a state of détente – neither our side or theirs will be mad enough to instigate a war of mutually assured destruction.'

Dakota listened, horrified, staring at Arbenz who looked like he'd just been asked to take charge of the Second Coming.

'But you're wrong,' Corso pointed out. He'd managed to haul himself to a halfway-upright position against the wall. Kieran glowered at him threateningly, but stayed where he was. 'It *can* happen, because it's happened before – in the Magellanic Clouds.'

Every pair of eyes in the room, except Dakota's, turned to focus on Corso. Dakota kept her gaze on the rest of them while Corso explained.

'We all know about the novae in the Magellanic Galaxies,' Corso continued, to dumbfounded silence. 'One after the other, all within roughly the same sector of a neighbour galaxy, more than a dozen stars detonated with no explanation. More than that, they were stars that shouldn't have exploded. Most of them were the type of main sequence star any life we've ever encountered needs in order to survive. There was always the possibility the novae explosions were the product of something intelligent, but that was never more than wild speculation. Well, now we have the proof, in the navigational and historical records on board the derelict. On that basis, I don't see any reason to doubt that the Magi weren't refugees from a war of absolute destruction.'

'And you know this for sure?' Gardner demanded.

'I can only tell you what the records themselves say. But it explains a lot.'

'You're lying,' Arbenz hissed.

'Listen to yourself!' Corso shouted. 'The Magi fled from a war that destroyed a fair chunk of an entire galaxy and *you* think you can control the weapon used to do it?' He laughed weakly. 'Finding that derelict is the worst thing that happened to the human race. If the Shoal don't decide to destroy us, we'll do it to ourselves, I guarantee you.'

Dakota couldn't help resenting Corso for keeping so much back from her – even though she knew she'd have done the exact same damn thing. Arbenz was blinkered to the point of insanity, but Gardner was a different matter: he could see how deep they were all dug in now. No wonder the Shoal were terrified at the prospect of their client races discovering the secret of faster-than-light travel: the result might be war on an unbelievable scale. Star after star, after star . . . exploding in the endless night, spreading deadly, life-destroying radiation throughout the Milky Way, a brief mystery to be pondered in the night skies of a million unknown worlds.

There could be heard a surge of static-laden speech, and Dakota glanced over towards one of the Freeholder troops, who stood with one finger to his ear.

'Senator?' interrupted the soldier. 'We're getting a report from the base on Theona. The ground team say the derelict is starting to move.'

Dakota realized in that moment that Trader was not yet gone. Although possibly the derelict was acting under its own volition, it was much more likely Trader had wormed his way inside the Magi vessel's computer systems. The alien craft, she didn't doubt, was entirely capable of supporting the full weight of an alien artificial intelligence.

Dakota experienced a sharp spike of pain in one temple, and glimpsed a flash of light out of the corner of her eye. It was a visual glitch she might have paid little attention to, if she didn't remember experiencing exactly the same reaction every time Trader had taken control of her during the past weeks.

Piri's work on her implants had brought back the clear memory of those minuscule visual glitches, and the horror that had followed each and every time. On such occasions, her conscious mind had entered a kind of unquestioning limbo, reducing her to little more than a somnambulistic flesh puppet.

But this time was different: this time she was more aware of it happening to her than ever before.

Something of Trader still survived inside her implants – and it was trying to gain control of her again.

Arbenz and Gardner were bickering together while a disgusted-looking Kieran Mansell stood over to one side, conferring quietly with the three troopers.

Josef Marados had once said she would be crazy not to acquire some kind of countermeasure against the possibility of someone trying to control her through her implants. He had been right: both right to say so, and right in thinking she'd find a way of dealing with such an eventuality.

The cost, however, was high, and she'd never seriously imagined she might be forced to take such drastic action.

Nevertheless, this was the time.

'April is the cruellest month,' she whispered, the words emerging from her throat as a bare whisper. She saw one of the troopers glance towards her suspiciously.

In response, a visual cue flagged up in the corner of her vision, a warning flag she'd put in place long, long ago.

Next, she murmured: 'I will show you fear in a handful of dust.'

The trooper who had looked over stepped towards

her, and she ducked her head down so he couldn't see her lips move.

Another warning flag appeared in the corner of her eye, followed by a request for confirmation.

Granting that request was the simple matter of a half-whispered affirmative.

The trooper lowered the snub nose of his weapon towards her. By now, Kieran glanced around as well.

She said: 'Consider Phlebas, who was once handsome and tall as you.'

Another flag came up, flashing red in the foreground of her vision. A final warning.

All she needed to do was utter the last sentence.

The *Piri Reis* spoke to her.

<Dakota, you must now directly confirm to me your request to create an irrevocable erase and destroy loop in your Ghost implants before proceeding. However, the approaching fleet is now in weapons' range, and is spreading out in what appears to be an attack pattern. Their computers have targeted the *Hyperion*. If your implants are destroyed, your ability to interact with the *Hyperion* and carry out defensive manoeuvres against hostile forces will be gone.>

Thank you, Piri, she replied. *Nonetheless, I confirm.*

The trooper stepped forward to where she still crouched, barking something she did not understand, before bringing one booted foot up and using it to nudge her shoulder. Kieran stood staring at her with hard eyes for a moment, then his hand flicked back towards the knife sheath hidden inside his jacket.

She stared up at the trooper.

'Shantih shantih shantih,' she snarled up at him, completing the sequence.

The changes inside her skull were abrupt and violent, the higher functions of her implants fading away to leave only a dim, insensate void.

'Sir,' one of the other troopers was saying to Arbenz. 'Theona base camp reports that the enemy fleet is now in range and moving in for an attack.'

'That's ridiculous,' Kieran snapped. 'If that was the case the *Hyperion*'s automatic systems would have . . .'

Gardner, Kieran and the Senator all stared at each other at that same moment. Suddenly, emergency klaxons began sounding the length of the ship. Kieran shouted something incomprehensible, and stamped over to the door, but it refused to open.

'We're locked in.'

'Bullshit,' Arbenz retorted. 'Blow the damned thing open if you have to.'

The troopers exchanged glances with each other, then stepped forward, lowering their weapons to aim at the door's locking mechanism. A moment later, thunder and light filled the room. As Dakota watched, the door held for just a few moments, before fracturing at the hinges and falling outwards into the corridor.

I'm losing my mind, thought Dakota miserably, as her Ghost continued its self-immolation.

It felt a lot like dying, like plummeting into an endless abyss where one's soul had previously resided.

Then, just when she thought it was all over, something else slid into the vacant space inside her skull. Something dark, heavy and alien.

She writhed uncontrollably, gasping for breath.

Whatever this was that had settled into her brain, it wasn't the Shoal AI. Something entirely different had replaced the higher-level Ghost functions she'd just erased.

From somewhere far down the corridor sounded a series of loud, echoing booms, accompanied by a grating, rolling roar that grew louder second by second. It didn't take a lot of guesswork to figure they were listening to the sound of explosive decompression. The *Hyperion*'s entire atmosphere was being violently dumped into space.

Dakota had her filmsuit to protect her, but Corso's pressure suit had been torn from his back and discarded as soon as they'd been brought back on board the *Hyperion*. Keeping him alive over the next few minutes wasn't going to be easy.

'Is this your doing?' Arbenz screamed at Corso. 'A thousand generations of Freeholders are going to grow up using your name as another word for traitor – or don't you get that?'

'*You're* the traitor!' Corso screamed back. 'You're a murderer, a gutless opportunist.' The roar of air had become deafening. A powerful wind tore at Dakota as she tried, with difficulty, to stand up.

'It's no wonder we're trapped on a useless backwater rock being told what to do by a bunch of psychotic assholes like you,' Corso continued. 'The Shoal know everything, Senator. And they probably have ever since you got here.'

Arbenz looked apoplectic. 'What are you talking about?'

'Listen to him,' Dakota shouted from behind the Senator.

Arbenz whirled around to face her. 'They know everything that's going on,' she continued. 'They planted software spies in the *Hyperion*'s stacks long ago.'

There are worse ways to die, Dakota reflected. It was clear neither she nor Corso was going to leave this room alive. At least, before the troopers blew their heads off or the last of the air was gone, she'd had the satisfaction of seeing the look on Arbenz's face.

Ignoring them both, Kieran grabbed the Senator's shoulder. 'We can get to the bridge!' he yelled. 'We can seal it off manually, and try and retake control from there.'

The Freehold troopers had begun pulling breathing apparatus out of their uniforms and fitting masks over their faces. Kieran pointed to two of them. 'Barnard, Lunghi – you're coming with me.'

'What about them?' Gardner shouted, gesturing at Corso and Dakota.

'Fuck them,' Arbenz replied. 'They—'

Everything went black.

Pandemonium reigned. Dakota blindly fought her way over to Corso, but the darkness went deeper than just the lights going out. There was an emptiness now that Dakota hadn't felt inside herself since her first set of Ghost implants were ripped out.

Corso fought against her at first, until she identified herself by yelling in his ear over the cacophony of raised voices and howling air. He stopped struggling immediately.

'This is our chance,' she urged him, her mouth pressed right up against the side of his head. Her words sounded thin and indistinct as the atmospheric pressure rapidly dropped.

She dragged him away in what she hoped was the right direction, blindly crashing into other bodies. Hands grabbed and punched at her, and she lashed out in return, taking a savage bite at someone's hand when she felt it grab her face. Despite the near-total darkness, her eyesight was starting to adjust. Something thudded against her shoulder. She reached up, and it felt warm and sticky to the touch.

The confusion got them out through the door, where it was just as impenetrably dark. She could hear Corso's laboured panting next to her as she took an educated guess on which way to head to get back to the cargo bay. There was a fifty-fifty chance she'd made the wrong decision, but it was still infinitely better odds now than before the lights had gone out.

And all the while, Dakota struggled to understand what had just happened.

She had no doubt Trader was responsible for this shipwide systems failure, yet she was sure beyond a shadow of a doubt that she had destroyed whatever remained of the Shoal AI inside the *Hyperion*. Without the semi-organic machinery she had tracked down and destroyed, the *Hyperion*'s stacks couldn't possibly allow the alien's intelligence to function or survive.

Which led her to the conclusion Trader had left boobytraps in case of just such an eventuality. After all, it was exactly what she would have done.

The air got thin enough for Dakota's filmsuit to activate automatically, swallowing her bruised and battered body in its oily embrace. She felt Corso's hand jerk away for an instant, as it touched his skin where he clung on to her.

She realized to her chagrin that getting out of the storage room would have been a lot easier if she'd activated the filmsuit as soon as the lights went out, because the lenses over her eyes were starting to pick up the infrared heat signatures of the walls and machinery around them, making it far easier for her to find her way.

Corso's flesh glowed a dull orange beside her, while the corridor was transformed into a hellish tangle of hidden power conduits and circuitry overlaid with the ghostly cool sheen of the walls. But at least she could see they were heading in the right direction.

Corso was floundering badly, struggling to breathe. The howling sound was becoming fainter. Another minute or so and they'd be in vacuum.

She grabbed hold of Corso, dropping them both straight down the middle of a drop shaft that she remembered would take them most of the way.

Then, thankfully, dull red emergency lighting flickered on.

They got to an airlock, and she hauled both of them inside it, feeling her bruised and exhausted muscles protest. Fortunately the airlocks were all equipped with emergency manual switches that would pressurize them within a couple of seconds, and they ran on circuits independent of the ship's central stacks.

She hammered at a switch and waited for what felt like long, long seconds before she heard a faint hiss that gradually built up into a roar that lasted several seconds.

She let herself slide down against the wall, almost crying with relief. Corso lay slumped beside her.

That empty silence inside her, where her Ghost had been, was no longer so silent. The alien presence she'd felt entering her now filled up her skull, grating against her senses as if it quite literally didn't fit.

She listened carefully to its voice, and realized the creature that had entered her mind was the same as the intelligence she'd previously sensed within the derelict's stacks. And with this came other knowledge.

She could hear other voices – like that of the derelict, but different – calling from deep within the inner system.

It seemed there was more than one derelict in the Nova Arctis system.

Without thinking about it, she tried to summon a mental image of the cargo bay on the far side of the airlock. But instead of the perfect, accurate, three-dimensional map she would once have expected, there was only a half-formed notion drawn from her own frail human memories, inexact and unreliable.

She opened a locker, hoping to find an emergency suit there, but it was empty. She cursed and slammed the door closed. She glanced at Corso lying half dead beside her, and knew they had no choice but to exit into the vacuum of the cargo bay regardless.

If she remembered – if her frail, human memory served her right – the *Piri Reis* was located very close to their current position.

'Corso? Corso, can you hear me?' She shook his shoulder frantically.

His eyelids fluttered, and Dakota thanked the heavens as his eyes focused on her.

'Listen to me,' she said. 'There's only so much air in here and hard vacuum out there. Understand?'

His head moved slightly in what passed for a nod. 'I hear you,' he rasped.

'The cargo bay is just on the other side of this airlock. We're going to have to move fast, and I mean *fast*.

But it shouldn't take more than half a minute or so.' She forced a weak grin. 'Think you can last that long?'

'But I don't have a suit.' His eyes focused more clearly. 'Dakota, no—'

'That's exactly what I mean,' she said, reaching up to the airlock's control panel. 'When I say, take a couple of deep, rapid breaths, OK? Suck it in, hyperventilate, and then let your lungs empty. I'll get you there in a couple of seconds, I swear.'

'You're insane,' he murmured.

'Right, and back on your blessed Redstone people don't try to prove they're the ultimate fucking warrior by seeing how much poisonous native atmosphere they can breathe without passing out or dropping dead?'

'That's not the same thing.'

'Like hell it isn't. It's dangerous, and so is this – except this time you don't actually have a choice. Unless you'd rather sit here in this airlock and wait for those maniacs to find us again.'

'There's no other way?'

'Like you don't know that already!' she snapped. 'No more time for arguments.' She hit the panel, and it began counting down the ten seconds to depressurization. 'Now, Corso! Draw it deep, blow it all out. Hard and fast. Do it!'

Corso staggered to his feet. 'Crazy bitch,' he yelled, then forced his chest in and out, drawing air deep into his lungs. For all his apparent anger, Dakota could see just how terrified he was.

A bell chimed, followed by a loud hissing that got rapidly fainter. Corso's eyes widened in alarm and he emptied his lungs one last time. Absolute silence fell and the outer door swung open on a cargo bay that was tinged hellish red. Corso propelled himself out of the airlock and into the interior of the bay with manic energy.

Dakota followed. For a heart-stopping moment she couldn't figure out which way to go, but then she managed to make out the *Piri*'s dim shape. She boosted across the empty space, towards a spinning and flailing Corso, and collided with him.

They sailed together across the bay, crashing into a bulkhead only a short distance from the *Piri Reis*'s hull. Dakota stabbed towards it with one oilslick hand, Corso kicking after her.

He almost made it, heading the right way, but then he started to drift. The frantic pedalling motion of his arms and legs grew weaker moment by moment. Dakota pushed back towards him in a panic. For far too long, they'd both been running on nothing but sheer adrenalin.

As he finally drifted up against the *Piri*'s hull, she reached for the emergency access panel and slammed the release switch with her fist. An airlock flipped open a few metres further along, and Dakota manhandled him inside.

Corso lay beside her, apparently unconscious, as she waited for the pressure to stabilize. She shook him, out of fear and frustration as much as anything else, but got no reaction. She pinched his nostrils and blew air deep into his lungs. After several seconds he jerked away from her, his chest rising and falling more noticeably.

The inner door finally swung open and Dakota's filmsuit dissolved back into her pores. '*Piri*,' she shouted, 'get the medbox ready!'

She looped one of Corso's arms over her shoulder and dragged him inside, weeping from the effort. To her eternal gratitude, the status lights on the medbox showed it was already activated. She cracked the lid open and started to lift Corso inside with one last, strenuous effort.

He pushed weakly against her with her hands. 'Dakota. I'm fine. It's fine. I'm—' He curled up in a ball and started coughing violently. 'Oh God, I never want to go through anything like that again. I thought I was dead.'

'Take it easy. We're safe for the moment.' She put one hand on his shoulder, in an effort to reassure him.

A few moments later he passed out. Dakota closed the lid on the medbox and went through to the command module and sat down at the console. Her stomach twisted to think of piloting the ship without her Ghost anticipating every thought and action.

'*Piri*,' she spoke into the air. 'Respond only to voice commands from now on.'

'Acknowledged.'

It all seemed so clunky, so difficult, with none of the

speed of thought reaction she was used to. But it would have to do.

'Primary systems are currently down on board the *Hyperion*. I want you to seek out any localized automatic or override systems for the cargo bay doors. Then open them and prepare to exit the *Hyperion* on my command.'

'Acknowledged.'

Dakota waited in silence as seconds stretched into minutes. Meanwhile she ripped up an old shirt and used it to bind her shoulder and help stop the bleeding where Kieran had wounded her during their scuffle in the dark.

Finally, laboriously, the cargo-bay doors began to swing open.

Dakota sank back into an acceleration couch and guided the *Piri* out through the doors, slowly remembering half-forgotten piloting skills that didn't involve the use of her Ghost implants. After slipping out of its cradle, the *Piri* moved inexorably towards stars framed by the huge open bay doors. The *Hyperion* slowly fell away behind them, and she instructed the *Piri Reis* to set a course for the inner system.

If anyone on board the *Hyperion,* or its sister ship, was bothering to pay any attention, it wouldn't have been difficult to shoot them out of the sky. But if the Senator and his buddies were still alive, maybe they were too busy trying to stay that way.

TWENTY-FIVE

Arbenz did not relish having to sacrifice the lives of the three troopers.

But they were soldiers and, more, they were Freeholders, men brought up to appreciate the necessity of sacrifice in the face of war. Without his personal command, the Freehold forces arrayed in the Nova Arctis system would fall into disarray. It was therefore militarily essential that he himself stay alive. The same went for Kieran, the most deadly weapon the Senator possessed.

Gardner was another matter. He should have been considered entirely dispensable but, unfortunately they needed the technical and financial support he represented.

That meant sacrificing a trooper, which was no small matter. For that, Gardner would find himself paying a price one day.

One of the troopers resisted, and Kieran had to slay him against his will. Another looked like he meant to resist, but Kieran's dispatching of him was swift and merciful and clean. The third had a look in his eyes the

Senator had seen before, during Challenges. It was the look of a man who knew with absolute certainty he was about to die.

As the last of the air drained out of the *Hyperion*, Gardner, Kieran and the Senator hurriedly set to pulling the combat suits off the three dead troopers and putting them on. The suits were of a standard size, but designed to expand, contract and reshape themselves according to the physique of the individual who wore them.

Arbenz was pleased to feel his own suit fit itself tentatively around his contours, adjusting itself for maximum comfort and freedom of movement. All three of them next pulled on light, foldable helmets.

He stared at the corpses of the three troopers, floating lifelessly nearby, and decided that one day children would be taken to see their commemorative statues standing tall and proud in public parks on Freehold worlds scattered throughout the furthest reaches of the Milky Way.

Kieran led them along darkened corridors and via drop shafts towards the bridge, with nothing untoward occurring on the way. His soldier's instinct assured him that whatever had been responsible for the sudden depressurization was finally gone.

Once they reached the bridge, Kieran managed to reactivate the main systems without too much trouble, but it was clear that much data had been wiped from the *Hyperion*'s stacks. It was even clearer that the approaching fleet was almost upon them.

Once Kieran had the emergency doors locked down and the bridge repressurized, Arbenz pulled off his helmet. 'Kieran, see if that fleet is trying to hail us. Can you take us out of orbit if necessary?'

'Propulsion systems are down for the moment, Senator, but the weapon systems remain fully functional.'

'What if they start shooting?' asked Gardner, his face white and eyes wide with alarm.

'They'll be waiting for us to start shooting first,' Arbenz reassured him. 'That way, history would record us as the aggressors. Kieran, hail the *Agartha*. I want to know if that fleet out there has identified itself yet.'

Kieran nodded absently and tapped at a screen. He spoke up several moments later. 'Senator, the ships are owned by Alexander Bourdain. They've requested our immediate surrender, or they'll begin firing on us.'

Gardner took a step forward. 'Senator. We have to do *something*. We can't just sit and wait!'

Arbenz hustled over to a command console, which had a map of the Arctis system displayed above it. The approach vectors of Bourdain's fleet were overlaid in lines of glowing green. Kieran meanwhile stepped over to man the weapons station immediately next to it.

'Kieran, do you think—?'

'I make sure to keep up my simulation training, Senator,' Kieran replied, anticipating Arbenz's further question. 'There are three ships approaching, but only one of them is armed. More than likely the others are nothing more than troop carriers. My best guess is they didn't anticipate us moving quite so many of our orbital military resources to this system.'

'You're saying they didn't think we'd be so well armed, then?' asked Gardner from behind them. There was a nervous edge to his voice that Arbenz didn't miss.

Kieran ignored his interruption and continued to address the Senator. 'To all intents and purposes, the *Hyperion* appears to be still crippled. We could use that to our advantage.'

'Where is the *Agartha*?'

'Relative to Bourdain's fleet, it's been maintaining a position out of sight on the far side of Theona,' Kieran informed him. 'That means they're using up a lot of fuel, but I'm fairly certain Bourdain's fleet don't know about her yet. Their approach vector is focused solely on the *Hyperion*.'

Arbenz nodded, pleased once more with Kieran's natural instinct for warfare. 'We'll wait until they're closer, then we can spring a little surprise on them.'

TWENTY-SIX

Corso was dreaming of his family back on Redstone, who were all glad to see him. He hugged his father, who was still wearing his prison uniform, his face streaked with blood from the prolonged torture sessions he had been forced to endure. Lucas recognized uncles, aunts, nieces and nephews he hadn't seen in months.

One by one, they all waved goodbye to him as, smiling and happy and holding hands, they lined up along the edge of a ditch. The children all wore brightly coloured breather masks, from which rose plumes of steam. But, after a few seconds, half a dozen armoured troopers stepped suddenly out from under the shade of a canopy tree, and mowed down every last one of them with repeated bursts of fire from their weapons.

As Corso watched his kinsfolk tumble lifelessly into the trench, from nearby came the sound of an earth-digger engine roaring to life.

He woke feeling weak and dizzy, and the increasing gees from their rapid acceleration away from the *Hyperion* and from Theona didn't help any. The *Piri Reis* was now boosting at maximum speed towards the inner system, putting as much distance between them and the Freehold as possible. He'd have actually preferred they headed for Newfall, but it was situated on the far side of Nova Arctis, and therefore out of range of the *Piri*'s fusion propulsion systems.

When Dakota had explained how she'd deliberately fried her implants, a long silence followed that particular declaration.

'So now you're going to tell me where we're going?' he prompted. 'Since, as far as I can tell, there's nowhere else to go.'

As he stirred, Corso found himself securely strapped into one of the acceleration couches. Dakota's attention had been focused on a display of the invading fleet manoeuvring into orbit around Theona.

The *Hyperion* appeared to be inactive, yet somehow he couldn't help but believe the Senator was still alive. They'd know soon enough, once the fleet came within proper range of the frigate. Meanwhile, the *Agartha*, for reasons unknown, was only just beginning to move out from its orbit on the far side of Theona.

'I'll explain in a minute,' she replied. 'But first I want to tell you something – and then you can tell me if it sounds crazy or not.'

Corso was too exhausted to argue and waved at her to go on.

'Let's say there was some kind of war a long way off,

using some kind of starkiller weapon,' Dakota continued. 'Then the survivors escaped here, but the Shoal wiped them out, thereby establishing a technological hegemony.' She looked around at him. 'Why would the Shoal *do* that?'

'Self-preservation?' Corso shrugged. 'Maybe the Magi were aggressors.'

She shook her head. 'Too simple. Everything changes now that we know the transluminal drive is also a weapon. It's the one great question of the age: why do only the Shoal possess the secret of faster-than-light travel?'

'Because they stole it from the Magi,' he replied, as if stating the stunningly obvious.

'But if the Magi figured out how to do it, why not the Shoal? Why did they have to steal it from someone else?'

'What's your point?'

'My point,' Dakota answered, 'is if *one* race can develop a transluminal drive, then why not a dozen races? Or a thousand, for that matter? By all rights, based on what we now know about the drive, half the Milky Way should be barren and lifeless. The skies should be filled with battlefields thousands of light years across and littered with dead worlds.'

Corso smiled wryly. 'Maybe it is, and we just don't know it yet. You're also assuming other species would be as aggressive and expansionist as we humans are.'

She laughed, the sound dry and pitiless. 'And you reckon they aren't?'

Corso peered at her. 'What happened to you that time I put you in the interface chair? I could tell you were holding something back.'

'All right,' she relented. 'I saw a lot. It was like I was actually on some world within the Magellanic Clouds. I know the link only lasted a couple of seconds but, believe me, it felt like longer. *Much* longer.'

'What do you mean?'

'I've hardly had time to really think clearly about it.' Corso smiled at that. 'It felt like waking from a dream where you feel like you've spent ten years of your life in a place that doesn't exist any more. It felt like knowing everything about it, instantly. That's what it felt like.'

'But were you able to hang on to any of it, once your Ghost was wiped?'

'Only what I could remember with my *natural* memory. Even with my Ghost fully operative, most of it didn't make sense – at least, not at first.' She shook her head. 'You know, I don't think even the Magi developed the transluminal drive themselves. I think they found it somewhere.'

Corso didn't look as surprised as she might have expected.

'There were hints of something like that in the derelict's historical records,' he confirmed. 'It didn't make much sense at first, but—'

'But it does now?'

'Worryingly so, yes.'

She nodded. 'All right, here's another idea for you. What if the Magi, when they discovered their first transluminal drive, had actually walked into a trap?'

Corso looked at her disbelievingly, but she hurried on.

'Look, say you want to get rid of potential competitor species, for whatever reason. Maybe to prevent them from becoming powerful enough to end up effectively ruling a galaxy the way the Shoal now do. So what you do is leave something very like that derelict hidden away somewhere it might eventually get discovered by a species possessing the ability to get into space, but only at a sublight crawl.'

'This is the most paranoid thing I've ever heard in my life,' Corso guffawed. 'What could possibly make you think—?'

'One thing I learned while I was in that chair is that the Shoal may own the transluminal drive, but even they don't really understand how it works. The derelict on Theona isn't one of those traps I suggested, but I think the Magi themselves found something very like it a long time ago – and that *was* a trap.'

'You know, even when we were on board the derelict, I had no idea of the drive's destructive capacity. It sounds to me like maybe you already had some idea of what it could do.'

'No, Lucas, I didn't. But once the Senator forced you to admit what the drive could do, all those fragmented bits and pieces of knowledge from the derelict started to make sense. Think about it: a cache of technology left hidden on some uninhabited world, like bait for a rat.'

'And you know all this from only a few seconds in that chair?'

'Why not?' Dakota demanded. 'You can't deny it makes a lot of sense, once you put the evidence together.'

'So why haven't the Shoal managed to wipe themselves out, in all this time?'

'Because they've been careful. Very careful. Maybe only a select few of them ever know the truth. Whatever created the cache the Magi discovered intended that the drive would eventually wipe out any aggressive, warmaking species that later stumbled across it.'

'So the Magi got wiped out.'

'Yes, but some of them survived and escaped here. Now the Shoal roam the galaxy, looking for the same kind of caches wherever they might still be hidden. Not necessarily because they're greedy, and not just to retain their power, but maybe because, if they don't, someone else might find the technology and initiate a war like nothing we could ever begin to imagine. The kind of war that usually doesn't leave any survivors to pass on a warning.'

'You're starting to sound almost like you're on the side of the Shoal.'

'No, I'm saying that once you begin to take into

account the things we now know, the overall picture gets a lot more complicated.'

'I don't know.' Corso shook his head. 'It's a lot to accept.'

Dakota twisted her head around to eye him triumphantly. 'All right, here's the killer proof. Clause Six, in the Shoal's colonial contracts.'

Corso gazed at her quizzically. 'How do you mean?'

'We don't really know why the Shoal insists on that clause, because it doesn't seem to make any sense. They gave the Uchidans a world of their own, and a couple of decades later they took it away from them again. But why?'

'Go on.'

'Because the Shoal found another cache there: the same kind of thing the Magi once stumbled on. It's the one explanation that helps everything else make sense.'

Corso looked thunderstruck. 'But a solar system is a big place, Dakota. Why—?'

'Even the Shoal can't search through every solar system in the galaxy. Easier to wait until one becomes inhabited, and *then* scour it thoroughly for evidence of a cache. Even if they don't find one at first, they know they're going to be frequent visitors there aboard their coreships, since no one can get to that world except through them. And this gives them plenty of time, in the long run, to survey every last boulder and grain of sand within a system. So when they found one in the Uchidan home system, they didn't want any witnesses, and they weren't taking any chances whatsoever.'

Corso shook his head and looked away. 'Maybe you've got something there.'

'No, Lucas, I'm more sure of this than I've ever been of anything.'

'So,' he asked carefully, 'what are you proposing we do now?'

She studied him carefully as she spoke. 'I don't know. I really don't know. At first I just didn't want Arbenz to get his hands on that Theona derelict, and now I realize you don't either. But there's even bigger reasons now to make sure he doesn't win this.'

'That's a given, but it's not what I meant,' Corso replied. 'Say, for argument's sake, you got your hands on that derelict. Do you destroy it like the Shoal presumably want, or do we take possession of it and make humanity into a true star-faring species?'

'I'm still not sure,' Dakota admitted. 'But right now our priority is staying alive. Your Senator has that fleet to deal with, and I don't know who's going to win the fight, but once it's over, the survivors are going to come after us.'

'Now you're going to tell me just why it is we're headed into the inner system.'

'Do you remember when I came to you in the medical bay, and I said the derelict had fired out some kind of signal at the same time it attacked you?'

'Yes,' he said guardedly. 'But I never had the chance to find out what that was all about.'

'It looks like our derelict isn't alone: it might have been part of a fleet. Well, that transmission was fired directly toward Nova Arctis' innermost world, Ikaria.'

Corso took a moment to absorb this information. 'But you don't actually *know* anything's there,' he said finally.

'It's a chance.'

'A chance at what?' Corso protested. 'There's *nowhere* for us to go. You saved my life. I'm grateful for that.'

'We'll never get control of the derelict that's on Theona,' Dakota replied, 'but I've got reason to think we might do better with whatever other derelicts are on Ikaria. Maybe, if we're very lucky, we *can* survive this one.'

Corso stared at her, speechless.

She grinned. 'But, if you'd rather turn back and surrender . . .'

Corso shook his head. 'No, Let's just maintain this course. At least we'll gain ourselves some breathing space before the fusion piles give out.'

TWENTY-SEVEN

Bourdain's fleet fell into the Nova Arctis system like a swarm of avenging silver angels, the hull of his centre ship bristling with plasma weapons focused on the silent shape of the *Hyperion*, still locked into its tight orbit around Theona.

They had crossed the system at the highest speed possible, and were currently locked into a high-gee deceleration, their engines pointed in-system as they braked hard to avoid overshooting the gas-giant Dymas altogether. Warriors in dull-grey liquid body armour were couched in racked acceleration couches inside the two accompanying craft.

The three ships began to turn as they came out of deceleration, each slowly spinning around until they dropped towards Theona nose-first, their automated weapons systems swivelling to maintain their line of fire on the *Hyperion* itself and the base on the moon's surface, far below.

Arbenz frowned, glancing across the bridge to where Kieran still maintained his post at a console. Gardner sat a little way off, in a couch at one end of the bridge area, watching them both with a contemplative look. *Contemplating how to get rid of us, more than likely*, the Senator mused.

Kieran looked up. 'Sir, I'm concerned about what that woman Merrick said, about the Shoal placing software spies inside the *Hyperion*'s stacks—'

'We can worry about that later,' Arbenz responded dismissively. 'Right now, we have this fleet to contend with. In the meantime, I'd love to know who was responsible for leaking information about the derelict's existence to Bourdain.'

'Senator?'

Arbenz glanced over at Gardner, who was peering down at a comms console with apparent fascination.

'What is it, Mr Gardner?' he snapped, his voice full of irritation.

'It's the derelict, Senator. You might want to take a look at this.'

Arbenz turned to Kieran, who then brought up what Gardner was seeing to the main screens.

There were severe tremors evident on Theona, bad enough to rupture the ice, and all centred on the derelict. The officer in charge of the surface base had already ordered an evacuation.

Doubt assailed Gregor Arbenz for the first time in a very, very long while. Things were starting to move far faster than he would have anticipated.

*

The staff and troopers stationed inside the Theona base had barely a few seconds to register what at first appeared to be a major 'quake. Then they registered nothing at all, when the base, along with several cubic kilometres of ice and rock, was vaporized in an instant, leaving the churning ocean below exposed to the stars and the cold of space for the first time in half a billion years.

A hole had appeared in the pristine white surface of Theona, a vast chasm with foam churning at its bottom, as water boiled on contact with the near vacuum of the moon's atmosphere.

From the centre of it all arose a shape like a night-marish expressionist sculpture of a squid, carried upwards by incandescent bursts of energy. Water cascaded from its hull, freezing instantly and shearing off in great sheets, as the derelict fought its way through the clouds of debris and superheated steam that rose in a great mushroom above Theona's fractured horizon.

'Senator,' Gardner's tone became harsh and clipped, 'I am asking you again to order the *Agartha* to fire on the derelict.'

Arbenz sighed and forced himself to turn away from what he was seeing on the overhead screens. So far, Bourdain's fleet hadn't fired on them, and Kieran had regained nominal control of the propulsion systems as well as the weapon banks, but hadn't activated either. They were going to run silent for as long as possible.

The *Hyperion* still looked like it was mostly inoperative: dead in the water, as they used to say.

So far it looked like their strategy was working, while the approaching fleet appeared to be heading for a rendezvous. Arbenz couldn't help but wonder what they would make of the alien craft that had just wiped out an entire Freehold base.

Meanwhile, the *Agartha* was due to reappear, any minute now, from its hiding place on the far side of Theona.

'Mr Gardner, you have no power aboard a sovereign Freehold military vessel. Your role here is purely advisory – and I'd counsel you to remember that.'

Gardner came round to stand directly in front of the Senator, thrusting his face forward. 'If you don't shoot that thing out of the sky before it jumps out of this system, our entire arrangement is over. All support for this expedition will be withdrawn, and you can pay your own damn bills.'

The Senator stared at Gardner, and then burst out laughing. 'Why in the name of Christ do you think we would destroy the one thing we came here for?'

Kieran stood silently nearby, awaiting his orders. It seemed Gardner had forgotten about him for the moment. Good.

'That derelict is clearly under the control of some alien force,' Gardner persisted. 'What if it jumps right inside the heart of this system's star and turns it nova, Senator? *What if it tries to destroy us all?*'

The Senator gave him a pitying look. 'Or you might consider the more realistic possibility that Dakota Merrick is controlling the derelict herself.'

Gardner stared at him, almost bug-eyed with horror. 'You think this is just a matter of someone simply stealing the derelict?' he choked. 'We don't have any reason to think it isn't about to destroy this entire system, you fucking lunatic. Merrick said the Shoal knew from the start what we'd found and now, by the looks of it, they're busy protecting their secret. If you don't act right now, there's a very good chance we're all going to die.'

The Senator bristled. 'Outside of you and the woman pilot and Corso, there isn't a single human being in this entire system who didn't fight to the death at some time to prove they were good enough to be here. We aren't afraid of dying, Mr Gardner. But if we do die, at least we die with honour. Maybe you should think about that.'

'No.' Gardner shook his head furiously, taking a step back from the Senator. 'No!' He shook his head again. 'You're insane. I want to communicate with my partners. *Now*.'

'That's not possible. We're under attack, hadn't you noticed?'

'You have a duty—'

'I only have a duty to the Freehold,' Arbenz replied wearily. 'You can return to your quarters. We're going to catch and disable the derelict, but only once we've dealt with the fleet. It might possess transluminal capability, but until it decides either to jump or not jump, it's no faster than either us or the *Agartha*.'

Arbenz turned away from Gardner, implicitly dismissing him. But Gardner just stepped back around to confront him again.

'Who the hell do you think you're talking to, Senator? What exactly do you think you're going to do without my help? You're going to kill us all!'

'Frankly, I don't trust you, Mr Gardner.'

Gardner's face darkened. 'To hell with you. Corso was right: you're going to kill us all, just to satisfy your fucking honour.' He spat the words out with maximum derision. 'Our relationship is over.'

Arbenz stared at him, his face twisted into a mask of fury, and then he burst out laughing.

'Have you ever had those occasional moments of absolute clarity, Mr Gardner? I genuinely did wonder who was responsible for telling Bourdain about the existence of the derelict. Now that I think about it, I wonder how I could ever have harboured any doubts that you were the one responsible.'

Gardner said nothing, but Arbenz could see the truth hidden in his cowardly eyes.

'Kieran,' signalled the Senator.

Kieran came forward, quickly grabbing Gardner around the neck and pulling him back until he was bent over a console. Gardner flailed and twisted in his grasp.

Arbenz then stepped forward and punched Gardner

hard in the stomach. The man slumped, winded, then redoubled his struggles when he saw the long, heavy knife Kieran had withdrawn from its sheath. He handed it over to the Senator.

'Don't take this personally, David. You're a braver man than I thought, going behind our backs like that. But if we can't trust you, we can't take any chances either. We took the life of a loyal Freeholder just to keep you alive, and now it's time for you to pay him back.'

Kieran yanked Gardner's head back hard, exposing his throat. Arbenz wasn't a sadist, so he made it quick. He took the knife and cut a deep slice across Gardner's throat as Kieran kept a hand firmly planted over the man's mouth. A spray of blood spattered on the deck. Gardner's body twisted and jerked momentarily before it collapsed.

Kieran gave his superior an accusing glare. 'You should have let him defend himself, Senator.'

'This isn't the time and place for observing tradition,' Arbenz snapped. 'Have you readied the systems yet?'

Kieran nodded. 'We should evacuate straight away.'

'Not yet.' Arbenz shook his head. 'Not until whoever's in charge of that fleet is just about ready to board us – if that's what they're intending to do. Until the *Agartha* shows up and draws their attention, we'll be an easy target if we abandon ship too soon.'

*

Dakota had already told Corso about the uninvited guest inside her skull. They'd watched, appalled, as a dome of dust and debris expanded across the face of the receding moon.

'The derelict?'

'It has to be, surely? I think Trader must have taken it over, now there's nowhere else for him to hide. But the derelict itself – the machine intelligence in the heart of it – can still communicate with me. It's the same with the other derelicts on Ikaria.' She looked at Corso. 'It's like they *want* me to come to them.'

'But your Ghost—?'

'The physical circuitry still functions.' She smiled. 'With all the protocols and routines I built up gone, it means the other Magi ships will accept me as a pilot. No interface chair required whatsoever. Just me.'

Corso shook his head. 'I don't know what to say. I know I don't have any choice but to believe what you're telling me.'

She stared off into space, far away for a moment.

'I'm not crazy, Corso. Trader might have control of the Theona derelict, but maybe there's a way to persuade one of the other ones on Ikaria to take us out of this system.'

The surface of Theona was hazed by cloud, pale tendrils slowly wrapping themselves around the surface of the little world, spreading outwards from the gaping hole the derelict had blasted through kilometres of encompassing ice. Dark and silent, the *Hyperion* drifted far above.

The three ships comprising Bourdain's fleet manoeuvred to come alongside the inactive vessel, while sporadic automated mayday alerts and warnings of cataclysmic life-support failure continued to broadcast from the Freehold craft. Warnings blasted out from Bourdain's fleet that the *Hyperion* was about to be boarded.

There was no reply. Before he and the Senator had departed the bridge, Kieran had deliberately left several communications channels wide open that permitted those in charge of the invading fleet to access the bridge's video feeds and witness the carnage within.

In the meantime, on the far side of the *Hyperion* from the nearest ship of the attacking fleet, there was a brief burst of energy as an emergency rescue pod, carrying two people, jetted away.

A few moments later, once the central ship of Bourdain's fleet was within a thousand metres, the *Hyperion*'s engines blazed into unexpected life and it began to move. Slowly at first, but then faster, heading for an intercept with the fleet's command ship.

At that same moment, the commander of Bourdain's fleet picked up the *Agartha* on long-range telemetry, approaching from over the curve of Theona's horizon.

Missiles raced away from the *Agartha*, closing in on the other two vessels in Bourdain's fleet.

TWENTY-EIGHT

'Something's happening,' remarked Dakota.

Corso peered over at a display of figures scrolling in tight columns as the *Hyperion* unexpectedly powered into life. They'd watched closely the destruction occurring on the surface of Theona, now barely more than a distant pinprick of light as they accelerated away. Dymas itself was beginning to dwindle as the *Piri* used up most of its remaining fuel to blast them halfway across the Nova Arctis system.

The images they were now watching were fed through a deep-space optical scanner system set up by the Freehold. It allowed them to watch the approach of the three unmarked vessels, as they carefully vectored in to match the *Hyperion*'s orbit and velocity.

'Why aren't they shooting?' Corso wondered out loud.

'Because there's too much valuable information on board the *Hyperion*. At least, I reckon that's what they're assuming.'

'I didn't mean the other ships,' said Corso. 'I meant

the Senator. He's not the type to go down without a fight.'

'Assuming he's even still alive,' Dakota replied dismissively.

'You couldn't kill him that easily. And look.' He pointed at the screen, as the *Piri*'s detection systems picked up and isolated the image of a tiny vehicle exiting the *Hyperion*.

'Yeah, he's up to something,' Corso mused, leaning in closer.

The *Hyperion* had been programmed for a basic intercept course with the fleet's command vessel. Under any other circumstances, the crew of the command vessel would simply have plotted a course that took them out of the ageing warship's path. But that didn't take the *Agartha* into account, preceded by three nuclear-tipped missiles.

Bourdain's command vessel was now caught in a classic pincer movement. Its beam weapons swivelled in their ports and fired outwards, destroying each of the missiles in a flash of bright fire.

Too late: the command vessel's crew had hesitated a moment too long. The *Hyperion* had ramped its engines to maximum acceleration – a far higher rate of gees than would have been possible if anyone on board had still been alive.

The command ship tried to boost itself out of the *Hyperion*'s path. And it almost made it.

The *Hyperion* surged forward, slamming into the command vessel, whose hull crumpled like paper under the impact, releasing puffs of atmosphere. To an outside observer, it would have appeared as if the two ships were actually melting into each other.

More missiles had been launched from the *Agartha* in the meantime, also targeted at the two subsidiary vessels. The command vessel's fusion propulsion systems meantime exploded under the force of the *Hyperion*'s impact, releasing all their energy in one single, devastating blast.

Lines of light spread along the length of the *Hyperion*'s vast bulk, rapidly moving from fore to aft as the craft's magnetic containment chambers ruptured, spilling raw plasma into space.

Corso chewed at his knuckles as he watched intently on the *Piri Reis*'s main screen. The destruction of the *Hyperion* and the largest vessel in the enemy fleet had caused an explosion bright enough to overwhelm the *Piri*'s filters for a few moments. He was forced to partly rely on numerical feeds and communications traffic analyses to give him a true picture of what had just happened.

The battle thereafter degenerated into a straightforward shooting match. The *Agartha* was decelerating now, and one of the remaining two enemy ships was drifting lifeless, set into a slow spin by a missile strike. Judging by the way it had been ripped open, it was extremely unlikely that anyone on board had been left alive. The *Hyperion* and the command vessel had merged into a tangled, burning mass, twisting slowly as Theona's gravity sucked them downwards.

Corso next turned his attention to their passage across the Nova Arctis system. The *Piri* was already moving at enormous speeds, its tiny mass, relative to ships like the *Agartha*, allowing it to zip between worlds at an almost uncanny pace. The danger of interference from any other ships that might be orbiting Newfall was nonexistent: at the moment, that planet was far on the other side of the system from them, putting any other Freehold vessels far out of reach.

The innermost world, Ikaria, was however a lot more reachable. It lay almost directly ahead, locked into a tight, Mercury-like orbit around its parent star, close enough that any atmosphere it might once have possessed had long since been burned away.

Dakota's ship was fortunately equipped with a small cache of micro-probes, tiny automated things that could be boosted to far higher speeds than a ship like the *Piri Reis* or its fragile human crew could withstand. They were already most of the way toward Ikaria, getting ready to dive downwards and relay back images and data pertaining to anything they found or saw.

The battle above Theona was over almost as soon as

it had begun, the *Agartha* firing further missiles that destroyed the remaining enemy ship. The *Agartha* was already altering its course to come after the Theona derelict, which had by now left the moon's orbit. It would inevitably pass within only a few million kilometres of the *Piri Reis* as it dived towards the heart of the Nova Arctis system.

Long-range detection systems showed the crackle of plasma around the derelict's skin. The *Agartha*, meanwhile, was already accelerating so hard it was a wonder its crew could survive on it at all. Regardless of this, the derelict still had the clear advantage.

It didn't take much guesswork to figure out that the derelict was powering up for a transluminal jump.

Corso was willing to bet any amount of money the alien craft's destination was the fiery heart of Nova Arctis itself. It seemed Dakota's Shoal AI was about to destroy an entire system, all to wipe out the evidence that the Shoal had stolen their transluminal technology from a far older civilization.

More information flashed up before him: tachyon relay signals from Newfall were being targeted at the derelict, presumably in a desperate attempt to slow, stop or divert it, using communications protocols he himself had helped develop. Whoever was behind the signals knew what they were doing. Almost certainly that meant other Freeholder scientists like himself. But whoever they were, they surely understood they were fighting for their lives.

Corso stared at the board in front of his acceleration couch, sensing the power in his hands. Using his own copy of the same protocols, he could block those transmissions from Newfall.

He felt a sensation like ice being clamped around his heart. He could do it: he could prevent his own people from finding a way inside the first derelict.

Yet he found he didn't want to do that.

The extremists back on Redstone had been toppled. There could be no triumphant return for Arbenz, not even with the transluminal drive in hand. Only arrest and disgrace for his murderous ways.

Perhaps, then, there was still the chance the Freehold could rise back up out of obscurity and become part of the Consortium in a way they never had been before.

He carefully pulled his hands away from the board, glancing over at Dakota who lay asleep in her own couch, a remarkable feat considering the gees they were both still subject to as they blasted across a solar system.

But it wasn't really sleep, she had informed him when her eyes had briefly fluttered open a little while back: more a kind of trance state.

Whatever was happening inside her head, or within the empty vaults of her Ghost circuits, was beyond his comprehension. To Corso that was the most frightening thing of all.

TWENTY-NINE

For Dakota, it felt strangely like stepping into someone else's dreams.

For several hours now, her Ghost had been slowly flickering its way back into life. There was no trace of the highly personalized routines she had built up over so many years – but *something* was trying to speak to her, its voice reaching out from distant Ikaria.

Most of the sensations she was currently experiencing within her mind were entirely incomprehensible: synaesthetic flurries she strongly suspected were intended for sense organs entirely different to her own. But within that chaos appeared nuggets of information that were startlingly clear.

She was learning to understand the Magi.

The derelicts on Ikaria reached out to her, across the cold and lonely void. They had been waiting for someone like her for a long, long time.

She felt rough, hot rock pressing against her skin. She lay at the bottom of a deep valley, a kilometres-deep crack running along an ancient fault line in Ikaria's crust.

There were three of her . . . no, of *them*. They were machines, the same as the Theona derelict – partly organic in nature: not alive in any way she could understand, but certainly aware nonetheless.

She opened her eyes and looked around. Corso had finally fallen asleep in his couch despite his grumbled complaints earlier about the constant acceleration. Her brain felt like cotton wool, and she knew she'd been communing with the distant derelicts for far longer than she'd realized.

She could see from the readouts that the *Agartha* was accelerating fast in the same direction. Catching the *Piri Reis* wouldn't gain them anything, so they could only be chasing after the derelict.

She laughed to herself. Did they actually think they could outrun it?

Directly ahead, Nova Arctis was steadily growing larger, though still barely more than a particularly bright pinprick in the unending night. Very soon, the *Piri* was due to flip on its axis mid-course, as a prelude to heavy deceleration.

The *Piri*'s miniaturized probes, in the meantime, were sending back initial reports from orbit above Ikaria. She stared at blurred images of what looked like, yes, three more craft identical to the Theona derelict, but buried deep within a chasm on Ikaria's crater-pocked surface.

The probes circled lower and lower in their orbits, gaining higher and higher definition images in the remaining time before Ikaria's gravity finally sucked them to their doom.

By now Corso had woken up.

'They're just the same as the first derelict we found, aren't they?' he commented.

'Looks that way. Have you noticed the course the Theona derelict is taking?'

Corso tapped at a console and stared up at a screen. The first derelict had now adjusted its trajectory to bypass Ikaria, clearly having set a course for the heart of the sun.

Corso pulled himself up with a strap and swore, his muscles bunching with tension. 'No, it'll get there too soon. We don't have enough time—'

'Stop panicking,' Dakota snapped. 'It's still too soon for it to make the jump. It could take hours, even days, right? Assuming it even *can* make a jump once it's this deep inside a system.'

The most interesting aspect of not being real, Trader's virtual doppelgänger had long concluded, was the lack of concern felt for one's own self-preservation.

The recesses of the derelict's information stacks were near infinite in their storage capacity, far surpassing just the satisfaction of mere curiosity. Within their depths Trader had discovered the accumulated knowledge of a culture that had undergone endless expansions and contractions within the Magellanic Clouds for very nearly two million years. Their empire had ruled countless worlds before collapsing into half-remembered dust, only to rise again with passing aeons, and spreading yet further outwards.

The humans liked to call the cloud-dwellers 'Magi', and it was as good a name as any, given the miracles of which they were capable. But even so, some things had yet remained far, far beyond them. Their empire had been built with excruciating slowness, taking hundreds of millennia to spread incrementally across their galaxy at a sublight crawl. That empire had fought itself to the death a thousand times, as vast civilizations, locked into war with each other, failed to recognize their common ancestry until long after the combat was over.

In the meantime, the derelict hurtled towards its destination deep within the heart of Nova Arctis. The virtual Trader felt no concern, no sense of loss, and no fear over its own imminent destruction.

Here I am, embodied within the mind of this craft, contemplating the end of my existence in a very short time indeed. Does that lack of concern deny me as a true thinking being, or is my ability to be aware of myself – to exist – suggest that I am just as alive as the original me?

When these philosophical questions grew tiresome, Trader dived deep within the derelict's stacks and the endless realms contained therein – fully-fledged interactive environments representing a million worlds over a spread of uncountable aeons. He lived virtual centuries within these environments at an accelerated pace, while in the greater universe outside the derelict crawled towards its ultimate destination.

The tragedy was that the flesh-and-blood Trader would never know of the rich experiences being partaken of by his doppelgänger. All evidence that the Magi culture had even existed had been deliberately destroyed some millennia before. Better to consign an entire civilization to the dust than risk the revelation that yet more caches might be found scattered throughout the cosmos.

The Magi had been seduced into destroying themselves.

They had stumbled across a hidden cache of high technology in much the same way as the humans had stumbled across their derelict starship. It had been buried in the heart of an asteroid, within a chamber of clearly artificial origin, seemingly a gift of sheer providence.

Trader idled a century away in the abyssal, kilometres-deep chambers of a world-library the Magi themselves had called *Sadness of Lost Memories Recovered from Damaged Media*. Therein he found the stories of a hundred mighty interstellar civilizations to rival the Shoal and far beyond, of their rise and fall and rise again, like the steady beating of a god's heart – all lost in the depths of ancient time.

Of all the theories Trader had heard, ranging from the drily sober to the irredeemably insane, one appealed above all others. Not because it appeared to have any greater validity than any other theory, but because it scared him more than any other.

The theory held that the transluminal drive had been created by a race of beings responsible for the construction of the universe itself – a race generally referred to by the Magi as the Makers. The drives appeared to tap into the same infinite energy that fuelled the primordial chaos from which all reality had sprung: therefore it was not unreasonable to assume the drive had been a means by which those ancient godlike beings could tour their creation.

Unfortunately, after some billions of years had passed, the Makers found rats in the cellar: life, in all its astonishing fecundity.

And so they had set out traps, nets cast wide and deep in the hopes of snagging the unwary.

If some of those ancient Magi cultures had bothered to check the records lost deep inside their own world-libraries, they might have been able to prolong their existence by the simple expedient of hunting down those carefully hidden caches of dangerous technology and destroying them before they were found by others, much as the Shoal had now been doing for almost the entirety of their recorded history.

It was only stunningly bad luck that the humans had discovered a Magi ship, rather than one of the original Maker caches.

Trader had been present during the Twelfth Schism, some seventeen millennia before (a mere stripling a few thousand years old, and only just beginning to grow weary of existence), when the Maker Cult had swept through the younger ranks of the Shoal ruling elite. Thousands had been put to death or assassinated over the next millennia to prevent knowledge of the star drive's destructive potential from becoming more widely known.

And if this star and all the ancient Magi ships hidden among its worlds were destroyed, how long before some other species discovered an actual Maker cache, before the Shoal could get to it first? This was the wearying reality – that the Shoal were only delaying the inevitable, galaxy-spanning conflict that even the Dreamers agreed must eventually come.

Let the stars die, Trader thought, drifting aimlessly through the long-dead shadows of a forgotten race. Let it all start again, until, a few billion years from now, other species rise from our ashes and wander through our own discovered memories and ancient ruins, wondering how we came to destroy ourselves so quickly, before themselves re-enacting that same history.

And then came a signal, disturbing its long years of idle wandering.

Finally it was time.

The Shoal AI prepared itself for non-existence.

The *Agartha* was closing on them, shadowing the *Piri Reis*'s cross-system vector. Dakota had altered their trajectory so that they kept Ikaria between them and the star it orbited. This helped prevent the *Piri Reis*'s external systems from becoming overwhelmed by Nova Arctis itself as it spread across their viewscreens.

They were deep into deceleration now, the last of the *Piri*'s fuel blasting towards Nova Arctis, and bringing them into an insertion point for orbit around Ikaria.

As the hours had finally become days, Nova Arctis began to appear on their screens as a ball of yellow incandescence with a dark blemish at its centre. This blemish gradually grew as the hours passed, turning the star into a halo of fire around the circumference of Ikaria as it grew larger and wider.

Long-range telescopes threw Ikaria's mottled, broken surface on to the *Piri Reis*'s screens as they dropped towards it, using filtering technology to pick out a visual map of a vast chasm on the approaching planet, the result of a massive impact some billions of years before. It was a crack running two-thirds of the way around the dead world's equator.

Their destination.

Dakota stared at the high-res video that floated in the air between the two acceleration couches. All they had to do was get down to that chasm, find a way on board one of the other derelicts, persuade it not to kill them, figure out how to fly it, and escape this system at light speed before the entire system detonated.

Easy.

She was conscious of Corso saying something to her.

'. . . the chasm those other derelicts are in?' He was pointing at the holo display between them. 'That thing makes the Vallis Marineris on Mars look like a furrow. Something must have hit that planet hard enough to just about crack it in half.'

Dakota shrugged. 'So?'

Corso sighed. 'Look closer.'

He gestured, and a 3D model of Ikaria replaced the video showing the chasm.

Its rotation was slow enough that a day on its surface was longer than one of its years. Sunlight crept over its horizon at a snail's pace, one hemisphere crisped by its extreme proximity to its parent star, the other dark and frozen until the inevitable arrival of a ferocious sunrise.

'There are places on the dark side where that trench goes down very, very deep: maybe eight or ten kilometres. We could hide down there if the derelict does blow the star.'

Dakota couldn't hide her incredulity. '*Hide?*' She laughed. 'From a *nova*? Lucas, we're practically next door to the star as it is. If you shouted it would probably hear you. Ikaria would be vaporized.'

'But not immediately.' As Corso replied, his eyes were bright with an unpleasant mania from the quantities of stimulants he'd been pumping into his blood stream just in order to stay alert. 'That could take up to a day or two, right? In the meantime we might be able to buy ourselves at least a few extra hours down inside that chasm.'

Dakota tried to frame a suitable reply, but it was getting harder to find the words. Instead, she just shrugged her shoulders and looked away, overwhelmed by a sense of increasing hopelessness. She was at a point where she wasn't even sure if she really cared whether she lived or died, just so long as events came to some kind of conclusion.

Each of them was turning into a basket case while the other one watched.

Readings showed the incipient transluminal energies crackling around the hull of the Theona derelict, and the possibility had occurred to Dakota that coreships rarely approached the inner part of any system they visited for reasons other than the ones most often assumed. Perhaps the Shoal were simply nervous about getting too close to any star while they were on board a transluminal vessel.

It seemed incredible that something so tiny could cause so much destruction, yet as Dakota sank further and further into the dreamlike thoughtscape of the remaining Magi ships on Ikaria, she found it harder to deny.

Then there was the question of physically landing on the surface of Ikaria. If Corso were not so stressed and so thoroughly doped to the eyeballs, he might have been aware of the obvious problem: the *Piri* was simply not designed to land on any planetary body; they barely had enough fuel to make the approach into orbit and, even if they could somehow make a landing, the stresses involved would tear the little ship apart.

So they were going to have to think of something else.

Whenever Dakota closed her eyes, instead of darkness, she saw alien starscapes; vast citadels spread across the faces of entire worlds; and great world ships that dwarfed even the Shoal's own interstellar craft.

'The derelict!' Corso shouted hoarsely. 'It's gone. It's off the screens!'

Dakota switched her attention to a tracking view. The Theona derelict was indeed gone from every reading.

The *Agartha*, however, was still marked on a map of the system by an advancing red line, still shadowing the *Piri Reis* at every step. It was following them into Ikaria's dark side, just as she'd expected.

PART THREE

PART THREE

THIRTY

Nova Arctis was a standard G2 class star, mostly hydrogen and helium and a scattering of trace elements that had been moving in its long, slow orbit around the galactic core, accompanied by the other stars of the Orion Arm, for the better part of three and a half billion years. It might easily have expected to last five or six billion more before entering its red giant phase, at which point it would have slowly expanded to swallow the majority of the rocky worlds that comprised its inner system.

A moment before Corso noticed the Theona derelict was gone, a shell of exotic energy formed around the ancient Magi craft, tearing a hole in the universe, through which it then fell. The translation into transluminal space produced gravitational shock waves that rippled outwards, precisely as if a planetary body had materialized within the inner system and then disappeared again within the space of a single moment.

If the men and women in charge of administrating the Consortium had known what Corso and Dakota now knew, they would have understood that a coreship penetrating this deep into any populated system could only ever represent an act of war.

The Theona derelict rematerialized deep within the core of the star, a swirling mass of fusing hydrogen and helium that burned at fifteen million degrees.

By this point, Trader had stretched subjective time aboard the derelict to its absolute limit. He witnessed the violent plasmas penetrating the hull like bright tentacles, vaporizing the exterior of the craft in a millionth of a second.

From Trader's accelerated point of view, the super-heated plasma moved at a leisurely yet measurable pace. He felt the derelict's systems shutting down around him as the vessel was reduced to a collection of free component atoms, merging with the violent thermonuclear dance beyond the evaporating hull.

The Shoal AI wondered, in the sliver of eternity before it ceased to exist, if it was the first intelligent creature ever to die directly within the core of a star.

Two millionths of a second after the derelict had materialized within the core of Nova Arctis, a vast burst of neutrinos shot outwards as the core of the craft's superluminal engines collapsed. Then followed a phase change – a shift in the fundamental properties of the matter immediately surrounding the derelict, which now spread outwards in the form of a devouring black sphere, transforming the fifteen-million-centigrade plasma into something much closer to the primordial energy from which the universe itself had been born.

Yet barely more than a few seconds had passed since the ancient starship had materialized within Nova Arctis. At its point of maximum expansion, the phase-change volume encompassed several tens of thousands of kilo- metres within the star's core. It began to collapse as the cosmological constant reasserted itself.

It made no difference to the fact that Nova Arctis was doomed. The final legacy of Trader's virtual doppelgänger came in the form of a whirling storm of singularities spinning outwards from the wreckage of the phase-change bubble, adding hugely to the destruction already wreaked.

Arbenz and Kieran had enjoyed a narrow escape from the *Hyperion*, moments before its destruction. There had been barely seconds to spare as they had crammed themselves into an escape vehicle and launched away. A few hours later, they were brought on board the *Agartha* in time to witness the *Hyperion*'s final plummet down towards Theona's surface, which was now entirely wreathed in white clouds.

Following the destruction of Bourdain's fleet, the path of action had appeared to be clear. But that changed irrevocably when the derelict had disappeared on its way into the inner system, even as the *Agartha* began falling along an almost identical trajectory.

On the bridge of the *Agartha*, Senator Arbenz gripped a railing tightly as he witnessed the derelict's disappearance. Just then a roaring sound, like a water-fall, filled his head and occluded his thoughts.

'Perhaps,' he muttered quietly, to no one in particu-lar, 'we deserve to die.'

'Senator?'

He turned to see Kieran's puzzled frown. Mansell had been speaking with a very grim-faced Captain Liefe, commander of the *Agartha*, and heir to one of the Freehold's most powerful ruling families. Liefe, like Kieran, had lost much back home because of the recent coup.

Liefe wasted no time. 'Senator, the derelict that took off from Theona has just disappeared from every sensor system. It's clearly jumped into transluminal space—'

'I know.'

Liefe nodded. 'But we've been continuing our analy-sis of Ikaria, and we're definitely picking up extremely low-powered encrypted telemetry that matches that of the derelict. There's clearly something else down there.'

Arbenz nodded. Along with the rest of the *Agartha*'s crew, Liefe knew nothing of the derelict's more destructive capabilities, or that its disappearance might very well mean it had dived into the heart of Nova Arctis itself.

He caught Kieran's eye, and saw the same thoughts mirrored there. If Liefe suspected that the entire system might be about to detonate, he might not continue per-forming his duty to the best effect.

Arbenz blinked his tiredness away. They might have

just minutes still to live – or days. There was no way of knowing, but that didn't mean inaction.

'Then that settles it,' he said, speaking more to Kieran than Liefe. 'We destroy the remaining derelicts before they too have a chance to jump out of this system. Similarly, we destroy the machine-head woman's craft before it can manage to rendezvous with any of them. That's clearly what she's planning.'

Liefe blinked, looking perplexed.

'Senator—'

'Remember who's in charge here, Captain,' Arbenz replied mildly. 'Kieran here will be overseeing the operation.'

Arbenz saw the shudder that passed through Liefe as Kieran caught his eye. The latter's deadly reputation extended far.

Emotionless bastard, thought the Senator, not without admiration. A machine in flesh-and-blood form, all the way to the bitter end.

'Senator, I must—'

He cut Liefe off again. 'We lost the first derelict because we were careless with the machine-head pilot. We were infiltrated, right from the very start. That doesn't mean we can allow our enemies to win what we have lost.'

Liefe wasn't a coward. His voice became more determined as he turned his back on Kieran.

'Senator, with all due respect—'

'With all due *respect*, Captain,' Arbenz snarled, 'if

that derelict somehow just jumped into Consortium space with Merrick on board, we've lost this fight already. But I really don't think that's the case, given we're still chasing her ship. We can clearly see where she's heading, and the only possible reason for her current trajectory is because she thinks there's something down on the surface of Ikaria that she can steal from us. I am *not* prepared to go down in history as the one who allowed that to happen.'

Liefe's nostrils flared in anger, but after a moment he nodded sharply, saluted, then turned away to address one of his crew.

Arbenz meanwhile turned to Kieran, and saw a death's-head smile creeping across the man's face. The Senator felt a thrill of the same emotion Liefe must have felt when confronted with that same smile.

'Merrick has altered her course to stay well inside Ikaria's shadow-cone,' Arbenz muttered, 'and it's not hard to guess why. If the worst happens, we might be able to find some shelter from the nova's initial expansion by keeping that rock between the sun and us. I want you to watch Liefe's every move in the meantime. The last thing we need now is insubordination.'

Kieran nodded. 'She killed my brother,' he half-whispered, eyes glistening. 'If we're to die, she dies with us, rest assured.'

There were shouts and exclamations from the far end of the *Agartha*'s bridge. They both turned to see Liefe and the rest of the bridge crew gathered around a floating display that showed an image of Ikaria, and Nova Arctis beyond.

Something was clearly happening.

'Corso?'

As he woke, he could detect the strain in her voice. He blinked himself wider awake, trying to make sense of what she was now seeing on one of the displays. His body still ached from the constant stress of the gees they were being forced to endure.

'Look,' she said, her voice thick. 'Nova Arctis – it's changing colour.'

The filters that processed incoming data from the ship's external cameras were shifting to accommodate a sudden radical shift in the star's appearance. It was becoming redder – darker. As they watched, a vast loop of plasma, long and wide enough to cut through a Jupiter-sized mass, arced outwards from the star's surface. Numbers flickered constantly next to the flare.

They continued diving down towards the surface of Ikaria, still locked into their acceleration couches, as the *Piri*'s engines used up the last of their fuel to drop them into a low orbit around the little world.

Corso glanced for the millionth time at the torrents of information sliding across the screens and the holo display, but the figures resolutely refused to change into something more accommodating to their continued survival.

He looked back over at Dakota, whose attention had drifted again, as it had done more and more frequently over the past twenty-four hours. The times she was fully aware of her surroundings were becoming rarer. It was getting easier to spot whenever the Ikarian derelicts were communicating with her: her face would become slack, eyes focused on some nonexistent horizon.

Corso had trouble figuring out what it was about this that so disturbed him, until he realized she looked less human every time she slipped into this strange fugue state.

Was it possible, he wondered, for her to slip so deep inside whatever dreams the Magi craft generated for her, that she lost track of where she actually was? Or was that just the voice of his own paranoia in the face of something he couldn't begin to really understand?

He spoke her name gently, hoping she might respond. Nothing. Just that same, calm, semi-blissful mask.

'*Dakota,*' he repeated, a little louder this time.

At last an acknowledgement: a blinking of her eyes as her head turned towards him

'You do realize we don't have enough fuel left to land on Ikaria without crashing?' he said. 'That's assuming we could land all the way down inside that chasm, in the first place. We used up too much fuel just getting here.'

She smiled with a faraway look, like she was actually listening to someone else. 'We don't need to land.'

'What?'

She focused more clearly on Corso. 'We don't need to land. We'll just bring one of the derelicts to us.'

Within Nova Arctis, the cloud of singularities began to condense, adding to the core collapse. The collective gravitational attraction of the condensing cloud was more than equal to Nova Arctis in its entirety. Within minutes, superheated plasma that had flowed along the same convection patterns for millions of years would be sucked inward to the void at the star's heart, drawn downwards at a considerable fraction of the speed of light.

In the end, Arbenz decided to tell Liefe the truth. It was obvious something fundamental was happening to the star anyway. Besides, all of Liefe's crew deserved to die as warriors, with full knowledge of the fate that lay before them.

'Inside its *core?*' Liefe stuttered as Arbenz finished. The faces of the crew around them were pale with shock.

For a moment, Arbenz could see, the Captain actually suspected he might be joking. Then the truth of it all began to sink in.

Arbenz put a hand on Liefe's shoulder. 'I'm sorry we didn't tell you before: the drive doubles as a weapon of unprecedented power. We need to destroy any remaining derelicts located on Ikaria, because if they're allowed to get away they could be used to subjugate the Freehold—'

'Arrest him!' Liefe shrieked at his security officer. Liefe drew his own weapon and stepped back quickly, levelling it at Arbenz. 'You should know that there were contingency plans in case you weren't able to handle this mis—'

Kieran moved from his static position with dazzling speed, his Challenge blade appearing in one hand for the briefest moment before it went hurtling across the bridge to land squarely in the middle of Liefe's back.

The Senator watched the commander hit the deck, the hilt of Kieran's knife protruding from his spine. The security officer fired his own weapon, catching Kieran on the shoulder. Kieran spun backwards, landing hard a few metres from where Liefe now lay twitching in his death throes.

Arbenz moved forward without a moment's hesitation, pulling the pistol from Liefe's dying fingers and firing three shots at the security officer. Two hit the man in the chest, while a third landed in his skull. The side of his head exploded messily.

Arbenz went over to Kieran and discovered he'd suffered no more than a bad flesh wound. He fanned his pistol around the remaining crew, most of whom stood in various poses of shock. Several appeared undecided whether they should try rushing the Senator or not.

'Listen to me,' Arbenz shouted hoarsely. 'I am still

your commanding officer by seniority of rank. Don't forget that. What Liefe tried to do just now was an act of mutiny. Nova Arctis is dying because of a Magi weapon. You can see that clearly. I don't know how long we have, but if you want to make your peace, make it now.'

'You've killed us, Senator,' said a young Lieutenant, stepping forward, his face full of cold fury. 'We believed in you, and you've killed us.'

Arbenz stood, staring at the younger man angrily. 'What's your name?' he demanded.

'Klein, Senator.'

'Fine,' Arbenz spat, throwing Kieran's knife down at Klein's feet. 'I killed your Captain, and you have the right to try and execute me for that. My rank is civil, after all, not military. But you knew the risks, all of you, when you came here.'

He nodded towards the display showing the distorted, flaring face of Nova Arctis. 'Just remember, in no time at all you'll all be following me to hell, and nothing you do can change that.'

Arbenz punched one hand into the other. 'Or we can make sure the ship directly ahead of us has no chance of escaping with what is by divine right *our* prize. If we die, they die. Wouldn't you rather go out fighting?'

Klein stared back, his jaw trembling. Arbenz could see how scared he was, though he was handling it well.

After a moment the younger man nodded, a defeated

look crossing his face. He bent down and slowly picked up the knife, stroking its sleek dark surface as he spoke.

'All right,' said Klein. He held up his hand when some of his fellow crew began to protest, and they fell silent.

Arbenz waited while Kieran watched from where he sprawled nearby, obviously experiencing great pain with every breath he drew.

'We'll obey your orders, Senator, because we can see for ourselves the evidence behind your words – but if you're wrong, and we do survive this, we'll make sure that people know your death was protracted, and we'll be recording your pleas for mercy for prosperity. Do we understand each other?'

'We do,' was the Senator's grim reply.

Dakota led Corso back through the command module, and then into the claustrophobic tunnel leading past her sleeping quarters towards the ship's rear, just fore of the engines. He crawled through after her, cursing when she managed to kick him in the head as he was squeezing through. After several appalling seconds they emerged into a space so tiny their heads were forced together.

'Listen,' said Dakota, 'see this door?' She pointed to a hatch next to Corso's shoulder. 'There's a one-man lifeboat on the other side, and here's the plan. I'm going down to Ikaria while you stay here in orbit. I get on board the first Magi ship I come to and bring it back up.'

'Uh huh,' Corso replied, appalled. 'That easy.'

'Yes, that easy,' Dakota snapped at him, grabbing him by the ear hard enough to hurt. 'Don't you think I can do this? I can't believe I'm saying it, but I should have scrubbed my Ghost out of my head long ago. What I've got in here now is infinitely better. It's like there's an entire world inside my head, do you understand me?'

'Not really, no.'

Dakota made a disgusted noise, her lips curling. 'Then you're just going to have to accept it. The *Agartha* is right behind us now, so there isn't time for anything else.'

'And what if you don't come back?' Corso demanded.

'Then I guess we're all dead.'

THIRTY-ONE

The foam of miniature singularities began to evaporate, but the killing blow had been dealt. The central mass at the heart of Nova Arctis was sucked inwards, becoming dense enough to strip the electrons from every atom and compacting what remained into a supermassive ball of neutrons, releasing a wide-spectrum blast of radiation in the process.

The result was cataclysmic.

The outer layers of Nova Arctis instantly exploded outwards, leaving behind a tiny neutron star barely a few dozen metres across. The star's dying throes released a level of energy equivalent to that of the entire Milky Way, within the space of a few seconds, and releasing a second blast of neutrinos in the process.

The wave front of plasma blossomed outwards from the neutrino core, moving at approximately one-tenth the speed of light.

The *Agartha* moved towards Ikaria's shadow, still decelerating to avoid overshooting the planet itself.

Arbenz looked up at a display showing the *Piri Reis* as a blip now falling into a low orbit.

One of the science execs stepped forward, looking pale and drawn as he glanced towards the still forms of the security officer and then at his dead Captain.

'Senator, there's just been a second neutrino burst from Nova Arctis.'

'What does that mean?' Arbenz replied in irritation.

'It's a phenomenon highly congruent with records relating to the Magellanic Novae some years back.' The man cleared his throat. 'Basically . . . it means the sun just went nova.'

It had occurred to Arbenz, as he waited here on the bridge, that sometime in the last half hour Kieran had quietly gone insane. The man stood at attention, gripping the dead security officer's weapon in both hands, but there was an almost dreamy look upon his face.

'It doesn't look any different,' Arbenz frowned, turning back to the science exec.

'Neutrinos move at the speed of light,' the man replied. 'The plasma wave front will be moving a lot slower, but still at a fair fraction of light-speed. We won't know it when it hits, but it won't be long. Our only hope of at least temporary shelter is getting into Ikaria's shadow. However, the chances of our survival for very long even there are very, very slim indeed, assuming we get into orbit and fully inside the shadow cone before the wave front hits Ikaria. And increasing our acceleration towards Ikaria isn't an option either, because if we did, we'd just crash into it at a couple of thousand kilometres an hour.'

Arbenz watched as another member of the crew stood up suddenly, threw a piece of equipment at a nearby screen, then bolted off the bridge. The piece of equipment bounced off and rolled away harmlessly. No one said anything.

'How many missiles do we have left?' Arbenz asked.

'Three,' said another member of the crew. He was sitting at a weapon's station and looking over towards them. 'What are you—?'

'Fire them.' Arbenz gestured at the blip representing the *Piri Reis*. 'They can reach that machine-head's ship long before we could. Fire them *now*.'

'We're out of range,' the crewmember replied. 'There's no guarantee—'

'That doesn't matter, damn you! It's all we have,' Arbenz yelled, fear finally evident in his voice. 'If it's the last thing we manage to do, just kill them.'

A moment later, three tiny blips raced towards the *Piri Reis* in rapid succession.

Dakota felt a hammering lurch, then nothing. She was crammed into the escape pod like a baby in a steel womb, having stripped off her clothes and then activated her filmsuit before climbing inside.

She was all too aware of being far beyond the point

of no return. The only light came via the feeble glow from a data screen that displayed the surface of Ikaria rushing towards her.

They had identified a wide shelf, deep within the chasm, on which the three Ikarian derelicts lay. The shelf itself was about twenty-five kilometres in length and about two kilometres wide, and surprisingly level. She watched as the pod drifted down on a tail of fire between canyon walls that dropped away into darkness. But she rapidly lost any meaningful sense of perspective.

The pod hit hard, and began rolling. She screamed once, and then listened for a few seconds to the sound of her own frantic breathing. Status lights blinked on, while static fuzzed across the data screen.

But at least she was down, and alive.

She cracked the pod open and it split in half like an egg, releasing her onto the frozen surface of Ikaria, deep down within the chasm. The vast stony walls rising around her were far more intimidating than she'd expected. With the stars appearing only as a thin sliver of light above, it felt like standing within the maw of some vast mountain-toothed monster that was frozen in the act of consuming the universe.

She could feel the derelicts brushing against her mind even before she spotted the nearest of them, less than half a kilometre distant from where she'd landed. It was easier to get an idea of the size of the thing when it wasn't looming out from murky, subterranean waters.

She realized with a start that it was powering up in

anticipation of her arrival, readying itself for trans-luminal flight. She felt strangely drawn to it, despite its nightmarish appearance, like the bleached skeleton of some apparition from deep within the recesses of her id.

She thought of Corso, from whom she had snatched one last kiss before closing the pod's hatch around her. It had been a small intimacy but, given the likelihood of failure, it had assumed for her an overwhelming importance.

She could still taste him on her lips but, now she was actually down here, her ship felt a long way away.

Corso stared aghast at the screens on board the *Piri Reis*. One showed a second flood of neutrinos emanating from deep within Nova Arctis, while the other displayed what could only be missiles rapidly closing the gap between the *Agartha* and Dakota's ship, though still some considerable distance away.

'*Piri*!' he yelled in panic. 'We need to take evasive action, now!'

'Not possible,' the *Piri Reis* replied. 'Further course alterations would use up too much fuel and we would rapidly lose orbit. Alternative courses of action are required.'

'I can't think of any!' Corso yelled, literally tearing at his hair. 'For God's sake, isn't there something we can do? If one of those hits us, there won't be anything left to hit the ground!'

There was an agonizing pause, for four or five seconds. 'All possible courses of action result in fatalities. I recommend we maintain our current position. The missiles may not have enough fuel to strike us. Also, we represent only a small target.'

'Can't you scramble their brains?' Corso yelled again. 'They're just missiles, for God's sake! Tell them to hit something else!'

Another agonizing pause.

'Attempting,' *Piri* replied.

The first missile missed the *Piri Reis* by just fifteen metres. The onboard systems showed its path, spiralling down towards the surface of Ikaria. The second, arriving a minute or so later, was entirely on target, however. Corso watched numbly as it drew closer and closer, accelerating towards him. The blip wavered slightly while the *Piri* attempted to subvert the device's internal instructions remotely.

Corso realized it was too little too late. He remembered how he'd quickly gone over the *Piri*'s systems in order to understand how the ship functioned, and had found there were manual systems just aft.

A few seconds of scrabbling located them.

He found what he needed. The only option for survival was performing a manual fuel dump. It was tantamount to suicide, but there weren't any other options.

He tapped at a manual interface with shaking fingers,

more than a little aware just how quickly the seconds were ticking by. A few moments later the *Piri Reis* shuddered as half its remaining fuel was jettisoned into space, causing it to veer slightly in its orbit.

He listened to the sound of his own frenzied gasps as he waited to be blown to smithereens.

And waited.

I can't still be alive.

He crawled back through to the command module and laid shaking hands on the back of an acceleration couch, before peering up at a display.

A blip was closing fast on the *Piri Reis*. Corso didn't even have time to open his mouth to scream.

A thousand hammers slammed into the hull.

Dakota looked up at a tiny flash of light far above.

Oh please no, she thought. *Piri?*

<I am here, Dakota.>

Dakota had never felt more relieved. *Where's Lucas?*

<I am not sure. We were fired upon by the *Agartha* and subsequently hit by a missile. I have lost contact with the cargo area, and analysis of footage recorded at the moment of impact suggests it may have either been damaged beyond repair or entirely sheared off. There has been loss of pressure from some internal spaces, and internal communications are currently offline. It may take fifteen minutes at current estimates to re-establish

contact with the command module and ascertain if he is still alive.>

Dakota felt the bottom drop out of her stomach. *Find out now, Piri.*

<Until contact with the command module is re-established, I cannot—>

I get the idea, she replied, cutting the connection.

Light filled the chasm.

The edges of the valley were thrown into stark relief. Her eye filters dimmed to their very darkest, but even at that setting she was blinded. Every surface, every grain of rock and sand was brilliantly lit up.

At the very edge of the horizon, she thought she saw the edge of a mountain melt.

The third missile's guidance systems were sent into confusion by the sudden, overwhelming increase in albedo from the direction of Nova Arctis. The missile strayed towards the edge of the cone of shadow cast by Ikaria, and was turned to a puff of superheated gas in a fraction of a second. This was carried outwards by the advancing storm of energy expanding in a shell around the neutron core where a star had been.

The expanding wave front of plasma rushed on towards the *Agartha*.

*

Kieran stepped towards the Senator, who looked up at him.

'We only have a few moments, Senator,' he said. 'The wave front will reach us very soon.'

The Senator nodded tightly; it was clear he was barely holding himself together. 'I hope it's—'

He shook his head. *I hope it's quick*, Kieran knew he'd meant to say.

Kieran reached out, almost lovingly, and cradled the surprised man's face in his hands.

'I hope it is, Senator. But it may not be.'

He broke Arbenz's neck with a sudden, swift twist. The Senator didn't even have time to look surprised.

Kieran lowered the dead man's body to the deck with due love and respect, before standing up straight again to wait for the end with the rest of the crew.

The shell of plasma swallowed the *Agartha* totally, tearing it apart and transforming it into superheated vapour in barely more time than it had taken to envelop the missile.

It continued to expand, racing towards Newfall, a hundred and thirty million kilometres distant, carrying the gaseous remains of the Freehold ship and its crew ever outwards, as it would continue to do for many tens of thousands of years.

On the sunward side of Ikaria, the effect was devastating. The amount of energy slamming into the planet was equivalent to several thousand nuclear warheads exploding every few seconds, as plasma that had been trapped within the photosphere of a star for untold epochs was unleashed instantaneously.

Ikaria's crust literally began to melt away, turning white-hot and then vaporizing, the overwhelming fire digging deeper into the planetary crust at a rate of hundreds of metres every second. Ragged mountain peaks, which had formed long ago during asteroid impacts, exploded under the pressure as they slowly turned from the night side to face the rage of the dying sun.

Within hours, rather than days, the planet would cease to exist, joining the wave of expanding gas as it was reduced to its constituent atoms and spread through the local constellation.

The ground trembled under Dakota's feet. She broke into a run, bounding under the low gravity straight towards the skeletal alien ship.

She couldn't help but feel, as she approached, that she was somehow tumbling into a trap. The ship's spines were too much like the reaching cilia of some hungry sea creature. The beckoning space that had opened beyond the spines in anticipation of her arrival was too much like a gaping, expectant maw.

She kept her eyes half-shut and focused on the ground, her thoughts filled with the terrible, pervasive light slowly seeping over the horizon and turning the top of the valley a dull orange-red.

<Dakota. I am maintaining a position as close to directly above you as possible. However, it may be only minutes before there is insufficient fuel to prevent drifting sunward. My records indicate there is further danger in the form of sunlight reflected from the dust and debris now being thrown up around Ikaria. The energy output from Nova Arctis is currently several billion times the average, and when reflected from clouds of particles it may prove extremely lethal.>

Almost there.

She threw herself forward, as the terrible light began to overrun even the filmsuit's filters, dashing through the derelict's spines and into its interior.

The impossible light began to fade as the entrance behind her flowed shut. There were no open spaces beyond the entrance. Instead, the body of the derelict began to enclose her, entombing her like a dinosaur that had stumbled into a swamp.

She felt it cool and soft against her skin and realized in a moment of terror that her filmsuit had somehow shut off by itself. She struggled to draw breath as her lungs kicked back into action, but there was no air in here to breathe.

She was buried alive, deep within a chasm on a dead world orbiting a dying sun.

Madness began to seep into her thoughts.

Then she saw stars rushing towards her.

*

Several minutes later, the shockwave reached Newfall.

Shallow oceans were turned to superheated steam, and the very atmosphere burned. As one hemisphere facing Nova Arctis dissipated under the equivalent of ten billion suns beating down on it, Newfall began a process of losing mass that would last, at most, a day or two.

It was like taking a flamethrower to a crumpled ball of paper. As gases burned away and the nova dug deeper towards the planetary core, Newfall's gravity would drop, making it easier for burned-away atoms and molecules to achieve escape velocity under the intense pressure of nova heat.

Newfall would soon be little more than a memory.

Corso had cried out in terror as the *Piri* lurched. Then he heard a high-pitched whistling that tore at his nerves, and felt air rush past his face, tousling his hair.

The *Piri* was losing atmosphere. The lights had gone out.

He grabbed fistfuls of wall-fur as the air vented, sucking him in the direction of Dakota's sleeping compartment. If he didn't do something now, he'd be dead in seconds.

He let go of the fur, twisted around and landed just next to the entrance to the space where Dakota slept. He saw where the hull had been ripped open, sucking out half the contents of the room. He found the emergency-seal button and slapped it, waiting while the compartment was sealed off.

The howling ceased abruptly and he gasped for air. Automatic pressure sensors had picked up the oxygen drop, and hissed quietly as they replenished the supply from the *Piri*'s depleted supplies.

Corso paused there for the next minute or so until he had stopped shaking too violently. Then he pulled himself over to a console that still appeared to be active, though unresponsive. He couldn't even tell if the *Piri*'s stacks were still functioning.

There was enough basic systems information, however, to tell him the worst had happened. He was drifting now, and in another twenty minutes or so, the *Piri Reis* would orbit into Ikaria's sunward side, and then straight into the path of the nova.

THIRTY-TWO

Dakota awoke naked between cool sheets.

She sat up with a start and looked around. Tall windows looked out over an azure sky.

There was no sign of the derelict, of Ikaria . . .

After staring about herself for a while, convinced she'd gone mad, she stepped over to the window and looked up to where the sun should be. Instead there was only a black dot surrounded by a visibly expanding ring of fire.

She looked down, at the empty city below her, and crumpled to her knees.

Below the window lay a chasm of such magnitude that it made the valley on Ikaria look like a crack in the pavement. Lights burned all the way down as far as she could see, illuminating windows and verandas all the way down into an apparently bottomless pit.

On the other side of the chasm. a vast alien metropolis spread out yet further.

Without knowing quite how, she became aware she was now the only living thing on this entire world.

She moved away from the windows, and from the sight of the pitiless chasm below, and noticed a door at the far end of the room. She raced over and tugged it open, finding a corridor stretching beyond. Everything – the shape of the corridor itself, of the doors, of the windows – suggested this place had been designed for creatures larger than humans, and of entirely different proportions.

Dakota wandered down steps not designed for human legs and constantly peered about her. When she reached ground level, she saw that a street stretched away into the distance.

Something about her surroundings made her sure this city had been abandoned for a long, long time. She wandered about, naked and still in shock, then turned back for fear of losing her way. Eventually she found her way back up to the room she had woken in.

The bed was of entirely human proportions, as was the data book that stood on a plinth to one side of it. She had no idea if it had been there or not when she'd woken.

She picked up the book and began to read the words there.

Some hours later, she wandered back into the empty streets in a daze. She was still naked, so clothes appeared to be a concept alien to whoever or whatever had brought her here. She didn't feel cold, however. And though she felt hungry, the actual need to eat, just in order to stay alive, appeared to be absent.

This entire world was a library: the book had told her that. The library obligingly shaped itself to her memories of human libraries, giving her information in the form of words on electronic pages. It had also told her she was still inside the derelict, and still on the surface of Ikaria.

This, then, was how the derelict chose to communicate with her. Corso's interface chair seemed laughably primitive by comparison.

As months passed, she learned how to summon the ghosts of the dead Magi Librarians and quiz them about their history. In turn, they taught Dakota her true purpose: the one they believed she had been brought to Nova Arctis to fulfil.

After a few years, she began to understand just how much was required of her, and just how much would be at stake throughout the galaxy if she failed.

Corso listened to the desperate sound of his own breath, as he counted down the seconds to his death. He was sufficiently preoccupied, and it took a moment before he realized a comms light on the command console was blinking.

Someone was trying to communicate with him.

He lurched upright. Information was scrolling across a screen, too rapidly for him to follow.

It appeared something else had taken control of the *Piri Reis*.

'*Piri*!'

No answer.

He hammered at the controls, but they failed to respond.

The ship lurched violently.

For millennia, the three Magi vessels had lain in their silent graves, waiting for the arrival of a Pilot.

The first Pilots were older than dust, half-forgotten Magi who had flown these ships to this lost, lonely system even as the Shoal hunted down the last of their numbers. Those first Pilots had enjoyed countless virtual years within the memories of these three craft, but even that near-eternity of subjective experience eventually gave way to the gradual pace of external time and entropy.

In the end, death had claimed even them.

Bright rivers of white-hot lava spat and flowed in the depths of Ikaria's great chasm, sending searing light up towards the ridge on which the three derelicts lay. The one Dakota had entered finally rose from its resting place, bright energies flickering around its skeletal spines.

As the ground fell away from beneath it, pockets of gas detonated from deep within the chasm walls, sending boulders and debris tumbling down on the two remaining vessels.

Vast fissures began to tear through Ikaria's crust, and the planet shifted in its orbit as it rapidly lost mass to the searing heat of the nova.

Above it all, the *Piri Reis* floated like a dragonfly above the open door of a furnace.

THIRTY-THREE

'Corso? It's Dakota. Can you hear me?'

Corso jerked around, astonished. For a moment he'd thought she was right there beside him, but the voice he heard had come through the *Piri*'s comms system.

'I'm here, Dakota. I really, *really* hope you've got some good news.'

'Can you activate the external cameras?'

'I don't know,' Corso admitted. 'I can't get the *Piri* to respond. Where are you? Are you still down there? I'm deaf and blind up here. I have no idea what's going on.'

'What's going on is that it's a fucking miracle you're still alive. I need you to do something. I can see from where I am that the *Piri Reis* is badly damaged. The cargo section and aft, right?'

'Yeah, part of it's been sheared off, best as I can tell. I think you're going to be sleeping in the command module for a while.'

'A lot of primary systems can still be controlled manually, just not very efficiently. You understand?'

'I do.'

'I'm on my way up, aboard one of the derelicts. I'm going to tether it to the *Piri* and then we can get the hell out of here.'

Corso hesitated. The idea that she had somehow succeeded was strangely difficult to accept. It was only at that moment he fully realized just how thoroughly he'd expected to die. That he might actually survive . . .

'Now listen to me, Corso. There's an extendible cable system at the back of the *Piri*, same stuff they use for building skyhooks. The only problem is the winch system, and how badly it got damaged during the missile impact. The Librarian thinks the cable itself might be fine, though. All I need you to do is release the cable manually, then I can take care of the rest.'

Librarian?

'Release it how?' he demanded.

'You won't need to go outside. Are the lights on – on the main console?'

'Yeah.'

'OK, key in this sequence.' She recited a list of numerals and letters, and he entered them. More lights began to flash, and Corso felt a low vibration pass through the deck.

'OK. Something happened, but I can't tell what. Dakota . . . who's this Librarian?'

'Long story. I'll be over there in maybe ten minutes. There'll be time to explain later.'

Corso stared at the console. *You don't say.*

*

The derelict shot upwards, achieving escape velocity within seconds of lifting off. Beneath, the shelf on which the derelict had sat for so very long finally collapsed into the fire far below it.

A blister formed on the Magi ship's skin as it rose towards the *Piri*, which was still spinning helplessly. Once it had achieved orbit, a black figure emerged from within the blister, crouching low against the hull, peering out from amid the twisting spines.

Dakota stared out beyond the derelict's flickering energies towards the *Piri Reis*, allowing the zoom on her filmsuit to pick out the cable steadily extruding from the tiny craft. Her thoughts then merged with those of the derelict, whereupon the Magi vessel altered its course minutely.

The derelict matched speeds with the *Piri*. Meanwhile the instructions Corso had already entered had caused the cables to extend from her ship. Dakota watched as the near end of the first cable slid between the spines and came towards her. She scuttled aside, watching as the cable was absorbed into the derelict's hull.

The cable became taut, and slowly – very slowly – the *Piri Reis* was drawn in towards the derelict.

Dakota didn't need to see the surface of Ikaria to know what was happening there: the Librarian was feeding images directly into her implants. Vast explosions rippled across the planet's molten surface, rising upwards like fiery blossoms. Burning dust rose upwards, filling the space around the brilliant corpse of Nova Arctis with deadly light.

As long as she stayed there within the shelter of the spines she was safe – at least for the moment. The space–time distortions generated by the transluminal drive, still powering up, acted only as a temporary shield at best.

Come on, come on.

The *Piri* was drawing closer, pulled tail-first in between the spines, like prey reeled into the mouth of a space-borne predator.

The Librarian spoke to her.

In a civilization as old as that of the Magi, knowledge was paramount. When a civilization had millions of years of accumulated cultural wisdom to draw on, some of its most powerful citizens were inevitably those who controlled access to that knowledge.

The Librarians, in a sense, *were* the Magi. Their membership had been drawn from dozens of now long-extinct species, but their purpose – their recognized collective identity – had been in existence longer than many of the cultures that once supplied its members in the dim and distant past. They had always been jealous guardians of their knowledge.

Creating the ships Dakota had until very recently known only as derelicts had been their idea – the Magi's gift to posterity: a way for minds on worlds not yet born to understand the nature and the legacy of the Maker threat.

The *Piri Reis* was finally drawn fully inside the embrace of the derelict's spines. Dakota pushed her way over the hull to her own ship, then grabbed on to the cable and pulled herself along towards it.

They were still deep within Ikaria's shadow cone, sheltered from the full force of the nova blast, but that wouldn't be the case for very much longer.

The temperature of the Magi ship's hull was rising rapidly, towards levels that would far exceed even its astonishingly high tolerances. And as they drew away from Ikaria, accelerating with increasing force, the cone of shelter cast by Ikaria's shrinking shadow cone grew narrower and narrower.

She had now to make sure the *Piri Reis* was thoroughly lashed to the Magi vessel. Otherwise it might not survive the final, hard burst of acceleration prior to the transluminal jump.

There were other cables that could be manually wound out from the *Piri Reis*'s hull and attached around the much larger vessel. It hurt her to notice where the missile had ripped part of the hull away. She estimated it had lost almost a fifth of its total mass.

No time now for regrets. She watched while the end of another cable was drawn into the derelict's pale flesh.

The *Piri Reis* was finally as secure within the derelict's embrace as it ever would be.

*

She found her way to an airlock on the exterior of the *Piri Reis,* and was thankful when she found it still opened. She cycled through, letting her filmsuit melt away as she climbed naked back inside the command console that she'd been so sure she'd never be seeing again.

Pale-faced and wide-eyed, she looked like a ghost to the staring Corso.

I *am* a ghost, she thought. The old Dakota was gone for ever. She'd lived a lifetime amid the derelict's stacks while her fragile body had nestled within its pale flesh.

'There's no time for questions,' she stated firmly, pushing by him. It was strangely like walking into a house remembered from the earliest days of childhood and finding it unchanged, everything exactly where she had left it.

She tried to match her memory of Corso to the man standing before her, pale and frightened. She remembered him with fondness, but in too many ways he was a stranger, someone she'd known a long time ago.

'Dakota . . .'

She glanced at him, saw he was looking at her strangely.

'Long time no see,' she said awkwardly. He frowned in confusion.

'Excuse me.' She stepped past him and towards a console.

There were things she'd forgotten – the smell of her ship's interior, for one. It smelled . . . stale. She closed her eyes for a moment, then opened them again, and remembered.

'We need to use the *Piri Reis* to help boost the derelict, and we need to do it quickly,' she explained.

She saw the befuddled expression on his face and reached out, touching his chin with her fingers. After her long sojourn in the Library, it felt like an eternity since she'd touched – let alone spoken to – another human being.

'The best way I can put it is that we're going to *tow* the derelict,' she continued. 'It needs to pick up a certain velocity before the drive will fully activate, which is where the *Piri Reis* comes in.'

'But that'll use up the last of our fuel . . .'

He was feeling too confused to be any help, so Dakota hit a button. She pictured the *Piri Reis* suddenly leaping forward, the cables taking up the strain, and the derelict nudging up behind, its own sublight engines powering it silently forward. The whole process was entirely inertia-free so long as they remained encompassed by the derelict's spines.

She could see that Corso hadn't even realized they were accelerating.

Outside, the *Piri* strained at the cables buried in the derelict's flesh like a dog straining at its leash – the last of its fuel now burning up in intense fusion heat that sprayed across the Magi ship's spines.

They slid out of the shadow of the dying, shrinking world and into the full glare of the furious inferno beyond. At first the superheated plasma flowed around the localized distortions created by the Magi ship, but even that would not prove sufficient.

The derelict's primary structure had been manufactured on the surface of a neutron star, deep within a stellar factory complex that had spanned light years. Even so, it couldn't survive indefinitely in such an overwhelmingly extreme environment. Slowly, very slowly, as the hull became superheated, it began to bubble at the extremities, revealing the skeletal structure underlying its spines.

THIRTY-FOUR

'So are you going to try and shoot me now?' Dakota asked mildly. 'Or are you going to be sensible and wait until we're out of here?'

Dakota had turned her back on the console, facing him with arms folded across her naked chest. There was something so bizarre about this situation, Corso found it hard not to think it was made some kind of joke. He watched as the filmsuit flowed back out of its hidden recesses and totally coated her body within moments.

'I don't know what you're—'

She punched him with one black-slicked fist, the assault so sudden and so unexpected he simply went reeling away from her. Corso bounced off the opposite bulkhead, then grabbed on to the fur there and stared back at her in shock.

'*What* the hell are you doing?'

'No, Lucas,' she told him. '*You* listen to *me*. You were going to try and take the derelict away from me. I won't be happy if you deny it.'

'What? No, I . . .'

She pushed herself away from the console and was

across the cabin in a moment, pinning him to the wall with one hand at his throat.

Under other, better circumstances he might have been able to defend himself, but he'd had too little sleep for too many days, and had been put under too much stress. Corso struggled, but was held firmly in place.

'Listen, I don't know what you think I was going to do, but for God's sake . . .'

She smiled with sad amusement. 'Don't worry, Lucas, I'm not going to hurt you. But you're not going to lie to me any more.'

She twisted his arm with her other hand, and flipped him over until his face was pressed deep into the velvety fur lining. Keeping one of his arms wrenched painfully back between his shoulder blades, she quickly reached inside his pocket and withdrew the weapon. It was a tiny thing really, but he'd known all along it would be his only real bargaining chip if by some miracle they managed to survive this far.

Dakota suddenly let go of him and he whipped around, glaring at her. She pushed herself back over next to the command console, the slim oblong shape of his weapon in her hand.

'All right,' he said, trembling. 'Exactly how did you know?'

She shrugged. 'I didn't.'

Corso stared at her in confusion.

She shrugged. 'I just figured it was likely you'd try something like this. You and me, Lucas, we've got different aims in mind for the transluminal drive. All along, you knew something like this had to happen, sooner or later.'

Corso thought over his options, and realized he didn't have any. 'All right, fine. I understand what you're saying. But you have to believe me when I say I wasn't going to harm you.'

She laughed. 'You came on board my ship with a gun hidden away, and you weren't going to harm me, yet the survival of your shitty little planet was at stake?' She glared back at him.

'Just let me explain myself.'

She nodded for him to continue.

'The Consortium is corrupt,' he explained. 'You already know that. It's an empire in everything but name.'

'You think I'm going to give this derelict to the Consortium?' She laughed in derision. 'Don't you understand? The derelict's whole purpose is to find booby-traps, caches of alien technology. It's a weapon for destroying other weapons.'

Corso looked back at her blankly.

'I was inside that derelict for a *long* time. Not in objective terms – purely subjective. There used to be Pilots for the Magi ships, creatures utterly unlike us which lived for millennia. Their job was to find Maker caches.'

She saw the look of comprehension that passed briefly over his face.

'You've heard that name before, haven't you?' she said excitedly.

'A progenitor race?'

'The ones some of the Magi races believed created the universe.'

Corso was staring at her with something like awe, as if he'd only now allowed himself to believe she'd been telling the truth about her experiences on Ikaria.

'What's important is that *something* left caches of high technology scattered throughout their galaxy, and ours, and maybe others. It's exactly like I said, Lucas. The drive was seeded in this way specifically to entrap fledgling spacefaring cultures like their own. Any race that finds a cache soon figures out the drive's potential as a weapon. If they're aggressive, war is inevitable, whether it's after a hundred years or a hundred thousand. In the process, they wipe out other species, either by accident or deliberately. Destabilize enough stars, and it's going to wipe out higher life forms throughout the local stellar neighbourhood. The caches are bug traps, high-tech flypaper. The Magi created these ships, the derelicts, to track down those caches and destroy them, and also the knowledge they contained.'

She smiled. 'Which is pretty ironic, when you consider the only way for them to do that was to use the same drive technology that destroyed their own civilization.'

Corso put his hands to his head. 'For God's sake, Dakota! Do you really think knowledge like this would be better off with the Shoal?'

'I've got no love for them. But in all their history there's never been a war in our galaxy like the one that wiped out the Magi. I'll give them that much.'

'As far as you know.' He grinned nastily. 'Maybe they're lying.'

That stalled her. As her lips quivered, he knew she'd been wondering exactly the same thing.

'I'll tell you this much, Dakota. Before I even met you, I was terrified of you. I thought you'd be some kind of monster. I realize now you're not, but you're way, way out of your depth. How far do you think you can run with something like this, before someone catches up with you? As long as you live, somebody is going to be looking for you, whether you have the derelict or not, just so they can have the information tucked away in your brain. They'll do whatever they can to get it all out of you, and then they'll dispose of you.'

'And what would *you* do?' she asked quietly.

'Look, things are changing in the Freehold.'

He ignored the disbelieving look on her face.

'I *mean* it,' he insisted. 'The people who founded the Freehold are long gone. With Arbenz dead and his controlling faction out of power, we have a chance now to gain real legal status within the Consortium. Everything will change, but with the transluminal drive, we could be a power player. We won't be sidelined any longer. And we can protect you, Dakota, seriously. Without our help, I don't know if you stand a chance.'

'Nice try.' She smiled sadly. 'But I don't think the human race should have the drive at all.'

'You're condemning the whole human race to an eternity of despotism!' Corso bellowed in frustration. 'We'll always remain at the mercy of the Shoal.'

She shook her head. 'No. That's not so bad if the alternative is extinction.'

Even as they spoke, Dakota could sense the urgency within the derelict's thoughts. She could almost feel the near-invulnerable flesh of the ship being abraded away by the constant, high-energy assault of plasma rushing away from Nova Arctis' core. It was as if it were her own skin being burned away.

The *Piri Reis*'s engines began to blast intermittently, then fell dark and silent as the last of its fuel was gone. Despite the shelter afforded within the derelict's spines, its hull was beginning to glow a dull red.

Chunks began tearing away from the hull of the Magi ship. Much of the hull coating had already been eroded from the spines, till they had become entirely skeletal in appearance, like slender bony fingers reaching out to grasp the *Piri Reis*.

Vast plumes of light began to radiate outwards from the derelict, almost indistinguishable from the burning plasma that roared past on all sides.

*

They waited in silence while Dakota slid rapidly back into her fugue state. But the moment he so much as twitched a muscle towards her, she became suddenly alert again, the tiny weapon aiming towards him.

Corso shrugged and relaxed again. Her eyes subsequently unfocused once more and she went back to wherever it was she went at such times.

And even if he'd been able to gain control of this situation, what then? He himself wasn't able to communicate with the derelict. And even if he had been, he was pretty damn sure it wasn't going to go anywhere he wanted it to go. No, Dakota had the upper hand – had *always* had the upper hand. She had always been the key to this whole operation.

Corso gave himself up to the inevitable. 'All right,' he said, 'at least tell me where we're going.'

She snapped back out of her fugue instantly and focused on him. 'I don't know.'

'You don't *know*? I thought you said you were that thing's pilot.'

'We can't jump this soon without taking some risks. But we don't have any choice either. If we wait any longer, any minimal protection we have against the nova will be lost, and we'd be dead in an instant. So we jump now, but where we end up . . . hard to say.'

Corso took a deep breath. 'Frankly, I'm surprised we even got this far.'

'I just wanted you to know before—'

He raised a hand. 'I appreciate it. Really. But after we get there, can you let me off at the next stop?'

She laughed fiercely at that. 'I don't want to be enemies,' she said.

'Neither do I.'

Dakota felt the *Piri Reis* rumble beneath her. At the same time, she saw her ship from the outside, smashing hard against one of the white-hot spines, the confining cables whipping about.

The derelict surged forward, crashing against the *Piri*'s engine block, sending it spinning. The derelict's inertialess zone was the only thing preventing Corso and Dakota from being smashed to pieces in an instant.

If they didn't jump now . . .

The derelict with the tiny ship cradled in its spines flickered out of existence, and fires unimagined even in hell filled the void where it had been.

When the plasma shockwave reached Dymas, the outer layers of the gas-giant's atmosphere were stripped away within only hours. The planet was literally smeared across the face of the Nova Arctis system.

As it shrank, the gas-giant's gravitational grip on its satellites – including Theona – weakened, and these worlds spun away into space, burning and boiling under the lethal assault of the dying star, their rocky cores vaporizing over the following hours.

Vast streamers reached out from where a star had

once been. If anyone had been there to witness it, they would have recognized that they were witnessing the birth of a nebula.

It was over.

Dakota crawled through the darkness until she found Corso's warm body. She put one hand on his chest and felt it rise and fall. Then she let her head fall against his chest and wept.

After another little while, the lights began to flicker back on.

'*Piri?*'

'Dakxxx—'

She tried again, rerouting her ship's language circuits. They were still running on emergency power; still cradled within the half-melted spines of the derelict.

But they were alive . . . and somewhere far, far away from Nova Arctis.

Corso was badly concussed, constantly slipping in and out of consciousness. The medbox had given her some of the necessary medication, but it was still going to be a while before he made a great deal of sense.

'xxzzz-ota. Dakota.'

'*Piri*, good to hear you.'

'Our stellar maps appear to be out of context with the observed local area,' the *Piri* advised.

Dakota patted the console. 'Yes, *Piri*, that's right.'

'We also appear to be attached—'

'No more questions, *Piri*. We're safe, at least for the moment, and that's all that matters. I know we're out of fuel. How are we for everything else?'

'There are sufficient supplies for another one hundred hours,' *Piri* stated, 'at normal rates of consumption by one person.'

Not so great then, and now for the important question. Dakota licked her lips, and felt her heart hammering as she asked it.

'Where are we, *Piri*? Do you have any matches in your stacks for where we are just now?'

There wasn't any sign at all of the burgeoning nebula where Nova Arctis had once been, and the last time the derelict they were lassoed to had travelled through this part of the Milky Way had been long enough ago for its own stellar maps to be wildly out of date.

'I have found a match,' *Piri* declared after a few moments.

'You're shitting me,' she mumbled. 'Where?'

'We are in Bandati space,' the *Piri Reis* declared. 'On the edge of one of their colony systems. Analysis of current tach-traffic indicates they are aware of our presence. What appear to be a fleet of mining ships has departed in our direction from an outlying world. Would you like me to initiate an emergency broadcast to them?'

'No, wait.'

What now, Dakota wondered? What now, indeed?

'Call them,' Corso mumbled from somewhere behind her. 'We don't have any choice. You heard the *Piri*. We don't have enough supplies to stay alive. Not even if you dumped *me* overboard.'

There's always the derelict, Dakota thought. It was out there, waiting for her. But it had been too badly damaged, and was now engaged in a long process of self-repair that might take months.

'Call them,' Dakota agreed after another moment's hesitation. 'Tell them it's an emergency.'

Perhaps, she thought, it was enough just to be still alive.

For a hundred thousand years, throughout the Milky Way, creatures with eyes – or something that fulfilled the same function – would turn their faces up to the sky and see a new star burning brightly in the night, before it gradually began fading after a few days. The sight of that light would inspire wars and poetry and philosophies that would live for a thousand years more, long after the memory of the nova itself had passed on.

That same light would shine down on other worlds at far greater distances, even in other distant galaxies, and inspire curiosity and terror in equal parts.

In time, other stars would join it, blossoming and burning briefly all across the face of the Milky Way, like a fiery portent of doom.

extracts reading groups

competitions books new

discounts extracts extracts

competitions

books

new

events

events books extracts

new reading groups

interviews

events extracts

discounts

new books events

events new

discounts extracts discounts

www.panmacmillan.com

extracts events reading groups

competitions books extracts new